Praise for The Last Keeper

What's your favorite tactile treat? Truffles? Granny's choco chip cookies? Vintage wine? Kobe beef?

Well, *The Last Keeper* is like that. It's so good I have to pace myself forcibly and take small portions of Michelle Birbeck's book to postpone its eventual ending. The synopsis alone ensnared my imagination, and I knew I had to read this story. Serenity Cardea's eyes are luminescent green and just like Superman to his kryptonite, I fell into its depths. I was immediately sucked in to her life, the complexities of being one of the remaining Keepers, the promise of true love at the expense of her life. How does one choose bliss in exchange for one's death? Are you ready to give up a lifetime in exchange for a few years of happiness with your true mate?

I have read a lot of Vampire-Hunter books, and definitely too many romance stories, but I have never come across a story like this. Michelle's play of words is simple, but her pull is magnetic. I'm not one to highlight words, but I found my copy lit up by it.

Braine - Talk Supe Blog

The Last Keeper

By
Michelle Birbeck

Michelle Birbeck

TWCS
PUBLISHING HOUSE

First published by The Writer's Coffee Shop, 2012

The Writer's Coffee Shop
(Australia)   PO Box 447 Cherrybrook NSW 2126
(USA)   PO Box 2116 Waxahachie TX 75168

Paperback ISBN- 978-1-61213-347-8
E-book ISBN- 978-1-61213-079-8

A CIP catalogue record for this book is available from the US Congress Library.

Cover image by: © Francois De Beer I Dreamstime.com
Cover design by: Jennifer McGuire

www.thewriterscoffeeshop.com/aallred

Dedication

To James, I wish you could have seen this

Book One

Chapter One

London, 1940

London had changed a lot over the last hundred or so years. Once it had been little more than an overgrown playground for the rich and snooty society of the time. Well, perhaps it hadn't changed *that* much.

As I stood on London Bridge, looking out across the city, I noticed that life seemed to go on as normally as it could in these times. The sun had set and the people were retiring for the night. They drew their blackout shades and bedded down to another night of waiting. Waiting for news of loved ones sent to war. Waiting for news that the war was over.

Silence surrounded me, making me feel as though I was standing in a gallery admiring a painting. Just like patrons of a gallery, I too was an observer, watching as the world passed me by. There were times when I simply glanced at the picture, gaining a general idea of what was happening before moving to the next one. And there were times when I saw everything. Every minute detail that the painting had to offer came alive before my eyes, but only if I took the time to look.

It came alive before me now in the form of a vampire skulking down the road. The dark colour tinting his aura stood out clearly in the darkening streets, marking him for what he was. I'd seen the face before, standing tall by the side of the London Seat of Power, one of the vampires' ruling bodies.

Ducking my head, I intended to walk straight past him, heading home before more creatures began prowling the night for something tasty to kill. He spotted my quickened pace and thought I was on the menu. I wasn't, but

I also wasn't in the mood for a confrontation, not when I was so close to the London Seat. Following my instincts was bad enough—I'd spent hours staring at a map before being drawn here—but now they'd forced me into the heart of a raging war and the home of the one Seat I couldn't abide. The last thing I wanted to do was show up on their radar.

The first thing one of their lackeys would do would be to attack me. If they survived, they'd go running straight to their masters, all too eager to give up information about where I was. If they found me, they would try to kill me, or worse, have me followed home and target my family.

Avoidance was better. I wasn't supposed to kill them all.

Still, I could do what I did best and plant a few ideas in his mind before he passed me by.

No sooner had I reached for his mind, intending to influence him into a change of direction, than I made the mistake of glancing up. Closer than I thought; he was staring right at me, eyes wide with recognition. My emerald irises and flame-like red hair were too much of a calling card not to be looked at twice. My appearance was well known among the lackeys.

I shuddered to think of how many humans had been killed in the pursuit of the vampires' famed Angel of Death. Or how many more would fall because they were fated to appear too similar to me.

"Hey, I know you."

"I think you're mistaken."

"Well, well, well," he drawled, slowing to a casual saunter. "Too much knowledge on your face to not be who I think you are."

Working in his mind as fast as I was able, I clung to a fraction of hope that he'd change his mind.

I took one step past him; one more and I'd escape.

His pale hand shot out, gripping my arm. "No. I've seen you before." His voice dropped to a whisper. "Imagine what I'll get for bringing the body of Azrael to our king."

I sighed. It was time to live up to my name.

Part of me enjoyed it, especially after everything the vampires had done, to my race, to me—to my sister.

"If I am who you think I am"—I pried his hand from my arm—"then what makes you think you'd win?"

"Finding your mate makes you sloppy."

My loud laugh filled the night air, echoing off the empty buildings. "Perhaps, but then, *I* wouldn't know about that."

Whoever they were getting their facts from didn't know anything about me. Had I found my partner, my mate, I wouldn't have been within a hundred miles of any Seat. Clearly they weren't offering a high enough price for information. They never did . . .

The first blow almost surprised me; a laughably feeble fist thrown towards my side. Blocking it easily, I stepped away, luring him to the alley beside what had once been a factory.

He followed me, his eyes tracking my movements. When we were hidden from the prying interest of any passers-by, I was free to do as I pleased.

Which meant killing the thing before he reported a sighting.

My family was here. I would not risk them.

Yet I wanted to draw out the fight, wanted to make it last until the lights died, draining the colour away and leaving the city blanketed by darkness and fear. When he came at me, smiling brightly in the fading light, I shook my head and went in for the kill. I ducked another fist and laughed when he took a chunk out of the wall, sending dust and shards of brick into the air. The confidence I sensed in his mind faltered, but only for a second.

"If you wanted an easy kill, go find some other redhead to throw at your master's feet!" My words did nothing to deter him. He pivoted back to face me, features glowing.

The vampire's fist came flying towards me again, and I grabbed hold of it, using his momentum to swing him off balance and send him tumbling to the ground. A moment later, I hooked my arm around his throat . . . and pulled. The snap was loud in the quiet alley. His body went limp in my arms, the fight leaving him in a rush of stagnant breath.

But death was never a sure thing with a snapped neck, not for a vampire.

Helen, my sister of sorts, wouldn't be impressed if I dismembered the body by hand. She'd never get the blood out—or the smell. The best and only way to make sure a vampire was dead was fire, but a fire would draw too much attention. Head and heart were the next best things.

Pulling a small knife from my purse, I knelt in the rubble and turned the vampire over. He looked dead enough, eyes fixed and staring, breathing ceased, but I couldn't take the chance. One stab to the heart, up and in under the arm, and another to the brain, straight through the ear.

The sun would incinerate the body as soon as it spread its warmth on another day, burning the overfed vampire until all that remained was ash. So I tucked him out of sight of the road. It was either that or the river.

A good fight normally did wonders, easing my tattered nerves, but not tonight. Tonight my mind was filled with a dread that had little to do with the dangerous times.

The mere thought that such petty human battles could affect me was laughable. Wars were fought. They were won, they were lost. And still I lived on.

Heaving a sigh, I began my walk home.

A large townhouse awaited me in the heart of the city. From rich coloured Indian rugs to antique furniture, it was filled with some of my most prized possessions. But it was the basement I wanted most—so I could cram it tight with our records, piling the books high until it was fit for bursting.

"Did you run into any trouble on your way?" Helen asked as soon as I walked in. Her shrewd green eyes watched me closely, checking for injuries.

I shrugged out of my jacket. A distinct chill was in the air despite autumn having not quite arrived. "No, not at all. It just took a while longer to wind down than I thought."

"And yet, you are as tightly wound as when you left," she commented, taking my coat.

"I feel that something is about to go terribly wrong. Perhaps it's because we're here. It's been so long since I've been this close to the heart of things."

"Being close to a Seat of Power will cause you stress, but it has never caused this reaction in you before. When was the last time you slept? Ate?" She narrowed her eyes and refused to let me further into the house until I answered.

"I ate with you and Jayne three nights ago, and I'll sleep when it comes." Although what I ate was very little, given the rationing.

"You ate, but you didn't taste the food. And you haven't slept in months, well before we moved. Not long after you made the decision to move here."

"I'm perfectly fine." I turned my back to her, trying to head for the stairs.

"That's a matter of opinion." She meant well.

Helen and I had a unique relationship. To an outsider we were mother and daughter, but I had watched her grow, as I had her mother and her mother before her. We fought, on occasion, like an old married couple, and we could sit for hours discussing her thoughts about the world. She worried about me like any mother would, and I worried about her in the same fashion. We were the best of friends and the closest of sisters. Our relationship had changed so much over the years, moving from my being her aunt, while her mother was still with us, to her being my daughter. And now she was my most trusted companion. The cycle had been the same with her mother, as it would be with her daughter.

She was right about one thing, whether or not I was fine was a matter of opinion, and she could see straight through my falsehoods. I was far from "perfectly fine."

"Oh, Serenity?" I stopped, one foot on the stairs. "The charity auction is tomorrow evening."

"Do I really have to bother?" I asked, turning to look at her.

It was part of the price I had to pay for moving to London. My contacts were kind enough to "forget" about Jayne being here instead of being evacuated on the condition I put in a generous appearance at their fundraising evening—including helping to pay for the affair. The money I would have to spend wasn't an issue; it was the event itself I dreaded.

"Unfortunately, but I'm sure it won't be as bad as you fear. Perhaps you could woo some of the boys that are yet to be sent to war with your dancing skills."

"I would rather waste it than be forced to dance with those pompous idiots," I muttered as I climbed the stairs.

"Shall I inform Sam that he'll accompany you?" she called after me, and I sensed smug satisfaction in her voice.

"Actually," I turned to face her again, "I'll be taking *you*."

"Oh," she gasped, sounding pleased. Not quite the reaction I was hoping for. "I best organise another dress for the evening, then."

"Damn it."

"Language . . ."

"When you're as old as I am, you can use whatever language you please," I said.

Why would I have a need to dance? I wasn't built for spending an evening daintily dancing around a hall. I was built for protection, for keeping the peace between the races.

"Damn it," I muttered again. They were slowly becoming my favourite pair of words.

The sun was rising once more, and yet another night had been filled with nothing but thought and pointless mind chatter. That made more than six months without sleep by my reckoning. At least. Not a record, not by far, but worrisome.

The last time I'd gone longer without sleep, it was because I was fighting for the lives of my brothers and sisters. Trying to get them to safety before . . .

"Auntie?" a small voice asked. "Are you awake?"

"I am," I answered, matching Jayne's volume. "What's the matter, sweetie?"

Jayne was Helen's five-year-old daughter. She was a beautiful little creature, the mirror of her mother. Of me, as well. Dark red hair tumbled to her shoulders, framing a heart-shaped face and a bright pair of green eyes. She was going to be on the short side, all the women in the family were, but that wouldn't affect her in the slightest. Already she was feisty.

Crawling onto the bed with me she whispered, "I couldn't sleep, and I didn't want to wake Mama."

"Well, you came to the right place. How about a story?" It always helped her after she'd had a nightmare and I hoped a story would ease her back to sleep for a while.

She never told me when that was the problem, but I could see it in her eyes. The light that shined out of them would dull, and she would stare off into space. Her nightmares didn't come often, but they were occuring with regularity since the move to London.

Jayne sighed and snuggled deeper into the warm blankets. "Yes, please."

"Shall I choose?"

When she nodded, I reached into the antique bedside table and pulled out an old, battered book of fairy tales. It wasn't the kind seen on modern shelves with princesses and princes. These were special stories, and though I didn't need to read the words, Jayne did.

"Let me see. How about I tell you about two little twins who lived a very long time ago? They were the first twins in the family, the whole race, in fact. But they were not the last . . ." I wasn't sure why, but I'd chosen my own story to tell.

A couple of hours later, we rose for the day. Jayne had fallen into a light sleep partway through the second story, and she slept peacefully until Helen came to find her.

It hurt her when her daughter came to me like this. It wasn't the fact that Jayne had come seeking comfort; it was the fact that she needed to seek comfort at all.

"Did she have another nightmare?" Helen whispered, reaching out to stroke her daughter's cheek.

"She didn't say, but I think so." She was worried. "I'm sorry."

"Whatever for?"

"You cannot tell me you haven't noticed the increase in her dreams since moving here? *I brought you with me.*" It was something I was starting to regret, deeply.

"And we chose to come. It has always been a choice. We were never forced to come with you, Serenity. You make that clear each time we move. Always have. Now, enough of this talk. You *will* join us for breakfast today." It was apparent in her tone and hard look that blaming myself for Jayne's unrest was not acceptable. It didn't stop me. Probably didn't stop her, either.

We all were quiet at breakfast, though Helen tried to start a conversation about the auction that evening—the one where dancing played an uncomfortably large part of the entertainment. It was a futile attempt. All I wanted to do was show up, do my part, and leave. But there was no doubt in my mind I would be forced to endure the entire evening.

"There was some mail for you this morning." Helen was smiling as I helped clean up after breakfast. Only one reason caused such a joyous response.

"William?" I asked, hardly able to contain my excitement.

She nodded, just once.

I grinned, then raced off to see what was in the letter. Correspondence from William was always the highlight of my day, especially considering how hard it must be to get a letter out of France. He was my brother in every way that counted. Fifteen hundred years younger than me, and the only other remaining Keeper. We weren't related by blood, only by race and purpose, but we were as close as I'd been with my own sister. My twin. I smiled as I read his words.

Dearest Serenity,

I hope this letter finds you well. Of course, I do not expect you to be anything but.

I am sure the dance will not be as bad as it seems. Nor will the attending dandies, as you used to be so fond of calling them. Look at it from their point of view. You are a beautiful young lady with the ability to donate a great deal of money to their cause. I am sure they are just jealous. And if they knew your real age, I am sure their wives would be even more so.

In another matter, I have some news for you. The first is very trivial, really, but I am excited all the same. I found my first grey hair as I write. It is a monumental occasion, I assure you. It is a strange feeling to be growing old after all these years. A strange but good feeling.

On to my other news, Alison is expecting again, so we will have another birth to add to the records before the end of the year. I hope for a girl this time, a miniature replica of my Alison, providing the troubles she is having pass. I love our sons, but a girl would complete the family nicely.

Should this letter arrive before your dreaded occasion, please relax and try to have fun. The toes you step on will heal in time, I promise.

I look forward to hearing of your exploits and injuries.

Love always,
Your Brother,
William

Injuries. That was a long-standing source of amusement between us. In order to avoid these dreaded things, I used to pretend that I had no skill at all when it came to dancing. The truth was I could dance the night away without so much as a thought, but I hated it. It had become a means of torture over the years. On this one occasion, I accidentally stepped on some poor fellow's toe, breaking the thing . . . well, it had been a running joke ever since.

"Serenity?" Helen asked from the doorway. I hadn't realised that I'd stopped what I was doing. How long had I been sitting here staring off into space? "Is there news?"

"Alison is expecting again." I smiled and handed her the letter. "William has also found his first grey hair. I am thinking of making a comment regarding his age, though he'll no doubt come back with something worse."

"You are a few years older than him," she said. "Anyway, I came to tell you it's time to get ready."

Already? Time must have slipped away from me.

"Must I go?" I grumbled again.

"You must keep up appearances. Come now, I picked out your green dress." She handed me the letter. "I know how much you enjoy wearing it."

I rose and did what I did with everything I received from my brother: I burned it in the fireplace. He did the same with those I sent him. Short of never contacting each other, it was the easiest way to ensure safety. We'd decided once there were only two of us, that we needed to keep in touch in case anything happened. And it was nice to be reminded that I was not yet the last.

"Serenity?" Helen called.

I hadn't realised I'd stopped, thinking again. It was something that was happening more and more often. And it wasn't a good thing. Getting caught up in my thoughts at the wrong moment could cost someone their life, or it could come as close to costing my own as was possible.

"Perhaps we should move," Helen said. The words crashed through me, sending the strangest feeling of fear racing through my veins.

"Don't be silly. As soon as I know where the London Seat are, I'll be fine. If Jayne doesn't improve, then I'll start looking. However, I feel I need to be here. You're free to use any of my properties if you wish to leave. This isn't exactly a safe city at the moment."

I already knew what her answer would be. Helen would be wherever I was, and that included her daughter and her brother, Sam, who was no doubt retrieving the car for the evening. Sam had been with us for years, choosing to stay with his sister since the death of her husband.

"You already know the answer, Serenity. Besides, we have a wonderful event to attend this evening." Helen smiled widely, but it didn't hide the concern in her eyes.

Getting ready for the ghastly event was a complicated affair. Hairpins and makeup. Undergarments and accessories. Literally hours of primping before everything was ready.

How I longed for simpler times when a dress was something you wore day to day and your best was only worn on Sundays and at weddings. One day a week was by far more agreeable, and that was only if I happened to be going to church. Though, I had to admit that my dress for the evening was beautiful.

The floor-length cocktail dress was one of my favourites. Its gentle lines and satin-smooth finish were both comfortable to wear and stunning to look at. The high, jewelled neckline was encrusted with emerald-coloured stones that matched the dress. The colour took some of the attention from the bright shine of my eyes. It allowed me to observe the room without being overly noticed, because most people were too busy staring at my body to notice to my shifting gaze.

Sam drove us to the hall where the event was taking place. With a reluctant final sigh, I followed Helen out of the car. We were expected and Mr. Wilson, the organiser, was eager to greet us.

"Miss Cardea, so glad you could come."

"I could hardly miss such a worthy event, could I?" His slight floundering amused me. He always had a problem with the air of authority I carried.

"Of course," he said, ignoring my sarcastic tone. "Let me introduce you to some of our contributors tonight."

"Go, have some fun," I whispered to Helen. "Find someone you like."

"You know Steven was the only one for me," she said, her voice low enough for only me to hear.

"That doesn't mean you can't have some fun." I smiled, knowing she would never do anything of the sort.

Mr. Wilson held his arm out for me. "Shall we?"

We walked through the crowd, and I was introduced to what felt like half of the people there. Many of them were faculty members, though the university was currently closed. Most of them were too old to be sent to war, Mr. Wilson included. Sharp minds and wandering eyes were the main feature of them all.

"Ah! There he is. Miss Cardea, I'd like you to meet the best ancient languages professor that I have had the privilege of working with. Professor Issac Baruti."

I stopped dead in my tracks and beat back the vicious hiss that tried to force its way out of my mouth. I hadn't known *he* was in the city. I was well aware of who the professor was, and *what* he was. But it wasn't the Egyptian professor I was worried about. It was his wife, Poppy Baruti.

The name "Poppy" had been given to her because of her preference for draining the last bit of life from men on the battlefield. She was one of the few who'd left the Seats of Power. Willingly. Though I firmly believed that people could change, I had my doubts about someone who was so ruthless in the taking of life. Surely anyone who had built their reputation by spilling blood and littering bodies across the centuries didn't have it in them to give up such power. Yet, when she found Issac Baruti, she stopped. At least, that was the claim.

"Professor Baruti, it's a pleasure to meet you," I lied, offering him my hand.

"Thank you, Miss Cardea. It is an honour to meet the fine young woman who has helped us so much." He seemed genuine as he took my hand in his slightly cooler one, showing no signs that he knew what I was. His pleasant smile reached his eyes.

Just as I was starting to feel uncomfortable at having a vampire so close, even one whose reputation was apparently free from death, we were interrupted. A stunning brunette with piercing brown eyes glided towards us. His wife. I'd recognise her anywhere, though we had never met.

"Issac, my dear, look whom I found wandering about."

"Have you met Mr. Synclair?" Professor Baruti asked before turning to his wife.

Behind her stood two figures. Both were blond, though I couldn't see much of the man. The woman was lovely with her hair pinned up in an old-fashioned style. It suited her perfectly. Her steel grey eyes made her appear older than she was, giving her an air of wisdom.

"I don't believe I have." The same anxiety that had been plaguing me rose again. Perhaps the great Poppy being in the city was what had caused it.

"Then you must allow me to introduce you. This is Mr. Ray Synclair and Mrs. Synclair."

Fantastic, another wife to avoid if her husband decides to stare.

"You must be Miss Cardea. My son has not stopped talking about the wonderful woman who helped to set up this event. Ray, dear, you must finally meet Miss Cardea."

Son? Well, I hadn't seen that one coming.

As he turned to face me, excusing himself from his conversation, the first things I noticed were the cane he used to support himself and the hand resting atop it. It must have been why he hadn't been drafted. He leaned heavily upon the cane, though I couldn't see why. His hand clutched it repeatedly as he moved forward, as though his entire weight were resting there. I stared at him, taking in his short blond hair, gunmetal grey eyes, the nicely defined muscles under his shirt, his close to six-foot frame . . . *every* inch of him.

When our stares met, I was left without words.

Never before had I been rendered speechless. Standing before me was the reason I hadn't slept in months. He was why I was here, and every part of me knew it in that second.

The room faded away until there was nothing left. It was there in his eyes, that feeling, that need . . .

"It's a pleasure to meet you, Miss Cardea." He smiled, striking me dumb once more. He didn't extend his hand as everyone else had. It was resting atop the cane, and I got the impression he needed it more than he would like.

"Serenity," I managed to whisper, reluctantly tearing my gaze away.

"I'm sorry?"

"Serenity, my name. Miss Cardea is so formal." My voice was hardly audible, and it barely held as I forced the words out of my mouth.

"Would you do me the honour of dancing with me, Serenity?" he asked, smiling.

"I . . ." Could I say no? I didn't want to. But I needed to. I needed to get out, to clear my head and think about what had happened. "I'm sorry, but I'm not feeling very well. Would you please excuse me?"

Without waiting for an answer, I blindly turned away and searched for Helen. I found her chatting quietly with some of the gossip-hungry wives.

"I won't be home tonight."

She looked towards me, startled by my sudden appearance. "Aunt Sere, is everything all right?" Her voice was only a whisper.

Clearly I appeared as rattled as I felt. It was a rare occasion when Helen resorted to calling me "aunt."

"No." I didn't bother to elaborate; I just walked out of the dance and left it all behind.

How could I feel so dumbfounded, yet so at ease with a person this quickly? Something about Ray Synclair had shaken me to my core. In the depths of my heart I recognised the feeling. I had recognised it the second our eyes met. The feeling of not being able to look away, of losing all sense of self.

I had found my weakness, my mate. The one thing in the world that would make me happy beyond compare.

And the one thing that would ultimately destroy me . . .

Chapter Two

It was one of those rare occasions when I hoped for trouble. It wasn't something I found on a regular basis, but being in the city, so close to one of The Seats, I was sure to find some.

Vampires tended to gather near them, hoping to be the next in a long line of hangers-on. They were mostly lackeys who were sent on menial errands, never actually part of the main goings on, but close enough to feel the rush of power. Any of them would be eager for a chance.

I was betting on someone, anyone, getting on the wrong side of me—anything to distract me from my thoughts of Ray Synclair.

The entire time I wandered, I berated myself for leaving him there, in the same room as one of the most notorious vampires in the world. Surely he would be safe; there were far too many people around for her to try anything, but . . .

Stop it.

I was overthinking everything. Of course nothing would happen to him. He would be perfectly fine surrounded by the people at the hall. No doubt some other woman would want to dance with him, and though the thought made me want to return to ensure that didn't happen, it caused me to wonder. Exactly how had he planned on dancing with me? Surely that cane of his would hamper any such attempts.

There were so many questions I wanted to ask him when I saw him again.

Wait, when? There isn't going to be a when.

There was no chance I'd felt that accursed connection. It couldn't be that this was the time and place for me to find my weakness. It just couldn't. There had to be more time left for me. How else were we supposed to survive?

Fear lanced through me, making it so hard to breathe that I had to stop. If he truly was my . . . no. I squeezed my eyes shut, as though closing them would make everything less real. The possibility was too much. Having my life linked so intimately to another when there was so much left to do was almost unbearable. To be so close to the brink of extinction and then find my partner . . .

No! It just couldn't be that connection.

If it was, and our lives were linked so . . . what if he died?

The thought almost brought me to my knees. Yet it was all too real a possibility. The vampires had hunted our partners for fifteen-hundred years. They would stop at nothing—because killing him was the only way to kill me.

I gripped the wall beside me, my fingers making rubble of the stone as I tried to calm myself. I had to be wrong.

If I wasn't then the reality was too horrific to contemplate.

I needed to speak with William. He would know. He would tell me how frivolous I was being.

Helen confronted me the second I stepped through the door. "I don't suppose you would care to elaborate on why there was a very concerned Mr. Synclair chasing after you last night?"

It was a question I didn't want to answer. Not yet.

"Would you wake Sam for me?" I asked, ignoring her hard tone and worried stare. "I need him to do something for me."

With the way she glared at me, it was clear that the subject was not closed. She wanted answers, and knowing Helen, she was going to get them. One way or another. If I were being honest with myself, which I absolutely wasn't, I didn't want to share that answer with anyone. If I was wrong, and I adamantly hoped I was, then I didn't want to admit how much he affected me.

If I were right . . . the possibility was frightening.

Write . . . that was what I needed to do. If I were to get an answer, either way, then I needed to write to William. It took me a few moments of deep, calming breaths before I was able to put pen to paper and write out my worst fear.

Dearest Brother,

Congratulations, both on your first grey hair and the news of your family addition.

First, please accept my apologies for the delivery of this letter. I knew that, due to its content, it needed to reach you and only you.

I am in dire need of your advice on a matter I know you are well versed in. While attending the function you so kindly inquired about—no injuries to report I am afraid—I encountered a young man.

I am sure by now you have realised the importance. The young man I met has had a profound effect upon me, and I require your advice on whether I am correct.

Upon meeting him, for the first time in my life, I found myself speechless. Not only that, but I couldn't tear my gaze away and I think I finally understand the meaning of looking into someone's eyes for the rest of time.

I cannot accurately put words together to describe the depth of the feelings that coursed through me in that single moment. One word from his lips and I was enraptured.

Part of me is praying I am incorrect and I have been bewitched by the spell of infatuation. However, the greater part of me is concerned that it has finally happened. As you well know, this is my greatest fear. If I am not, then I am afraid the end is almost here. There are a great many things we need to now discuss, and I believe seeing you in person would be the best way.

I am rushing things again, aren't I? My apologies. You know how I can be. The messenger has been instructed to wait until you have finished this and composed a reply.

Please write back as soon as possible. I would greatly appreciate your help with this matter.

And, as always, please take every step to ensure this letter is destroyed.

Kindest regards,
Your Sister

It took me far too long to write the letter, and by the time I was finished, Sam was awake.

"You need me?" Sam asked, half asleep. His dark hair was tousled, but his sharp eyes missed nothing. He looked a lot like Helen, but his father was apparent in the hard line of his jaw and the deep reddish-brown of his tight curls.

"Yes, please, Sam." Rising, I handed him the envelope. "You know how to get to William's house safely, I take it?"

"I do."

"Good. Take my horse, and get there as soon as you can. My boat will be ready for you at the docks. Do *not* let anyone see this letter. Once you arrive, please wait for a response."

As much as I'd have preferred him to take the car, getting it across the channel was a problem. Thanks to my contacts, borders weren't an issue, but traveling could be.

William lived with his wife, Alison, and their sons, David and Michael, in a small village skirting the border between France and Switzerland. The journey would take Sam a minimum of five days by horse, but that meant pushing Tara to her limits. I also expected William to insist he stay overnight before returning.

"I'll be back before you know it." He smiled, heading for the door.

A couple of hours later, I finished with the first pile of the notifications and had updated our records. They were death notices—all of them. The number of our un-matured descendants dying had increased since war had been declared, and although it was a concern, there was little we could do about it.

I picked up another notification. It was a request for assistance—recognisable by the insignia on the back of the envelope.

The nearest Seat had probably dealt with it, but I needed to make sure. There were times when unruly vampires fell through the cracks and we ended up picking up the pieces, but The Seats were good at keeping our rules. I was loath to admit it, but I needed them. I needed them to keep their own in check so I could do what I had to do with as little help as possible.

Still, requests for assistance couldn't be ignored. I tried to think of something other than this problem that would likely require me to leave the country—it was too close to William for comfort—but when I let my mind wander, all I thought of was the night before.

All roads lead to Rome. All thoughts lead to . . .

I almost hurled my pen across the room. I would have, anything to stop my thoughts from going there again, but Helen said, "Are you accepting visitors?"

There was a strange look in her eyes that I couldn't quite place. "Why not?" It would grind away the hours. "Who's visiting?"

Glancing at the clock, I saw it was just after lunchtime. I'd spent the entire morning wading through my pile of notifications. Perhaps the waiting wouldn't be as hard as I'd thought.

"A certain Mr. Synclair."

My heart stuttered in my chest for the briefest of moments. What reason did he have for visiting me? I'd met him only briefly, and only once. Surely my sudden departure couldn't have worried him enough to visit.

Maybe he felt the same way. Maybe he'd felt that connection, as well.

I sighed. What a silly notion. How could he possibly feel anything for me after meeting me only once?

I had hoped to hear from William before I was once again confronted by the enigma that was Mr. Ray Sinclair. The Fates were turning against me, a collaborative, determined effort to bring about the end of my race.

"Serenity?"

"Sorry," I answered automatically.

My heart raced with the sheer anticipation of seeing him once more. It made me want to run away from everything.

I followed Helen out of my study and to the sitting room. Even as I paused in the doorway, Helen scampering off to attend to something, I lost all ability to form a coherent sentence. And he hadn't noticed I was there yet.

He had his back to me, standing by the glass display cabinet where I kept my collection of precious stones. Every few seconds he leaned forward slightly, looking closer at one stone or another, perhaps trying to figure out what they were. It took a rare and knowledgeable person to be able to identify the uncut gems. Only I knew their origins, having collected them throughout the years.

His hand fluttered over the dark blue of the lapis lazuli, almost grazing the rough surface. Then he pulled back, as though he thought he shouldn't be touching it.

Clearing my throat, I forced myself to speak. "Mr. Sinclair, to what do I owe this pleasure?"

He straightened up, his shoulders tensing as he turned around and repositioned himself. "Miss Cardea, please, call me Ray. I'm sorry for intruding, but you left early last night . . ." He paused, struggling for words.

"I'm sorry about that. I felt unwell. I'm fine now." It was a lie. Fortunately, I had years of practice.

"Are you sure? You know we still have some excellent doctors at the hospital." His playful smile was infectious, and I found myself smiling brightly at him.

"I'm quite fine. There were just a few too many people, that was all." Even as the lie left my lips, guilt washed over me, which was a first.

"Would you come for a walk, Miss Cardea?" he offered, a faint blush creeping up his cheeks as he spoke.

"Serenity. I'd much prefer for you to call me Serenity."

I should have refused his invitation. I should have waited for William's reply, but I couldn't. I felt it again, that burning desire to stand with him like this forever. How could I possibly deny him? He looked so unsure of himself as he spoke. There was no way I could watch the uncertainty in his unusual eyes grow into something more when I had the power to stop it.

"We can take a walk through the gardens, if you wish."

I kept a reasonable distance between us while we walked. It was a pleasant and clear day, and with the warmth of late summer in the air, we didn't need to bother with coats. The nights were starting to turn chilly again, with the season starting to wind down, but there was one thing I still took pleasure in: the full blooms of my exotic flowers. The gardens of the few houses I had dotted around various countries were considerably larger than this one, but it suited my needs.

"How are you liking the city?" Ray asked, after a few minutes of comfortable silence.

"It's not the same as it used to be," I blurted out.

It had been years since I was last in London, though that information wasn't commonly known. I cursed myself for not thinking before speaking.

"You've been here before?" His tone was curious, but I felt as if he'd read more into my words than he was letting on.

"Many years ago," I admitted. It wasn't an easy task to avoid looking at him, not when I was drawn to him so.

"I don't think it's changed that much, but I didn't get out a lot when I was younger," he said quietly.

"But you have lived here your whole life. The differences would be less noticeable to you."

"I suppose that's true," he conceded.

Neither of us spoke again as we toured the small gardens. Ray never enquired about the more unusual plants I'd planted nor did he try to close the gap between us . . . though he wanted to. Whenever I looked down, his hand was twitching, as though he was contemplating reaching for mine but hadn't quite summoned the courage. What scared me was if he had, I wouldn't have stopped him.

"May I . . . ?" I paused, nodding towards the cane he was leaning on.

We'd come to a stop by the back door, but I wasn't ready to go inside yet. There were so many things I wanted to know about him, and for a moment, I was going to indulge myself.

"You don't have to answer," I added when he didn't say anything.

"I don't remember a lot of it. Any, really. Flashes now and then of what happened in the years after," he began, staring intently at his hand, a small scowl on his face. "It happened during the Great War. I was very small at the time, and my mother didn't get to me in time. No one was expecting the first wave of bombs, and our house was caught in it. The only reason the doctors saved my leg was because they thought it would strengthen as I grew."

"Did it?" I asked gently when he stopped.

"Yes," he said, glancing up. "I couldn't walk at all when I was a child. It's why I spent so much time surrounded by books. They were my best friends, and I still love them. Before this mess started, I was training to be a history teacher." He was smiling brightly again, and it was clear he was set on that path for life.

"Why are you really here, Ray?"

He winced. "The truth?"

"That would be a good place to start."

"I honestly don't know. I have no idea why I was so excited to dance with you. I don't know why I had to come by today to make sure you were well. There were so many stories about you from the other teachers, and something in me told me that I absolutely had to meet you. That somehow I had to get to know you. You must think me mad." He didn't meet my eyes when he spoke, opting for staring at the ground instead.

"Thank you," I whispered, causing him to look up.

"For what?"

"For checking on me today, for wanting to dance with me, and for telling me. I've enjoyed your company." I stopped myself right there. It would be so very wrong of me to continue.

"As I have enjoyed yours. More than I should admit."

"Join me for dinner." It was supposed to be a question, but it came out more like an order.

The day had shown me beyond any doubt that I couldn't wait for William's reply before seeing him again. I doubted Ray would keep away for a whole week, especially when I'd already offered dinner. As much as I wanted to fight what I felt, as much as it terrified me, I needed to keep him where I could protect him.

For now.

"I'd love to." His smile was so wide that I grinned back.

The twitching of his hand told me just how nervous he'd been about admitting the depth of his infatuation.

I wanted to tell him everything, and it took a great effort to keep from doing so. He would surely run if I were to blurt out my deepest secrets without any warning. Or he would be off to the asylum before I could stop him. Neither were reactions I wanted. And again, I was getting ahead of myself. There might not be a need to tell him everything.

Hope was a wonderful thing, even if it seemed increasingly unfounded.

After extending the dinner invitation for two nights' time, I watched as he walked down the road, presumably to his home. There was a bounce in his uneven step, and I could almost see the grin he was surely wearing. When he glanced back at the corner and saw me, the smile I'd envisioned was shining brightly as he raised his hand slightly before walking on.

I would need to find out where he lived, and soon. I wouldn't go there unless I was invited, but I wanted to check the area surrounding his home, in case there were any threats that needed dealing with. Just as I would watch the people close to him for any signs of anyone more than human.

"And you said you would never find him," Helen accused, closing the door.

"I don't know that," I said, hoping to avoid the subject.

"You invited him to dinner?"

"Yes, two nights' time. Will you join us?" It would be more comfortable if there were more than just the two of us.

"Yes, but you're avoiding the point, Serenity."

"I know."

"You know what William's reply will say. Why are you trying to fight it?"

"Because this is no life for him. This is no life for anyone human. And I'm scared." My reply was but a whisper at the end.

"What in heaven's name for?"

I hung my head as I answered her. "He'll run away."

"Serenity Cardea! Don't be so foolish. Ray has a good heart, and he will be as accepting of who you are, as of what you have to do to keep him safe. I know that look in his eyes, Sere. He may not know what he feels just yet, but he does feel something. Nothing is going to be able to change that." It was rare that Helen became this confrontational, but when she did, she was serious. "As for this being no life for a human, what is it you think we are?"

"Keepers."

"Un-matured Keepers. Essentially human. We're vulnerable. We don't have the kind of senses or immortality that you do. And I do quite well for myself in this world, thank you very much!" Her indignant tone was on the verge of dissolving into laughter.

She did more than "quite well" for herself. I'd lost count of the times she'd patched me up and ordered me about over the years. Jayne would end up the same, with a tough streak a mile long, three miles high, and the world wide.

"Don't fight this and tell him."

She was right, of course. It was the same advice I'd given William when he came to me about Alison. He'd been so frightened about telling her. Scared she would run off or think him insane. For hours he'd paced around our sitting room, all the while pouring out his deepest fears. It used to be such a beautiful time when we found our partners, but after our numbers started to dwindle, it became a fear. Finding our partner meant our lives were over. As the only two left, it was hard to know our days were numbered.

If Ray were the one for me, how could I possibly tell him that our lives were linked so absolutely? How could I tell him that he would be hunted because of our connection?

I *would* tell him, but not yet. I'd wait for William's reply, and cling to that last shred of hope that I was wrong. Not for my own sake, but for Ray's. Knowing his life would become a deadly game of cat and mouse would be hard enough to understand. Accepting the existence of mythical creatures like the professor was enough to scare anyone off.

And though no one had ever run before, there was always a first time.

Chapter Three

I sat by the window almost every day after that first week, eagerly awaiting Sam's return. It had also seen me by Ray's side more often. I wasn't putting up much resistance where he was concerned. There was still a small part of me that was attempting to fight the connection and praying I didn't have to force him into the world of myths and legends. However, the more time I spent with him, the more I realised Helen had been absolutely correct; I did know the answer William would send.

The dinner we'd shared together, two nights after our walk in the garden, had resulted in some interesting conversation, and an amusing introduction to Jayne.

"Hi, Uncle Ray." She'd practically attacked him when they first met, throwing herself at him and wrapping her tiny arms as high around his waist as possible.

"Erm, hello," he answered, awkwardly patting her head.

"I'm Jayne."

I'd stood back, watching the whole exchange with an amused smile on my face. She hadn't even let me say my own greetings. Instead, she'd taken a firm hold of his hand and almost dragged him into the dining room, chattering all the way. It was all Ray could do to keep up with her. After those first few seconds of unexpected contact, he was completely comfortable with her, quite content with letting her talk his ear off until dinner was served.

"Jayne, it's time for bed," Helen said, not long after dinner was finished.

"Good night, Uncle Ray. Good night, Aunt Sere," she sang, giving us each a peck on the cheek.

"Good night, Jayne," we both answered, though Ray had a slightly confused look on his face.

"Thank you," I mouthed to Helen as she went to tuck in her daughter.

Turning my attention to Ray, I apologised for the exuberant nature of Jayne. "I'm sorry about that. She tends to get overly excited when she meets new people."

"She is absolutely adorable. I thought she was your sister?"

Ah, there was a question I didn't want to answer. Jayne had told him many things about the short life she remembered with me. Everything from the secret passages I had shown her in our old house to the frequent "trips" I took. Fortunately, a quick look had silenced her. She hadn't mentioned anything about our relationship. Mainly because she was not yet old enough to understand the complexities. She knew I was her aunt and Helen was her mother. Outside of that, she didn't comprehend the need to differentiate between who I was and who I was supposed to be.

"In a way. She's Helen's daughter, and I've known her since she was born. They're family." There was no need to add that I had also known Helen since her birth.

"You're very lucky."

"Yes. I don't know what would have happened without them." That was a lie. I knew exactly where I'd be if William hadn't suggested taking Lona's daughters in all those years ago. Only one of my sister's children took me up on my offer, and I'd never looked back. "Tell me about your family."

"You met my mother at the auction. Her name is Liza, and she is the most wonderful woman. It's a good thing she likes having me around the house. I can barely cook anything beyond burnt toast, so I'm fortunate she enjoys cooking for me. In all honesty, she's been there for me more than I could've hoped. I can't imagine someone more kind and loving." The picture he painted of his mother was done with absolute reverence. It was clear he loved her very much. "Of course, it's been just the two of us since my father died."

"Do you miss him?" I asked, gently laying my hand on his arm.

"I don't remember him. He died in the first year of the last war. He'd been in the army before the war, and from what my mother has told me, it was what he loved to do. All I have is the book he left for me before he went away to war," he said, smiling. His eyes had a faraway look about them, as if he were trying to find even the briefest memories of his father. "Do you remember your parents?"

I took a deep breath, fully prepared to lie, to relay the same falsities everyone was told: my mother died in childbirth and my father soon after. But I didn't. I should have, but something stopped me.

"Yes. They were wonderful people. I do miss them, but they led a good life, and I know they're happy. Helen has been in my life for so long now that she is my family."

If he was aware of the lie that had already been told countless times in the city, he didn't say anything. For that I was grateful. The reasons behind my falsehoods were simple: people asked fewer questions when they thought you never knew your parents.

"I'm sure they would be very proud of you." His response surprised me. There was plenty for them to be proud of, but nothing Ray knew about. "You have made such a difference in the time you have been here."

It all became clear then. He was referring to the donations I'd made to aid the evacuated children. It was a meagre amount in the grand scheme of my life, but enough to ensure that Jayne and Helen were where I could protect them and that Sam was overlooked when it came to the war.

"I was brought up to help those I can." How true that was. "It's something I do wherever I am." It felt good to tell Ray the truth. Seeing the sparkle in his eyes when I revealed even the smallest piece of information was exhilarating.

It was one of the numerous things we discussed that night at dinner, and many an occasion afterwards. Our conversations gave me the distinct feeling he knew something was off.

ᛏᚼᚳᛘᚦᛉᚳᚠᛏᚷᛁᛈᛏᚾ

"Tell me more about the places you've lived," Ray said eagerly.

Jayne had been talking to him again, telling stories of the places I'd seen. But I couldn't tell him that yet. How could I explain the wonderful and amazing cities I'd lived in, when most of them were nothing more than rubble now? Rome, one of those many places, still stood, but it was desolate compared to its original glory. How could I describe America at a time when its existence was unknown and India back when the humans thought the world was flat? He must have noticed the change in my expression as I contemplated what to say.

"Forgive me. I didn't mean to upset you." His voice was a whisper, his eyes downcast.

"It's not your fault, Ray. Mine is a long and complicated story, the places I've lived and the things I've seen . . . I want to tell you, and I will, just not yet." I forced myself to meet his gaze.

"I understand."

I had to look away. He shouldn't understand so much while knowing so little. "Let's get you home. It's getting late, and I don't want to be responsible for your mother fretting over you," I said, rising from my chair.

"Come for dinner," he suggested as we reached the door.

I was all prepared to decline his offer when I heard the approaching hooves of my horse. Glancing down the street, I spotted Sam. He rode up quickly and came to a stop right outside the gate, a smile on his face. He knew what was in the letter he was surely carrying. His expression said so.

Without thinking, I sprinted forward, helping him from the saddle. He'd clearly been riding hard all day in an attempt to get home before nightfall.

It was only when Sam was safely leaning on me that I realised my mistake.

Ray had seen everything.

He looked shocked as Helen moved past him, racing to her brother's side. It wasn't right for me to have done what I had. Women weren't supposed to be able to help grown men from their horses. I was mentally berating myself as Helen led Sam into the house. The letter could wait.

My mind was working overtime, trying to come up with some lie to explain the strength he'd clearly seen, as well as my ability to recognise the hoof-falls of my horse from a distance.

Ray's mouth remained agape for a moment longer before he carefully navigated the stairs and asked, "Dinner on Friday?"

"Friday," I agreed, after realising he hadn't actually asked the question I'd been expecting.

It was a couple of days away, so that would give me time to think about the mistake I'd made and what I would tell him about it. It also gave me time to read the message from William. After reading that, everything would be clearer.

I swore there was a spring in his step again. Listening harder, I heard the faint tune of whistling. It was a light, happy song, perfectly suited to him. Though I was concerned about him walking home alone, I kept that firmly to myself. He would no doubt refuse any kind of escort, especially one from me. He struck me as stubborn—and curious. I continued to watch him until he turned the corner after a brief glance back in my direction.

"Helen, would you take Tara around to her stable?"

She'd been standing behind me for a couple of minutes, quietly observing. As she wandered off to take care of the horse, she was muttering under her breath. "No point in sending the poor thing halfway around the world. Should've just listened to me in the first place."

Turning back to the house, it was my turn to smile. There really had been no need to send Sam to France for an answer I was now certain of. Whatever shred of hope I'd clung to was gone. It was impossible to deny the feelings that were stirring within me.

I found Sam in the kitchen sniffing at the leftovers.

"Any problems?" I asked as I took over preparing something for him. "Go on, sit down."

"None at all. Just took longer than I thought. Six days there, six days back. William insisted I stay for a day before he wrote his reply, but you expected as much," he answered, adding a thank you for the food.

"That's good. He wrote a reply then?"

Sam let out a laugh as I hovered, eagerly awaiting his answer.

"He did." He paused briefly, before pulling a sealed envelope out of his pocket and placing it on the table in front of me.

Grabbing the letter, I gave Sam a brief kiss on the cheek and turned towards the sitting room. Helen had come in moments before and was preparing a bath for her brother. Jayne was snoring quietly in her bed, unaware of anything that had happened, and Tara was stabled.

"There was also a message from William," Sam said, as I reached the kitchen door. "He says: take your own advice."

Turning back, I stared at him for a second. Sam's dark hair was full of bits of leaves and dirt, but he didn't notice. All of his attention was focused on his home-cooked meal, but the telling smile on his face between bites, accompanied by the verbal message, sent my heart soaring.

Take your own advice. The message was as clear as if William had been standing in the room chastising me for being so stupid. I'd given William the same advice upon meeting his wife.

He'd fought so hard when he met her. As soon as he stopped fighting, their lives had come together beautifully. He told her about us, about everything. William had asked me to be there. She sat there quietly while he explained. Afterwards, she rose from her seat, took his face in her hands, and scolded him for not telling her sooner. Neither of them had looked back since.

Eager to open the letter, despite already knowing its contents, I took the nearest seat.

Dearest Sister,

Of course you are correct in your assumption, and I am so very happy for you.

I trust that my separate message has also reached you. You are well aware of how hard your life, and his, will become if you choose to ignore that advice. I cannot stress how important it is that you listen to your heart for once and not your head. I know you far too well, my sister, and I know how you think. Do not let your fear of this cloud your mind. For both your sakes.

You are correct about rushing our meeting. I feel that the times, as they are, may be too unstable for us to meet safely. When things have settled, we shall arrange a safe place for us to do so.

One day I would love to meet the young man who has finally managed to render you speechless. You always were the most outspoken of us, and I know it is a sight I would relish. I am sure he must be a wonderful man to have affected you so deeply.

On a final note, I am pleased to hear you did not injure anyone during your most recent social outing. Perhaps this is a change for the better?

I hope to hear from you soon.

Always,
Your Brother

He was right. As if I expected anything else. There was an uncontrollable urge when Ray was around. One that demanded I tell him everything. I needed to stop hiding it. He knew there was something about me that was as far away from normal as possible.

But as much as I wanted to tell him, there was also so much I needed to do. Most important of all, it was time to prepare for the inevitable outcome of my numbered days. William and I would need to meet, the sooner the better, and we would have to exhaust any option we hadn't already looked at for resurrecting our race. But he was right; we would wait until the war was over.

Panic flared through me at the thought of leaving the world to fend off the vampires on its own.

Pushing those thoughts to one side, I concentrated on how nice it would be to stare into Ray's eyes and not have to look away. After reading the letter once more, I placed it in the fireplace.

My life had been going along the same path for so long, me being somewhat careless in my encounters with The Seats, or any vampire actually.

All that had to change. Ray's safety was my highest priority, immediately followed by his happiness and well-being.

Changing my life wasn't an issue, but it wasn't just my life that was going to be twisted around like a knotted tree root. There were so many things I would have to explain, now that my decision was made, and all of them required me to choose my words very carefully. More so when I explained to him that his mother could never know of my world. That was for her protection more than anything else.

I changed into the dark-coloured men's clothing that I had for such occasions, made my way through the quiet house, and paused for a moment in front of my study. It was tempting to stop in there and open the metal cabinet that was hidden away in the back of the room.

"You're going hunting?" Helen's voice startled me.

"No. Not tonight. I'm going to sweep the area around Ray's house." There was little point in lying to Helen about what I was planning.

"Then you do *not* need what you're thinking of getting," she told me, crossing her arms over her chest.

"I was only considering the possibility."

"Good. Now, will we see you for breakfast?"

"Yes."

Helen smiled, and we exchanged our goodnights before she headed up the stairs for bed. Leaving the door to my study as it was, I slipped out into the night.

Ray's house was easy enough to find. He'd tried, unsuccessfully, to invite me over and had insisted on telling me where he lived. I took note of his directions and reminded myself to check that there were no threats nearby.

It would be easier to start with the streets a few over from his house and work my way right up to his next-door neighbours. The task would take me most of the night, but it was worth it. Although I didn't expect to find anything of significance, I'd sleep . . . *feel* a lot better knowing there were no immediate threats.

When I'd glanced over my map of London, I had overlooked the fact that Ray's home was only four streets over from some of the places I frequented most. It was often visited by thirsty vampires. That area of the city was heavily populated with humans—all out after dark and none with families or people to miss them. It was close enough to the river that any bodies could be disposed of. And who would listen to the drunken ramblings of a vagrant who claimed to have been attacked by vampires if they were left alive?

Vampires weren't designed to let their meals live.

And a thirsty vampire on the loose could wreak all kinds of havoc. So despite Ray's house being as far away as it was, it was still too close for my tastes.

It looked as if I would be making trips to this part of town on a nightly basis.

I let my senses roam out around me as I walked, eager to get out of the area and closer to Ray's house. Things had been quiet of late, but there were at least two vampires who would need to feed regularly, and human blood was the only thing agreeable to their palates.

It was possible to live off animals, but animal blood alone was simply not an option for most. Feeding from humans meant they needed blood twice a week, and that was if they didn't kill their meal. Living off animals took a strong will, a poor palate, and an ability to feed on an almost nightly basis.

"I still don't understand how you have never killed. You should try it sometime," a hauntingly familiar voice said. It was barely above a whisper, but it was close.

"My dear, you know I will never take the life of someone. If I had the stomach for it, I wouldn't drink from them at all." It was Issac Baruti. Of all the places for him to be, and for his wife to be with him.

Hiding in the shadows cast by the nearest building, I eavesdropped on their conversation. It was clear they were out to feed, though that wasn't my main concern. With Poppy Baruti being who she was, even though she'd left The Seats, I couldn't let them have the slightest inclination of what I was. Being so close to a Seat of Power was bad enough, but Ray knew these two. He'd been training at the same university at which Issac Baruti taught. It was far too close for comfort, and having them in this part of town . . .

"Ah, I know what you mean, Issac, I do. I cannot believe you convinced me to give up killing them." Poppy's voice was as stunning as she was, the old Roman accent barely noticeable in her words.

"Power is not everything," he answered.

Such true words.

The sounds that followed were ones I'd heard many times. The sound of drinking blood. It normally resulted in a dead body floating down the river —or whatever convenient dumping location happened to be nearby. However, when the sound of feeding vampires ceased, there was a slight moan from a distinctly human throat.

They'd left him alive. Perhaps Poppy Baruti *had* changed.

Sinking farther back into the shadows, I waited, fully prepared to follow the professor and his wife home. Knowing where they lived had become my priority for the night. Since Ray was friends with them, it was entirely reasonable that he would want to socialise. Unfortunately, not arousing suspicion meant I might also have to spend time with them. Perhaps I could keep Ray occupied enough that he would have no time to see them.

Following the freshly fed couple proved to be easy. They were distracted with each other's company. They teased one another as they went, talking about their upcoming evening.

"You know what we haven't done in too long," Issac said, pausing in the shadows of an alley. "We haven't had someone to play with for a while."

I wasn't sure I wanted to know, and judging by Poppy's slight squeal, she understood exactly what he meant and was looking forward to it. Whatever it was, they didn't act on it and continued heading home.

As I expected, they were living on the outskirts of town. Their house was nondescript, nothing to distinguish it from its few neighbours. At least they were a fair distance from Ray. That was the most comforting thought.

After watching them retire for the evening, I raced back towards town. Now that the task had been completed, I needed to continue with my sweep.

Ensuring Ray's safety may have just become a full-time job.

Chapter Four

The nights following my invisible encounter with Poppy and Issac Baruti, I wandered the streets around Ray's house, watching. Most of my time was spent thinking about what I'd say to him, how I'd break through the cloak of secrecy surrounding my world. Death was the usual punishment to anyone who found out. At least where the vampires were concerned. The Weres weren't so strict with their rules, though only humans mated to one were told. The witches kept to themselves. Scattered and scared after the burning times, there were few of them. Risking persecution again wasn't an option.

"Stop it," Helen scolded me.

"What?"

"You're pacing again. It's going to be fine. There's no need to tell him everything tonight. Just ask him to join you on a ride tomorrow and tell him you want to talk to him."

Friday had come too quickly. Nervous about dinner with Ray's mother, and dreading his reaction to my secrets, I was as highly strung as I could get. Helen was sure I was going to wear a hole in the rug.

For two days I hadn't seen him, and I had been deeply tempted to stalk his back garden in the night so I could catch a glimpse. The only time I'd been brave enough to chance a trip that close to his house, I found him watching out of his bedroom window. After that, I vowed never to spy on him again.

Other than the distinct upset I felt at being away from him for any length of time, things had become better.

Since accepting the connection, I'd never been more at peace. Though peace was clearly a laughable concept as I began to pace yet again.

"Sam is getting the car," Helen informed me, placing herself in my path.

She stood there, hands on hips, staring me down. It was about the only way she was going to stop me.

"Oh, tell him not to fuss. I'll walk."

"I'll do no such thing. Ray's mother will most likely insist he walk you home if you turn up on foot. Then where will you be? Following him out into the night again. You are taking the car."

She had a point.

"Fine, but if I'm a mess now, which is a clear fact, then I'll be even worse if I don't get to walk for a while." She knew full well how I got when I was like this.

"You'll be perfectly fine. Now stop worrying and go enjoy your evening." With that, she all but pushed me out the door and into the waiting car. I expected to be a complete mental wreck by the time we pulled up outside Ray's house, but I was surprised to find I was perfectly at ease.

It was Ray. He was the reason I was suddenly so relaxed.

So this is what it feels like, I pondered.

There was no nervous shifting as I waited for someone to answer the door. Even when I saw it was Ray's impeccably dressed mother who'd opened it, I simply smiled, calm and collected.

"Miss Cardea, it is a pleasure to see you again," she greeted me, smiling brightly as she took my shawl.

"You, as well, Mrs. Synclair. If you would, please, call me Serenity."

"Of course, but I must insist that you call me Liz, dear. Mrs. Synclair makes me feel so old, and Liza was my mother's name."

Mrs. Synclair, dressed in a simple skirt suit with the same hairstyle she'd worn to the auction, stepped to the side, allowing me in. She and her home were a matching pair, both elegant.

Their house wasn't as grand as some of the ones I'd lived in, but it was just right.

There were a couple of family portraits adorning the walls—large, heavy-framed things. Yet everything else was relatively simple. Matching carpets ran up the hall and stairs, thick and fluffy under my feet, and were more modern than the house led me to believe. It was exactly how I'd imagined Ray's home.

Ray was in the dining room, setting the table with one hand, a wistful look on his face. I smiled as he shuffled around, grabbing a fork or knife from the sideboard then setting it carefully down in place. He was dressed as his mother was, impeccably. Dark trousers and a light shirt, neatly tucked in at the waist. The colours highlighted his hair, and no doubt the pale shirt would bring out those eyes of his.

"Ray, dear?" his mother prompted.

For the first time in my life, I felt embarrassed as he caught me staring. My head dipped when he looked up, straight at me, but I lifted it again, unable to keep my gaze from him for long.

Dinner went well after that. The slightly awkward silence that had developed as we stood staring at each other was soon cleared in the form of Liz. She truly was a wonderful woman, and she did everything possible to make me feel at home. She was more than happy to exchange a couple of interesting stories from Ray's childhood, much to his displeasure and my amusement. Though when he insisted I should share some of mine, I refused. Those would come in time.

"Dinner was delicious, Liz," I complimented her as we cleared the table.

"Thank you. I must apologise about the vegetable mash once again."

I laughed. It had been the worst part of the meal, and the only part Ray was responsible for.

"It was fine, really. You should have seen some of the concoctions I created when I first started cooking. I swear, you couldn't feed them to the animals." Of course, practice made perfect, and I'd had almost three thousand years of practice.

"I'm sure it wasn't as bad as that." Ray's voice startled me. I hadn't heard him enter the kitchen.

"They were far worse, I assure you. However, that's a story for another time. For now, I'm afraid I must be heading home. I promised Jayne I'd read her a story before bed this evening."

"Well, it has been wonderful having you, Serenity. You must come for a visit again, soon," Liz insisted, grasping my hand tightly in hers.

"I have a feeling she'll be spending more time here, Mother," Ray interrupted, stealing me away. He led me to the door and just . . . stopped. He seemed worried.

"Is everything all right, Ray?"

"Yes. I wanted to ask you something," he mumbled, looking at his shoes.

"You can ask me anything, Ray."

"I . . . I wanted to ask if we could make this, us, official," he said, finally glancing back up. "I'm enjoying your company so much and find that you are almost constantly on my mind. My birthday is coming up and Mother is insisting on throwing a party. I would like you there with me, by my side."

"Ray, I'd love to, but . . ." I wondered how to explain it to him.

"*But?*"

"There are some things I need to tell you before you accept me. Things you may not understand. Come to my house tomorrow morning. We can take a ride out, and I'll tell you everything. Then after that, if you still want me, I am yours."

There was concern on his face, thoughts, perhaps, that I didn't want him. That was utterly ludicrous but I needed him to know what I was. I had to give him the chance to run if he chose.

"Does this have something to do with your parents?" he asked, his eyes searching mine.

"In a way. It's more to do with me and why my life is so complicated. Please, try not to worry. It's nothing bad, I promise." Hesitantly, I brought my hand up to his cheek, running my fingers down to his chin. "Please?"

"Tomorrow morning?"

"First thing," I said with a smile.

"Then I shall see you first thing."

"Thank you," I told him before I turned towards the car.

I felt his gaze on me as I greeted Sam and climbed into the back. Turning back to the house, I saw that Ray was indeed standing there, watching my every move. Smiling, I raised my hand and waved one last time before Sam shut the door and we were off. I toyed with the idea of roaming the streets again after I'd read to Jayne, but I would only be tempted to guard his home as he slept. It would be best if I avoided him for the night.

Most of my time was spent ghosting around the house.

By the time dawn was raiding the sky, I was ready for the day to be over with. I wanted to tell him everything, to get it out in the open and face whatever reaction he had. It wasn't until Helen reminded me that I realised I hadn't changed after dinner. It wouldn't do for Ray to turn up and find me looking the same as when I'd left him.

Once I was in proper clothes, I went to prepare Tara. Ray didn't have a horse of his own, or at least he didn't keep one at his house, so I readied my other horse, Falcon. We mainly used him to pull the carriage, but he was well-tempered enough to be ridden when the occasion called for it.

Not long after breakfast, Helen called down. It was barely loud enough for me to claim to have heard it down at the stables, but I answered anyway. Ray would soon find out exactly how much I could hear.

"Send him down, Helen," I called back to her.

It was a beautiful day with few clouds and little chance of rain according to the news. A perfect day for taking a ride through the surrounding countryside.

"Good morning, Serenity," Ray greeted me a few moments later.

"Good morning. Have you ridden . . . ?" I stopped speaking as I turned towards him.

How could I have forgotten?

"I'm not very good, but I have ridden before," he answered, saving me from embarrassment.

"I'm sorry, we can take the carriage or one of the cars if you prefer," I offered, not entirely sure how I managed to be so oblivious.

He smiled, giving me the impression I was forgiven. "So long as you have a step I can use, it will be fine. Which one will you be riding?"

"Tara. I prepared Falcon for you. He's getting on a bit now, but you shouldn't have any problems with him," I explained, pointing out the grey gelding.

Ray had little trouble mounting Falcon once he was provided with a step. It was fascinating to watch how he adapted to challenges so easily.

"Ready?"

"As I'll ever be." He smiled, looking uncomfortable.

"We'll take it slow."

There was somewhere I wanted to take him. It was a good hour's ride out of the city, but it was a safe place. Once there, I'd answer all of his questions and demonstrate anything he needed to see. I should have been terrified, but I was strangely calm yet again. It really was him. How had I ever seen him as my weakness? Even though I hadn't managed to sleep, I felt more alive and alert than ever before. That was all because of Ray.

Neither of us said much during our ride out of the city. He glanced at me every few minutes, but the silence we shared was comfortable.

Well, that's a new feeling.

It was just over an hour later when I steered Tara off the path and into the uncharted woods at the edge of London. Fortunately, I knew where I was going. Falcon was used to letting Tara lead and followed her into the trees. It wasn't long before we got to where I wanted to be. It was secluded and far enough from the city that we weren't likely to be disturbed by anyone, especially any travelling vampires.

"Where did you learn to ride like that?" Ray asked as I set up the blanket and food that I'd brought.

"I learned to ride when I was very young, many years ago," I answered truthfully. "I like the speed Tara is capable of, but I prefer my own."

"Your own?" he questioned as we sat down.

"Yes. Ray, what would you say if I told you there were things in this world far beyond anything you know and believe?" It was as good a place as any to start.

"I'd ask to which *things* you are referring," he said, speaking slowly.

"Creatures. The things nightmares and fairy tales are made of. Beings who walk the night preying on those weaker than they." I couldn't look him in the eye as I spoke.

"Are you trying to tell me that you're some mythical creature here to do some unspeakable deed?" he whispered, worry in his voice. At least he wasn't laughing.

"No. I'm not here to do unspeakable deeds, and I'm not a mythical creature. Myths and legends do not cover what I am." I glanced up to observe his reaction.

"You aren't human."

"No. Not in the sense that *you* are. I don't need to eat or sleep. I'm faster than anything you know of and I'm stronger than you could imagine."

"What are you?" he asked gently. There was no scepticism in his voice. It simply sounded as though he didn't want to offend me by asking.

"No one really knows. It's not clear exactly how we came to be. We've existed for as long as the other races, and at some point someone decided we were here to protect those needing it, to keep the balance. Our name came about long ago, but it's the title of what we do, not what we are.

Keepers. Immortal Keepers of Peace." I paused for a moment to let him absorb the information before continuing. "Ray, I was born in the year 1067 BC." I looked away as I finished my speech. This was where he would surely run or laugh or accuse me of creating some farce.

"You say you keep the balance between our race and the others. Who are the others?" he asked, shocking me. I'd expected him to question some part of my statement, but not that part.

"There are five races: humans, vampires, witches, Weres, and us," I began. "The witches and Weres are relatively reclusive. After the witch trials they kept to themselves, mostly out of fear. The Weres stick together, living in colonies in remote places. It's the vampires we have the most trouble with."

"Vampires? As in Dracula?"

"In a way. They have few traits in common with that fictional portrayal. Although they are somewhat more complex. The myth about them burning in the sunlight is only partly true. It depends on how powerful they are. The more powerful, the more potent their weakness is. Generally, they're as strong as I am and nearly as fast." The excitement of sharing this with him was almost enough to leave me breathless. "They aren't entirely never-changing. Their hair and nails grow, though at an exceptionally slower rate. They have the strength, the numbers, and the organisation to take over the human race without a second thought—"

"And you're the reason they haven't?"

"Yes." I paused for a moment, staring intently at him. "You're taking this very well, Ray."

"I guess it isn't much of a surprise, really. I always thought there was something else beyond what I was seeing—especially when it came to you." He shrugged. "Even before I met you, when I heard you would be attending the auction, I knew I had to be there. There were so many rumours about you, about what you did and the causes you gave to so willingly. Something in those stories intrigued me and made me want to meet you all the more. Then, when I did, you were like no one I'd met before. So it stands to reason that there's more to you than meets the eye."

"Still, I tell you I'm three thousand years old, and that vampires, witches and Weres are real, and . . . *This*," I gestured to him, all the while shaking my head, "is not a normal reaction."

"Would you prefer me to run screaming? Or fetch the men from the asylum?" There was a light, teasing edge to his voice.

"No, but you may do that yet." I sighed, not quite able to believe how well things were going.

"There's more to your story?"

"Much more. Life with me is never easy. It is full of danger, more so now than ever before. Every few years I'm forced to move. There are occasions when I'll be gone for days or weeks at a time, and I cannot always tell you where I'll be." This was the breaking point. Would he be able to accept me, faults and all, and without explanation when needed?

"Serenity, the feelings I hold for you are growing. Each day I spend with you finds me wanting more time. I understand things aren't as they seem, and I'm willing to accept that. More than willing. As much as I'd like to aid you in what you do, I know I can't. However, I'd like to be with you," he told me, taking my hand.

"There's still a lot for you to learn, but if you're willing, and you'll still have me, then I am yours. Completely."

"I'd like that. I'd like that very much."

Chapter Five

We spent most of the day sitting among the trees. I told him so much, but they were only a few of the things I'd seen in my life, what I remembered at least. Names and specifics faded over the years, but I still remembered the magnificence of the places I'd visited. However, my friends and family were always engraved into my mind, a constant reminder of what we protected. I fought to hold onto those memories, refusing to let them go.

Our conversation skirted around the aspects of how to avoid and identify the vampires.

"May I ask you a question?"

I laughed. He insisted on starting each question like that, asking if he was allowed to ask. "Of course you may."

"How are only some vampires able to walk in the sun?"

"It all depends on the lives they take," I explained. "Draining the life from someone gives them power. The more lives they drain, the more powerful they are. And the stronger they are, the more potent their weakness is. For those who insist on taking the life of their meal every time, it means they'll never see the sun. Even a cloudy day is too much for those vampires to risk. Although, if they stop taking lives then their power will wane."

"That makes sense. As the saying goes: the bigger they are, the harder they fall. Or similar at least."

Ray sat there, smiling, taking everything I told him at face value, with barely any questions. He leaned forward eagerly whenever I told him about my past, as if he couldn't get enough of who I was and what I'd done over the years. He was either burying his feelings so deep that I had no chance of finding them, or he really was taking things as well as he appeared to be.

"You mentioned something about Seats of Power earlier. What do they do?" he asked, lying flat on his back, staring up into the trees.

"They police the race. There are eight of them spread out over the various continents and hot spots. If we don't influence a vampire who's causing trouble first, then they'll inevitably be called for an audience with the nearest Seat."

It was a simple system they used, one created by Poppy Baruti herself. A vampire was called to the nearest Seat, given an opportunity to state their defence, and then effectively made to submit to their own execution.

"Few vampires survive an audience. For those who fail to attend, their fate is much worse."

"How so?"

"How about we save that discussion for another time? There's something I've been meaning to ask you." Detailing The Seats' preference for dealing with those who didn't comply was not something I wanted to discuss. It was gruesome at best. At worst . . .

"Ask away."

"Why history? You could teach anything you wanted. Why choose the one subject that you cannot ever truly know the answer to?"

"Exactly," he said, his eyes going wide and lighting up. "I can never know the answer. Over time things will change and new information will arise, but we'll never know for certain. There are so many glorious cities and cultures which have been lost to the sands of time. How can I not want to keep them alive in some way?" He spoke with such passion, such purpose. It was easy now to see why he'd chosen history as his subject. "Then of course, you would know more about that than I do. Would it be too much for me to ask hundreds of questions about the places you have seen?"

I had to laugh. The historian in him would want to know that. I could have sat with him for hours just talking about my life. It would have been an absolute pleasure to tell him of the party I had once attended in Rome. Or the mixture of sadness and relief as the people of Egypt buried their last Pharaoh. But there was the distinct smell of rain in the air, and I didn't want to keep him out in it.

"It must have been fascinating to have lived for so long."

"More like a curse." Eternal life wasn't something I would recommend. "For years I've watched my family grow and pass. It has been a joy, seeing each of them through their lives . . ."

"But you want that for yourself?"

"Yes. In my life there has never been time for relationships or families of my own. And I would never have wanted them. The way we find our wea— our partners is designed so that we cannot possibly miss them. We allow our instincts to guide us when we choose where to live, and then, when we meet them, we know. I cannot really describe it, except to say it's the feeling of wanting to stare into someone's eyes for the rest of time."

Even that wasn't accurate enough. Sometimes people met each other and they just knew they would get along, something in them called out to the other. It was like that with us, but deeper and more profound. And then that connection was made, that dreaded connection which was the end of us.

"You were going to say something else, instead of *our partners*," he prompted gently.

"I was," I admitted, looking away.

"Tell me? Please?" He sat up, reaching for me.

"Weakness. I was going to say weakness," I said quickly, glancing down to avoid his gaze. I wasn't able to lie to him.

He was gentle as he ran his fingers down my jaw, guiding my face back to his. "Is that because the vampires will try to use me against you?"

"No. Ray, what I have to tell you isn't easy, and I need you to know that I will protect you for as long as I live. No matter what happens." My words were slow and measured in an effort to make myself clear. I searched his eyes as I spoke, staring into them as though I could see his very being.

"Serenity," his tone was almost chastising, "nothing you can say will make me leave."

"Even so, you'll always have that choice." I paused, wondering if there was any point in choosing my words carefully now. "Our weakness *is* our partner. The only way we can be killed is through their death. There's an unbreakable link between your life and mine. When your life is over, by whatever means, so is mine." Taking his hand, I placed it over my heart so he could feel my heart beating, as I could hear his. "We used to have a saying: As your heart beats, so does mine. When your heart sleeps, so will mine."

"That sounds fair enough," he answered, leaving his hand where it was when I moved mine.

"I just told you that the only way to kill me, a three thousand year old immortal being, is to kill you and you say *that sounds fair enough?*" He was smiling, running his fingers over my collarbone. I frowned, wondering if he was sane.

"Yes. It makes sense. I assume you only feel this contact once. I also assume that each race has a weakness. Therefore, it's understandable that this connection is yours. From what you've said, and what I've seen, there's little that can harm you. I'm a firm believer that everyone has his or her time."

"I'm dumbfounded. I never thought it would be this easy." I was still in shock over what had been said.

"Of course, those beliefs were before I realised there were immortal beings walking the earth," he said, smiling.

He was fascinated when I explained our defences to him. How we couldn't be turned into a vampire because we were immune to their blood. How the witches' spells couldn't harm us. How each variation of Were was unable to shift forms when they were near us. And our biggest asset: the fact that even though vampires could read the minds of any race, they couldn't read ours—not unless we wanted them to. It was the same with their powers, those who had them weren't able to use them against us.

There was a kind of switch in our minds, something only we could see and use. One flip and a vampire could read our thoughts. Another and they couldn't. So simple, and so effective. It was there in our un-matured descendants, too, but the switch was permanently at work.

There was nothing but understanding, and occasionally confusion on his face as I spoke.

"Ray, I don't think you quite understand the gravity of how life with me will affect you."

"Then tell me. Serenity, I understand life won't be easy, but I want to be with you." His eyes were alive with the conviction of his words.

"There are only two of us left, as you know. But, I never told you why there are so few. The vampires know of our weakness, Ray. They have hunted us until there were no more to hunt. The only reason I'm still alive is because I hadn't met you. My last brother William is only alive because he moves so often and tells no one except me where he'll be. If they find you they . . ." As much as I wanted to tell him, I didn't want to scare him off.

"They'll stop at nothing to kill me."

"Yes. For some reason, when the attacks started, our descendants stopped maturing. Generations came and went, and nothing. Not a single one. William was the last to reach maturity. After him there have been no more, and we don't know why. The vampires show *no* mercy. They're cruel and have no regard for life." I searched his face as I spoke, looking for any sign of fear.

I found none.

"What do they want?"

"Dominance. Over everyone." My mind started to dwell on the problem that was our ever-dwindling numbers, and the consequences of the day we were no longer here.

"We should head back. There's a storm coming, and I don't think you would enjoy being ill," I told him, looking at the dark clouds which were closing in.

It took me only seconds to pack everything we'd taken for the day. It was amazing how comfortable I was around him now that he knew everything. I had no issues darting after a napkin that had been caught by a sudden wind or using my strength to load up my horse without help. It was only when it came to mounting the horses that we hit a small issue.

"Oh my! I never thought," I whispered as Ray stood staring at Falcon. "Would you be offended if I offered to help you?"

"Normally I'd decline your offer, but I don't think I have much of a choice."

"I promise not to tell anyone if you accept my help. How's that?"

He laughed. "I didn't figure you for the gossiping type."

It was a simple enough task to offer my hands as a step for him. He reluctantly put all of his weight on me, steadying himself on my shoulders.

"You won't hurt me," I reassured him when he paused.

"Are you sure?"

"Completely. If you knew some of the situations I've been in over the years, you would know I'm very hard to kill."

With only a moment more of hesitation, he clambered atop Falcon. Once I was settled in Tara's saddle, I dug my heels in and we surged into a pleasant trot.

"I want to ask you so much," Ray said quietly.

"Ask, though I may not always be able to answer."

"When you say Weres, do you mean *werewolves?*"

"In a way. The Weres are spread throughout the world, living in groups made up of the shifters, their mates, and any children they have. They don't all shift into wolves at the full moon, though. The ones in this country change into black leopards. The ones in Russia, on the other hand, they do turn into wolves."

There were other types of Weres: the Congo Lions of Africa, the Great Bears of Canada, and the Panthers of Brazil. Most of them migrated occasionally, but they stayed within their respective countries, rarely coming into contact with each other. Their numbers had stayed roughly the same over the years. They weren't a thriving species like the vampires, but they survived and were happy enough.

"They sound like fascinating creatures."

"Standing at almost twice the size of their animals, they are truly beautiful, and deadly. And they can be very hostile to others, preferring the solitude of their own, opposed to the social aspects of regular society, and they're fiercely protective." Stunning creatures or not, I avoided them unless I had to.

"Do they mature, like you? Or is it different for everyone?"

"All vampires were once human, but were created by the exchange of blood. Witches are born and inherit their powers, and Weres are also born, not made. The same can be said of us. Then when our bodies and minds are ready, we mature." It was the only way to accurately describe what we went through, a kind of growing up process. "Our bodies get stronger, faster. Our senses heighten, and our gifts make themselves known. It takes a couple of weeks, a gradual change so we can grow accustomed to what we are."

"So there's no set age? It just . . . happens?"

"Whenever we're ready, whenever that might be. My sister matured when she was only fourteen years old, whereas I was twenty."

"That was my next question." He was smiling eagerly, so excited that I was sharing this with him. "You mentioned earlier that the vampires often have gifts when they're turned. Do you have them, as well?"

"Yes, although ours are more defensive than aggressive. Where the vampires are telepathic, we aren't. We can see a person's thoughts when we enter their mind, but prefer to respect their privacy when possible, changing only what we need to. And we have our defences."

"They can do nothing to you?"

"Not that we're aware of." It was yet another thing they absolutely despised about us. "It will be a grave day if they ever gain the ability to touch us with their powers."

"And what of your gifts? Do they work on everyone?"

"They do. It's one of the reasons we believe we are here to keep the peace. If no one could touch us, but we could affect all, then surely we were meant to do as we do."

"Some would say you were here to rule all."

"Some would, but we aren't some."

"And what of your gifts? Are they the same as those of the vampires?"

"Some are. We used to have so many gifts. There were those who could read your mind without having to enter it and those who could look at any item and tell you how it worked. An aunt of mine had great precognitive abilities, and one of my cousins could form a physical barrier around anything. Our race has seen gifts ranging from the simple ability to move things with their mind to being able to create fire in the palm of the hand." It was a shame those times were gone.

"What's yours?"

"None of consequence."

"I thought you said you all had gifts?"

We did all have gifts. Mine was just . . . complicated.

"Long ago, my sister told me that my gift was *life*. Being my twin, hers was the opposite: *death*. Nothing in our records mentions them, and I have no idea where she found the information. As far as I'm concerned, whatever gift I do have, it's irrelevant." Most of what she knew of our gifts was the superstition surrounding the birth of the first twins in the race.

"Will you tell me of her? Your sister?"

"Not today. Talking with you has left me in an exceptionally good mood, and I'd rather leave that story for another day, if you don't mind."

"Anything you wish to share, any time you wish to share it." He smiled and reached for my hand, but quickly had to grab hold of the reins again.

In that single gesture I learned so much about him. His hand was warm in mine, and his hold was firm. He would be with me until the end, no matter how difficult things got. Still, perhaps he hadn't quite understood everything.

"I'm not entirely sure you quite grasp the gravity of how difficult life can be with me," I told him as we reached the house. "There are only two of us. The work that once took an entire race is now left to William and myself."

"Serenity Cardea," he said with a sternness that shocked me. "You seem determined to drive me away, and I won't have it. No matter how hard life will be, it is nothing compared to being able to spend it with you."

He continued while I stayed wide-eyed and silent. "If you will still have me, then I'd like nothing more than to call you my own. Regardless of what others may think, and regardless of how difficult the future may be."

He managed to dismount without any help.

"Ray," I whispered, afraid my voice would break.

He'd stripped me of my words. Nothing could come close to explaining how I felt or how much I truly wanted him at that moment. So I did the only thing I could think of.

I jumped from my horse, stood as tall as possible, and gave him a lingering kiss on his cheek.

"I'll always be yours," I told him, my hands still resting on his shoulders.

The new light in his grey eyes was enough to make me forget everything else. For once I let my mind wander into fantasies of our life together, of how we would raise our children and how I would read them our stories. For that moment, as I stared deep into those mesmerising eyes, everything was perfect.

Then I realised I was staring and was standing barely an inch from him, surely too close.

"Forgive me." I stepped back quickly, ducking my head to hide my blush. "I forget myself with you. It won't help that I have no idea what the rules of etiquette are in this time . . ."

"Rules were made for breaking," he said, smirking.

He pulled me back towards him, not a breath of air between us, and placed my hands back on his shoulders. "Feel free to forget where you are with me anytime you wish."

"I may have to take you up on that."

"Ah, I did hear the horses." Helen's quiet voice broke our happy little moment a couple of seconds before she appeared in the doorway. "Oh! I'm sorry. I came to see if Ray was going to stay for dinner."

I looked up at him. "Would you?"

"If we let my mother know, I don't see why not." He was flustered but smiled widely as he spoke.

"How about I go and ask Sam to fetch her and we can all have dinner together?" Helen was looking for an excuse to leave, and her offer was the perfect one.

"Thank you, Helen."

"Perhaps we should head into the house, as well?" Ray suggested, nervously shifting.

"She knows better than to say anything. If she does, I shall bring up some *very* embarrassing childhood memories of her."

He laughed long and loud at that. It came in handy, being older than everyone else. Things like childhood stories were something I tried to remember. I never knew when I would need them, or when they could be used as playful blackmail.

"I was wondering about something. Why do you eat if you don't need to?" he asked as we walked hand in hand back to the house.

"Appearances and habit. If food is scarce, then I'll forgo eating in favour of my family. If not, or the situation demands it, then I'll eat. It's also nice to sit down to a meal with my family on occasion."

"Sam is on his way over to Mrs. Synclair's house and Jayne is in the dining room setting the table," Helen informed me when we walked into the house after stabling the horses.

"Jayne?" I called. "Would you entertain Ray whilst I help your mother with dinner? He isn't safe to be allowed anywhere near the kitchen."

"Can I talk to him properly now?" Jayne giggled, rocking back and forth on her heels as she spoke.

"Yes, but don't scare him." She would do her best to remember any scary story she could. Though I doubted they would affect Ray, I pleaded with her not to delve too deep into the stories she knew.

"I'll try."

Reluctantly, I let Jayne drag him away.

She was an intelligent child, and she understood when to keep quiet about what I was. It was something that was instilled into all of our children—the need to keep our secret. It was as important to us as it was to the vampires. Only our reasons were different.

Once we were alone, Helen took one look at me and said, "It went exceptionally well."

She stood by the sink, leaning against the stone and wood, arms crossed and a knowing smile on her face. She'd known the answer long before I'd been willing to accept it.

"It did."

"No running. No screaming. Not even the smallest trace of fear. Am I correct?"

"Yes."

"You forget how well I can read people, Serenity."

"I know, but I still expected him to run for the hills, screaming all the way." It surprised me how quiet my voice was when I spoke.

"You deserve this, never forget that."

"I'll try."

It wasn't long before Sam returned. I heard the car coming up the street. The distinct sound of her engine telling me that it was ours.

"Jayne, dear, that's enough for tonight. Ray's mother is coming for dinner," I told her, carrying in the first of the plates.

"Can I tell him some more later?"

"Not tonight."

"Would I be correct in assuming that I cannot tell my mother?" Ray said, half asking, half stating.

"I'm sorry. If it was safe for her to know, then I would tell her in a heartbeat. It's best she knows as little as possible beyond the obvious." My smile was a sad one

"I understand. It wasn't something that should be discussed over dinner." Briefly, I kissed his cheek. "Are you ready to play human for the evening?"

Chapter Six

"Serenity, it is good to see you again," Liz greeted me. "Thank you for the invitation."

"It's a pleasure. I couldn't very well steal your son for the evening and not invite you."

"Between you and me, you can steal him anytime." She leaned in close as she spoke, whispering the words and casting a brief glance deeper into the house, perhaps checking to make sure Ray wasn't about.

"I may have to take you up on that offer."

Playing human was something I was good at, in more mature company at least. I struggled at making small talk with people of "my own age," but talking with those "older" than me came more easily.

I commented on Liz's dress and the style of her hair. We talked for a moment about how things were in the world. Anyone looking on would have thought we were simply two humans having a quiet chat. Even Ray was surprised at how easily I managed it.

"Serenity?" Helen called. "Dinner is ready."

"Shall we?"

I led Liz to the dining room where Jayne was finishing setting the table. She was struggling to reach the glasses she wanted. I grabbed them for her and set them down.

"Jayne, would you keep Ray and Mrs. Synclair company whilst I help your mother?" I asked her.

"I'll be good," she promised. Code for *I know I can't talk to them about certain things.*

I passed Sam on my way to the kitchen. He offered to help with taking the food through, but Helen had already told him to sit down, so I did the same. He'd done enough for one day.

"You need a towel for that," Helen reminded me when I went to pick up the casserole dish.

"Thank you," I whispered.

As good as I was at playing human in social situations, providing romance wasn't part of the setting, I was very forgetful at home.

I may not have had to hide from Ray anymore, but I would do everything I could to prevent his mother from being dragged into my world, as well.

"Oh, that smells scrumptious," Liz said when I put the casserole down on the table.

I offered her a plate. "Helen is an excellent cook."

"Is that where you learned?"

"Partly. Mostly I was taught how to cook by my mother." The smell of freshly cooked beef wafted around the table. I hadn't been eating much lately, only when we had company, so Helen had plenty to make a nice, thick casserole.

No one spoke as we ate, and it wasn't until the plates were being cleared away—Sam insisted on doing that himself—that the conversation began again.

"My son tells me you took him riding today," Liz said, glancing at Ray.

"I did. He knows how to handle a horse. Did you teach him?" There was still so much I didn't know about him, about his family.

"No. I cannot ride to save my life. The poor things despise me. The closest I get to a horse is when it's pulling the carriage." She laughed, a rich sound. "Our neighbour taught him. Wonderful man. Lovely wife, too."

"Have you known them long?"

"Oh yes. They moved in when Ray was only ten. Ray still couldn't walk well at the time but insisted he could ride a horse." There was a mischievous twinkle in her eye.

"I would've liked to have seen that."

"There are many stories I could tell you of his exploits. However, I don't think my son would appreciate it."

"Mrs. Walters, are there any stories you could tell us about Serenity?" Ray asked

"I'm afraid you'll have to ask her. Serenity is very good at keeping her embarrassing moments to herself." Helen paused for a moment. "Although, perhaps you should ask her how she broke some poor man's toe. . ."

"Helen!" I cried.

"I think I'd like to hear this." A mischievous smile accompanied Ray's words.

"No. Absolutely not. I refuse to embarrass myself with *that* story."

"You won't mind if I embarrass you, then?" Helen didn't give me a chance to answer. "When Serenity was younger, she hated dancing, despite being a beautiful dancer. She was forced to attend one particular event and had to dance with this awful man. He was a fine dancer, but he was rather pungent."

I groaned and hid my head in my hands as Helen continued her tale.

"To try to get out of dancing, she would pretend she was the worst dancer in the world, stepping on toes, missing steps. Well, when she *accidentally* stomped on the poor man's foot, he howled in pain. It turned out she'd broken his toe."

Ray and Liz burst into laughter.

"Thank you, Helen. Perhaps I should bring up some of your *finer* moments."

"How about we change the subject before we have a war between the two of you?" Sam offered.

"Excellent plan," Helen said.

"I agree. Would you mind if I asked how you met Ray's father?"

"Not at all." Liz smiled, a wistful look in her eye. "We were very young, not even as old as you two are now. I was playing the piano at an event hosted by my mother. Despite my reluctance, my parents insisted on introducing me to everyone there. When I saw Raymond, there was no going back. By the end of the next week, he had asked for my hand in marriage. We were married two weeks later. The time I had with him was short, just three years, but I will never forget him."

"I'm sorry," I whispered.

"Not to worry, dear. I could never see myself with another man. He was —still is—the love of my life, and I'm grateful for my years with him. Even more so for the fact that I have Ray." Her smile was a sad one.

"It was love at first sight, then?" I asked, trying to lighten the subject.

"That it was. A bit like the two of you."

"Mother." Ray shot a sheepish glance in my direction.

"Don't be shy, Son. I only say what I see."

"Well, as we're on that subject, I suppose now is as good a time as any . . ." He turned towards me with a look of mischief on his face. "We have an announcement."

"Ray, you don't have to do this now," I whispered. "If you need time to think about everything I told you, I understand. It's a lot to take in."

"Serenity," he sighed, "my mind is made up. You are the only one who can change it."

"Well, don't keep us waiting," Jayne cried, bouncing in her chair.

"Jayne," Helen chastised.

"Serenity and I are dating. I asked her this afternoon."

"I hope you asked permission," Liz said, only half joking.

"He did," Sam confirmed, earning a confused look from me. I hadn't known that Ray had asked permission from anyone. "I know my sister and I aren't Serenity's parents, however, I'm positive they would approve."

Suddenly, I was pulled into an embrace by Liz. The physical contact was strange, but nice. "Welcome to the family."

"Thank you." I awkwardly returned her hug.

As soon as she released me, I was gathered into another one by Helen and Sam.

"I suppose the ladies will be disappointed in a couple of weeks."

"A couple of weeks?" Helen asked.

"Has Ray not mentioned he's turning twenty-six in two weeks?" She was glaring at her son now.

"He mentioned his birthday was coming up, but not when it was."

"You must all join us. It will be nice to see the looks on those pretentious children's faces when they see what a beautiful woman my son has by his side."

"Mother, they aren't that bad."

"None of them were ever good enough for you, my dear." She turned towards me. "They were exceptionally cruel to him as a child because of his leg. As if it was his fault! Yet they insist on being invited to the celebrations."

"I'm sure they'll be green with envy when they see these two together," Helen reassured her.

"How about I show you around the house? I don't believe I've had the chance to do so yet."

Ray gave me a thankful smile as I led Liz out. It was clear that talking about certain aspects of Ray's childhood made him uncomfortable, and the least I could do was distract his mother for a while. It wasn't a surprise that he'd had some trouble when he was younger. Children weren't known for their subtlety, especially when it came to such an obvious injury.

Fortunately, my plan to give Liz a tour of the house worked wonders. She had a good eye for art and fell in love with some of the paintings that lined the walls. The large landscape at the head of the stairs caught her eye, and though I didn't remember the artist, I told her the piece was almost a century old. Jayne decided to join us, and she took great delight in telling her some of the more acceptable stories behind some of the pieces of work.

"It's the home of the fairies," she said, pointing out the tiny figures hiding in the trees. "They come out at night and make sure the house is safe from monsters."

Monsters being vampires. *Fairies* being the work that I did.

Jayne followed us around the house but ducked back into the kitchen when we came back into the study. She'd seen all the books before, and the ones that interested her most wouldn't be on show for Liz.

"You have such a wonderful collection," Liz said as I showed her around my study. "Have you read all of these?"

"Many times over in most cases. Books are one of my many passions."

"I can see why Ray has fallen so quickly for you. I see it in the way you look at one another." She trailed a hand across the spines of the old books. "You are just as I was with his father."

"The joys of young love."

"You do love him, then?" She paused by my desk.

"Oh yes. How could I not?" How, indeed.

By the time we returned to the sitting room, Sam was already bringing the car round. It was getting late, and it was time for Liz and Ray to head home.

"Will you join me for breakfast tomorrow, Ray?"

"I would love to. What time?"

"How does eight sound?"

"Perfect."

"Sam will take you home."

"There's no need to go to all that trouble, Serenity. It's not so far to walk," Liz said with a wave of her hand.

"We insist. It's getting late, and I'm sure Serenity would rather know you're home safe," Helen insisted.

She chuckled. "Well, now, we can hardly refuse if you insist, can we?"

Helen collected their coats, and though I was reluctant to see them go, I needed to talk to Helen before heading out for the evening.

"Thank you," Ray whispered, startling me.

"Whatever for?"

"Saying you'll be mine."

I stared at him for a moment in utter shock. "You're being ridiculous. I should be the one thanking you."

"And yet, here I am, offering you my thanks, regardless." He brought his hand up to cup my cheek.

"I'll see you in the morning, if not before."

He raised an eyebrow in question.

"Go, I'll explain tomorrow." I smiled.

Ray and Liz said their goodbyes and climbed into the car. Listening hard, I heard their hushed voices.

"She is a fine young woman, Son."

"She's one of a kind." There was a smile in his voice as he spoke.

"You do plan on proposing?"

"In time, yes. I'd like to get to know her better first."

"Tell me when you decide. I have something for you."

I stopped listening then, but not before I heard the faint whisper of Ray's voice. "Goodnight, Serenity."

I turned back to the house with the biggest smile on my face. Helen and Jayne were waiting for me, smiling brightly, also, and eager for more news of my day.

"Time for bed, Jayne," Helen told her, never looking away.

"Can I stay up a little longer?" she pleaded.

"She may as well. It's not like she'll sleep when she's so excited."

"One more hour," Helen said, finally glancing at Jayne.

She raced off into the sitting room, picked her favourite chair and curled up, ready for what I was about to tell them. Jayne was eager, though there were some parts that she wouldn't be able to understand. Like why I'd been so scared, or why I still was.

Jayne knew the stories of us, how in times gone by she would've become as I was, but she was too young to know the hardships we'd faced. Those stories were for when she was older, when she better understood what had happened, when she would want answers for why she wasn't maturing, and why she never would.

"I already know it went well today, but I want to know what you thought," Helen said as soon as I was seated. Helen and Jayne's poses were mirrors of each other, a matching pair of impatience.

"I told him almost everything." I smiled at the memory. "I told him of the others, my history, and even how old I am. He didn't flinch when I told him just how closely our lives were linked. He actually said that it made sense!"

It struck me then, as I watched them leaning forward, that just because I'd been dreading the day this connection was made didn't mean everyone else had. Helen knew what it was like. She'd also seen her parents together. Jayne had heard countless stories. They'd been waiting for me to find that missing part of my life.

"I like him," Jayne spoke up.

"I do, too."

"I think he's nice, and cute," she continued.

"He must be to put up with you, but I'm afraid he's all mine, so you better keep your hands to yourself."

"I will, Aunt Sere." She stuck her tongue out.

"You really thought he would run?"

"I did. I was so scared that he would." I sighed as I laid my head on the back of the chair. "But I have nothing to worry about. He knows the basics, though there will always be more to learn, and he took it in stride."

"I always knew it would take someone very special to capture your heart, and I was right. After the way I saw him looking at you tonight, I have to admit he is something special indeed."

"His mother said the same thing about me."

After three thousand years on my own, I'd started to believe there simply wasn't anyone out there for me. Helen had been right all along. I just hadn't found anyone pig-headed enough to put up with me. Until now.

"Are you going out tonight?" Helen asked after Jayne was tucked into bed.

"Every night as long as we're in the city. I can't risk him being found, even by accident."

"Be careful."

Two full hours after Ray had left, I was heading out for the night, locking the door behind me. We kept a spare key hidden in the porch eaves, out of sight. Someone would have to be well over six feet tall to reach it without jumping. Even then, they would have to hop to get up there. Regardless, it was ideal for me. The last thing I needed to carry around in the middle of the night was a set of jingling keys.

Since meeting Ray, I'd taken the same route every evening—around his house and sweeping out and back in again before dawn. I planned on changing the route slightly on occasion, but the overall area would be the same. If we were still here during the winter, I would make the rounds twice. Once after dark and again before dawn.

The sooner I persuaded him to leave the city, the better.

As I walked back towards Ray's house, with every intention of making a brief stop in his garden before heading home, something caught my eye. Or rather, two *somethings.*

Lurching through the dark streets, two over from Ray's house, was a vampire. He'd just jumped from the window of one of the houses and had a corpse slung over his shoulder.

Upon closer inspection, it was a young woman; she appeared to be about eighteen, at the most. It should have been easy to carry on and ignore whatever was about to happen. I couldn't stop vampires from feeding, no matter how hard I tried. I wasn't meant to save everyone.

But I couldn't let the vampire waltz off into the night with the poor girl. Not when I heard the faint fluttering of a beating heart in her belly. Chances were she didn't even know she was expecting.

I couldn't chance an altercation in the middle of the street, so I settled for following the vampire and waiting until he stopped to feed. There was an abandoned textile factory on the edge of the river. That was where he was most likely taking her.

Perfect.

Plenty of space and nothing but a few unlucky humans in the area—or a couple of vampires on the hunt.

I followed him straight into the derelict building. The quiet closed around me, and I hoped I could get this over with and be home before dawn.

The woman was blessedly out cold. The vampire must have clobbered her when he snatched her from her bed. If he did a good enough job, she'd be dead before she regained any level of consciousness.

I followed him up the rickety stairs, trying to avoid the creaking steps.

He kept on going until he reached the top floor. There was a light thump as he dropped the woman to the ground. That quickened my pace.

By the time I'd scaled the last flight, barely avoiding the gaping hole near the top, the vampire had already started feeding. It was too late to try to "persuade" him not to. I'd have to actually confront him.

The racket I made leaping over the last missing step did the job for me. As I landed, much louder than the vampire had, he spun around to face me, defending his dinner.

"You're not one of us," he hissed, prepared to fight for what he thought was his.

"No, I'm not, and I'll not let you kill her," I told him, advancing cautiously.

Just then, the woman let out a small moan, and for a moment I thought she was awake. Chancing a quick look in her direction, I saw she was still unconscious and the bite mark on her neck was already healing.

I didn't see the vampire charge straight for me.

I caught the sound of his footsteps only a fraction of a second before his body slammed into mine, sending us flying towards the nearest window.

It had to be the one that had an intact sheet of glass.

Sailing through the air after being attacked by a vampire was nothing new for me. Neither was diving out of a window.

As I hit the ground, the glass sliced straight through my shirt and embedded into my skin. There was a resounding *crack,* as at least two of my ribs broke, and my head snapped back. The force of the fall was too much, and knocked me out cold.

Chapter Seven

When I came around, it felt as if only a few moments had passed, but no matter how long I was out, it was long enough. Long enough for the vampire to flee and for my wounds to heal around the glass in my back. Whoever the vampire was, seeing me must have confused him enough to make a run for it.

With the glass embedded where it was, I wouldn't be able to get it out by myself. Helen would be upset I had put myself in this situation, but I wouldn't allow the vampire to kill the woman.

Unless he already has.

The thought made me grimace.

Forcing one step in front of the other, I went back into the building. Each step hurt more than the last, but I had to check.

I was relieved to find the woman unconscious on the floor, the shallow bite mark already fully healed, her breathing slow and steady.

It took a great physical effort on my part to hoist the woman's dead weight into my arms. I knew the address where I'd seen the vampire leaving. It would take me a while to get there. Being home before dawn had gone out of the window the same moment I had.

The trip to the woman's house was a long and agonising one. The two distinct breaks in my ribs would take a while to heal, a day at least, and that was causing me some trouble. Scaling the wall to get the unconscious woman back in her bed was near impossible. Instead, I had to pick the lock and sneak through her house, room by room until I found the one I was looking for. There was only a woman I thought to be her mother in the other bedroom. She was sound asleep, and I managed to get out without waking her. She wouldn't know I'd been there, and her daughter would think she'd had a nightmare, a very vivid nightmare—if she remembered anything at all.

There were few people on the streets this early, and I managed to avoid the few I saw. When I reached my door, however, I realised I couldn't unlock it. In the state I was in, I couldn't reach the key hanging in the porch.

"Damn it." I reached for the doorbell instead.

Waiting on the doorstep for someone to find me wasn't an option. If I passed out—I was feeling distinctly light-headed—and I ended up at the hospital . . . that would be very bad.

"Coming," Helen called when I rang the bell for a second time. "If that's Ray, then he needs to learn to tell time."

Her footsteps on the carpet were almost as loud as her grumbling.

"Serenity?" she asked as she opened the door. "Oh God! Sam!"

"I'm fine."

"Like hell you are! What happened?" She helped me into the house. "Jayne, can you get the medical kit, please?"

"Vampire, window, ground," I answered. "Honestly, I'm fine."

"No, you are clearly not. You are white as a sheet, and I can feel the glass sticking out of your back."

Seconds later, a very flustered, half dressed and half asleep Sam came charging down the stairs.

"Really, I walked back here. I'm fine," I tried to tell them, but I was going nowhere on my own.

"From the way you're standing, I'd guess at least one broken rib. So, no, you are not *fine*," he said, carefully linking his arm around my waist.

"Two, actually. At least." He accidentally moved a shard in my back, making me wince and hiss.

"Two. If we can't fix them here then a trip to the hospital may be needed," he said, sounding concerned.

"It's only my ribs. No punctured lung and no internal bleeding. I just need someone to get this glass out." I was deposited at the kitchen table, sitting the wrong way on one of the chairs.

"Jayne, would you take your breakfast to the dining room this morning?" Helen said when Jayne returned with the medical kit and a light dress.

"Yes, Mother," she answered. "Feel better, Aunt Sere."

The medical kit was one that had been collected over the years, and contained everything ever needed. Any injury that didn't require surgery, Helen had the supplies to treat.

"Can you take your shirt off?"

"It's not as bad as it seems."

"Take your shirt off and we'll see."

The sound of broken glass falling to the floor accompanied the removal of my shirt, and I felt a few smaller pieces dislodge in the process. It was a start, but there was far more glass decorating my back and neck, and some in my arms, as well.

"What happened?" Helen asked, looking over my injuries.

"I was checking the area round Ray's house. Spotted a vampire taking a woman. She was unconscious, but she was pregnant. I couldn't let him kill her. I don't think she knew." I braced myself for the pain as Helen picked up a scalpel.

When my wounds healed around something, I *felt* it. Every part of it. The width of the object, the depth, and even the texture. In order to remove it, it either had to be pulled or cut out. Pulling it out was far more painful than having a scalpel slice through my skin.

"You always were too kind for your own good. You know we don't get involved like that." She paused. "But I'm glad you did."

"There was no walking away. I just couldn't."

"I know. Now, this is going to hurt. A lot. You look as if you have the entire window in here."

When she removed the first piece, I gasped. "I think I do."

The worst part, and the hardest, was that I needed to calm myself in order for Helen to work. If I didn't, it would hurt twice as much. Forcing the muscles in my back to relax, I lowered my head and hoped it would be over soon.

I tried to concentrate on the thud of glass hitting the towel on the wooden table. The soft fabric muffled the noise, making it sound as if someone was knocking on a door in the distance.

The fresh wounds healed quickly but not before staining my back red. She didn't stop to clean up; she would do that once she was finished.

Helen was almost done when the doorbell rang. Jayne called out that she would answer it.

"What time is it?" I asked, wondering who was calling this early.

"Eight o'clock."

"What? I must have been out longer than I thought."

"You were *unconscious?*" Helen half-screamed. "Just how high was this window?"

"Fourth story, and I fell with the vampire on top of me." Then I realised who would be calling at eight in the morning. "Ray!"

"No you don't." Helen forced me to stay when I tried to stand. "You're going nowhere until I'm finished."

"May I at least put something on?"

"I'm almost done, Serenity. Then you can see him as if this never happened."

Her plan held some merit. I'd be fine in a couple of minutes, and if he saw me like this, he would worry. If *I* saw me like this, I would, too. The fact I was obviously unconscious far longer than I thought was already a concern.

"And after I'm done with your back, I want to take a look at your head.

Make sure there's no permanent damage." There was a smile in her voice, and I knew she was only joking.

But our plans of greeting Ray *after* my back was clean and free of glass didn't turn out how I'd expected.

"Serenity?" Ray's worried voice sounded from the doorway as the last piece of glass hit the towel. "What happened?"

I turned my head slightly to see him standing in the doorway, wide eyed. Jayne must have returned to the dining room.

"I'm fine. Really, I don't see why everyone is so worried." I was growing tired of it.

"There's so much blood," he whispered.

"Be thankful you didn't see her when she got home," Helen told him.

"May I *please* put my dress on?" I was well aware I was half-naked.

"Just a second. I need to clean your back." She walked around me to the kitchen sink.

Glancing behind me again, I saw Ray still standing awkwardly in the doorway, his face as red as my back. His eyes weren't full of disgust or fear at the blood; they were full of concern.

"Honestly, Ray, I'll be fine." I offered him a small smile.

He met my gaze but looked away quickly.

Sitting half-naked in any given room in the house wasn't a new state for me. Be it a piece of wood wedged into my leg or badly broken bones, it had all been done before in one form or another.

"Ray, she really is fine," Helen told him, when she returned with the cloth and a bowl of warm water. "Watch."

She ran the cloth down my back, ringing it out into the bowl. Repeating the process, she ran it down my back again and again. Then over my arms and up to my neck. Before long the water was cloudy, dirt from the glass and red from my blood mixing into a muddy brown.

"See? She heals quicker than you can imagine. Why don't you go into the dining room whilst we finish up?"

There were shuffling footsteps as Ray retreated.

"Now, how about we look at these ribs?"

"Thank you," I told her, not talking about my ribs.

"Not to worry, dear. You are, perhaps, somewhat blasé about your injuries. Though I think a demonstration could have been executed a little better." She chuckled.

"I wasn't going for a demonstration." I sucked in a pained breath as she prodded my side.

"You were right about there being two broken ones," she said. "Let's get them taped up."

She would have made an excellent nurse had she chosen to become one. Instead she insisted she was where she was needed, especially after the last time my ribs were broken.

A couple of minutes more and I was done, giving me chance to pull on the light dress Jayne had brought down with the medical kit. I needed a good soak in the tub, but it could wait until Ray had gone. There was some explaining I needed to do first. And an apology wouldn't be amiss, either.

"Ray," I said, standing in the dining room doorway. "Would you like some breakfast?"

"I'm not sure I can handle anything to eat right now." He smiled, just a touch.

"Come sit with me in my study?"

With a nod, he rose and silently followed me. There were two deep couches in there, making it my favourite room for reading. I took one, expecting him to take the other. I was surprised when he sat next to me.

"Are you sure you're fine?" His eyes were still wide. "There was a lot of blood."

"Apart from two broken ribs, which will be healed by tomorrow morning, I'm fine."

"How did it happen? Was it vampires?" There wasn't even a pause before the word *vampires.*

"It was a vampire, yes. I was trying to save a woman, and he caught me unawares. When I awoke, he was gone, but the woman was alive." I patted his hand gently. "He caught me off guard and charged, sending us through a fourth-story window. Helen had to cut the glass out of my back because I healed around it before I got home."

"Are you sure you're fine?" he asked again, running his hand over my arm.

"Really, I am. Broken bones take the longest to heal, but flesh wounds close up relatively quickly. Would it bother you if I said I've had worse injuries?"

"No. I'm just concerned. When I saw you in the kitchen with all that blood down your back, it scared me. I thought I might lose you." He glanced down, whispering his words.

"As your heart beats, so will mine. When *your* heart sleeps, so will mine," I said with utter confidence. "Ray, there's nothing anyone or anything can do that would mean you losing me. I'm here to stay until your time is up."

He smiled, but he was still squinting a little. I was used to having Helen worry, and even Jayne on the rare occasion, but having Ray anxious for me touched me. With Ray it was different. He wanted to protect me, to care for me, though I was the one meant to protect and care for him.

"Now, I rather fancy some breakfast." I took his free hand. "Would you join me?"

"I'd like that."

We ate breakfast in the dining room. I assumed Ray didn't want to be back in the kitchen so soon.

There was a slight pull on my ribs when I took a deep breath. They were healing nicely, and I'd be back to normal before dawn. But I wouldn't be going out tonight, not if Helen had anything to say about it.

After breakfast, Ray and I went to my study. I showed him some of our records, the ones I happened to be updating at the time. He hovered not out of interest over what I was showing him; he was hovering because he was still worried about me.

"Ray, honestly, I'll be perfectly fine by dawn." I'd been talking to him for five minutes straight without a hint of acknowledgement.

"I know," he whispered, suddenly looking embarrassed.

Oh! He wasn't thinking about the injuries I'd sustained. The blush in his cheeks told me exactly what was running through his mind.

I'd been half naked when he walked into the kitchen.

"Ray, please don't be embarrassed." I set my book aside. "You couldn't help but look. I understand that. And if it helps . . . I have every intention of letting you see much more at some point." My cheeks heated up.

"It was wrong of me to stare as I did."

"Regardless, you and I are together now, so seeing such things are normal, eventually. Or so I'm told."

After we got that embarrassing conversation out of the way, Helen called to say lunch was ready. I hadn't realised the day was passing so quickly. Just after lunch, Ray said he was due home. He'd promised to do some errands for his mother, as she had her own to run. I offered to walk him home, but he refused, as I knew he would. I wasn't overly worried about him walking alone. It was a gloriously sunny day, despite the chilly start, and most vampires would be hiding in the safety of their homes.

"He took that rather well," Helen said, when I returned inside.

"Better than I expected. He was more worried over the etiquette of seeing me half naked."

"I'll bet he was. You should have seen the colour of his face when I washed your back off. He would've fallen down had he not already been supporting himself with the doorframe." She joined me as I laughed.

We'd finished cleaning the kitchen, making sure all the glass had been swept up and everything put away, when the doorbell rang. In the hope it might be Ray, I raced to the door, almost tearing it off its hinges to answer it. I was surprised to see Liza Synclair standing on the doorstep with a parcel in her hands.

"Good afternoon, Liz. This is a pleasant surprise." I stood to the side and gestured for her to come in.

"Good afternoon, Serenity. I thought I would come and spend some time with the young woman who has captured my son's heart." She smiled brightly.

So that was why she'd asked him to do some errands.

"I also have something for you." She patted the lid of the parcel.

"You didn't have to do that," I told her, but I wondered what she'd brought.

"I realise you will have many dresses to choose from, but I saw this one and thought it would be perfect for you." She set the box down on the sitting room table, and tossed its lid to one side. "Go on, have a look."

Upon peeling back the layers of tissue paper, I found myself staring at a mass of shimmering fabric. Picking up the straps, I took the dress from the box, letting the material slip from my fingers.

Gorgeous was the first and only word I could use to describe the dress. Even *gorgeous* did it no justice at all. The light velvet was embroidered in bright, vibrant jades, oranges, and blues. The design of beautiful flowers flowed from just under the bust down to the waist and then swept down to the hem on the left. Matching embroidery adorned the straps where they met the dress.

"Liz," I breathed. "I can't accept this. It's beautiful beyond words."

"I was wearing this when I met Ray's father." There was a sad smile on her face as she reminisced. "My father brought it back from France, and the style was outrageous at the time. So much skin on display. My mother refused to let me out of the house unless I wore a stole with it. She was embarrassed that my father would buy something like this for me."

"Liz, I really can't accept this," I told her, touched that she would think to give me such a sentimental item.

"Nonsense. I will never be able to fit into this again, and I have no desire to. You're about the same size as I was, and it will be put to much better use with you than sitting in the back of my wardrobe gathering dust." Her hand fluttered lightly over the fabric. "Besides, I'm sure Ray will simply be stunned when he sees you in it."

"Thank you. It truly is beautiful."

"Come now, we had best make sure it fits you."

The entire afternoon was spent going over and over the dress. The second I slipped it over my head, thankful the tape from my ribs had been removed, I knew it was going to be perfect, if a touch long. Helen had then ushered me up onto a stool and told me to stay perfectly still. An hour of crawling round the floor and she was finally done. It had taken three attempts to adjust the hem, making sure it was the right length. The first had been far too long, the second just a fraction. I thought all of them were perfect, but Liz and Helen insisted it had to just brush the floor as I walked. The third attempt reminded Helen that I wasn't wearing any shoes and saw her scurrying to find the right pair.

"Apart from the hem, it's a perfect fit," Helen said.

"Doesn't she look stunning?" Liz asked as the two of them stepped back to admire me.

"It's missing something." Helen gave me a once-over.

"I know." I hopped down from the stool.

Before anyone objected, I raced up the stairs to my room, careful not to catch the delicately pinned hem. It was fortunate I'd spent some time reorganising my belongings one long afternoon over late spring just after we'd moved in. I knew exactly where to look. Two boxes, one with a necklace I rarely wore, and one with a shawl I'd never worn. It had been a gift from William in an attempt to get me to dance more often—an attempt that had failed. The necklace was one of my most prized possessions.

Taking both of the boxes downstairs, I carefully unwrapped the shawl first, draping the thin silk around my shoulders. The pattern wasn't an exact match to the dress, but they complimented each other perfectly.

When I brought out the necklace, there was a gasp of appreciation from Liz and one of shock from Helen.

"Would you mind?" I asked, handing Helen the piece.

"I don't think I have ever seen anything like it," Liz mused, as Helen swept my hair to the side and fastened the necklace in place.

"It has been in the family for years."

It was actually a gift from my sister and dated back to the Celts. The Celtic Butterfly, as she'd called it, was a beautifully made silver necklace with a single polished jet stone in the centre. The knots making up the design looked like a pair of butterfly wings. She'd laughed when she told me why she'd chosen that particular stone.

Calming.

She'd been teasing me. Out of the two of us, I was the calm one.

"You're absolutely stunning," Liz commented as I gave them a twirl of the almost-complete outfit.

Helen had a motherly smile on her face. "Ray will be mesmerized."

Chapter Eight

Two weeks passed quickly, and I managed not to get myself thrown through any more windows.

Ray spent every day at my house, or I spent the time at his. At least until I realised I hadn't bought him a present. After hours of rattling around the house wondering what I could get him, I eventually decided on something. It required me to spend several hours hunched over my desk, but it was worth every second.

Helen took an entire week to make sure the dress was a perfect fit. I lost count of the number of times she had me up on that stool in the dining room, checking and double-checking her work. Personally, I didn't know what all the fuss was about; Ray's eyes were hardly going to be on my hemline.

Naturally, Helen, Sam, and Jayne were also invited to the party, and Jayne had the time of her life getting ready with us. She was thrilled and promptly told her mother that she had to wear her lilac dress for the occasion. It was her favourite. Helen had chosen a simple, yet elegant, pale yellow one.

When the three of us descended the stairs, Sam let out a whistle of appreciation and told us he would be fighting the men off with sticks. That earned him a soft thump from Helen.

"Is everyone ready?" he asked, rubbing his shoulder playfully.

"Yes."

I was nervous.

This was the first birthday party I'd been to outside of my family. What if I tripped? What if he didn't like his gift? What if Professor Baruti was there and I managed to expose myself for what I was?

With a knowing smile, Sam went to fetch the carriage. I'd tried to persuade him to let me get someone else to take care of our transport for the evening, but he'd insisted. He wouldn't even let me bring the car from the garage, insisting that the carriage was the only way to travel to the event.

"Would you please stop pacing?" Helen asked me while we waited for Sam.

"Sorry," I muttered, not aware I'd started.

"What do you have to be nervous about?" She put herself in my path. "He knows about you. He clearly loves you, even if he hasn't said it yet. So take a deep breath, and stop fretting."

I sighed. "You're right."

"Of course I am. Now, we have a party to get to."

Music was already playing when we arrived, slightly late. Ray was mingling with the guests, mostly young women and older men with their wives, some from the auction. The second I saw him all of my worries evaporated.

He was so comfortable discussing politics. Everything they said to him, he had a rebuttal for. Every counter argument was met with either quiet approval or a disproving shake of his head and a fierce comeback. Over the few short weeks I'd spent with him, I'd seen how intelligent he was. None of these men stood a chance at winning the debate. No matter how light-hearted they appeared to be.

"Excuse me for a moment," he said after noticing our arrival.

"Of course," Mr. Wilson said, turning to continue his discussion with another man.

Ray greeted us with a warm smile on his face. Turning to Jayne, he said, "You look lovely this evening."

"Thank you," she told him before following her mother farther into the house.

"Serenity," he breathed, turning to me. "Lovely does not begin to describe you."

"You may be somewhat biased." I was well aware of the sudden silence as I reached up to kiss his cheek. It had become my habit of late.

"That may be so, but that dress is sublime on you. Have I seen it before?"

"Good evening, Serenity," Liz greeted me, interrupting Ray. "Helen worked wonders with the hem, I see."

"She did, though she spent most of the week fussing over it."

"This is the dress I was wearing when I met your father," she explained to Ray. "I thought it would make a wonderful gift to Serenity."

"You were wearing it in the portrait hanging in your room," Ray said, the pieces of the jigsaw falling into place.

"I was." She smiled. "If you'll excuse me, I believe the refreshments need tending to."

"Happy birthday," I told him once we were alone. "I have something for you."

"You didn't have to get me anything," he scolded gently. "You being here is enough of a gift."

"Nonsense, this is something I thought you might like to read." Having handed him the wrapped book, I watched as he opened it. "It's from a collection we made around five hundred years ago, but I only wrote the stories into it over the past week."

"Serenity, this is too much," he whispered, without having opened the book.

"Accurate, first-hand accounts of the rise of Rome, the burial of Cleopatra, the discovery of America, and some of the stories of my kind." Taking the book, I pointed out some of the tales. "Not all of them are about me, but they're all accurate."

"I'm at a loss for words."

"The stories of my kind are in our language, and you will only be able to translate them with the key that's in my study. The rest you're free to read whenever you wish, but promise me you won't share them too widely."

"I promise." He ran his fingers gently over the thick binding. "This will be for my eyes only."

"When you can read my language as well as I can, perhaps I'll let you see the rest of my history."

"What did I ever do to deserve you?"

"You never had to do anything, Ray. I'm yours, and I always have been."

"I must be dreaming."

His statement caused me to chuckle softly. "It's not a dream. This is all very real."

"Thank you. You have no idea how much this means to me."

"I think I might."

"May I show my mother?" he asked, eyes still on the book. "She would love to see what you've given me."

"Of course."

We made our way through his home, stopping occasionally to say a brief hello to some of the guests. The house teemed with people, and eager stares followed us everywhere. I heard the whispered comments about who I was and musings about our relationship. There certainly were some jealous women in attendance.

By the time we meandered into the kitchen, where Liz busied herself preparing more food, I had overheard at least two plans to steal Ray from my side. Those petty children would be in for a shock if they tried. I may have looked every inch the delicate lady, but I was far from it.

"Ray, dear, are you well?" Liz asked when she spotted us by the door.

"Very well, Mother. I wanted to show you what Serenity brought for me." He smiled as he handed the book over to her.

"Oh my," she whispered, glancing through some of the pages. "Where in heaven's name did you find such a treasure?"

"It was among some books we've had for a while." It wasn't quite a lie.

"I hope you plan on reading quickly, Son. This is something that needs to be put in the safe." She gently closed the book. "For now, I'll put it on your desk."

"Would you like me to do that?" I asked. "You seem very busy."

"Nonsense, it will only take me a moment. Go, have fun."

It felt strange, a human wandering off with one of our history books. She wouldn't know what most of it was about—neither would Ray without some assistance—but it still felt strange.

"I cannot thank you enough." Ray's whisper sounded loud in the silence of the kitchen. "It really is too much."

"Ray, you will come to learn that material things are just that—things—and nothing is too much. Not when it comes to you." I took his free hand in mine. "Would you dance with me?"

"Someone told me you despised it."

"Ha! Helen has been telling you more stories."

"Perhaps. You do dance then?"

"Come, I'll show you how much I can enjoy dancing."

It took us a few minutes of pointless chatter before we reached the sitting room. All of the furniture had been moved to leave room for the couples. Various young women were busy glaring at us from the side-lines. They may have taunted Ray for most of his life, but they were certainly able to see what they'd missed. He was an incredible young man: intelligent, handsome, strong . . .

I was, of course, biased in my opinions, but anyone could see what a wonderful husband he would make.

"Serenity, how exactly do you plan on my dancing with you?" he asked when we entered the sitting room.

"Do you trust me?"

"Completely."

"Then I promise not to let you fall."

There was a hint of confusion on his face as I reached for his cane. I'd never let him fall, but I wanted him to be able to dance, as he'd desired when we first met. Quite how he'd planned on dancing with me then was a mystery.

Taking a firm hold of his hand, I let my body absorb the weight of him as he leaned into me.

"Let me do all the work," I whispered. "Put your hand on my waist."

We didn't need to move from where we were, barely past the doorway, and the song that was playing was coming to a close. He did as I asked, hesitantly.

"Ray, look at me." I gazed deep into those consuming eyes and told him, "I won't let you fall."

He took a long breath, closing his eyes briefly. When he opened them, there was a look of determination on his face. He smiled, nodding once.

Leaning to the side, I placed his cane within easy reach of us. Though I was more than capable of supporting him in any dance, something simple was perfect.

Music filled the air, drowning out the whispered comments and jealous mutterings. He was apprehensive, but after a gentle reminder to look only at me, he relaxed. Our steps were simple, never moving far from where we started. We would only have the one dance together this evening, but from the expression on Ray's face, that would be enough.

By the end of the song, he was smiling brightly, laughing as we talked.

"Thank you," he told me, picking up his cane.

"It was my pleasure, Ray."

"I'm quite surprised I didn't step on any of your toes, with that being my first dance and all." We sat again, taking up one of the sofas along the sitting room wall.

"You never told me you hadn't danced before," I chastised him. "I would've had you practice had I known."

"Dancing hasn't exactly been my top priority in life." He tapped his right leg with a finger, smiling sadly.

I smiled wickedly. "Then perhaps I shall force you to practice on occasion."

One dance was all we were able to manage, but there would be other times, and practicing sounded like a fantastic plan. The rest of our time was spent sitting on that same sofa, talking.

Except for the occasional interruption.

Unwanted interruptions.

Especially when it came to a couple of the young women whom I'd overheard earlier in the evening. Having seen Ray with me, they thought it would be the perfect opportunity to ask him for a dance.

I was tempted to make comment on their treatment of him over the years, but that was information I shouldn't have known. So my mouth stayed firmly shut as they flaunted themselves in front of Ray—even when they took to sending supposedly evil glares in my direction after his refusal. It was Ray's birthday party after all.

For him I would play nice with anyone.

Even self-centred, stuck-up, pompous morons.

We heaved a sigh of relief when the party drew to an end. The sun was setting and everyone wanted to get home before nightfall. It was a dangerous time to be caught unawares, and not because of the vampire feeding ground a few streets away.

Sam insisted on helping Liz move the chairs back to their proper place before we left. She refused to let us help with the cleanup. The sight of Sam and Liz moving furniture was a humorous one. Jayne had fallen asleep on one of the sofas, snoring softly. She barely flinched as they dragged it back to where it belonged. We all let out a chuckle when she snuggled deeper into the cushions.

Jayne was still sleeping when we finished. Out of habit, I went to gather her in my arms for the ride home. She was too big for Helen to carry, and there was little point in waking her just to put her back to sleep in a few minutes' time. Sam stopped me, nodding discretely in Liz's direction.

It was so easy to forget myself, especially when I was around Ray.

"Thank you, Liz, I had a wonderful time."

"You will have to come for dinner one evening. I've enjoyed your company immensely."

Ray walked out to the carriage with me while Helen and Liz discussed their plans.

"Will you be going out again tonight?"

"I go out every night, Ray. The incident with the window was a rare occurrence."

"I wasn't worried. I wondered if you would . . . ?" He looked down at his hands as he often did. "Would you come by?"

Standing up on my toes, I whispered, "Leave your window open."

"Thank you," he said, kissing me on the cheek.

It was the first time he'd kissed me, the first of many I hoped, and that brief kiss had me smiling all the way home.

He knew of the single occasion when I'd trespassed in his garden in the dead of night. Of course, it hadn't bothered him in the slightest, and he insisted I was more than welcome to watch over him whenever I wished. An offer I refused. Unless there was cause for me to be there, I'd let him have his privacy.

Except when I was specifically invited.

"What has you so happy?" Helen asked once she'd tucked Jayne in bed.

"I'm going out tonight."

"You go out every night, why would tonight be . . . ? Oh! You're going to see Ray," she said, smiling as everything clicked into place.

"He asked if I would."

There were a couple of hours before it would be safe to return to his house. Once everyone was asleep I would go. The last thing either of us needed was to be caught by his mother. She may have a soft spot for me, but sneaking into her son's bedroom was bound to erase that.

Once Helen and Sam had said their goodnights, I took to wandering around my bedroom, looking for something to wear. As tempting as it was to spend the time wandering the streets around Ray's home, I didn't want to chance a repeat of the incident with the window. It would be worrying for Ray if I didn't turn up at his house.

In the end I settled on a lightweight, dark-coloured summer dress. It was more appropriate than the clothes I normally wore at night, clothes in which Ray had yet to see me.

I slipped quietly out of the house and hurried through the streets towards Ray's. It was quiet in every way. Most of the humans were sleeping, and I didn't encounter anyone of the nonhuman variety. Even the vampires were only venturing out when they needed to feed. Getting caught in the blast of a falling bomb might not kill a vampire, but getting trapped in the rubble could.

When I got to Ray's house, I silently scaled his garden wall and waited in the shadows. He was leaning on his windowsill, gazing up at the night sky, like he had the one night I'd dared to get close enough to see him.

When I'd asked, he told me it was something he did often, thanks to his grandmother.

With his father gone and no memory of him, she told Ray he was watching over him. So whenever he woke in the night, he would gaze at the stars for a while. They reminded him that he was never alone.

How true that sentiment had turned out to be. Even if it was in a way he couldn't have anticipated.

I understood the feeling of relaxation he got from them. The night sky had hardly changed over the years, and it was nice knowing that there was something as everlasting as I was.

When I stepped out of the shadows, it took him a long moment before he realised I was there. I had to laugh at the unobservant nature of humans.

"I'll get the door," he whispered, knowing I'd hear him.

Putting my hand up, I gestured for him to stay where he was. There was no point in making him walk to the door when I could easily scale the wall.

A couple of seconds later, I was standing beside him, following his gaze to where I'd been.

"That was fast. I would have opened the door."

"Climbing through your window is more discreet, and I did warn you."

"Yes, you did."

"You look tired." I reached up to trace the circles under his eyes.

"Long day."

"Go to sleep, then," I told him. "I'll be here in the morning if your mother is still sleeping."

He paused for a moment, leaning against the windowsill. "Would you . . . ? Do you mind if . . . ? Would it be too forward of me to ask you to lie with me?"

His question took me by surprise. It wasn't the question itself or the act of staying with him in his bed, or even the fact that he'd asked. I *wanted* to be with him. That was what shocked me. It was all so very new, and so very frightening.

Apparently I paused in my answer for too long. "Never mind, forget I said anything."

"Ray, this is new to me. I'm not sure what's appropriate and what isn't." Taking his hand in mine, I tried to find the words to explain. "I would love to, but I'm unsure as to whether it would be right to do so."

"This is new to me, as well." Slowly, he inched towards the bed and sat on the edge. "I did have an idea regarding what's proper and what isn't."

"You've been thinking about this?"

"I have, and I came up with a suggestion. In public we stick to the proper rules of society, as ever-changing as they seem to be. In private, I thought we could perhaps try things by your rules?"

"That sounds . . . very fair."

He had clearly put a lot of thought into our physical relationship, more than I had. I'd assumed things would progress at whatever rate they happened to. The rules of etiquette hadn't crossed my mind. Ray's suggestion took care of that. I'd be free to be who I was when we were on our own or at my house.

"So, you will?" He patted the bed beside him, a coy smile on his face.

"I will."

Being in Ray's bed, his arms wrapped around me, was like nothing I had ever experienced. We talked for a moment before he drifted off to sleep, a smile on his face. I heard his mother snoring softly down the hall, and Ray's heart beat out a slow, steady rhythm. There was nothing in the entire world I'd rather do than lie by his side, watching him sleep.

As I lay there, resting my head on his chest, I thought about our days together. Endless hours filled with questions and answers. We'd spent most of our time at my house or riding in the fields surrounding London.

My mind wandered from the things we'd talked about to what it felt like when he kissed me. It may have been a chaste peck on my cheek, but it made me wonder what it would be like to have him do it again. Letting my eyes drift shut, I thought about what that could be like. To feel his lips against mine, to have him kissing me. Properly kissing me.

Chapter Nine

I don't know when it happened or even how. I do know the last time I'd fallen asleep so easily was before I matured.

Sleep for us was almost always forced. When we did, it was exceptionally light, and it took a conscious effort on our part. Always.

Yet, as I came awake, I knew I'd fallen into a deeper slumber than I'd ever experienced. Normally, on the occasions when I slept, I was awake by dawn.

The first thing to catch my attention as I woke was the sound of Ray's heartbeat, and the second was his arms wrapped around me. My initial reaction to realising I was curled up in Ray's arms was to snuggle deeper into his chest, relishing the warmth.

No sooner had I moved closer to him than I heard footsteps in the hall. There was a brief knock on the door, swiftly followed by it being opened.

I shot up, and came face to face with Ray's mother. She was as shocked to see me as I was her. My only saving grace was the fact I was on top of the covers and wearing my summer dress.

"Morning, Mother." Though Ray's tone was sheepish and his voice quiet, a stray arm found its way around my waist, pulling me closer.

"Good morning, Son, Serenity. Breakfast will be ready in a few minutes." She eyed my dress briefly before leaving.

Stupid, stupid, stupid. I should have never accepted his invitation. I shouldn't have stayed in his bed.

We were both silent as I berated myself repeatedly for my mistakes. Mistakes cost lives; I knew that better than anyone. Mistakes weren't something I could tolerate, not where Ray was concerned.

The best scenario I could come up with was telling Liz everything. But

Ray would be in enough danger as it was; dragging Liz into my world wasn't an option.

"Serenity, I'm sor—"

"Stop. Please, don't blame yourself. I should have been more careful."

"No, I should never have asked you . . ."

"Ray, please. You couldn't have known I would fall asleep. Even I didn't know." Yet, looking at him, sitting in his bed, smiling, it wasn't so much of a surprise. I smiled back. "Perhaps I should go down, try to explain."

"Let me," he suggested. "I got us into this."

"Don't be silly."

"Fine, how about we go down together?"

I nodded and offered to wait outside his room while he dressed.

Pacing the short space between his door and the opposite wall, I stewed over what had happened.

How could I have fallen asleep? More precisely, how had it happened so easily?

It was something I'd need to ask William about. He would have the answer. I also needed to ensure it never happened again. That was, if we managed to get through this incident unscathed.

Yet, even as I strengthened my resolve, I had to admit I liked the sensation of waking up with Ray. More than liked. It was something I could happily get used to. Waking up alone did not compare.

"Ready?" he asked once he was dressed.

Nodding, I took his hand. "For what it's worth, I rather liked waking up in your arms."

"As did I."

We were apprehensive as we descended the stairs. I heard Liz humming in the kitchen. *Humming?* That couldn't be right. Yet, as we came to a stop in the doorway, there she was, busily finishing the eggs.

She spotted us hovering and laughed. "Oh, stop looking so scared. I'm not about to shout at you."

Taking our seats, we were silent, waiting. I wrung my hands anxiously. Surely what had happened went against almost everything that was expected of a young couple.

She placed our plates on the table then sat opposite us. "I'd like to tell you a story, and if you ever repeat this, I will deny it."

Ray nodded, tucking into his breakfast.

"Before your father and I married, he used to sneak out of his house and over to mine. Every night, after our parents were asleep, he would creep in through the front door and not leave until morning. I would wait up for him, and we would talk for hours." She smiled at the memory. "He continued making the trip to my house every night until we were married. It wasn't until our wedding day that our parents took us to one side and said:

'Now you don't have to sneak into each other's beds.' I cannot tell you how mortified we were, but they weren't angry. Apparently they had discussed telling us earlier, but they knew we were behaving ourselves. Unbeknownst to us, they had been checking up on us since they realised."

Of all the things I was expecting to happen when we walked down the stairs, that was *not* one of them. Both of us had stopped eating, opting to stare open mouthed at Liz.

"I do have one request," she said after a moment.

"Anything," Ray agreed quickly.

"I assume that you," she said, looking at me, "sneaked in the front door sometime after I went to bed and that you came on foot."

When I nodded, she changed her focus to Ray before continuing, "Then I suggest that you, young man, act like the gentleman I raised you to be and not let Serenity roam the streets at night. I'm not going to forbid you from sharing each other's beds. Lord knows, you'll find a way to do it anyway if I did, but it is not safe."

"I promise."

That was something we would have to talk about. It was all well and good promising not to let me wander the streets, but there was no chance in hell I'd let Ray wander them alone. If he insisted on keeping his promise to his mother, then I would follow him on his way to my house and then all the way back to his again.

"Good, now eat up before it gets cold."

She left us in the kitchen and headed out to the garden.

"That went well," I said once we were alone. "Better than."

Ray laughed. "I can't believe my father used to do that."

"I think I might be able to."

"Why is that?"

"If you are like your father, and I think you are, then you must have gotten your disregard for the rules from somewhere." I smirked, just for a moment, then went back to eating my breakfast.

I felt much better about the situation as I washed our dishes. There was still the niggling little voice in the back of my mind that told me I could never be so unaware of my surroundings again, but it was fading. Fast.

I kept sneaking glances at Ray as we washed. Every time I did, I saw him smiling brightly.

I was *home*.

Ray was my home.

He was everything I could have wanted and more.

"Do you think you'll be allowed to spend the day with me?" I didn't want to upset his mother.

"I don't see why not."

"Perhaps we should ask first," I suggested, "in light of this morning."

"Perhaps we should. I should get you a shawl for our walk anyway." He shuffled to the back door.

Liz was happy to see to her gardening and let Ray spend his time with me but insisted he be home for dinner. It was a condition I was quite willing to accept.

Our stroll was pleasant. It was the first time I'd walked with Ray to either of our houses. Though he was competent enough with his cane, it was slow going.

And I wouldn't have had it any other way.

There was a chill in the air, and though I barely noticed it, I would have looked strange had I not borrowed a shawl. There were few people on the streets and we quite happily talked the entire way. Hand in hand.

It was how we spent the rest of the morning, and most of the afternoon.

When we got to my house, I apologised to Helen for not letting her know where I was. All was forgiven, however, once she heard what had happened. She would have a good laugh over that for quite some time.

My mistakes were so rare that they were well documented when they occurred. It would be like the broken toe incident all over again. Something I'd never live down.

And it was worth it.

Waking up in Ray's arms had been heaven. *Why had I even considered fighting this?*

We were sitting in the library, having had lunch in the garden. Ray was attempting to decipher the first of the stories I'd given him. It wasn't going very well. He was still on the first page, and I hadn't shown him the expansive records yet.

"Would you like some help?"

I'd been watching him, knowing exactly what he was struggling with. Three of the letters had the same symbol, and another two also had the same. Common letters that could change the entire word. The only way to tell them apart was minute, almost invisible differences in the characters.

"I think . . . am I seeing things or are some of these the same?" He frowned as he tapped his finger against the pages.

"Some of them are almost identical." I bit back a laugh.

His frown deepened. "How do you tell the difference?"

"Do you see the tail of that character?" I pointed to what was supposed to be an *E.*

"Yes, it's the same as the others."

"Not quite. Do you see how it's longer, thinner?"

He squinted, leaning closer to the page. "Oh yes. Now I see it. It *is* longer."

"That one is an *E.*" I pointed out the next one, which was almost identical. "The short, fat tail is the *A,* and the short, thin one is the *I.*"

"How do you ever remember the differences? How can you even see them?"

"My eyesight is sharper than yours, and I've been reading and writing that language since I was little." It was a shame we'd stopped speaking it by the time I was born. "Why don't you take a break? Tell me something about you."

"What would you like to know?" He set the book aside, placing his reading glasses on top of them.

"Anything, something that no one else knows." Despite our endless hours on the same subject there was still so much about him I had yet to discover.

"All right, I have something. You must promise not to laugh, though," he said, with absolute seriousness.

"No laughing."

"Before I was born, my mother did a lot of knitting. She was off her feet a lot with me, and she cannot abide needlepoint. Anyway, she knitted me this toy in the shape of a hedgehog. His name is Herbie, and I still have him," he said, looking at his hands again.

"Why would I have laughed at that?" I thought it was quite sweet that he'd kept it.

"Most grown men don't have their childhood toys hidden away in their rooms."

"I happen to think it's rather sweet."

"He lives in a shoebox I turned into a bed when I was ten."

"And? It's something you're sentimentally attached to. I'm sure that if I'd had anything of the sort, I'd still have it."

"Tell me something about you?"

"What would you like to know?"

"Tell me a dream, something you've always wanted," he asked, his eyes sparkling.

"There is one desire I once had." More of a wish really. "But I need to explain some things before I tell you."

There was something I'd always wanted, but it had been pushed to one side after my sister had passed. For a fairly simple dream it was a complicated story.

"There has been much that I've seen in my life, as you know. More than anyone could ever understand. Everyone I have ever loved has grown old and died. Yet, since I matured, I haven't changed. My hair hasn't grown, I haven't gotten any taller, and I haven't aged. I can remember a number of details from my life and have had everything I ever wanted—except a love of my own. I never had someone to love the way I love you.

"The only things I have ever dreamed of, ever wanted, are children of my own and someone to raise a family and grow old with. It was the one thing I could never have. The one thing I had to put on hold until the right time. Until I met you. Yet, now that I have, I'm torn. On the one hand I have everything I have ever wanted. And on the other, I have everything I cannot have."

"Why?"

"Do you remember when I told you our descendants had stopped maturing?" I waited for him to nod before I continued. "Before that happened, it was a simple case of finding our partners, settling down, and raising the next generation. We retired, so to speak, when we found our partners. But then The Seats discovered how to kill us and everything changed. Now there are only two of us left. I cannot stop doing what I do, and yet, part of me tells me I have to. I have to protect you above all else."

Ray sat beside me and spoke softly. "There's more you aren't telling me."

"There is, but that's for another day." There was a lot more to the story, but I wasn't ready to tell him. I wasn't sure I'd ever be ready to tell him.

The story of my twin sister, Lona, was not one I enjoyed retelling. It was with her death that our children had stopped maturing. We still had no idea how to reverse the effects of her death. None of our records held any clues, and our psychic hadn't thought to check so far into the future before her own passing. There hadn't been a need to, not until it was too late.

ּ᛫ᚾᚲᛏᛟᛉᚲᛏᛉᛚᛟᛏ

"So, may I meet Herbie?" I asked, as I walked back to Ray's house for dinner. Apparently the invitation had been extended to me, as well.

"As long as you promise not to laugh when you see his bed." There was such concern shining in his eyes.

"I promise."

I almost broke my promise the second the words were uttered. I'd never make fun of his sentimentality over his toy, but I came very close to laughing at the desperate tone of his voice and his expression. He was so adorable.

"You promised!" he cried as a small chortle escaped me.

"Ray, I'm not laughing about your Herbie. I promise." It was hard not to chuckle as I spoke. "I laughed because the look on your face is too cute for words."

He watched me out of the corner of his eye for the rest of the walk, checking for any signs of laughter. He continued all through dinner with his mother. Every time I caught him, I would smile.

Being with Ray and his mother gave me hope. Though I couldn't change what I was, or stop what I had to do, perhaps I could still live my dream. Ray would be in constant danger when he moved with me, but that was an inevitable part of my world. I was starting to believe it was possible to have my dream. To be able to live my life with Ray by my side. Making the choice to grow old was something I could barely wait for.

Not yet, though.

There were things that had to be put in place before I considered it. Things I'd need to talk with William about. Perhaps a trip to see him in the near future would be necessary, though I was loath to leave Ray in the city alone. William would also have my head for turning up without arranging something safe.

Before I left for the evening, promising to return when everyone was asleep, Ray introduced me to his Herbie.

"Do you promise not to laugh anymore?" he asked as we entered his room.

"I promise."

He walked over to his wardrobe and reached for the pile of boxes that were sitting on top of it. It was tempting to offer him some help, but he managed fine on his own. I enjoyed seeing that he could manage most things without any assistance. Leaving the bottom one at the foot of his bed, he returned the others.

He dusted off the box as we sat on the ottoman, then removed the lid and pulled out the small hedgehog. "Serenity, this is Herbie. You're the first person to see him in almost fifteen years."

"I am honoured to meet you, Herbie," I said quietly.

"He seems so tiny now," Ray muttered as he held the toy in his hands.

"What are all the bare patches?"

"I used to gnaw on him when I was little. He was so much bigger then." He was still looking down at the toy.

"Ray, what's the matter?" He'd become very quiet all of a sudden.

"I was wondering about something . . . something you said earlier." He paused for a moment, awkwardly shifting in his seat. "You love me?"

"Yes," I answered, without hesitation.

"Is it strange that I love you, too, after such a short time?" he asked, putting Herbie back in his bed.

Cupping his hands in mine, I said, "Not at all."

We sat so still for so long, his face in my hands, his eyes boring into mine. It took only one moment for everything to change. I leaned forward, just an inch, and he reacted, brushing his lips against mine for a fraction of a second. Both of us froze. Hesitant. Each waiting for the other to act. Him wanting to be a gentleman, as he was raised. Me wanting nothing more than to feel his lips on mine again.

He moved first, just a touch, pressing his lips against mine, and I slid my arms around his neck, holding him close. Our lips moved together, gentle, exploring. It was all so new, and so beautiful. His hands were on my waist, pulling me closer to him, pressing his lips harder against mine.

It was better than I'd imagined—the delicious taste of him, the feel of his hands on my waist, and the urgency with which he kissed me.

"Ray, Serenity." The sound of his mother calling to us was the only reason we broke apart. "Sam is here."

I kissed him again briefly. "I'll be back soon."

Neither of us moved for a moment, both of us smiling brightly.

"I'll leave my window open."

My smile was still in place as I said my goodbyes to Liz, and for the entire ride home. Neither Sam nor Helen said anything about the bounce in my step or grin on my face, but they knew. It was clear from the sideways glances they gave me and their own smiles.

"Sam?" I asked as everyone was retiring for the night. "Could you have Tara ready in the morning?"

"Of course." He furrowed his brow as he fought the urge to ask questions.

There was something I'd put off, something that had been in the pile of notifications, and I should have dealt with it a lot sooner.

As I walked through the streets, my mind raced. It was filled with the memory of our kiss and the worries of what I'd tell Ray in the morning. When I reached his garden, he was waiting at his window once more. I scaled the wall without hesitation, appearing at his side before he had a chance to register the fact I was there.

"You know you could give me a heart attack doing that!" he whispered, clutching his chest.

"Your heart sounds fine to me," I laid my head where his hand had been, listening to the steady beat.

"How can you tell?"

"I've been around for a while, Ray. Though your heart is on the fast side right now, it's perfectly fine." I smiled.

We stood there for a moment as he leaned against the wall. It was the only way he could wrap both of his arms around me.

When he yawned, failing in his attempt to stifle it, I said, "Time for bed."

"Will you stay again?"

"Not for the entire night." As much as I wanted to, I couldn't. "I don't want to get you in any more trouble with your mother."

He fell asleep quickly, but not before insisting on a goodnight kiss. A kiss I was more than happy to oblige him with.

I took extra care not to fall asleep in his arms again, but it was harder than I expected. By the time the first light of dawn shined through the window, I'd figured out what I needed to do to keep him safe while I was away. I just hadn't worked out what to tell him. Ray stirred as I slipped from his bed. I quickly left him a note to come by after breakfast, and to come alone. That would give me plenty of time to change and prepare everything I needed before he arrived.

"Go back to sleep, my love," I whispered before I slipped out of his room.

Chapter Ten

There was a spring in my step. I was rather pleased with myself when I got home. Only Sam was awake. I hadn't fallen asleep and gotten Ray into any more trouble.

"Good morning," I greeted Sam when I reached the kitchen.

"Morning." His voice was light, but his stare was hard. "You going to explain why you only need one horse today?"

"I need to leave for a few days." Ignoring him was easy given my light mood.

"How long?" he asked, tucking in to his own breakfast.

"A week, maybe more."

"How long have you been putting it off?"

"The letter came just after I met Ray." I winced, expecting a rebuttal.

Instead of a lecture about letting things get out of hand, like Sam normally gave me, I was greeted with a heavy sigh. Nothing more.

There were times when I felt as though I was barely older than the twenty or so years I appeared. Whenever I left things too long, because we were moving or had plans of some sort, Sam would remind me of the consequences.

As if I needed to be reminded.

"He's your life now, Sere. He comes first."

Sam finished his breakfast and left to prepare Tara. I had a short time before I needed to change, so I began making breakfast for Helen and Jayne, a feat I rarely attempted. Despite my ability to cook, it wasn't often that I found the time or the motivation to do so. As I would be leaving for a while, the least I could do was cook breakfast by way of an apology for the short notice.

"Something smells good," Helen commented when she came down. "Looks good, too. To what do we owe this pleasure?"

I feigned hurt. "Can I not cook for my family without there being an occasion?"

"You can, but you *don't*." Picking at the cut fruit, she stared at me.

"I have to go away for a few days." I ignored her as best I could, while setting the kitchen table.

"And you would like me to keep Ray busy?"

"Please. I'd stay, but I'm afraid I've put this off for too long."

"Of course."

We would have talked more about what I was dealing with, but Jayne was awake and chose that moment to join us.

Some discussions we avoided when young ears were present.

It was a grand affair when I cooked for my family. Every breakfast food we had was on the table. Fruit, toast, a little bacon, cereal—everything they could want and more. No one would need to eat until dinner by the time they were done. There would be plenty of leftovers for Sam if he was hungry again.

I only had an hour or so before Ray arrived. There was something else I wanted to talk with them about first.

"As you know, I need to go away for a few days," I began once Jayne had gone to get dressed for the day. "I hope it will be a simple task; a few vampires near Lyon are causing trouble. It's too close to William for comfort, and I should have dealt with this when I heard about it."

"Does he know?" she asked, meaning William.

"No, and I plan to keep it that way. There's no point in getting him upset over something I'm quite capable of handling." He needed to concentrate on his family. "Besides, we agreed he would only help with troubles if I needed him."

"Did that not go out of the window when you found Ray?" Sam asked, giving me a pointed look.

The agreement was that when William got married, I would take over everything. Updating the records. Actively dealing with any issues. Anything I could handle on my own, I did.

"We never discussed it," I said, avoiding Sam's gaze. "There was something else I wanted to talk to you both about."

"Ray?"

"Not yet. He doesn't know I need to leave. What I wanted to discuss was what would happen to the records when William and I are gone."

"We have years before that happens," Helen hissed, taking me by surprise.

I'd been expecting a more rational response.

"Perhaps we do, but there's a chance we don't have that long left. I'd like to put things in place for when the time comes," I said as calmly as possible. "I need to discuss some things with William . . ."

"Serenity, you have been my mother, my sister, my daughter, and my best friend. You *will* outlive me, so there's nothing that needs doing now."

"Helen, please. It's not much that I'm asking, but it is something I need to ask now, *before* anything happens. If the records we have kept over the years fell into the hands of the vampires, they could wipe us out. Every name of every descendant we have is in those records. I just want to ensure they'll be protected and looked after by someone I trust, and I've trusted your family for longer than I care to remember." I hadn't expected her to argue the point at all, let alone so adamantly.

"Helen, Serenity is only trying to prepare for the worst. You know how she is," Sam said, attempting to soothe her.

"Fine, I'll listen, but I'm warning you now, you *will* outlive me and I will never need to put your plan into action."

Though I didn't understand her anger, I was happy she'd agreed to listen.

Sam ignored her. "What did you have planned?"

"If the time comes, then I want all of the records in one safe location." Preferably away from anyone who could use the information they contained. "In order to best protect them, I'd be grateful if your family looked after them. I'll have a house specifically designed for the purpose, in the safest location I can find."

"One condition," Helen said. "You are not to start construction on the house until necessary, which means years from now. If you want to draw up the plans, then fine, but I'll only agree if you stop thinking about it now and leave it until you absolutely have to."

It was a fair compromise. "Agreed."

She analysed my reaction for a moment. "You already have them made."

"The initial plans have been drawn up, the location hasn't been finalised, but it has been narrowed down. Land in each area has already been purchased." It never did me any good to lie to Helen.

"When?"

"As soon as I saw the reply from William."

She glared at me for a long moment before shaking her head and leaving the room. There was silence as I stared after her, until Sam broke it by laughing loudly.

"What's so funny?"

"You two are two-of-a-kind. Both as stubborn as the other, though I think you have the edge," he told me. "I'll finish preparing Tara."

"Thank you."

There wasn't much I needed to do to get ready. Dark trousers and a thick shirt were all I planned on wearing, accompanied by a decent pair of boots, suitable for riding Tara and running. An extra set of clothes and a small bag was all I needed. The spare clothing was essential; travelling while dressed as a woman could cause problems. Not every country I ended up in treated women the same. Money was the other necessity. I could get anything I needed with enough of it.

I was descending the stairs, changed and bag ready, when there was a knock on the front door. Ray had arrived.

Sprinting down the last few steps, I eagerly opened the door, forgetting I was dressed completely different.

I almost laughed when his eyes grew wide at the sight of me. "Good morning."

"Good morning, you look . . . different," he said, eyes travelling up and down my body.

"Yes, I need to talk to you about something," I stepped to the side so he could come in.

Helen was already in the sitting room, all trace of our earlier disagreement gone as she greeted Ray.

"Good morning, Helen. How are you?" he asked, taking a seat next to me.

"I'm fine, thank you."

"You seem worried," I told Ray, shifting closer to him.

"I am. You said you needed to talk?"

"Yes. I need to go away for a few days." Why was this so *hard?* "There's something I have to deal with."

"How long will you be gone?"

"A week, maybe more." Less if I could. "I was supposed to leave after the auction, but things didn't go as planned."

"Have you been putting this off because of me?"

"Perhaps, but that isn't the point. I'd like to put certain measures in place for you whilst I'm away."

"To protect me?"

"Yes."

"Whatever you need to do."

"Thank you," I whispered. "Would it be possible for you to spend your days here? Or at least let Helen know where you'll be?"

"Of course."

"I'd also prefer it if you didn't walk anywhere alone, especially in the evening. Sam will have the carriage if you need it, as well as any of the cars."

I was somewhat happier about leaving once we'd finished talking. Helen suggested they all take a trip out to one of the summer fairs. Jayne would love it, and Ray's face lit up when I mentioned one of the other cars I had. His eyes grew so wide I almost thought it was Christmas morning when I told him I had a Rolls-Royce Wraith. I'd need to ask Helen for details of his reaction when he actually saw the car. His face did fall some, when I said Sam was the only person allowed to drive and the only reason Sam was allowed was because I'd taught him myself. Helen still didn't like the car, but Sam was comfortable behind the wheel.

"You have to go, Serenity," Ray said as we walked down to the stable.

"I know. It doesn't change the fact I don't want to leave you."

He gave me a bright, teasing smile. "May I ask a question before you leave?"

I chuckled. "Always so polite."

"Why are you dressed like . . . well, as you are?" He gestured to my clothes. "Not that I'm complaining."

"It's more convenient in case anything . . . happens. Also, travelling like this is much easier."

"Well, I must say, they're very becoming on you."

"You're only saying that because you can see more of me than if I were wearing a dress." Smirking, I gave him a little twirl.

"That may be so, but you look beautiful, regardless," he said, making me smile even brighter.

We fell into an uneasy silence as I prepared to leave. There were no signs that anything would go wrong while I was away. Everything I could do to protect Ray in my absence had been done. No one besides my family and William knew I'd found my partner. There was nothing stopping me . . . except I didn't want to be apart from him.

"I wish there were another way." I leaned into his one-armed embrace.

"You have to, Serenity," he said, all the playfulness gone.

"I know." I pulled away and looked up at him. "As soon as I'm able, I'll be back."

"I'll miss you." He brushed his hand through my hair, smiling just a touch as he spoke.

"I'll miss you, too."

"May I kiss you goodbye?"

"No, not goodbye, but I would like it if you kissed me." Goodbye wasn't something I was willing to say to him, or have him say to me, even if I were only going to be gone for a few days.

He smiled briefly before lowering his head, his hand still in my hair. Every second away was too much. He'd kissed me mere hours before, but it didn't compare to the sensations that were running through me now.

"I'll be back soon," I whispered against his lips. "As soon as I can."

"Be safe. I love you."

"I love you, too. Always."

With one last, all too brief kiss, I mounted Tara and kicked her into a gallop. When I reached the gates at the bottom of the garden, I turned back for a moment. Ray stood watching me. There was a smile on his face and his arm was raised, waving, but even from a distance, I saw the worry in his eyes.

I'd left things too long, and there was a chance that the nearest Seat had already stepped in. If they were there when I arrived in Lyon, things could get . . . interesting.

Chapter Eleven

Running into any member of The Seats while I was away caused many problems. There may not have been anything physically different about me, but I was sure they would be able to tell I'd found my mate. They had a knack for knowing such things.

I'd managed to keep my family safe for centuries, and I would continue to do so for as long as possible. It meant I needed to be more cautious than I would normally be. There was no guarantee any of The Seats would be there, but there was always a chance. They all knew who I was, or what I looked like, at least. None of them knew what I was truly called.

They had a different name for me: *Azrael,* the Angel of Death.

Why they called me that was a mystery. I was no angel, and certainly no angel of death. Yet I preferred they call me that rather than know my real name.

If they wanted to find me, that would be all they would need.

It was only a matter of time. As long as they believed I hadn't yet found my partner, I'd be left alone. Reasonably. There would always be the odd confrontation that I found myself in.

I hope this won't be one of them.

Despite the war, traversing the Channel proved easy. It helped that I saw well enough to avoid other ships, and there were several places I could dock my boat relatively undetected. It wasn't a big boat, just enough space for a couple of people and a horse or two. For the longer journeys I had my plane, not that I knew how to fly the thing.

By the time I was halfway to Lyon, slipping by on the outskirts of war ravaged towns and cities, it was past midnight. Travelling at night always took more time, but there was little time to waste and no point in stopping. With Ray waiting for me, I wanted this over as soon as possible. No stopping, as little rest as I could manage, and the quickest work I'd ever done.

From the information in the letter, it appeared to be a relatively simple job. Just a few vampires in the area, numerous unexplained deaths, and a few other rumours that confirmed their presence. One thing all of our descendants were good at was spotting vampires.

There were a number of subtle differences humans almost always missed. The slight predatory grace with which they carried themselves. The way they would occasionally breathe a little too deeply when in close contact with someone. Their fangs were never seen, unless they were buried in someone's neck, of course.

Sometime before dawn, I found a place for Tara to have a brief break. I'd give her a proper rest when I dropped her off at Laura's house. Laura was my cousin, or rather Helen's cousin. Helen descended from one of Lona's twin girls; Laura descended from the other.

She currently lived on the outskirts of Lyon. The place where I was going was only a couple of hours outside of the city, but I'd stay with Laura until nightfall.

As the sun rose above the horizon, I mounted Tara once more and set off on the final leg of the journey. It would be early when I arrived at Laura's, but she would be there. Her home doubled as a small bed and breakfast.

I arrived after breakfast time. I didn't think to change out of my men's clothing.

An unfamiliar young man greeted me at the door. *"Bonjour. Est-ce que je peux vous aider?"*

"Ou est Laura?" Another advantage of living in so many places, and for so long, was the many languages I'd learned. Though I was not polite enough to ask anything more than "where is Laura."

He looked confused for a moment, before ducking inside and leaving me standing in front of the wide open door. I could hear his hurried footsteps as he went to fetch Laura. I almost laughed when I heard the conversation. Perhaps I should've changed into a dress before appearing on Laura's doorstep.

"Laura? There's a man at the door for you. Only I'm not sure he is . . . a he," the boy said, surprising me. I hadn't expected him to speak in English.

"Did you get a name?" Laura asked.

"No, I'm sorry. Would you like me to?"

"No, never mind." From the sound of things this was a regular occurrence. "Go and help that daughter of mine clear the table."

With my hat pulled down, most of my face was hidden from view until she was standing right in front of me.

"*Que puis-je faire pour—*" she began, pausing as she recognised me. "Serenity!"

"The one and only."

"Well, this is a surprise." She smiled brightly as she opened her arms. "How is my dearest aunt these days?"

"Busy, as always." I held her tight for a moment.

"I take it you're here on business then." Her smile faded as she let me into her home.

"It seems like all I do."

"Are The Seats slipping again?"

"No, not at all. They do their job wonderfully. I'm afraid it's me who's slipping," I whispered.

"Why would—"

"Aunt Sere!" A short brunette, Laura's only daughter, interrupted us.

"Annie." I smiled brightly at the young woman. "It's good to see you again."

"You, as well. You seem . . . *different.*"

"Trousers and a shirt will do that to you." It was a nervous joke.

I hoped it was only my clothes that had thrown her. If a sixteen-year-old child could tell that I'd found my partner, then the vampires would spot it immediately.

"I was about to ask why you were the one slipping, but I think I know."

"Is it that obvious?" I asked, wincing.

"Only if you know what you're looking for. That same smile was on Annie's face not two months ago." So that was the young man I had seen. Annie had found her partner.

"Tell me about him," Laura ordered, directing me to the sitting room.

There was little point in resisting. Laura always did have a way of getting information. A person could talk to her for hours about anything and nothing. She always listened.

So we sat in her sitting room and talked all morning. I described my first kiss to her, and the way I'd felt when he wrapped his arms around me. We spent an entire hour discussing the beauty of his eyes and how they shined whenever he was excited or happy. How I could get lost in them forever.

"You miss him."

"I missed him as soon as he was out of my sight."

"I was the same those first few years after I met my partner." She gently patted my knee. "Still am."

"How is André?" I hadn't seen her husband about.

"He went to war."

"Is there anything I can do?"

Where we could, we didn't interfere with human affairs. We didn't fight in their wars or work for their governments, or vote in their elections. The jobs we held were as far removed from having any influence as possible.

We ran our own small businesses, as Laura did, or we worked in low-profile jobs. Our entire race was well off, though most were only wealthy enough to have a comfortable life.

Our partners . . . some of them felt differently. "He went willingly, and he left with a promise to return," she said, smiling sadly. "I'll know if anything happens."

The connection wasn't as strong for those who hadn't matured, but they knew when they lost their partners, even if they were thousands of miles away. But unlike William and me, their connection wasn't one that killed them when it was severed.

"If there's anything you need . . ."

"I'll ask."

That was the end of the subject. As good as Laura was to talk to, she was never one for saying too much about herself. She preferred to listen. It was something that had been passed down through the generations. They'd all been listeners on that side of the family.

I pottered around the house with Laura for most of the afternoon and helped with dinner. It made me feel better. And it was the least I could do for turning up unannounced and expecting her to feed and water my horse.

"You know you cannot tell anyone about my partner," I reminded her when it came time for me to leave. "The only reason I've told you is because you're family."

"I'd never tell anyone." There was a promise in her voice and a smile on her face. "Will you be staying for breakfast in the morning?"

"Not this time. I want to get back as soon as possible."

"Of course. I'll make sure your horse is rested," she said. "Good luck."

"Luck has little to do with it."

Despite the dark night, I took extra care not to be spotted as I raced from the house, sticking close to the plentiful shadows. I'd already estimated it would take me almost an hour to reach the place Laura had said I needed to be. There'd been a number of unexplained deaths in a nearby town, one that Laura frequented because of her future son-in-law's family.

The night was clear, the stars glittering brightly with only a sliver of a moon to outshine them. When I arrived, it was peaceful. No one wandered the streets, and every house was dark and quiet, bedded down for the night.

Though no vampire stalked the moonless evening looking for their next meal, I knew they were here. Everything I saw and sensed pointed to an abandoned barn on the edge of the quiet town; its rickety boarding barely kept the vampires hidden. Not only did I smell the lingering scent of fresh blood in the air, but I heard them.

I stopped.

The wind was mild, winding its way through the trees, gently rustling the lush leaves. My breathing and heart sounded loud in the heavy darkness, making me strain to listen. All around me the night was alive with the distant sound of slumber and the closer whispers of vampires.

There weren't just the two vampires in the barn. It sounded as if there were at least half a dozen of them. Muffled voices filled the structure, all whispering quietly about plans and meals. Almost obscured in their midst were the quiet cries of two humans.

So much for this not being complicated.

"Would someone *please* check if she is here yet?" a hauntingly familiar female voice drawled. "This town has so little in the way of livestock."

There was a reason the vampire sounded so familiar. It belonged to the second most feared female vampire in the world, as well as the only female who held one of the Seats of Power.

Elena.

It was a trap.

chapter Twelve

Even as I realised the whole situation was a setup, there was little I could do about it.

I had no idea how long it would be before I was discovered, if I was spotted at all. If they wanted to lure me out, then it wouldn't be the first time, and I knew what was coming next.

If I didn't show, they would find or make more vampires and use them to bring me out again. That would result in more human lives lost.

Elena heaved a sigh; she was frustrated. "Who do I have to eat to get anything done around here?"

The only female left in The Seats had to be fierce, but Elena took it to a whole new level. She looked like a Greek goddess: tall, stunning, with blond hair and dazzling blue eyes. Looks can be deceiving. Beautiful she may have been, but a goddess she wasn't, unless her own opinion of herself counted. There wasn't a depth that Elena wouldn't sink to. If it fit her purpose, she would step on anyone to get where or what she wanted.

I didn't blame her for the hatred she felt towards the human race, or even the way she treated the vampires who broke their rules. Elena had been born into slavery, but not the kind where humans were bought and sold as servants. What the vampires in the barn were thinking of doing here had been done before. When Elena was born, it was into the arms of her dying mother. Dying because a vampire had latched onto her neck the second her baby had been delivered. The village, deep in the Russian mountains, had been taken over by vampires. How she had then become so twisted was a mystery.

It had happened before The Seats had been formed and was one of the many reasons they'd been created.

"I do believe she is here," another familiar voice answered.

Kiros. Elena's mate.

Well, that was the London Seat accounted for.

London was the smallest of The Seats, with only the two of them. The others ranged from three to six in number.

I decided a direct approach would be more entertaining. The rotting wood of the door did little to hide me. Not that I was trying.

"Is it that time of the century again?" I drawled, standing in the disintegrated doorway. "I do hope you've been waiting."

"Azrael," Elena greeted me. "What took you so long?"

"Moving, you know how these things go."

"And where might you be living these days?"

"Around the corner from Hell, where I've always lived." I smiled.

Anyone would think we were old friends if they looked at the two of us. She was the only one who ever kept calm when faced with me. Elena smiled, while everyone else in the barn glared daggers.

A subtle shift in the air made the hair on the back of my neck stand up and told me Elena was trying to use her powers. Hers was fear. When she chose, she could make everyone around her feel as though they were living in their worst nightmares. It was immobilising—fortunately, her gifts had no effect on me.

"Really, Ellie, do you never learn?" I asked, being purposefully condescending.

"Elena." She carefully pronounced each syllable. "My name is Elena."

"Oh, yes, so it is. Now, I have no business here, so what do you want?"

"You . . . Dead," Elena hissed, always the optimist.

"Come now, Ellie. You know as well as I do that I cannot be killed. Why do you insist on wasting my time?" It was a good thing I was a practiced liar.

Though technically, I was telling the truth. *I* couldn't be killed, unless Ray was . . .

"Yes, but your family can." Kiros sneered, leaning forward slightly.

"You've already killed almost all of my family. Or have you forgotten?" Goading the powers that be was such a wonderful pastime.

"Yes, and I had so much fun doing so," Elena told me, laughing as she did. "One day, Azrael. One day we will find your man, and we will take everything from you. Slowly."

"I'd tell you to hold your breath, but where is the fun in that?" As amusing as it was to torment them, I was rapidly becoming bored. "Would you get on with it?"

"No point. We just hadn't seen you in such a long time, and we thought you might need reminding that your time is limited," she informed me. "You . . . and your *brother.*"

"I should feel honoured," I said, gesturing to the vampires around me. "All of this just for me? Next time try calling."

Reaching out for the minds around me, I planted a seed of doubt here and there—little changes that swept away their plans with a hand so gentle they thought it was their own. Little things that would stop them from following me.

The influence we held over them was a beautifully complex thing. We could alter any thoughts in their minds, strengthen memories, prevent them from being remembered, as well as adding new ones.

"Oh, not only for you, Azrael. All this was never just for you." She chuckled, an irritating sound that made me want to cringe. "And you thought we wouldn't be able to see the change in you."

The threat was clear in her words. Not for me. Not for William either.

She knew.

And I had to leave. Now.

As I turned, Elena called out, "I never said we were done with you."

"You are done when I say you are, *child.*" Several shocked gasps filled the room. They didn't know what to think of me. To see someone talk to their leaders as I had was unheard of. Even more so to see someone stand up to Elena.

Fear flared through the room, forcing a shiver down my back. Several fearful noises were torn from unsuspecting throats as Elena's power washed over me and into them.

Leaving the vampires to deal with Elena, and whatever wrath she decided to wield in her anger, I walked away. Once the barn was safely behind me, I ran. I'd barely made it a hundred feet before the screams started. The humans were the first to die, their last breaths a weak whimper amidst the terrified cries of the vampires. They knew what was coming.

That was both good and bad. Bad for them; their lives were over and there was nothing I could do to change that fact. Nevertheless, it was good for me. By the time they were finished, I'd be far enough away that they would never find me.

I wasn't going back to Laura's after all. I couldn't chance leading them back to Laura's house, not without risking her life, and I wasn't willing to do that.

And William needed to move again.

It had been in the forefront of Elena's mind. They knew he'd found his partner. When she said his time was limited, she meant they were already working to find him. It had taken them ten years to find out, but now that they knew, all their resources would be geared towards finding him and killing his wife.

It was an hour and a half run from Lyon to William's home. He lived on the French-Swiss border on the outskirts of a small place called Ferney-Voltaire. He'd moved there only a few short years ago. It was a quiet little village that had never been troubled by vampires and was close enough to the mountains that he could disappear in a heartbeat.

But by going straight to William's house, I was putting him in more danger.

I slowed down, coming to a stop. Backtrack and detour was in order. If I timed it right, I'd be on his doorstep at dawn with not a single vampire in sight. So long as I didn't go anywhere near the barn, it would be safe. Time consuming, but safe.

Easing to a stop almost fifty miles away from the village, I waited, listening. It sounded as if no one was following me, but sounds can be deceiving.

After almost an hour in the same place, checking and double-checking everything, I decided it was safe to continue. Even then, I took a roundabout route to William's house, doubling back on myself several times before reaching the border. On the off chance I'd missed something, or a vampire had recently moved to the picturesque village, I circled the surrounding area.

When I was absolutely sure, beyond any doubt, that there were no vampires within a ten-mile radius of William's home, only then did I go to his door.

The sun was coming up over the horizon, and I could see myself living somewhere similar. A small town, peaceful and pretty. Quiet and undemanding. It was the sort of place where I'd be happy.

I was undecided about being there for only a moment as I listened to the beating hearts within the house. William was sleeping, as were his sons and wife. Alison, William's wife, was about five months along, and I could make out the fluttering heartbeat of their unborn child. After hearing that sound, I knew I was doing the right thing in warning them, and I hammered on the door.

I almost laughed at William's muttered cursing. Almost.

I heard him drag on some pants and stomp down the stairs. "Coming. Coming," he muttered, reaching the bottom of the stairs.

There was more shuffling as he unlocked the door, lock after lock sliding back.

"Yes?" He didn't quite look awake as he pulled the door open. His eyes were half closed, unfocused, and I could tell what he meant about finding his first grey hair. He was older than I remembered him.

When I attended his wedding, a decade before, he'd looked so handsome in his suit. His short dark hair had been brushed for the first time in what felt like decades, and he was smiling so brightly.

"William." I breathed a sigh of relief.

"*Serenity?*"

"May I come in?"

"Of course. Of course," he muttered, now wide awake and worried.

"I'd never have come but . . ."

"Do you need anything? Are you hurt?"

"I'm perfectly fine," I told him. "It's you who I'm fearful for."

"What happened?" He insisted on checking me over, just in case. "You ran here? I thought you were in London?"

"I was. There was some trouble outside of Lyon. I ran from there."

"You went alone? How much *trouble* are we talking about?"

I may have been quite older than him, but he had a tendency to act like my big brother on occasion.

"Just a report of some minor troubles. Nothing I couldn't handle on my own."

"You still should have come for me." His tone was hard. "Our arrangement was null and void the second you met him."

"Maybe so, but that's hardly the point."

"No, Serenity, that is exactly the point. What if something happened to you? What would happen if you had to crawl home, as you have done in the past, and led someone straight to your door? No. From now on, we do things together. No matter how mediocre it seems. You tell me."

"William, would you listen? The point is that it was a *trap*. One set a mere hour away from where you're living."

"All the more reason for you to contact me."

"They know, William. They know about Alison."

Chapter Thirteen

The colour drained from William's face, and he resorted to rubbing the stubble that had formed on his cheek overnight. His deep brown eyes were wide with worry, and a hint of fear.

It was a day he'd known was coming, and one we both dreaded. With his third child on the way, it was an even darker day.

"Are you sure?"

"Ellie said our time was limited, and she mentioned you specifically, William. I'm sure of it. They know." I laid my hand on his shoulder.

"Elena was there?"

"As were Kiros and half a dozen vampires. There's something else," I said, wincing as I spoke.

"What?"

"I was expected."

"Were they not just expecting one of us?"

"No. They were waiting for *me*. They knew I'd come, and I'm certain they knew I'd come alone."

"Do they know about Ray?"

"Yes. The moment I walked into their midst they saw the change in me." I could've cried, looking at my last brother and knowing we were both in such mortal danger now.

"Whatever happens, make sure they *never* find out who he is. They cannot know." There was a desperate urgency in his voice as he spoke.

"What do you know, William?"

"Just promise me. Promise me you will keep him safe," he stressed, pacing the room. "You must keep him safe."

"William, what do you know?"

"Only that my time is more limited than I'd like." He slumped into an oversized, well-worn chair.

"*Please,* won't you tell me what's wrong?"

"I won't be moving again."

Not moving? The stress of everything must have been too much for him. "William, we need to figure out who betrayed us, and you need to move. It may have been fifteen hundred years ago, but whomever it was is still working with the vampires. They must be."

The first of the killings were so random, starting with my sister. Then we stopped reaching maturity, and we noticed a pattern. They weren't random attacks. Only those with partners and children were being targeted and killed, leaving our families broken and scared.

"We covered everything. Short of searching the minds of every one of us, there's little we can do." He sighed.

"We may have to."

"*We promised,*" he growled.

"I know."

Those of us who were there when my sister was killed had made a promise. Unless there was only one of us, we would not actively look into the minds of our family and friends to discover the truth about what had happened. Their reasoning was sound: it would make us no better than the vampires if we stooped to their level. But just because their reasoning was good, and I'd promised, didn't mean I liked it.

"Serenity, we promised. You cannot do that," he told me again.

We ended up glaring at each other for a moment. "You think I don't know? Some of the very people we suspected have been living with me for centuries."

When I looked back, his stare had softened. "I know."

"That doesn't change the fact that you need to move, William. They were an hour away from your home. Had I not doubled back countless times, I'd have been here just after midnight." I knelt in front of him, pleading with him. "As much as I must keep Ray safe, you must do the same for Alison."

"Not this time, Sere. I am tired of running from them. And besides, my time is more limited than you think," he whispered, holding his head in his hands.

"You have years left. Just because you have started going grey, which suits you, doesn't mean you're doomed to death anytime soon."

I tried to laugh, but my laugh came out as a half-hysterical squeak. There was something more he wasn't telling me, and I had a feeling I didn't want to hear the answer.

"More like months, my dear."

"William, what do you mean *months?*"

"The doctors do not think Alison will survive childbirth again. She is struggling so much already." There was such a deep sadness in his voice. "Will you take care of them?"

He didn't need to tell me who *they* were. I knew. It was part of the arrangement we'd made. If anything happened to him, I would take his children, would teach and raise them. I would make certain they knew of their father and the wonderful things he'd accomplished. They would be told of the kind heart their mother had and the beautiful woman she was.

"You know I will. You never needed to ask. But the doctors don't know everything. How many advances have been made in the past decade alone?" I said, desperate for him to see sense. "Alison is a fighter; she'll survive."

"She may not, and I need to be prepared."

"When did you find out?"

"Three days ago. She's been having problems, and they don't know what's wrong. She is tired all the time, struggling to keep food down, and every morning she wakes up in pain, yet she is only a few months along. I'm losing her and there's nothing I can do," he whispered, looking lost. "Vampires I can fight against. Weres I can fight against. Witches I could ask for help, if there were any. But my own child?"

"She'll survive," I said. "She will."

"You cannot know that." He sighed, rubbing his jaw again. "No one can know that."

"That may be, but we can all hope."

He was so hopeless as we stared at each other in the morning-dark sitting room.

"Thank you," he whispered after a few minutes.

"There's never a need to thank me," I told him. "You're my brother. I'd do anything for you. Anything at all. But you need to move."

He sat there in his chair, looking at me for a long moment. His breaths were measured and even; his gaze never left mine. "It will do Alison more harm than good to move her now. She needs to be settled," he answered. "If they come, then I'll deal with them."

"And if they come in the night? Whilst you are sleeping?"

"Then I will not sleep. When was the last time you slept?"

"Not the point, William." Exasperated, I stood, shaking my head. "Will you stop being so stubborn and *listen* to me?"

He sighed, settling back into his chair. Those dark eyes of his closed for a moment, but when they opened the answer I wanted was there.

"We'll move up into the mountains. I'll need a couple of days to arrange everything and pack what we need. We'll be safe at my cabin for while."

Relief flooded through me. "Thank you."

He smiled sadly, but it soon brightened. "You didn't answer my question. When *was* the last time you got any sleep?"

He was trying to move our conversation to lighter subjects, and though I didn't want to, I indulged him.

William was the only one who knew all of my embarrassing secrets. He'd been with me for quite a few of them.

Before he'd met Alison, we'd travelled together. On many occasions we'd posed as husband and wife in order to circumvent the customs of the time. When he found Alison, that ruse had proved interesting. My supposed husband proclaiming his love for another woman! Her parents had not been impressed. Fortunately, neither of them cared what they thought and decided to run away together.

"You need to go," he said about an hour later.

"I do. I need to get back to Laura's. Tara is there, and I'd like to get home as soon as possible." I paused for a moment. Going back to Laura's was risky, but the vampires had shown little interest in targeting our descendants. "We still have much to discuss."

I didn't want to leave him when there was so much to do, so many plans to make, and apparently not much time in which to make them, but I needed to get home.

"I bet Ray is something else," he said, smiling as he walked me to the door.

"He's everything I imagined and more."

"Get out of here, then. Go take care of him. I can look after myself," he told me, holding the door open.

"Tell Alison I'm sorry I couldn't stay."

"I will. Take care of yourself."

"You, too, old man."

"Says she who was born almost fifteen hundred years before me!" He laughed, shaking his head.

"Well, you *are* starting to go grey around the edges there."

"Do you need a horse?" he asked, reluctant to let me go.

"No. It'll be quicker if I run, and the way is clear for a while." I laid a gentle hand on his shoulder. "Stop worrying. I'll take to the rooftops if I need to."

"And fall into another poor soul's bedroom?"

"This is true."

"Stop stalling and get back to your man." He paused. "I wish I could have met him."

"You will."

"We shall see."

I gave him one last sad smile before I left. As eager as I was to return to Ray, I was just as reluctant to leave William. It had been so long since I'd seen him, years in fact.

Looking back when I reached his gate, I spotted Alison standing at their bedroom window. She raised her hand and I returned the gesture. There was a strained smile on her face as I turned away, and the feeling I was missing something returned.

It had happened often over the years since William's wedding. There were times when he would be distant, thinking. I'd asked, on many occasions, but he insisted it was nothing.

Yet, the more distance I put between us, the more I knew I *was* missing something. It wasn't like William to think all was lost before it actually was. He was the optimist, always had been. Where I believed we were doomed regarding our race, he'd always said something would happen. He insisted the race would not end with either of us.

How wrong he was.

There was no hope I could see. Nothing that could be done to change what had happened. William and I were the last. The only thing that could change that fact was a miracle. And I'd been alive for far too long to believe in them anymore.

I took the same precautions on the way back as I did on my way to William's. Laura and her family couldn't protect themselves as William could. It was almost lunchtime when I arrived at her home, secure in the knowledge that no one had followed me and no one had seen me.

"Serenity!" Laura cried when she saw me. "I was worried about you. Are you hurt?"

"Sorry, and no, I'm fine," I reassured her. "Things were . . . complicated."

"Complicated?"

"Just a little. Nothing to worry about." There was no way I was going to tell her I had run into the entire London Seat mere miles from her home. Best not to say anything, in case Laura inadvertently gave away what she was.

Elena might not have known much about Ray, or that I was in the city, but it was only a matter of time before they found out. If Poppy Baruti had recognised me, then everything hinged on whether she chose to tell The Seats I was there.

If she had . . .

Poppy had already left The Seats when I was starting to gain a reputation with them. It was possible she didn't know me, or who I was. Possible, but it was a chance I couldn't take. The first thing I would do when I got home was look for another house. Or perhaps try to persuade Ray to move to one I already had—even if I had to take Ray's mother with us and tell her everything.

Either way, I wanted Ray out of London.

"I'm sorry I cannot stay." There were more important things on my mind. "You understand."

"Of course."

"Was Tara any trouble?" I asked as I saddled her.

"No trouble at all. She's well rested, not that she needed much." Laura was distant as she spoke.

"Something is wrong," I stated, turning to face her.

She looked shocked for a moment and . . . *scared.* She was quick to rearrange her features into a calm mask, but not quick enough. Her heart was racing, and I could see fear in her eyes.

"Laura?" I prompted. "What's wrong?"

"I am . . . concerned. About you."

Lie. Everything I'd ever learned about human beings, and our kind, said she was lying.

"There's nothing to be concerned about," I told her. "Last night was simply a complication, one that won't happen again."

My words came out harsher than I meant. I didn't like being lied to, by anyone. But especially not by my family. I knew Laura as well as I knew myself. If there was something going on she didn't want to tell me, then there was only one way to find out.

To break that same promise William and I had been discussing.

I hoped I'd never have to.

I was tempted.

But my issues were far greater than whatever secret Laura was hiding.

"I'm not worried about that. It's this man you've found, Ray . . . What was his name?" she asked, more curious than anything else.

"*Willis.* Ray Willis." I hadn't given Ray's last name out to anyone, and I wasn't about to start.

"So you will be Mrs. Willis soon?"

"If you're wondering about a wedding invitation, Laura, then you should know it will only be his family in attendance. You know why I cannot invite anyone else." Tara was ready and I wanted to leave.

"Well, I was hoping." I turned to see a small smile on her lips.

"Laura," I sighed, "you know you're family to me, flesh and blood family, but you also know that I cannot risk his life. The fewer people who know, the safer he'll be—the safer we all will be."

"I know. As I said, I was hoping." She was still lying, but I needed to get home. I needed to see Ray again. That need overrode everything else.

"Take care of yourself."

Without giving her a chance to answer, I mounted Tara and set off at a dead run. The sooner I got away from Lyon, the sooner I'd be home.

Elena and Kiros should've gone directly to London, unless they were camping out somewhere during the day. I'd known them to go for weeks without draining that last bit of life from a human, just so they could attempt to follow me during the daylight hours. Even then, they had to take precautions and avoid intense sunlight or they risked being turned to ash.

Normally they didn't go to the effort of being able to venture out into the sun. Unless a vampire didn't show up for their audience, or they had special cause, they simply stayed hidden during the day and drained the life of any human they wanted.

Even if they hadn't gone to the trouble of fasting in order to lure me out, I still needed to take care.

It wasn't worth risking Ray's life. I would've loved for my encounter with Elena to come to blows, but William was right. I couldn't turn up on my doorstep half dead. It would be all too easy for a vampire to follow me and find Ray.

I needed to protect those closest to me. Now more than ever.

All to prevent the ramblings of a dying woman from coming true.

When there were many of us, we were blessed with such a wide variety of gifts. Everything from my mother's gift of physical protection, to my aunt's gift of second sight.

It was when my aunt was dying, just over a thousand years after I was born, that she gave us three predictions. The first was a simple enough affair, if somewhat far-fetched: good among the vampire race. Someone born of blood that could change the darkest of souls.

Issac Baruti.

Barely six centuries old, he'd supposedly done just that.

If the rumours were true.

The second of her final predictions had been the most haunting, the one that was on the verge of coming true. She saw us extinct, a single remaining Keeper fighting the inevitable. She saw us losing.

But it was the final prediction that had shocked us all, and made everyone think that there was no truth in her words. All the races were supposedly connected. A single family, so diverse that each of the races held a piece of the heart of the whole.

Impossible.

The five races could never be connected as such. Vampires hated everyone, as did the Weres. Witches hated humans, and humans didn't know of any of us. And we were on the fringes, as always.

It was impossible.

It was after lunch, far too long after I'd left, that I arrived back at my home. Despite being overjoyed at the mere sight of the house, I took the precaution of checking the surrounding area. Just in case.

As soon as I was satisfied that it was safe, I rode as fast as possible until I reached the stables at the back of the house.

Sam was already there tending to Falcon. I barely stopped long enough to ask about Ray.

"Reading in your room," he answered, laughing at my eagerness.

With a thank you so quickly spoken he couldn't have heard it, I raced up to the house.

"You look a mess!" he called after me.

"I know!"

I shouted out a quick hello to Helen, who was in the kitchen, as I hurried past her. There was a hearty laugh from her, too. Neither of them had seen me so eager to be home before.

Taking the stairs two at a time, I was at the top barely a minute after dismounting Tara. Coming to a stop outside my door, I paused for a moment, not wanting to give Ray another fright by barging in.

When I opened the door, forcing myself to keep calm, I realised it didn't matter. He was lying on my bed, sleeping peacefully, an open book splayed across his chest.

Sitting next to him as gently as I could manage, I smiled. He looked so peaceful when he slept. I ran my fingers over his cheek and through his hair, smiling more as his eyes fluttered open.

"Hello."

"Serenity?" he asked, half asleep.

"I missed you."

"I missed you, too." His words came out mumbled as I pressed an almost urgent kiss against his lips.

Chapter Fourteen

We spent a few minutes lying together, enjoying each other's company. It felt so unbelievably good to have him next to me again. The warmth of his body pressed against mine was everything I needed to help me forget my trip to Lyon.

Only certain things couldn't be forgotten.

Something had plagued me as I rode in circles, crossing my own path too many times to count. Laura had blatantly lied to me, and if my suspicions about her motives were correct, then I couldn't bear to face that possibility. Yet regardless of her lies, with Ray was where I needed to be.

I sighed. "We need to go downstairs."

"We could just stay here," he countered, pulling something from my hair. "Do you always come home looking like this?"

"No, which is why we need to talk to Helen." I sat up.

"Should I be worried?"

"No." I stopped, thinking about it for a moment. "At least, I don't think so."

Ray didn't need to fret over what had happened; The Seats would never touch him.

Sam and Helen were already in the sitting room when Ray and I came down. Though they were smiling and chuckling softly at how delighted I'd been to be home, they were clearly worried. I was a little windswept. My hair was full of bits of twigs and leaves, making it look like something a bird might want to nest in for the summer. My clothes had seen fewer holes and frays, too, and I could've certainly used a bath.

"Tara will need resting for at least a week," I informed Sam. "She has had a long few days."

"She's eating. Once I've groomed her, she'll be able to rest for a while."

"Thank you."

"What went wrong?" Helen asked.

"Things turned out to be more complicated than I thought."

"Who was it?"

"The London Seat."

"Elena *and* Kiros?" Sam asked.

"Both of them, and another half-dozen vampires."

"Do we need to move?"

When I turned to look at Helen, her eyes were wide and she was fidgeting nervously. "There's no way they followed me here. I spent days riding around in circles through France. Had they, I would've known," I reassured her. "But I will search for another house before the end of the year."

"Are you sure you weren't followed?" Helen asked, glancing at Ray.

"I'm sure. Also, the area around here is clear, just as it was at William's." I was about to continue, when Helen interrupted me.

"*William?* I thought you were doing this on your own?"

"It was a setup, Helen. They were waiting for *me.* Somehow they knew *I* would be the only one arriving. And they know about Alison. I had to warn him." I heaved a deep sigh, plopping down in a seat next to Ray.

"Were you hurt?" he asked, gently.

"As power hungry as The Seats are, they don't have a death wish." I placed a reassuring hand on his arm. "They know better than to cross me. My temper is a lot shorter than it used to be."

"You ran to see William?" Helen pressed, wanting answers.

"Yes. Woke him up at the crack of dawn, after spending the night doubling back on myself." I chuckled at the memory of him half asleep. "Told him he should move. Took some persuading. Not that I blame him, considering . . ."

My pause hung in the air, thick with unspoken revelations.

"What are you not telling us, Serenity?"

"Everything? Are you sure you want to know how bad things are right now?"

It was rare that I was short-tempered with anyone, and especially my family, but the trip to France had taken a toll. Even being in Ray's arms again helped only a little.

"He deserves to know."

"I stayed at Laura's house until nightfall. When I got to the village outside of Lyon, there were half a dozen vampires waiting for me, along with Kiros and Elena. They were talking about me, Helen. They knew I was the one coming to deal with them."

I told her how I had entered the barn, spoken with Elena, and then left. I didn't leave out the screams I heard as I ran.

"William is reluctant to move, and I don't blame him. The doctors don't think Alison will live through the birth of their child," I whispered.

"He's given up, hasn't he?" Sam asked as he pulled Helen to him.

"Not quite, I don't think. He's taking them to a cabin he has until something more permanent can be arranged." If I could have, I would've insisted he return with me, but separate was better.

"Can you not find out who's giving them their information?" Ray was unfazed by my outburst.

"We've tried. For *years* we have tried. All we know is they keep receiving these letters with details in them. But when we trace them, we get nothing! The least they would have to know is our names and who had found their partners. With that alone The Seats could find us. But who knows that?" I sighed. "However, I think I have an idea of who it may be, but I won't voice my opinions on the matter. If I'm wrong, then I'd rather be the only one to take the blame. If I'm right, then I don't want to think of the consequences of their actions."

"Serenity, you know I could help. I know the records almost as well as you do."

"Not this time, Helen."

"You know you cannot do this alone! I can give you an unbiased opinion."

"*No!* There isn't a single person among us who could give an unbiased opinion on this matter. Not this time, and certainly not my family." There was no need to snap at her, but she needed to understand. I couldn't ask my family, not when I thought they were the ones responsible.

Everyone fell silent. The air was thick with tension. "Forgive me, Helen. These past few days have been a little much."

"Nothing to forgive, but I think you should tell him about Lona." Helen's smile was sad as she spoke.

"Thank you, and yes, I suppose it's time I told you that story." I turned to Ray.

"We can leave this for another day if you like."

"No, I need to tell you this." It was something I'd been meaning to tell him. There never was a good time to detail how someone had been murdered. "You know I had a sister once, she was named Lona. We were identical twins; the first twins to be born in our race. We looked the same in every way: red hair, green eyes, average build, but we were opposites in every other."

"You forgot beautiful." He smirked.

"Behave." I offered him a small smile as I playfully chastised him. "As I was saying, she was fourteen when she reached maturity, whilst I waited until I was twenty. She was so volatile, and I was always calm and collected. Even our gifts were opposites, though I have no idea what either does. Hers was Death, where I supposedly hold Life."

My story wasn't one I told often, not outside of the prettied-up version held in the book I read to Jayne.

Lona had found her partner when she was about fifteen hundred years old. Henry was a good man, from a good family, and I understood why she'd been so taken with him. He was the opposite of her: calm, cool headed. When they met, she retired. Whenever we found our partners, we stopped our work. Instead she updated certain parts of the records and raised her family.

I was going to visit her when I heard the cries. I hadn't known what it was at the time, but knowing Lona was in the direction of the screams, I took off running, not caring who saw me. It was only a minute later that I arrived at her home.

I was too late.

Two vampires were dead on the ground, hearts torn out, throats ripped to shreds, their insides staining the sandy ground. If there had been any others, they were gone.

Henry lay, broken and turning, his body suffocating one cell at a time. Lona lay next to him, shrieking in pain.

The shift from human to vampire wasn't a pleasant one. It hurt, a lot. The body changed, transformed, died. It only took a few short hours, but the entire time was spent in unimaginable agony. The vampire blood destroyed everything, changing every part of a person.

As Henry turned, Lona died.

For hours I held her, hoping she would survive the pain she was in. She was incoherent, apologising over and over, but making no sense at all.

It was sometime just before sunset that Henry took his last human breath. With his last breath, Lona took hers.

"She died in my arms," I whispered. "I have witnessed some of the worst plagues mankind has ever seen, and *none* of that suffering can compare to what my sister endured. *Nothing* compares to the change between human and vampire."

"Serenity," Ray said, pulling me closer to him.

"Henry was devastated. Those first few weeks after turning, a vampire is vulnerable. No matter how little they feed, they'll burn in the sun as easily as those who kill every day." My voice was barely above a whisper. "But the sun was almost set, and it wasn't enough to kill him, so he begged me to do it. He loved Lona so much, as much as she loved him, or I love you. He couldn't live without her, and I granted his wish."

"I'm sorry," Ray whispered.

"It was years ago. I'm still bitter over it, I always will be, but it's been centuries."

Word of what had happened spread quickly among our race. Many wanted vengeance against the vampires. I'd opposed it at the time. We would've been as bad as they were if we'd done the same to them. But wiping them off the face of the planet was a *very* tempting idea.

And I wondered why they called me Azrael.

"I watched my sister die, and I spared their lives." I pulled away from Ray and stood. "I gave them their lives, *and they destroyed us.*"

It wasn't enough that we were going to die anyway, whether from a slow illness or a quick accident. The vampires had to take from us the only things in our lives we looked forward to. They made us dread the day we found out partners. Knowing our lives were drawing to an end meant there would be one less of us standing between them and the rest of the world. And then they had to take away the joy our children brought. Because we knew what was in store for them: growing up in a world that would soon be at the mercy of bloodthirsty destruction.

"It wasn't your fault, Serenity," Helen said.

"Helen is descended from one of Lona's twin daughters. Laura, who I stayed with, is descended from the other."

"I'm so sorry," Ray whispered again.

He'd stood and wrapped his arm around my waist, and I hadn't noticed. "It was a long time ago."

"But you still feel it."

"It was one of them," Helen said. "You think one of Lona's daughters started selling us out to the vampires?"

"Yes," I admitted.

"You think Laura told them you were alone," she continued.

"Well, I know it wasn't you." There was little point now in trying to keep my suspicions a secret.

"When did you know?"

"As I was leaving Lyon." It was why I lied about Ray's name. "No one can say anything until I'm certain."

"Agreed. We don't need to inspire a mob mentality over a wrong assumption," Sam said.

"May I ask why it would cause such a reaction all these years later?" Ray inquired, shuffling slightly.

Taking his hand, I pulled him down to the couch again and sat beside him. He would be more comfortable that way. "Lona was the first to be murdered by the vampires. We all knew someone gave away our secrets. The vampire that killed her knew her weakness, how to kill us. I found out a few weeks later the village had been surrounded. William had been on his way to visit Lona, as had his sister. It was our birthday, and we were all meeting up for a celebration."

Another of my sisters had come across the water, intending to give Lona news for the records. She'd stopped a mile or so short of Lona's home, knowing what the sounds were and opting to keep watch in case there was more trouble.

There'd been five Keepers there, and in all the years since, I'd never believed one of them to be responsible. At first I'd thought it was an attack gone wrong, an accident that had revealed our secrets.

The years had passed, however, and still they found us. One by one we were slaughtered, and in the end there'd been but two left. William and myself.

By the time anyone realised it could've been one of our own, it was too late. Everyone there that day was dead. And how could I suspect my own flesh and blood? The daughters of my sister.

"If our race found out there was a chance it was Lona's daughters, and their daughters since, they wouldn't hesitate to kill the entire family," Helen finished.

"Including Helen, Sam, and Jayne." It was a possibility, but unlikely, that they would come after me as well. Helen wouldn't be so lucky. They would see her family's decision to stay with me as a way to have access to the records. It wouldn't matter that I knew for certain Helen wasn't behind this. "We aren't violent people by nature, but there are some things that are wholly unacceptable, and unforgivable."

"You really think it was Laura who told them you were coming?" Sam asked, eyes narrowing as he stared at me.

"Aside from you three, she was the only one who knew I was alone. If it was her, then I'll have proof soon enough," I told him. "If not, no harm done."

"Proof?"

"When the vampires come, they won't be looking for Ray Synclair."

After explaining a few more details, I excused myself. I hadn't had a chance to change, and there were still bits tangled in my hair. A hot bath always helped me to relax.

Helen insisted on drawing the bath so I could spend some more time with Ray.

When it was ready, I left him in the capable hands of Jayne, who was, as always, eager to share more stories with him.

Sinking into the steaming water turned out to be exactly what I needed, despite not wanting to be separated from Ray. I could've spent hours steeping in the water, just lying there letting my fears wash away.

When the water started to turn cold, I dragged myself out of the bath.

Once I was dressed again, back to wearing my normal dresses, I went back downstairs to Ray.

Seeing him safe after so much worry had a profound effect on me. He was part of my very being, something I could no longer live without. Literally.

I wouldn't have it any other way.

Chapter Fifteen

"How long can you stay?" I settled into Ray's waiting arms, feeling a deep sense of relief.

He felt so warm, my skin having cooled since being in the bath. His heart was beating steadily, and I closed my eyes so I could listen to it. The sound was so peaceful. The even thud was a wonderful background to the gentle sounds of life carrying on throughout the house.

When he whispered his answer, his breath was a warm ruffle in my hair. "My mother is out of town for another day."

He had a wide smile on his face.

"Are you staying home alone?"

He shook his head. "No. My mother didn't trust me to feed myself properly."

That I well believed, having seen his lack of skills in the kitchen.

"I'd planned on staying with Professor Baruti, but Helen was kind enough to offer me your room." He was still smiling, but mine had slipped. "I hope you don't mind?"

Realising he thought my frown was because of him, I quickly answered, "No, not at all. I was thinking of something else." It was time I sat down with Ray and told him *what* his professor was. Good friends or not, I couldn't chance him ending up as Issac Baruti's next meal. Or worse, Poppy's. "I'm wondering how to tell you something."

"Do you need to leave again?" He couldn't quite hide the sadness in his voice.

"No, not at all. It's about Professor Baruti."

"What about him?"

"Have you ever noticed anything unusual?" I watched his reaction carefully.

"He isn't . . . human?" Ray asked, sounding unsure.

"No, he isn't."

"What is he?"

"The professor is a vampire who was turned six hundred years ago. He was an emissary, travelling from Egypt to Yemen when he was attacked. Poppy found him soon after and turned him."

Poppy had reportedly not killed a single person since the day she turned Issac Baruti. It was hard to believe. It was harder to believe that Issac Baruti had never taken a single life. What was it about the tall Egyptian that was capable of changing so much about not only the worst vampire in the world, but also our knowledge about vampires?

He wasn't the only one, of course. There were a handful of vampires who refused to kill. Most didn't last much longer than a century, having been hunted down by their own and slaughtered as a disgrace to their race. Had Issac not been so deep in Poppy's favour, he would've gone the same way. They were amusing for a while, entertainment for the killing vampires that wanted to test the convictions of those who didn't. But after that, they were entertainment in a different way.

"It's his wife I need you to be careful around." I couldn't stress the point enough. "She has connections in very high places. When she found Professor Baruti, she was the only other female vampire in The Seats. She may have left the Egyptian Seat soon after, but she still holds a lot of power with them. All of them."

Ray took the news that his mentor was a vampire surprisingly well. He sat there, calm and collected, nodding when necessary, and accepting my explanation quietly. When he spoke, it was to promise not to see the professor unless he had to. He would not, however, arouse suspicion if approached. It was a fair compromise. Professor Baruti was sure to know something was wrong if Ray ran away every time he got too close.

That didn't mean I was overly happy with it.

"What would you like to do today?" I asked, changing the subject to something more agreeable.

Helen had gone out with Jayne and Sam was taking the carriage to get it fixed. Ray and I were alone in the house.

"How about we sit here like this all afternoon?" he asked, a wicked glint in his eye.

That particular expression in Ray's eyes had become a regular occurrence. We may not have progressed much further than kissing, but I was more than happy to spend the afternoon in his arms.

Every part of him pressed against me as he took hold of my waist and pulled me closer, the heat of his body radiating outwards and blanketing me. He was the only man I'd ever kissed, and the only one I ever wanted to. As his lips moved with mine nothing else mattered. Time no longer existed and all there was in the world was Ray. The taste of his lips was sweeter than anything I could have ever imagined, or had ever tasted.

"I love you," he whispered, pulling away so he could breathe.

"I love you, too."

He was pressing gentle kisses along my jaw and down my neck when Helen called out from the front door, having just returned. Ray immediately straightened up, looking sheepish. I just laughed.

Helen knew I cared very little for the rules of whatever year it happened to be. They changed so often that there was little point in learning them all, and when it came to Ray I was more than happy to throw all of them out of the window.

"Good afternoon." Helen tried hard to hide her smile.

She couldn't hide it for long.

Ray looked far too worried for either Helen or me to be able to hold back our laughter. It was the first time we'd been caught doing anything other than simply sitting together. He couldn't have known it didn't matter to Helen what we were doing. I was happy, that was all that mattered to her.

"Do you have any plans this afternoon?" she asked, finally able to catch her breath.

"I thought I might show Ray some of the records. If he wouldn't find that immensely boring." I was teasing. Ray had spent hours poring over the book I'd given him, determined to decipher the stories in my language. He would find our history anything but boring.

"Come with me."

"You really keep them with you?" he asked as I led him into my study.

"I keep everything that needs updating. Just over half the records are kept here. The rest are with William." It saved me looking after books I didn't need. "You may want to stand back."

The locked cupboard that was situated against the far wall covered the entrance to the basement. I'd had the cabinet cast out of solid steel so it could hold some of my weaponry.

"Before I open up, there's something else I should probably show you," I said, reaching up for the hidden key. I kept it high, out of sight, and hidden in a specially designed rut so someone had to know it was there to find it.

Unlocking the door, I tried to suppress the shiver that ran down my spine. I only used weapons when I needed to. The only reason I hadn't destroyed them was because the time would come, when I was gone, when my family needed them.

"The key is always on top of the cupboard. If you ever need to defend yourself when I'm away, aim for the heart, the neck or the head. A blow to any of them with one of these is an almost guaranteed death for a vampire."

"They look like they're made of bone," he whispered.

"They are."

Their pale colours almost glowed in the darkness, standing out against the dark backdrop like twisted stars in the night sky. Each was older than I was, some as old as our oldest records. There were dozens of different weapons, everything from a sword and daggers to arrowheads and spear tips. They were all made from the bones of vampires, and that fact alone haunted me. I shuddered every time I saw them.

It was bad enough I couldn't bring myself to destroy them, but it was worse knowing that because I couldn't, some poor souls were trapped in between this life and the next, forever. It was widely believed that unless a vampire was burned in their entirety they wouldn't be able to cross over. Stuck for eternity, or longer, because of a single missing piece.

"Before The Seats were established, there were terrible wars among the vampires. Land and human life were brutally fought over, and as punishment for those who opposed the winning sides, their bodies were used like this." I gestured to the rows of weapons.

"I can understand why you have so many problems with them. If they're willing to do this to their own, I cannot fathom how they would treat us."

"If they ever got the chance . . . it's not a world I'd want to live in."

"How about you show me those records?" he asked, changing the subject.

"Are you sure?" I toyed with him a little, staying where I was instead of making a move to uncover the stairs. "They're only a pile of dusty old books with records of our lives dating back more than six thousand years. They might bore you to death."

"Open the damned door!"

"Ray!" I cried. "Watch your tongue! There are ladies present."

"Shall I go and apologise to Helen and Jayne?" he asked, laughing.

"You have some cheek," I said, pretending to be outraged by his words.

"Well, you're like no other lady I've ever met." He sure did a good job of changing the subject.

"Flattery will get you nowhere."

"It isn't flattery if it's the truth."

With a final chuckle, I closed the cupboard and heaved it to one side. Ray stared in awe as I shifted the heavy cabinet out of the way. Hidden behind it was the door to the basement.

The first thing I'd had done was have a steel door fitted. The excuse was that it was a bomb shelter. The truth was that no human could get down there without help, and I hoped no vampire either. There were no lights in the basement. The harder it was for anyone to see what was down there, the better. I grabbed the oil lamp that was on my desk, took Ray's hand, and led him down the dark stairs.

"Close your eyes," I whispered.

I left him standing in the middle of the room for a moment while I cleared a space for him to sit. I wanted to see his face when he saw the records. It was the first time I'd shown them to anyone besides my family. My heart raced as I thought of what Ray's reaction to them might be.

I gently guided him to the only seat. "Sit."

Once he was seated, I told him to open his eyes. He couldn't see everything that was in the room—the light wasn't strong enough—but what he could see . . . His eyes grew wide as he glanced around, trying to decide where to look first.

"The oldest books are there," I told him, pointing towards the back of the room. "These are our family trees. The one next to you . . . that's my own."

"I don't know where to start." His wide-eyed stare met mine and I laughed. "It would take me a lifetime to read all of these."

"You have a lifetime. Why don't you start with my family tree?"

He was so excited! He clutched his cane to his chest, gripping the wood as though holding it would prevent him from racing around the room.

"How far does this go back?" he asked, glancing over some of the earliest names of my family.

"I believe it dates back to my great-grandmother, some six thousand years ago," I answered, pointing out the first name. "Before then, we didn't keep records."

"Is your name in here as well?"

"About halfway through is mine."

Flipping through the pages, I stopped on my own, next to Lona's. Ray squinted at the paper for a moment, tracing the names as he tried to read what they said. The name next to my own was his.

"You put my name in here?" he said, looking back up at me.

"The day I got William's reply. I would have put it in sooner, but I needed to be sure."

He nodded once before going back to flipping through the volume. He would stop on occasion and ask what a name was, or confirm what he thought it was. I perched on top of a stack of books, passing him various ones to go through and pointing out how I had everything organised. Completed ones were at the back, oldest to newest. Family trees were in alphabetical order split into two sections—one for those that needed updating and one for those whose families had died out. Fortunately, that was a relatively small section.

Apart from a trip to get Ray some more light, we spent the entire afternoon in the basement. I read some of the older texts out loud to him; they'd been written so long ago he was wary of touching the books in case they fell to pieces.

"Can we stay longer?"

"They're not going anywhere," I told him. "You're free to look over any of them whilst you're here."

"You may never see me again."

"I would." I smirked. "I have to update the records every so often."

When we eventually emerged from the basement, dinner was ready. Ray was reluctant, but when Helen asked how he'd enjoyed himself, he beamed. I smiled as he explained the wonderful time he'd had being surrounded by our histories.

"What would you like to do for the rest of the evening?" I asked, once we'd finished washing the dishes.

"Spend some time with you?" He started wringing his hands.

"Come on. We can sit in my room, it's warmer than here." We walked slowly up the stairs, taking them at our leisure. Ray continued to avoid my gaze.

"You seem nervous about something."

"I am. I wanted to ask you something, but I'm not sure how you'll react." He looked at his hands as he sat on the edge of my bed.

"Ray, you can ask me anything."

"I know, it's just that this is something I've never asked anyone before, and I wanted to get it right," he said, wincing.

"Take a deep breath, and ask me." I patted his arm gently.

"You mean the world to me, Serenity," he said, after calming himself for a moment. "In the short time since I met you, I've fallen in love with you so deeply. There are so many things about you I'll never understand, but I want to spend the rest of my life trying to. I want to know everything about you, even though I know that's impossible. I realise being with you comes with its challenges, and you have your obligations, but I'd love it if it were me you were coming home to every time. Serenity Cardea, I want you to be my wife. Will you marry me?"

I was stunned. I'd expected him to propose at some point—it was part of the rules of his time—but I hadn't expected to be so moved by what he said.

"Yes," I whispered.

A smile lit up his face for a moment before I pounced on him. Wrapping my arms around his neck, I crushed my lips to his. He kissed me back eagerly. In one swift move he gripped my waist and dragged me onto his lap, never breaking the kiss. I felt every inch of him as he pulled me closer. We stayed like that for a long time before Ray finally pulled away.

"I have something for you," he said, out of breath.

He reached into his pocket and brought out a small gold and diamond ring. I recognised the rose window setting and the delicate band immediately; his mother had been wearing it the last time I'd seen her.

"Ray, is that your mother's ring?" I asked, staring at the beautiful piece of jewellery in his hand.

"It was my grandmother's. When I told my mother I was planning on proposing, she insisted this would be exactly right for you." He slipped it onto my finger. "A perfect fit."

"It's beautiful," I whispered, stroking the tiny stones.

"Not as beautiful as you." Ray drew me into another kiss. "I cannot wait until we are married."

"Then don't," I said against his lips as the feelings of desire grew.

He moaned. "Serenity, if I don't stop now, I won't be able to lie beside you tonight without taking you."

"I thought we were playing by my rules when we were alone?" I asked in between kissing his neck and jaw.

"You're trying to kill me, Serenity."

"I think you'll find I'm doing nothing of the sort." I sighed, loving the feel of his body pressed against mine.

"You're such a temptation."

"And you're too desirable for your own good."

"We should stop," he told me, moving his lips to my ear.

"We should, but only if we are playing by your rules."

"And if we're playing by yours?" He pulled back for a moment and gazed into my eyes.

"Had I found you when I matured we would've been together in every way before the end of the week. Marriage didn't exist in my time, not as it does for you. You found the one you were meant to be with and you took them. You declared your intentions and made them yours. I want you, Ray. More than anything. We can do this by whichever rules you want. If you want to wait until we're married, then we'll wait. I'm yours, in every way, whenever you want me, in whatever way you want me. I've waited a long time; a little longer won't do me any harm."

"I think you have waited far too long," he said.

His hands were at the buttons on the back of my dress, pulling each one open slowly. He was giving me the choice to stop him, the choice to back out, to wait. His lips were on my throat, his breath coming in gasps as he reached the last of the buttons. As his hands slipped inside the back of my dress, I let out a low moan.

He broke away from his kisses for a moment, watching as he slipped my dress from my shoulders. I was naked underneath. I blushed, glancing down as he gazed at me. It was the first time that anyone had ever looked at me as he was.

Now *I* was nervous.

"Beautiful." He ran the tips of his fingers across the top of my breasts.

"You are wearing too many clothes," I whispered, not trusting my voice.

Reaching for his shirt, he let me ease it over his head before I ran my fingers down his chest. He felt so lean under my hands, every inch of him defined and sculpted through years of supporting himself. The strong shoulders I'd merely glimpsed before were solid under my touch.

Before I had a chance to reach for his pants, he picked me up and laid me on the covers of my bed. With only a little struggle, he pulled the rest of my dress off, discarding it in a pile on the floor.

Never had I been as exposed as I was lying naked before him. I was ready; I had been since he first kissed me. Every time he held me close I felt it. I still had butterflies fluttering about in my stomach.

Ray removed his pants and lay next to me as naked as I was. Admittedly, he wasn't the first man I'd seen naked—when you've lived as long as I had, that was an inevitable part of life—although he was the best looking man I'd ever seen, and the only one I'd wanted to pay any attention to.

And pay attention I did, to *every* inch of him. From his solid shoulders to the silvery scars that decorated his right leg. They crisscrossed over and over each other, running down and around his thigh, almost as low as his knee and not quite as high as his hip. They were raised slightly, making his thigh feel odd when I ran my fingertips over it. I'd never touched a man so intimately before, and the more I felt of him, the more I wanted to feel. He shivered, his hand resting on mine while I caressed him. I thought for a moment that he was uncomfortable with my fingers there, but he drew away and nodded once, eyes closed. I hesitated only a moment more before continuing.

There was a fine trail of hair running down his stomach, soft under my touch and pale like the hair on his head. I wanted to tangle my fingertips in it. Everything was so new and so very different.

He stopped me before I got any lower. "My turn."

He was gentle as he began kissing me, touching me. He copied my movements, running his fingertips gently over my thighs, capturing every inch of them as he went. Such overwhelming sensations from such delicate touches. His hands were warm against my skin, making me tingle in anticipation. He brushed the backs of them against the underside of my breasts, causing me to moan and arch up against him. My mind was filled with the intimacy and tender warmth in his touch and the delicate strangeness of the experience. His measured caresses felt wonderful, but I was ready for more. So was Ray.

With only a little struggle, he was above me, gazing down.

"Tell me if you want me to stop," he whispered.

I nodded, and he pushed forward, slowly. The feel of him inside me took my breath away, making me gasp. It was utterly unique.

"Are you all right?" He paused for a moment, allowing me to adjust to the delightfully new sensation.

I looked up into his eyes, which were filled with concern, and whispered, "Yes."

I wrapped myself around him, holding him close as we moved together. It was like nothing I'd ever experienced, and Ray's moaned breaths whispering across my skin made it all the more enticing. Never before had I felt something so intimate, so incredible. I wanted nothing more than to spend the rest of time like this, in his arms, joined with him.

With a few more deep, powerful thrusts, he moaned my name, tightening his arms around me.

I ran my hands gently down his back. We lay together for a while, relishing the feel of each other, before Ray pulled the blankets around us.

"I love you," he whispered, holding me close.

"I love you, too." Snuggling deeper into his arms, I smiled. "You were worth waiting for."

Chapter Sixteen

For the second time since moving to the city, I awoke in Ray's arms. The memories of his proposal and our evening together came flooding back, making me sigh and snuggle deeper into his embrace.

He obliged me by pulling me closer. "Helen came by to say that breakfast was ready. She seemed jubilant."

"Oh?"

"Yes, as soon as she saw you sleeping, there was an undeniable smile on her face."

"It's been a long time since I've been able to find the peace to fall asleep." Being with Ray must be the key to a good night's rest, as well as a few other things.

"Maybe I should share your bed more often then," he suggested just as a loud gurgle announced his hunger.

"I think you may be hungry, especially after last night."

"May I blame you for wearing me out?" His voice was teasing, but it sent a thrill through me. It was entirely my fault we'd ended up as we were. Not that I regretted it for a single moment.

"I suppose you may." We smiled at the memory. "Perhaps I should get dressed before I'm tempted to do the same again."

"Or we could skip breakfast and have an early lunch in say, an hour? Or two?"

His offer was very enticing. Too much so. Helen was expecting us for breakfast and Ray needed to eat. Before I was tempted any further by the naked man who was suggestively eyeing me, I sprang up and raced into my dressing room. Only a few moments later, I was clad in the same summer dress I'd been wearing when I was caught in his bed by Liz. He was leaning back on his elbows, staring after me in shock.

"You are too fast for your own good," he grumbled.

"That may be so, but you do need to eat, and that's not going to happen with you sprawled across my bed," I told him, laughing at his sullen expression. "When we're married, I plan on keeping you there all day, but in the meantime . . ." I trailed off as a sound outside caught my attention.

A horse had stopped in front of the house. It wasn't unusual for us to get visitors, and Sam was busy fixing the gate so he would see to it. But as I turned back to Ray, the front door banged open and Helen's panicked cry echoed through the house.

"Stay here, and do not leave the room unless I come for you," I called over my shoulder.

Leaving Ray slightly startled, I raced downstairs. Something was gravely wrong. The echo of the sound rattling around in my head sent a chill down my spine and all traces of my good mood vanished.

At the bottom of the stairs, I was confronted with the sight of Sam struggling under the weight of an unconscious child.

In his arms lay David, William's youngest son.

"What happened?" I demanded, taking him into my arms.

It was a five-day ride for a grown man to William's house. Minimum. David was nine years old, barely. There was no way he should have been unaccompanied on my front doorstep. How had he crossed the channel? Or the war-torn landscape of France?

"Where is William?" I asked, panicked.

"He was alone, and he was holding this." Helen handed me a piece of paper. The words on it made my blood run cold.

"Take the children up to my room. Don't leave until I return," I ordered.

Helen knew not to argue when I started giving out orders. Before they left, I pulled Sam to the side. "Do not let them out of your sight, and I want you armed."

He nodded gravely, racing up the stairs after Helen and Jayne.

If he'd been followed, then we had to get out of the city before nightfall. I needed to check, to make sure David was alone.

There was a house up north we could use until it was safe to leave the country. The others could go ahead.

Almost an hour later, I ducked back into the eerily quiet house. There were no signs of more vampires in the city, but that didn't mean everything was fine. Things were far, far from fine.

"Helen?" I asked as I gently knocked on my bedroom door. "It's safe."

Seconds later the door swung open to reveal a very worried Helen and Sam, a terrified Jayne, a still unconscious David, and Ray. His eyes held fear, but it wasn't fear for himself.

"I'm sorry I scared you, sweetheart," I said, addressing Jayne. "I thought there was something wrong, but everything is fine."

"Serenity, what's going on?" Helen whispered, glancing at the note that was clutched in my hands.

"Jayne, will you sit with David for a moment? I need to talk to your mother." Regardless of the fact that I'd scared her more than ever before, she did as she was asked without question.

"The Seat isn't in the city," I said, as we gathered in the sitting room.

"How is that relevant to this?" Sam asked, putting a calming hand on Helen's shoulder.

"Dearest Serenity," I read aloud. "I do hope this note has reached you in time. If you truly value your last remaining brother, you will arrive at his home in a timely manner. If not, then your William will die, as will your partner, Ray. It is time you stopped trying to beat us. Yours, Elena."

Helen gasped, leaning into Sam for support, her hand coming up to her throat. "They have William."

"How do they know?" Ray whispered.

"Laura. It must have been," I said. "Ray, I have a house up north. I'm sending you up there whilst I go and make sure William is safe. When your mother returns this evening, tell her everything. I don't think it would be safe to leave her here."

"Are you sure?"

"If they know who you are, she's not safe."

There was nothing more I could say. I couldn't guarantee anyone's safety as long as we were in London. Hell, it was likely that I couldn't guarantee it no matter where we were. The best option was for us all to disappear. People could make whatever assumptions they wanted after we were gone.

Leaving Helen to explain to Ray what would happen, I returned to my room. David was awake, talking quietly with Jayne. I smiled sadly. There wasn't time to stop and chat with them, not when William's life was so precariously balanced.

"Stay here until your mother comes," I told Jayne.

In mere seconds I was changed, wearing the same clothes I'd worn just a day before. My hair was plaited down my back, ready for running. Apart from crossing the channel, I planned on going on foot. I was quicker than any horse, and time was so very precious.

My next stop was my study. Reaching for the key I'd shown Ray so recently, I unlocked the steel cupboard. One knife went into each boot, another on my belt. One of the tiny arrowheads was tied to the bottom of my plait, and two more were placed in my gloves. They sat perfectly between my fingers, turning a normal punch into a deadly one.

"You're going, then?" Helen asked, standing in the doorway.

"What choice do I have? I won't stand by and let them slaughter him. His eldest son is still with him. *I have to go.*"

"Be careful, Serenity."

"I always am, but this is William's life. Please, be out of the city by nightfall."

There was little time for a proper goodbye with Ray. He stood awkwardly by the sitting room door.

"Come back soon," Ray whispered, wrapping his free arm around my waist.

"I will," I promised. "I'm so sorry."

"This isn't your fault, Serenity. If we need to move, then we shall move." It was now that his acceptance of the life I led would be tested to the fullest.

I kissed him one last time before racing out of the door once more. If Elena had William, then what she could do to him was irrelevant. What she could do to Alison . . .

Getting out of the city on foot, dressed as I was, proved to be far simpler than I'd expected. I headed straight for the Thames. My boat would be waiting for me, as it always was. The boat journey was the most tedious part; agonisingly slow. It gave my mind time to wander and let me dwell on the fears I'd been holding back.

Fear for William's life.

Fear for the lives of his family.

Fear of being the last of my kind.

Fear for my own life.

But above all else, there was one fear that outweighed all of them combined: fear for Ray's life.

They knew who he was. Although they'd only mentioned his first name, there was no telling how much they knew about him.

It was possible this whole thing had been orchestrated as a trap. The Seats could very well be moving against Ray. It was why I'd insisted on him being out of the city by nightfall. It didn't matter if we lost everything in there. The entrance to the basement was hidden, so the books would be safe until I could get to them. Ray was what mattered most..

As soon as I was off the boat, I started running, fast as I was able. There would be bloodshed, and I could only hope the blood wasn't from someone I loved.

It was almost dark by the time I approached the border between France and Switzerland. Though there was little time to waste, I checked the surrounding area. Ten miles in all directions. Living on the outskirts of the village, as William did, provided privacy, but it also provided the perfect setting for an attack.

There would be no witnesses.

Elena was waiting when I eased through the open front door of William's home.

"*Serenity Cardea.* How nice of you to join us." Elena's voice caused a snarl to tear through me. "Now, now, there is no need for such hostility."

I didn't have time for games. Springing forward, I caught Elena by the throat and slammed her into the wall. In the same instant I went for one of the knives, pressing it into her skin.

"What have you done to them?"

"Who said *I* did anything to anyone?" She laughed, the action causing the blade to draw blood. Not enough to kill her. Shame.

I heard Alison's laboured breathing and William's grunts of pain. I didn't need Elena to tell me what she'd done. That much was all too clear. But, I couldn't hear William's eldest son.

"Do not toy with me, Elena."

"Oh, but I am not toying with you. Do you really think drawing my blood will alter the course of the things we have set in motion?" There was amusement in her eyes as she taunted me, forcing the blade deeper into her neck.

Letting her drop to the floor, I raced in the direction of the sporadic cries of pain. I knew this house as well as my own. It was one of the stipulations of knowing where each other was.

"Oh God," I muttered when I found William and Alison. "William? How much did they give her?"

The laboured breathing. The tossing and turning. The inexplicable pain William was in. It all pointed to one thing. Alison was going through the change, and there was very little that could stop it.

"Too much," William grunted between breaths.

"No. Please, no. William, I need you to fight for me," I begged. *"Please."*

"Not this time, Sere." His breaths were coming quicker now, each a pained gasp counting down the seconds he had left to live.

Alison was too weak to survive being turned. Her body was already struggling so much with their unborn child. It was too much for her. Too much for William to bear. Too much to take in. So I did the only thing I could. I begged over and over again for something, anything to save them.

As Alison's overworked heart came to a stuttering stop, I waited in silence, my breath held.

One beat.

A second.

Silence.

A third beat.

Then absolutely nothing.

William let out his last breath, and all fell still in the house. As the quiet dragged on, the breath I'd been holding came out in a rush. As it passed my lips, it turned into an inhuman cry, full of pain, suffering, and anger.

Unbridled anger.

"How sweet." Elena's voice hardly registered in my mind.

All I felt was the agony that came with losing one of my own and the burden that now lay with me alone.

"So, when is the wedding?"

That did it.

I turned away from the rapidly cooling bodies of the last of my family and pinned her to the wall once more.

"You will *never* lay a finger on him."

"I think we will. There is no one to fight with you, *Serenity.* You are all that is left. You can't win."

"If you think I'll give up, then you're sadly mistaken. As long as I'm alive, I will stand against you. Even if it means killing every last one of you."

"When you become Mrs. Willis, we will find you, and then we will kill you. That, I promise you."

And there it was. The piece of the puzzle that had been missing for so long. Absolute, unwavering proof of our betrayal.

"Thank you." I smiled, letting her go.

"Why would you *thank* me?"

"You just gave me the proof I need to stop this," I informed her, knowing there was nothing she could do about it.

"How do you know I did not torture your *brother* for the information?"

"Because William knew only his first name, and his surname is not *Willis,*" I said, still smiling. "Leave, Elena, and give your brethren a message. My race doesn't end with me. I'll find a way. That, I promise *you.*" I didn't have time to mess with her. There was too much I needed to do, and I had to get back to England.

"We will find him." Her promise meant little, but I felt the need to make myself clear.

"*Over my dead body.* And we both know that's not going to happen."

It was fortunate for her she decided to leave then. Had she stayed any longer I might have been tempted to kill her. It tore me apart to listen to her retreating footsteps. She'd murdered the last of my brothers, and in the most brutal way possible. It wasn't something I was inclined to let her live for. But live she would, at least for now. I needed The Seats reasonably stable, and killing Elena would compromise that.

Also, she'd given me that final piece of the puzzle.

I knew.

After all these years, I finally knew where it had begun.

It was rather fitting that William and I were the last. The first twin and the last of us ever to mature. William had been convinced we would both play a role in the revival of our race, that there was meaning in who we were and the path our lives would lead.

He was not a seer.

And whatever significance he would've played had died with him.

Chapter Seventeen

The sun was rising when I dragged myself from the floor to go in search of William's eldest son. His room was the first place I checked, and I found him there, neck snapped. He must have been sleeping when Elena arrived. At least he didn't feel any pain.

David had his own room, and I stopped there briefly, gathering some of the things he would need. It was a good thing William had a large carriage. He had refused to upgrade to a car, believing it was a phase the human race would soon grow tired of. A car would've been far too small to fit everything in.

William held the smaller portion of the records, though it was sizable enough. The entrance was in a similar place to mine and hidden in a similar way. It was easy to find.

Clearing it out would take time, but it needed to be done.

We never did discuss what would happen when we were both gone.

It was a simple task of picking up the boxes that were in William's basement and loading them onto the waiting carriage. There'd never been any point in him unpacking them as the books he kept needed no updating. They were neatly stacked into three large trunks that I strapped to the top of the carriage. The rest were in smaller boxes that I crammed into every available space I found.

There would be no second trips to gather anything else. It would already take too long passing through occupied France, and would take more influencing humans than I cared for.

The last book I retrieved was William's family tree. One of two copies. We'd agreed it was too dangerous to send any notifications to me, even though our postal system passed mail through the hands of several families before arriving. Personal letters were different, and rarely contained information that would identify us for what we were. So he kept a copy, and I had a second. It would need updating. A final entry for his family.

That could wait.

The sun was setting for a second time before I was ready to leave. The burning house created a warm glow on my back as I rode away. There would be no trace left of William or his family by the time anyone got to the house. They would assume they all had died in a tragic accident.

It would take me days to get back to my home. There was little point in stopping overnight, and William's horses had been trained as my Tara had been. Still, I was reluctant to push him to the limits when he was pulling a fully laden carriage.

Plus, there was a stop I needed to make.

Now that I knew who was giving the vampires their information, I had to stop it. They would take no more lives, and they would *never* find Ray.

Dawn was breaking by the time I reached Lyon, bringing with it a red glow of promise. It was the colour of blood on the horizon, the colour of the anger that was running through me, and the colour of the blood that had been spilled.

Just after breakfast, I arrived in front of Laura's house. I was still numb from watching William die, but my anger was slowly rising as I sat staring at the building.

"Serenity!" Laura called when she opened the door. "I didn't expect to see you again . . . so . . . soon. What happened?"

What happened? She had the audacity to ask me that as I sat in front of her house with William's records strapped to his carriage while he was nowhere in sight.

"I want a word with *you*," I snarled, hopping down from the carriage. "And you better pray you have some good answers."

"I-Is everything . . . all right?" she stuttered, backing up into the house.

Stepping inside and slamming the door behind me, I growled at Annie and her partner. "Go to your room, now."

"Aunt Sere?"

"*Shut up*," I hissed, "and leave. I need a word with your *mother.*"

"Serenity, w-what is . . . ?"

"Why did you do it?" I demanded when we were alone.

"Do what?"

"*Do not lie to me!*" I shouted. "William is dead! They *murdered* him."

She closed her eyes and whispered, "I'm sorry."

"No. You do not get to say you are sorry. *Why?*" My fist came down on the dining room table as I circled it. The feeble wood cracked under the pressure. "He's dead because of *your* family."

"My family is your family, too, Serenity."

"Not anymore."

"W-what a-are you g-going to d-do?" She stepped back until she was up against the wall.

"I'm going to do something I *clearly* should've done a long time ago." It was a promise I was more than willing to break, especially after what had happened. "Your family will know nothing of us. You will know nothing of what lives in the world around you. First, you *will* tell me why."

"Y-you cannot do that!" Laura cried.

"There are things you cannot know about us until you mature. Now you will tell me why you did it, or I will get the information myself." I was quickly losing my patience.

Cowering against the wall, Laura paused for far longer than my liking. "My family knew that if they killed Lona that way it would stop us from maturing," she whispered, hanging her head.

I stared at her, frozen in shock for a moment. "*What?*"

"She didn't want it—your life, maturing. She wanted a normal life, so she told the vampires what they needed to do. It was in one of the books your sister held," Laura explained, every part of her shaking with fear.

"Where is it?" I demanded. If the book still existed, it could save us.

"It was destroyed. Burned."

Frustrated, I took a step towards her and cried, "Why carry on? Why tell them everything, let them hunt us down and slaughter us? Do you have any idea how many of us have lived in fear because of what you've done?"

"They paid us," she whispered. "Promised us we would be safe."

"And you believed them! They *murdered* my sister! They *murdered* William! Do you have any idea what the pain is like when someone turns? It consumes them, killing every part of them! I had to watch as my sister felt the pain of a change that wasn't even happening to her!" I was screaming as Laura stood cringing away. "I just watched as William's nine-year-old son was carried unconscious into my home. We found him clutching a note from The Seats. They'd already snapped his brother's neck whilst he slept. At least you had better pray it was done whilst he was sleeping. When I got there they'd already started turning William's *pregnant* wife."

"I'm sorry."

"Not good enough." My voice was laced with hatred and anger. "Who do you think is going to stop them once I'm gone? No one will be able to."

"I'm *so sorry,*" she tried again.

"How can you be *sorry?* Do you know what you've done? Can you even comprehend what the world will be like when I'm gone? When there's no one stopping them? Sorry isn't good enough."

Though I repeated over and over again in my head that I'd be as bad as the vampires if I took her life, I was still tempted. Instead of killing her, I stepped out onto the porch. I needed to be away from her so I could concentrate. If I was going to wipe her memory of our race, concentration was a must. Looking at her while I was doing so would only make my anger return. I was barely under control as it was.

Entering the minds of our own was something I'd never done. Taking their memories was something we were told never to do. *Ever.*

When I finished, Laura wouldn't be able to pass on stories of our kind to her children, and she wouldn't have any knowledge of who we were. Annie and her partner would remember nothing. Their lives were now to be lived as if they were human, never knowing that something was missing.

If the time came when we started to mature again, if I managed to reverse what had happened, I would *consider* seeking them out. Until then, they were no longer part of our race.

When I went into Laura's mind, I was shocked. Everything was there. I hadn't smelled any vampires around her house because there were none. Laura's family had been part of our postal system; a complex arrangement that passed details through the hands of several different families before they came to me. Every time she received a letter regarding partnerships, clearly recognisable by the insignia we'd used for centuries, she'd simply looked inside and passed the information on. She'd been posting them information for years. Communicating via a third party who knew only of the vampires. That was a loose end I'd need to take care of at some point.

It took time to sift through the minds of three people, taking only certain memories, pulling them out like loose threads on a knitted jumper. Each one was connected to something else; pull too much and the whole mind would unravel, leaving nothing behind. It was a delicate job, easing the various memories from their minds one at a time, but it gave me time to see what they'd done and how they'd planned to continue. The Seats knew everything about me—my name and the fact that Ray was my partner. It was only a matter of time before they tracked me down. I'd need to disappear. She'd done her job well. There would never have been a trace of what she was doing if I hadn't given her the wrong name when she asked about Ray. I couldn't see what Laura's mother had done, but everything else was there. They had their own stories that had been passed down. Stories of their betrayal and how it had been "for the good of everyone."

The enslavement of the entire human race and anyone who happened to be filled with viable blood . . . That was *really* for the "good" of everyone?

Lona's daughter had been naïve to think that, and Laura was even more so to continue believing. She'd seen how things had gone in the past decade alone. Things were slipping all over the world because William and I had been fighting a losing battle.

Now there was no one left to help me.

As I took the last of their memories, an overwhelming tide of guilt washed over me.

This is for the protection of our race, I thought.

Our survival depended on Ray surviving as long as possible. Everything depended on that. When I was finished, I walked away without looking back. Laura wouldn't remember that I'd been there. Any remaining memories would be but the ghost of a dream. Nothing more.

On my way, I passed a young man wearing a sullen expression. He was clutching a telegram. Slipping into his mind for a moment, I discovered that it was a note regarding Laura's husband.

She had just lost her race, and she was about to lose her husband. At least she had been spared the physical pain of his death.

My mind was riddled with guilt as I travelled home. So much had happened, and all I wanted was to be home, to see Ray, and to be with my family once more. But the world was in a difficult time and those times encompassed everything, including me.

As I was riding out of Lyon, one of the many check points loomed ahead. Most that I'd encountered had been manned with soldiers easy enough to influence.

Not this one.

By his uniform, he was an officer of some kind. Why he was there I didn't care. His mind was already in my grasp as I approached, but not all minds are equal, and some are harder to influence than others.

"Halt!" He stood right in my path, blocking me from going any further. "What is your purpose here?"

There were so many answers I could have given him, just to placate him whilst I carried on with influencing him to let me pass, but I was so very tired.

When I didn't answer he demanded, "State your purpose."

With a shake of my head, and a deep seated need to be as far away from Lyon as possible, I did again what I had not long done. I made the man forget he'd ever seen me and carried on straight past him.

A feeling of dread was heavy on my heart as I saw London rise up before me.

Or what was left of it.

The German army had been busy while I was away. London was deserted. So many buildings had been razed to the ground. There were a few people wading through the rubble of what had once been a home and a shop. Then I passed the university. The same building I'd met Ray in.

Its neighbours were all but gone, and parts of the university were destroyed, as well.

Trudging past the ruins, I went straight to my home. I didn't intend on stopping long, just long enough to pick up a few things.

But when I opened the door, Helen was standing there. "Helen, are you . . . ?" I rushed over to her side, looking her over for injuries.

"We're fine," she promised. "But…"

"Why are you still here?"

"I'm sorry, Serenity," Helen whispered.

"Helen, why haven't you left yet?"

"Sam's missing, and Ray went to fetch his mother the day you left. That was last Saturday."

Chapter Eighteen

"*What?*" I whispered. I couldn't have heard her right. Ray couldn't have been gone that long. He was supposed to have left the city, gotten to safety.

"He left to get his mother . . . Serenity, Sam went after him."

"Where is he?"

"I don't know." Her voice shook, her calm slipping. "He never came back."

"Look after the children. I have to find them," I told her, racing to my room to change. Searching for someone would be a lot easier if I were dressed appropriately.

The first place I went was his house. There was no answer as I rang the doorbell again and again, so I let myself in. It was clear that no one had been there. There was a thin layer of dust covering everything and the air was stale.

He must have gone to the university, I thought, *but he has to be fine. I'm still here.*

Locking the door behind me, I raced through the streets towards what was left of the university. There were hardly any people about. Most had fled the city, and those who'd stayed were at the hospital with loved ones or helping to sift through the wreckage of various buildings.

I tried to get a closer look, but the police stopped me at the edge of the rubble.

"You can't go in there, miss," one of them said.

"Do you know if Liza and Ray Synclair were in there?" I asked.

"I'm sorry," he answered, shaking his head. "There were a few people inside at the time. They've all been taken to the hospital."

"Thank you."

It wasn't as crowded as I'd thought it would be. It had been a few days since the first bombs had fallen and most people had been released. Or had died from their injuries.

"Please, let him be safe," I whispered, approaching the receptionist.

"Can I help you?"

"Can you tell me if any of the Synclair family has been admitted? And Sam Cardea?" I asked, hoping that they were all fine.

"Just a moment."

It seemed like an eternity as she searched through various files and names. Each second ticked by, passing too quickly and too slowly at the same time.

"Yes, Mrs. Liza Synclair was admitted for a short time."

"And Ray Synclair?" I asked, practically begging. "Where can I find him?"

"The morgue."

I blanched. "I'm sorry?"

"Ray Synclair was taken straight to the morgue." She spoke slowly, which made her words that much worse. "Mrs. Synclair died of her injuries shortly after she was admitted. And we have no record of Sam Cardea."

That couldn't have been right. I was still alive, still breathing. My heart was still beating, so Ray couldn't be dead. I hadn't felt anything either. No jolt of pain or sudden realisation.

"Miss Cardea?" I heard someone call. It was a voice I hadn't expected to hear in the hospital.

"Professor Baruti," I greeted him, not wanting to deal with more vampires.

"Did I hear you asking about Ray and his mother?"

"Yes," I admitted. "Ray is . . . he's my fiancé."

"I am so sorry," he told me, unfathomable sadness in his eyes.

"He cannot be dead," I whispered.

"I'm afraid he is, Miss Cardea. I didn't know the two of you were so close." He led me to one of the seats in the waiting area. My mind was dissolving into panic as I tried to grasp what had happened.

"He cannot be dead," I said again. "I would *know*. Why was he even there?"

"He was picking something up," Professor Baruti informed me. "He and his mother were going away for a couple of days."

"No! He can't . . ."

"I am sorry," the professor said again, placing his hand on my shoulder. It was supposed to be a gesture of comfort. All it did was remind me of what he was.

"There has to have been a mistake." I shook off his touch and stood up.

"I'm afraid not," he said. "I was with him when it happened."

"And yet you appear uninjured," I hissed.

"If I could have done anything—"

"I don't want to hear it!"

The last thing I heard as I fled the hospital was Professor Baruti whispering, "I am so sorry. I did not know."

There had to be another explanation. I would've known if anything had happened to him.

I came to the only conclusions possible: either he'd already gone up to my other home, he'd left me, or he really was dead. I prayed it was the first explanation. The logical part of me was telling me it wasn't. That perhaps he hadn't taken everything as well as I thought.

Because no one was that calm.

Alison was, I thought, but pushed it to the side.

What if it had been too much, and he'd gone to Professor Baruti for help? After all, a vampire *would* understand needing to disappear from other mythical beings. Even if he hadn't told the professor what I was, the man had been a friend to Ray. It would explain why he was there. But on the chance I was wrong, I couldn't go to him to find out, because of Poppy.

Unless Ray was dead. But if he was, then how was I still alive?

There was a quiet voice whispering inside my mind, trying to tell me something I didn't want to be true. *Life,* it whispered, making me shake my head.

I hadn't realised where I was heading until I was standing outside of his house again. I stopped, staring at the front door. Part of me wanted to go in, to make sure he wasn't there waiting for me as though nothing had happened. The rest of me stayed rooted to the spot, refusing to move.

Was I wrong? I thought. *Was he really meant for me?*

Everything hurt. There wasn't a single part of me that wasn't blazing with pain. More than holding my sister as she died. More than watching William as he writhed in pain. Even more than seeing his house burn and knowing it was my own family that had caused it.

Tears ran down my face, soaking my cheeks. I *knew.* He wasn't waiting somewhere safe, away from everything that could go wrong.

He was gone.

But he was the one who was supposed to stand by me for the rest of my life. I was supposed to grow old with him, have him by my side as I felt the dread of leaving my family behind. We were supposed to watch our family grow.

We were supposed to stay together.

My mind screamed that I didn't want to go back into that house. I didn't want to see it empty; I wanted to remember things how they were.

The house was empty. There was no one waiting in any of the rooms. There were no signs anyone had been there since Liz had left on her trip. I couldn't tell if Ray had been back before going to the university.

What had he wanted?

There wasn't any reason for him to go there.

I ended up standing outside Ray's room. There was something I wanted.

He was supposed to have put it in the safe, but he'd spent hours trying to translate it. I couldn't have that falling into the wrong hands.

As I rifled through his drawers for the book I'd given him only weeks before, I bumped into his wardrobe. When I glanced up, I spotted the box that was on top of it. With tears streaming down my face, I reached for it.

He couldn't begrudge me that one small thing.

On my way out, feeling the sting of loss running through every part of me, I picked up one of the portraits that were scattered through the house. The most recent one of Ray and his mother.

The glances from passers-by as I walked home with Ray's things clutched to my chest were not my concern. I was a mess—tear-streaked face, wild eyed, and my hair still plaited.

I didn't care.

Couldn't.

"Aunt Sere?"

"Not now," I whispered. My voice was as lifeless as I felt.

In one week I gained a husband-to-be. And in one week I'd lost everything.

"Do you need anything?" she asked gently.

"Ray."

She placed her hand on my arm for a moment. "Sam?"

I shook my head.

Dejectedly, I walked past her, heading for the stairs. When I got to my room, I went to my wardrobe, putting the things I was so desperately clutching in it. Before I closed it, I lifted the lid of the shoebox, taking out the tiny hedgehog. Clutching it to my chest, I turned to face my room . . . and my mind went blank.

My bed. *Our bed.* So many memories in such little time.

My knees gave out and I collapsed to the floor, sobbing. Screaming.

No one disturbed me, and no one came to comfort me. My throat was raw by the time they faded to nothing but a whimper. I didn't feel it. All I felt was the pain of knowing he was gone.

It was dark before the tears stopped and I managed to crawl into the bed. My mind kept going over what had happened. Was there something I should've done? Maybe I should've gotten him out of the city *before* I'd left for William's.

My thoughts were spinning in circles, trying to think of something, anything to explain what had gone wrong.

Could he really be gone? Did my gift, so useless for so many centuries, mean I had to spend eternity knowing what love felt like only to have it ripped away?

Time ceased to exist as I lay on the bed.

Minutes passed with excruciating slowness. They turned, slowly, into hours. Those hours turned into days. Helen tried to talk to me so many times, but I couldn't bring myself to answer her. Life went on in the house; I heard everything, yet it was as if I was no longer there. Just a ghost listening to life pass by.

Helen received word that the London Seat had relocated due to issues in Spain. She was checking all of my mail, not that I cared what was in it. When that piece of news came, however, I felt my hope return.

I lay in the bed, waiting. Hoping. Yet the seconds passed. The minutes came and went. The hours dragged on and on. Night turned to day. Day drifted back to night. And nothing changed, not even the nightly bombardments. There was no call. No letter. No anything. The only words I spoke were urging Helen to leave, but she refused.

Part of me hoped he *had* found it all too much and decided to run when the dangers of my life became all too apparent. He deserved so much more. Could I deny him that?

Yes.

I'd never deny him the freedom to choose. I'd have let him go if he'd asked. *Had he asked* . . . But he didn't. He hadn't given me any indication he wanted to leave. He'd asked me to *marry* him! He'd said he wanted to know everything. That he understood.

How could anyone ever understand?

What we were went beyond the realms of anything that was known. I was a creature of myth and legend . . . *No,* I wasn't even that. I was just . . . a creature. A being trying to protect those weaker than me. Someone hoping to find love, yet hoping that day never came. My day had come.

And now it was gone.

Yet, as I thought of all the things I could have done wrong, the persistent voice in the back of my mind told me to stop being so stupid.

He wasn't alive somewhere, waiting for me. How could he be?

But as my mind cleared and began accepting that perhaps my gift had a use, all I could see was a future knowing the pain of losing my partner.

Every unneeded breath I took reminded me of it. Every time I inhaled Ray's fading scent from my sheets it stabbed me again, sharp as a knife, deep as an arrow.

I stopped counting as the days passed. I stopped thinking about what I could've done differently. I stopped hoping I'd ever see him again. I stopped thinking about him. I didn't wallow. I didn't mope. I wasn't miserable. I wasn't inconsolable. I didn't speak. I didn't eat. I didn't do *anything.*

Christmas was fast approaching, and yet I cared not. Not about presents for my family or dinner in front of a roaring fire. I knew I needed to move on. There was no one else to keep the peace anymore.

What was the point? It would make little difference in the end.

I had a duty to fulfil. I *knew* I needed to drag myself out of bed and get things done, but I couldn't.

Was there a point to protecting the human race when it could be so unbearably cruel?

"Aunt Sere?" a small voice asked from the door.

It was Jayne, and I couldn't bring myself to answer her. I didn't know if my voice would work.

Instead of leaving, as everyone else did, she stepped into the room, closing the door behind her. She clambered onto the bed and lay facing me. Looking into my eyes, she wrapped her arms around me and whispered, "I miss Uncle Ray, too."

That was all it took for me to lose control. One sentence. Five little words. The tears I'd been holding back since I first returned broke through. Every emotion I'd buried in an effort to stop the pain came roaring back to life, taking me, overwhelming me, forcing me to feel everything. Pain. Fear. Anger. Loss. Love.

I cried so hard I thought I'd never stop.

Through all of it, Jayne held me, never saying anything. She just held me, her tiny arms wrapped tightly around my neck. It felt like hours before I realised she was crying with me.

"I'm so sorry," I whispered, wiping her tears away.

"I just want my Aunt Sere back."

"I'm not sure if I can come back," I told her, unable to offer even the smallest of smiles.

"We can help," someone said from the doorway.

"I don't know if I can do it." Helen was standing there with tears in her eyes. "I don't think I'm strong enough."

"Let us help."

"Thank you." I opened my arms to them both. "I miss him so much."

"We all do," Helen said, hugging me.

"What am I supposed to do without him?" I asked.

"I don't know, Serenity. I can't answer that question."

"Will you come down for dinner, Aunt Sere?" Jayne asked, sniffling.

"I will, sweetheart."

Having my family with me made me realise something. I had to be strong. Not for me.

For everyone else . . .

Chapter Nineteen

1974

"You be careful with that, young lady," Helen said from her seat by the front door.

"Yes, Nana." Lizzy rolled her eyes as she passed me, gingerly carrying the box containing her grandmother's picture frames.

"I saw that!"

I smiled, but it was merely a fraction of the smiles I once wore.

Thirty-four years had passed since I was happy, since I'd smiled and laughed without it being forced. The house was ready, and it was time to move again. Everything had been packed and shipped from our last house in America. All of our descendants had been informed of where we were, just in case. Lizzy was enrolled in the university of her choice, Newcastle, Jayne was content with a receptionist job at a local hotel, and David had decided to stay behind with his newly-found partner. Everything was ready.

Except me.

Either I'd be in this house for a very long time, watching the world pass me by, having known only a glimpse of true happiness. Or my life would end, and the house would be needed. It wasn't a home; it was a safe house. Somewhere for my race to go if the time came.

When the time came.

A lot had happened over the years. My family changed the day we were told Sam had been found buried in the rubble of a demolished building. Helen was the one to stay strong then. I couldn't, and it had almost destroyed me again. Jayne was never the same.

The world around me had changed. I saw no point in growing older. Not that I saw a point in anything I did.

I still did what I had to, though I leaned towards killing more vampires than I influenced. I'd earned my name with them of late, though The Seats themselves tended to avoid me more often than not. I filled my days with hours of translations and stories. Jayne and Lizzy were to be left with the records of my race, but neither of them knew our language like I did. Translating it helped me to concentrate on something other than the pain I felt every day. It calmed my thoughts to know that whatever happened, any future generations would know who we were.

The years had seen me moving all over the globe. Nigeria. France. America. I'd even spent some time in Siberia. Anywhere, except London. I would never return there, not if I could help it. I preferred sunny places when it came to choosing a new town or city to live in.

The sun was something I needed, craved. It put the faint trace of a smile on my face and gave some warmth to my bones.

Not even the thought that it could all soon be over could make the pain go away.

The inevitable. That was what I'd taken to calling it. *My death* was a bit too morbid and melodramatic for my tastes. That was exactly what it was, though, my death. Either I'd die slowly, one day at a time on my own, or my life would come to a sudden end with the death of another.

Either way, it would come.

I'm a firm believer that everyone has their time.

Except me, that little voice in my head added.

It was an annoyance at times, that little voice.

Lizzy wanted to go to university, and though she could've gone to any in the world, she'd chosen Newcastle.

Why she was interested in studying history was a mystery. She didn't talk about her chosen degree often; it was a painful subject for me.

Newcastle wasn't the best option for her, and I'd offered to pay for any costs she would need to go to any university she chose, but she insisted on staying. The thing about Lizzy was that she always got what she wanted. Not in the way a spoiled rich kid would get everything they desired; no one could accuse Lizzy of being spoiled. She had a knack for knowing exactly what to ask for and how to ask. Jayne always said she should go into politics.

Still, we hadn't moved to the north of England for Lizzy. We were here for me. It was one of the places I'd chosen back when I first met . . . *a long time ago.* It was one of the safest places in the world for someone wanting to avoid vampires.

Despite the current political situation, Russia had been my first choice. The Wolves there would've been ideal, had they not found themselves on the wrong end of a group of upset vampires. The few that were left had fled deep into Siberia in the early sixties. The Great Cats were my next choice.

They avoided humans as much as possible, but above all else, the vampires knew little of their existence. The Cats were a myth, even to those who were legends themselves.

And if the time came, the best place to be would be among the myths.

In my mind, it was only a matter of time. We'd been fighting a losing battle for centuries as our numbers dwindled. Eight Seats of Power. Eight groups of vampires who needed to be *reminded* every decade or so that it was a good idea to stay hidden. I'd taken to visiting them on a yearly basis. One each year, every year, just to keep my hold over them. It had been a struggle for William and me to maintain our influence. Alone, I was failing.

"Leave the heavy ones to me, Jayne," I said, catching a box as it slipped from her hands. "I'm a little stronger than you."

"That you are, dear." She laughed as I sprinted off, box tucked under my arm.

Of the four of us, only Jayne, Helen, and I could've been identical triplets if not for the "age difference."

Lizzy, on the other hand, though cursed with the short stature of the family, was lucky enough to avoid the bright red curls, ending up with deep auburn hair that fell straight to her shoulders instead. She did, however, have my eyes. In reality she was the perfect mix of the Cardea bloodline and her father's.

The box of books was left in the basement, and I went back to grab another one. There were plenty of them. The van we were unpacking was the second of three. The furniture had already been unloaded, mostly by me, and it was in place in the house. The last van, the one Lizzy was working on, held all of our personal belongings. It was the biggest of the three.

Without taking note of the box I was picking up, I hefted it into my arms, only to find it was the lightest of them, and the oldest. As I picked it up, the bottom gave way. My breath caught as the contents tumbled to the ground, landing with a clatter.

It was the one box that was never opened, never talked about, and never, *ever,* looked into.

Lying on the ground were three things I never wanted to see. Three things that I thought about far too often for my tastes. It was a small gift that the picture frame had landed face first on the gravel, though the faces were ones I made sure to remember. The book was written in my own hand, and was the first book I'd translated. But it was the small box that had tears springing to my eyes.

I would always know what was in that box, and I would always feel guilty about having taken it.

"Serenity? Is everything . . . ?"

Helen rose and slowly crunched her way over the drive. She was by my side when she noticed what was on the floor.

"Oh dear! Come here."

She gathered me into her arms as the tears ran down my cheeks, unable to be contained any longer.

"I miss him *so much,*" I cried.

She knew whom I meant; I never needed to say his name. Never would if I could manage it. Not out loud. Ray's name was my most frequent thought.

"We all do, honey. We all do. You'll see him again, I promise," she said, trying to soothe me.

I wasn't the only one who believed, at least in part, that he was still alive. Some days I was more convinced than others.

"You can't know that. What if . . . ?" I began, dredging up the same arguments I used every time she or Lizzy told me I would see him again.

"Yet, I do. That grandchild of mine has been telling me that since she first knew of him. You of all people know not to argue with her," she told me sternly.

Even after all the years, Helen still had it in her to make me smile, if only occasionally.

"I know."

It was a few moments before I calmed myself enough to continue with unpacking the van. Reaching down to pick up the dreaded items, I felt Helen take hold of my arm. "I'll do that," she said.

"Thanks."

Nothing more was said about my slight emotional breakdown. They'd been coming more often over the years. Little things would happen and my whole world would collapse, shattering into a thousand pieces. After the first time I cried over him, I promised myself I wouldn't do it again. When Helen found me sitting by Sam's grave in tears, she made me promise never to hide again. A promise I'd managed to keep. One of only a few.

Most of the time I kept a carefully constructed façade in place, and I rarely let anyone past it. Other than my family, there was no need. My extended family, of sorts, all knew what had happened, and they knew better than to bring it up.

Sammy, the daughter of a family we'd lived near before we moved, had mentioned it. She'd been asking Lizzy about it and I'd overheard. The sound of Ray's name, spoken out loud for the first time in almost thirty years, had caused me to collapse in the hallway, unable to move . . .

It hadn't been pleasant for anyone.

It took most of the day to unpack the vans after my little breakdown. The house was bigger than anything we had lived in before. I'd specially designed it, and it was absolutely perfect. I'd included three stories, a basement, and plenty of loft storage. The top floor was mine for the moment. Not that I needed the obscene number of rooms that were up there. But the house wasn't for me. It was for everyone else.

For everyone else . . . That had become my mantra of sorts over the years.

The first floor was perfect for Lizzy and Jayne, the ground floor had rooms for Helen. They each had an en-suite bathroom, a study, their own bedroom, and a spare room. It was big enough that they had all the space they needed, and small enough that they were close to each other should they need anything.

Other than Helen's rooms, the ground floor of the house was fairly standard: kitchen, dining room, living room, and bathroom. Of course, the living room was about the size of a tennis court, and the dining room could seat more people than there ever would be here.

It was a safe house. Similar houses had been set up in various places. All had the same purpose, and all had at least one family residing in each. If the time came . . . *when* the time came, they would be needed.

Any day now. Any day.

The niggling voice was right. He would be fifty-nine if he was alive. If . . .

Perhaps it was for the best. If he was alive, and I couldn't find him, then The Seats were as helpless as I was. They were resourceful, but I was better.

Every time we moved, I'd searched. Each country we visited, I'd checked. Each new home that I acquired, I'd looked. Just in case.

Someone had cleared his house out not long after I moved away from London. But by the time I found out, the house had been sold, and any paperwork on the matter had disappeared.

"Excited about starting university?" I asked Lizzy when she came nosing around for something to eat later that evening.

"Not really. I can learn anything I want from you, and without the stuffy professors." She started rummaging through the refrigerator.

"Then why don't you take me up on my offer?" I suggested, and not for the first time.

"Because, you need a piece of paper to get a decent job, and I might want to work at some point. How else can I afford to travel the world?" She straightened, a piece of ham in her hands.

"You'd get more accurate knowledge from me, and I can get you your *piece of paper.* As for money, you know you can have anything you want. Anytime."

"That might be true, Aunt Sere, but I want to work for it myself."

I really did try to spoil her. It didn't work.

"Well, the offer is always open."

Her attention shifted suddenly, from the piece of ham to me. "There is one thing I want."

"Oh, do tell." I was hoping for a distraction.

"When will my Firebird be here?"

"Three days."

"Can I borrow your bike until then?" she asked, sweetly. Batting her eyes wasn't in her nature, but the look she gave me came damn close.

"Remind me what happened the last time you borrowed my bike?" Holding her stare, I tapped my foot lightly, waiting.

"That was three years ago, Aunt Sere, and I said I was sorry. It's not like I *meant* to wreck it. And it wasn't even my fault, not really," she muttered, glancing away.

I'd loaned her my bike, my personal, customised motorbike.

Not a full hour after she left, we got a phone call. My bike was on the side of the road, deep in a ditch. Mangled. She'd been going a touch too fast, had taken the turn wrong, and ended up crashing. It wasn't so much her fault as a lack of experience at handling speeds, but Lizzy had been lucky enough to survive without any broken bones. She'd been banned from ever riding my bike again. As well as being grounded for breaking the speed limit and had her own car taken for three months.

"Lizzy?" Jayne called.

"In the kitchen." I was careful not to call too loud; Helen had not long ago retired for the night.

"So, is that a yes?"

"Tell me you're not considering what I think you are?" Jayne interrupted, a look on her face that made me think about reconsidering. Just for a moment.

"Not at all," I answered, before turning back to Lizzy. "Two days."

"For what?"

"The bike." I smiled a semi-genuine smile.

"Are you shitting me?"

"Language!" Jayne and I chastised her.

"And keep your voice down," I added.

"Sorry, but *really?*"

"Conditions. First, you stick to the speed limit at all times. Second, scratch, crash, or damage her in any way and I'll make you work off every penny of it. *Every single penny.*"

"Anything. I'll do absolutely anything if you let me use your bike for a couple of days." She was practically begging now, bouncing up and down.

My motorcycle was not only the star of my collection, but it was my most essential item. She was sleek, fast, and perfect for what I needed her for. I had several cars and bikes stored around the world. It was often handy to be able to change cars in the middle of a journey, and it normally stopped anyone who tried to follow me.

"Two days, and I'm serious. I'll own you for a very long time if you damage her in any way."

"Right, time for bed for the humans. You should try to get some sleep, too," Jayne suggested, effectively ending the discussion.

"When do I sleep?"

"Still, you should try." She was too much like Helen on occasion.

I should. Thirty-four years was a new record for me. But the last time I slept had been after the most wonderful night of my life. It didn't matter how long I tried, or how hard, or how worn out I was, there was no sleeping without him.

It wasn't like I actually needed it. Or so I kept telling myself. But I was running on empty. Permanently.

It wasn't long before I was pottering about the books in the basement. Heavy books as old as I was. Smaller ones that were as new as the shelves. All of them held a piece of history, a piece of my life.

They'd gone into the boxes in order and they came out the same way. Two hours was all it took to put them on the sturdy, oak shelves that lined the walls.

That was exactly what they were going to become. History. They were currently an ongoing record of what I did, but soon they would be nothing more than a record of a time gone by, a race extinct.

Though I planned on keeping the books, they still needed to be translated, and it wasn't long before I turned my attention to the task. Set up in the corner was a brand new Mag Card Executive. It looked like the typewriters I'd seen countless times, except it wasn't as pretty. Aesthetics weren't the reason I'd bought it. The countless stacks of magnetic tape cartridges were why. When I'd told Jayne what I wanted to do, she found me the best available. I could translate the records, keeping them safe on devices few people could make use of, and I could update them.

Translating kept my mind busy. It kept it off other, more depressing matters.

It was nice to see some of the things that happened before my time, like the exploits of my mother and how she met my father. When I delved into the records, I remembered my sister and the situations she'd gotten herself into. I recalled us at our best, instead of at our worst.

There were books upon books of the stories that were passed down through the generations. Tales I'd wanted to pass on to my own children.

Stop it, I scolded myself.

There was no point in thinking like that. My dreams and hopes were long gone. There was no point in dwelling on them.

The hours of my life ticked away, each faster than the last. The saying goes that tomorrow is a new day. Tomorrow may be a new day, but each new day could be my last.

Chapter Twenty

I was standing in the back garden, watching the sunrise, as I did every morning. It marked the passing of another day. One I'd lived through.

"Morning, Aunt Sere. You want a weather prediction for the week?" I glanced over my shoulder to see Lizzy standing in the doorway in her pyjamas.

"If you think a prediction will get you my bike for any longer, you can think again," I said, knowing full well what she was after.

We used to play a game when she was younger. She would give me a series of predictions and I'd give her something in return for each one she got right. It started with trivial things like the weather or the news. Then we went on to bigger things, the types of people she would meet in school or a conversation I would have.

It had been a while since we'd played that game, but she tried to resurrect it on occasion. Especially if there was something she really wanted.

"What am I going to do if my Firebird takes longer than a few days to get here?" she asked, laying her head on my shoulder.

"How about you predict whether it will turn up on time?" I suggested.

"Worth a try." She sighed. "You want some breakfast?"

"Not today."

"You know, one day I'm gonna ask you that and you're gonna say yes."

"Not likely, and it's *going to,* not *gonna.*"

She asked me the same question every morning, and every morning I gave her the same answer. I rarely ate when we had company, and I never ate when I had the choice. What was the point in eating when nothing had any taste? It wasn't like I needed the nutrients.

Helen called out her goodbyes soon after breakfast, and left to join one bus tour or another for the day. She'd taken to her day trips, maintaining that it was a good way for her to get out and make new friends.

I stayed in the back garden until it was time for Lizzy to leave. Moving into the hall, I watched as she raced down the stairs, running late as always. It was strange seeing her dressed in my leather jacket. Fortunately, I'd remembered to take all of the essentials out of it. It would do her no good to turn up on her first day of university with pockets filled with cash and passports in various names.

"You know, for someone with such wonderful precognitive abilities, I would've thought you would be able to get yourself ready on time." She was double checking her bag, flustered slightly.

"Sure I can't persuade you to join me?" That was another question she asked on a regular basis. Did I want to join her at university? The answer? Absolutely not. There wasn't a point in gaining a higher education when I was more than capable of teaching any of the classes.

"No, I do not want to come to university with you. This is your first time through, you might learn something."

"Well, I best be off then. Not a good idea to be late on my first day." She grabbed the keys off the hook and raced out to the garage.

"Hey! Hold up!" I called, following her.

She barely turned around. "I know, I'll be careful."

"Come here."

She walked slowly, head down, shuffling her feet. When she was standing right in front of me, I handed her a small parcel. She looked up, startled.

"What's that?"

"An early birthday present."

She frowned. "My birthday was five months ago."

"A late one, then."

She ripped the wrapping off eagerly, then frowned once more at the little red book in her hands. When she turned it over, her brow furrowed in confusion.

"But I already have a driver's license."

I nodded to the book. "Open it."

Inside was a full entitlement for any car or bike. The license she had was fine for driving in America, but the rules here were different, including the recently instated helmet laws.

She threw her arms around me, squealing. "Thank you!"

"One endorsement for *anything,* and I'll take it off you," I warned. "And don't forget, you need your crash helmet here."

She nodded frantically, kissed me on the cheek, and raced out the door again.

"Be careful!" I shouted over the roar of the engine.

If I was lucky her car would arrive early. It wasn't her ability to control the bike that I was worried about—she'd learned a lot since the last time— it was the other people on the road. One mistake; that was all it would take.

It was fine for me to race around the world on a bike with nothing but a pair of jeans and a leather jacket. If anything happened to me, I could survive it. I also had sharper reflexes than she did. If anything happened to Lizzy, Jayne would be devastated.

"What are you planning on doing with your time?" Jayne asked when I returned from the garage.

"I was going to see if I could find some of the Great Cats."

"Do you know where they are?"

"Roughly."

"I could help," she offered.

"I'd like that."

There was a lot of work to be done. The Cats were the most reclusive of all the Weres, preferring to stay away from everyone else as much as was possible. It would be hard to find them, and harder to convince them to help me. As reclusive as they were, they were even more suspicious.

Rumour had it they'd gone into hiding during the witch trials and that most of them were related to various witches. I couldn't prove or disprove that one, but it was highly unlikely. With the recent rise in popularity of the occult, the many people claiming to be witches were nothing more than dabbling teens.

The true witches, those immortal weavers of magic, were underground. They were even further hidden in the shadows than the vampires were. The chances that one of them had mated with a Were was slim.

"Where do we need to start searching?" Jayne asked, spreading out a map of the area.

"Last I heard, they were somewhere in the Pennines. Rumour was they'd moved somewhere near here. After the Wolves were attacked, they decided to live closer to humans. For safety, of all things." I pointed out our search radius on the map.

"I can see their logic. If someone came to the middle of nowhere in the dead of night, you wouldn't notice the damage until morning. Living nearer to civilisation would cut down their ability to run free, but it would mean someone would notice them going missing." It was sound reasoning, but we couldn't exactly go around asking if anyone had seen any giant black leopards.

"I don't suppose we'd be lucky enough to have any news reports on sightings?" I sighed, staring blankly at what looked like a hopeless task.

"I thought you would never ask." Jayne smiled, rising from her seat and riffling through a bunch of papers on the desk. "It just so happens I kept an eye on local news for the past couple of years, and kept a few things you might be interested in."

"You're a star."

"Aunt Sere, you know I'd do anything to see a smile on your face. Even if it's a work-related one," she told me with absolute sincerity.

"I'm trying, Jayne. I really am," I whispered, all traces of my mood gone.

"I know. Now, how about we split these and go through half each?"

"I'll take the bigger half."

We split the pile of papers. Most of them were nothing more than a brief glimpse, or the history of big cat sightings in Britain. Then I found the one that brought almost a true smile to my face . . .

Teenagers today are being urged to avoid rural outings, especially overnight. Local specialists confirmed recent sightings of big cats in the area earlier this week. The sightings have become more recent over the past decade, and have gone so far as claims of actual attacks by the animals. Experts insist the animals will not attack a fully grown adult unless there has been extreme provocation but are urging teenagers hiking in the area to use caution. The animals are reported to have been around twice the size of any other big cat spotted in the country. Though there has been no official comment, it has been stated the breed appears to be that of the black leopard.

"Here we go," I said, comparing the area to the map. "Otterburn, Otterburn. Ah! Here we go. *Nice.*"

"What?"

"Looks like they're living on the outskirts of the National Park, right outside an army base." I beamed. "What a perfect place for them to have picked. All that space for running, and all that protection just around the corner."

"When are we going?" Jayne asked.

"I think I need to do this on my own. It's going to be hard enough to convince them that I am who I say. Most of the world believes us to be dead. As much as I'd rather keep it that way, I need to talk to them, and they can be hostile."

"I understand."

We spent the rest of the day looking at various other places they'd been spotted, but none of them were as good as the National Park. In the end I decided I'd go over on the weekend. It would take a whole day to find them, and even if I found them straight away, I needed time to talk to them. That was going to be the hard part.

"Lizzy should be back soon," Jayne whispered when the clock struck five.

"She's not going anywhere." I tried to give her a smile, but it didn't work very well. "As much as she says she wants to travel the world, she doesn't want to leave you."

"You can't know that." She started dabbing at the tears that were threatening to overspill. "Look at me. I'm turning into my mother, aren't I?"

"Just a bit, though I don't remember Helen being this emotional." That got a smile out of her.

The day Jayne left home for the first time I had to almost drag her mother back into the house. Helen was such a wreck that day, and for days afterwards. Jayne had seen the whole thing and almost decided to stay at home. Anytime since then when Jayne got overemotional over one thing or another regarding Lizzy, I reminded her about her mother.

"She was hysterical," she admitted.

"And you're nothing like that. It's normal, getting emotional when your little one leaves home. She's growing up, that's all," I reassured her. "I saw the same thing with you and Helen and her mother. Even I used to get emotional about it."

"And you will again."

"Can we not talk about that?" I asked, not wanting to ruin the good mood I was in.

"Only if you admit my daughter is right."

"How about we leave it as: we'll see what happens?" I asked, hoping that was the end.

"I'll drop it, *for now.*"

She only did so because the roar of the bike announced Lizzy's return from her first day at university.

"First words she says?" I looked at Jayne, hoping for a distraction.

"I can't wait to tell you everything?"

The door swung open, clattering against the wall. Lizzy laughed as she shut it, then bounded into the room. There was a huge grin on her face and her eyes were wide with excitement.

"I cannot wait to tell you absolutely everything, and we're going out this weekend."

Jayne and I burst into laughter, though mine was somewhat forced.

"Can I talk now?" she asked, staring at us as we calmed ourselves.

"Please, tell us everything." I gestured grandly to the nearest chair.

"You could at least pretend to be interested."

"Damn, and here I thought I was."

"Anyway," she began, ignoring my attempt at sarcasm. "Classes were, well, they were all right. That's not important, though. I made the best friends. We arranged to go out this weekend."

"You are *not* going to any discos," Jayne interrupted.

"Yes, Mum, I'm going to hop into your old miniskirt and go out with all the boys I met." She rolled her eyes. "No, we're not. We're going hiking!"

That was a good thing. She wasn't the kind to spend her evenings dancing and getting into trouble. Hiking was the sort of thing she'd enjoy. Though . . .

"Hold up, where are you going?"

"*We.* We're going up to the National Park."

"No. Not this weekend." I had things I needed to do.

"Aunt Sere, I already know about the Cat sightings. The boys might know a couple of them. That's why I told them I was bringing you."

Jayne scowled at the mention of *boys*.

Lizzy smiled brightly, arms crossed over her chest, and I knew I'd lost whatever argument I planned on using.

"How well?" I asked.

"James's second cousin is called Martin. They're related via their grandmother, and apparently he lives with some people who might be the Cats you're looking for," she proclaimed.

That was too good of an opportunity to miss out on. If they were the Cats, then having someone who knew them would be an advantage when it came to talking to them. And any advantage would be helpful.

"Besides," she continued, "I'm pretty sure James is a witch."

"Regardless, if I agree, and that is *if,* then I want you to promise me you'll stick by my side unless I tell you otherwise. I don't want you going anywhere near them alone." Neither Jayne nor Helen would forgive me if Lizzy got hurt. "We don't know if they can change around you, and I will not take chances with your life."

"Absolutely. I'll stay with you, unless you say otherwise," she vowed.

"Then it looks like I'll be hiking this weekend. Now, what about the rest of your day?"

Having Lizzy with me when I went anywhere near the Cats wasn't something I wanted. They were known to be hostile when it came to people outside of their families. All Weres were. The only outsiders they admitted were those to whom any of the Cats were mated. It was the same for the other Weres, too.

After our conversation, I spent the entire night searching through the oldest of our books. It was a worthy task, no matter how laborious it would be. What would happen after I was gone was never discussed again between Helen and me. She refused to hear any more on the subject after making me promise not to start on the house until it was time. Then after we lost William it was never discussed again until she found me working on the plans for the house. No one dared to go near that subject for fear I'd either break down or snap.

Why was it all my memories of that time were bombarding me now? Just when I'd rather forget them. Just when I wanted this pain to be over with.

ⲧⲓⲥ੮⊗℥CⲦⲝⲗⲯ੮੮

"Aunt Sere?" It was morning already, and for once I wasn't found in the garden watching the sun. "You want some breakfast?"

"Not today, Lizzy," I said, going straight back to my work.

She paused for a moment in the doorway to the basement, never actually venturing down. She was thinking about telling me something, if I had to hazard a guess.

Then she was gone again.

I should apologise for my behaviour towards her—my predicament wasn't her fault—but I couldn't. Doing that would mean admitting I wasn't coping.

Instead, I stayed in the basement, working on the translations. Even when Jayne came to say goodbye before she left for work, I stayed. Always working. Doing anything to keep my mind off the rest of my life.

When the doorbell rang, echoing ever so slightly throughout the house, I reluctantly went to answer it.

"Good afternoon, I have a delivery for Miss Serenity Cardea?" the young man said when I answered the door.

The cars had arrived early. Perhaps my luck was changing for the better.

Smiling, I asked, "Where do I need to sign?"

Ten minutes later the cars were signed for, and all but one were in the garage. Lizzy's pristine Firebird sat in the drive, waiting for her. As much as she loved riding my bike, when I let her, and when the weather or her mood suited her, she much preferred her Firebird.

Where I wanted the solitude of my motorcycle, she loved the fact she could ferry her friends around in comfort.

Actually, why not drop it off for her?

She wouldn't mind if I intruded for a moment to collect the keys to the bike. It would only take a second, and then she could show off her car that much sooner.

With my decision made, I grabbed the keys, picked up my spare helmet and jacket, and drove to the university.

I got there and parked easy enough, but when it came to finding someone who could tell me where Lizzy was, I ran into difficulties.

"I'm sorry, but we can only allow family members into the university when classes are in session," the irritating woman behind the reception desk told me. The third to tell me that.

"And as I've said, I'm her sister. I *am* family. She needs her car, and as I have the keys, and she has the keys to my bike, I *have* to see her." I was quickly losing my patience. "Look, I know she has European History now, so if you would point me in the right direction, then I won't be more than five minutes."

"I really shouldn't," she said. At least this was the nicest of the three.

"I promise I'll only be five minutes. No more than that. I just need to exchange keys with her."

"History is in the second building, and Miss Walters is in the first room on the right."

"Thank you."

I left the tiny, constricting office before I decided the human race didn't deserve to live. Second building, first on the right, I told myself. Easy.

Knocking once, I waited for someone to ask me to enter. The voice that called out must have been that of her history professor, she never did tell me his name, and it wasn't on the door.

"Come in."

"Hi, I just need to change keys with Lizzy Johnson," I said, glancing around the room for her.

"*Serenity.*" The whispered voice startled me, causing me to whip my head around.

Impossible!

It couldn't be. It just couldn't.

With shaky legs I walked up to Lizzy, handing her the keys with trembling hands.

"I'm sorry," she muttered but stopped when I shook my head.

After taking my keys, I tried as best I could to calmly walk to the door. I paused for only a second. "I'm sorry, Ray. I can't do this," I whispered, before running from the room.

Chapter Twenty-One

I did the one thing I tried never to do. *I ran away.*

How was it even possible? How was it possible that after all these years Ray was . . . ?

Nothing could have prepared me for it. Nothing at all. It just wasn't possible. But he'd been standing there, looking almost exactly the same as when I'd last seen him. That aura marking him for what he now was shining clear around him, screaming that he was a vampire.

How? I kept asking myself. *How?*

By all rights, I should've been dead years ago. I shouldn't have survived if he'd been turned. William had proved that, Lona had proved it.

I abandoned the bike outside the house. Then, as I stormed in through the front door, the memories I thought I'd buried rose to the surface and took over. Issac Baruti's words came back to me, whispering through my mind like long dead ghosts.

"I was with him when it happened."

"I am so sorry, I did not know."

It had to have been him that turned Ray. If only his words had made sense at the time.

Not that I would've believed them.

I still didn't.

But I loved Ray. Even though it was impossible, and he couldn't possibly have been meant for me if he'd been turned, I loved him with everything I had been, and with everything that I still was.

How?

That was the only question running through my mind. Even as I practically climbed the shelves to retrieve the box Jayne had put away, I knew I didn't need to see his family portrait to know it was him. He hadn't changed much. His eyes were the same. That beautiful grey colour that shined like moonlight. His hair was longer, pulled back in a ponytail now instead of cropped short. But he was the same.

Hugging the picture of him to my chest, I collapsed in the middle of the basement. All the fear, all the pain, and all the longing I'd felt over the last thirty years washed over me. I ached to go back to the campus and confront him. I longed to go back and talk to him, to say something, anything.

Yet, I feared he didn't love me anymore. I was afraid he'd changed when he was turned, as so often happened.

And that thought hurt more than all the years of not knowing. The thought he could be so different from what I'd known that he wasn't *him* anymore.

But he was teaching a history class. He always did love history.

Maybe he hadn't changed. Maybe he did want me.

Still, I shouldn't want him. Not now. They were always the ones we had to fight against, and I'd killed so many of them. More over the last few years as I let my pain take me to dark places.

But I would always love him. *No matter what.*

That was my conclusion.

It didn't matter.

And yet, that answered nothing.

"Serenity?" Helen called out, sounding worried. "What happened?"

"I found him," I whispered as she carefully joined me on the basement floor and wrapped her arms around me.

"Oh my dear. How long?" she asked gently, assuming he was still human.

"He's a *vampire.* But that's impossible." I sobbed, letting my emotions roll over me in wave after wave of confusion, longing, and bitterness.

"Is it?"

"Yes. It isn't possible. If it were, then why is Lona gone? Why did William have to die? If it were possible, then why am I alone?"

"Is that what they did to William?" she asked gently. "You never told us."

"That isn't the point. I don't know if I can do this anymore. I'm alone. There are no more of us, and there will be no more. And now I find that Ray, *my Ray,* is a vampire!"

"You aren't alone, Serenity." Helen's tone was hard. "You have us."

"I don't know what to do!" I wasn't in the mood to explain exactly why they didn't count. I needed to know what I was going to do.

"You'll figure it out; you always do."

"How? All these *books,* all these *stories,* and *nothing!* Not a single answer!"

"Did you talk to him?"

"No." I half-laughed. "I ran away."

"Go talk to him. Maybe this is what your gift does, lets you live through him being turned. Did you think of that?"

"The gift of Life," I scoffed. "What use is that when I can't keep fighting on my own?"

"Talk to him. You can work it out together."

"What do I say? *Hi, what have you been doing for the last thirty years?*"

"Well, *hello* would be a start. Go," she insisted. "Talk to him, see what he says."

"I don't know if I can. How am I supposed to face him? I still love him, so much, but how can I?"

"Tell me something, what did you notice about him when you saw him? What's changed? What's stayed the same?"

"I only saw him for a second."

She narrowed those shrewd eyes. "Answer the question, Serenity."

"His hair is longer; it was in a ponytail. He wasn't using his stick to support himself, so the change must have fixed his leg. He was taller. Not by a lot, just an inch or so. His shirt and pants were the same style he used to wear. His eyes were so bright, still the same colour." I rattled off an entire list of things I'd noticed. "He's the same."

"Exactly. Now go on. His address is by the door."

"How?"

"A certain granddaughter of mine called and said I needed to give you an address. She didn't tell me why, but I can only assume this was the reason." She beamed, deep wrinkles showing on her face.

"Thank you," I said, giving her a kiss on the cheek and offering her a hand up from the floor.

There was a war going on inside of me. I was so torn over what I was going to do. Even as I scanned the address Helen had written down, I wondered if I'd actually make it there. A part of me desperately wanted to throw myself into his arms and forget the last thirty-four years had ever happened. But the logical side of me said that wasn't such a good idea. He was a vampire.

That was what it came down to.

He was *a vampire*.

He was part of the race of beings that had plagued us for centuries.

No, he was more than that. He was the man I loved, the man I'd always love, no matter what.

As I shoved the keys into the ignition of my car, not trusting myself to be safe on my bike, I paused for a moment, hand on the steering wheel.

I had a second chance. This didn't have to be the end for me anymore. Maybe Helen was right; maybe this was what my gift did. Allowed me to survive his change, his technical death, and stopped me from having to leave everything behind.

But the longer I drove, the more my feelings of hope turned to anger. By the time Ray's house came into view, set back off the road on the outskirts of the city, anger was all I felt. Issac Baruti had known Ray was alive, I was sure of it. For decades I'd wondered whether he'd truly perished in the rubble of London or whether something else that I didn't want to think about had happened.

Pulling up in front of the house, it took me a minute to realise the car I was parked next to was Lizzy's. I'd need to send her home. Jayne would worry about her if she didn't return soon.

Taking a deep breath in a vain attempt to calm my already shattered nerves, I got out of the car. It was another couple of minutes of staring at the eclectic mixture of modern and Victorian structure before I had the courage to knock on the door.

"Hello?" I looked up when I heard the familiar voice.

And came face-to-face with Poppy Baruti.

"I'd like to speak with Ray Sinclair, please," I said, forcing myself to keep calm. "Or Issac Baruti, if he's available."

"Of course. Ray has stepped out, but Issac is here." She opened the door for me.

Her polite smile made me wonder if she'd recognised me.

She led me into the living room, leaving me alone with two reluctant hosts. It was clear the house didn't normally receive visitors. It was all sharp lines of colour and modern furniture, and though it was neat as a pin, there was nothing homely about it.

The two vampires sitting on the sofa, watching me from the corner of their eyes, were obviously uncomfortable with my presence. They kept shifting slightly, as if waiting for something to happen. It was also clear the male was protecting the female. A couple, or so it appeared.

She was tall and elegant with chin-length brown hair. He was taller, with a mess of black curls and a distinct German air about him. There was no way to tell how old either of the vampires were, but age didn't matter as much as power. And considering the afternoon sun streaming in through the windows, neither of them were overly powerful.

I was about to say something to them when Issac stepped out of the kitchen, looking exactly as he had the last time I saw him. I honestly didn't know what I expected, but seeing him just as he had been shocked me.

"Miss Cardea?" he asked, clearly as shocked by my appearance as I was of his.

"You *lied* to me." I took a step closer. My shock faded as quickly as it had risen, replaced by the anger I'd been trying to suppress. "Do you have any idea what could've happened when you turned him? What *should* have happened?"

"Miss Cardea, how . . . ?"

"For thirty years I've lived wondering which day would be my last. And now, after all this time, I find I should already be dead!" Every bit of anger I'd felt over the years, all directed at myself, came bubbling to the surface. Before anyone had a chance to react, or I had a chance to catch up with my actions, I crossed the space. Everything in me came pouring out as my hand connected with his face, the slap resonating around the room.

"*Why?*"

No one gave him a chance to answer. There was movement behind me, and suddenly I was restrained by two sets of strong, cool arms. Poppy positioned herself in front of Issac, barely glancing at him to make sure he was all right. Her sights were set on me, and she didn't look happy.

"Get off me!" I growled, more than prepared for Poppy to strike.

"Al, Leo, it's fine. Poppy, please?" Issac was rubbing his jaw slightly but otherwise was fine. He wanted to prevent any further attempts at bloodshed.

"Why?" I demanded again.

"He was dying. Ray and his mother had come by the university before dark to collect some things. Said he was getting out of the city. The warnings came too late, and the bomb hit the building before we could get into the shelter. Liza was too badly injured, and Ray only just survived. He would have died before any medical help arrived, and something in me told me I needed to turn him." He was still rubbing his jaw and shaking his head a little. "I didn't know the two of you were engaged. Had I known, I would have done everything I could to save him any other way."

"Ray was engaged? To *this?*" Al, the male vampire, said, sounding shocked.

Ignoring him, I hung my head. Ray had been dying and I wasn't there for him.

"He couldn't have had a relationship with a human. Telling you he was dead seemed the only way to offer you a new start."

"He never told you anything about me, did he?"

"Just that you were engaged and that he would never love anyone else." There was a hint of curiosity on his face.

"Well, I'd think it's clear I'm not exactly human." So much for the brilliant intellect of Professor Baruti.

"Do we really have to let all the crazies in the house?" Leo sighed, tightening her hold on me.

"Azrael is hardly crazy," Poppy snarled.

So she did know who I was. *Great.*

"Who else knows?" I asked, looking directly at her.

"Only me."

"Neither you nor Ray said anything about me?"

"As far as I was aware, you were his human fiancée. There was nothing more to it. You're not a vampire, and you're certainly not a Were. If you're not human, then I am at a loss." Issac shook his head, trying to work it out. As old as he was, I had to wonder why he hadn't recognised The Seats' name for me.

"I didn't think you'd ever recognised her, Poppy." Ray's voice filled the sudden silence. "Al, Leola, please let her go. And, Poppy, I'd appreciate it if you stopped looking like you want to eat my fiancée."

"She attacked Issac. Completely unprovoked," Al said, not letting me go.

"I know. I have to say I'm rather impressed. I always imagined she'd just kill him." There was no humour in his voice.

"Told you so," Lizzy spoke up from behind Ray. "Pay up."

I laughed at that, and everyone's attention shifted to me. It was typical of Lizzy to have placed wagers on whether I'd go so far as to kill someone or not.

"Lizzy never loses," I told Ray, seeing him for the first time.

As far as awkward moments went, I wasn't sure I'd seen worse. The silence stretched on as I allowed myself to stare. It was difficult, with me being restrained and facing away, but worth every second.

"Leo. Al. Really. I don't want to see you two hurt, and Serenity has a temper to match any of The Seats, so please let her go," Ray said, finally breaking the silence.

Reluctantly they backed off, freeing me, but not before Leola got in the final word. "That's right, Ray. Keep going with the secrets, why don't you? Get us all called in for an audience."

Lizzy stepped in. "The Seats don't have a death wish, sweetheart."

"I think an explanation is in order," Issac said.

"That can wait. Serenity and I have a lot to discuss before we even think about telling you anything." There seemed to be little affection between these vampires. Perhaps it was more of a convenience that they were together than anything else. "I have a lot of explaining to do first, anyway."

"Just a bit," Lizzy muttered.

"Go home, Lizzy," I ordered.

"Not a chance. I already missed you slapping my languages prof. I'm not missing the rest of what's going to happen."

"Lizzy, you are going home."

"For once, I'm gonna have to disagree with you, Aunt Sere." She crossed her arms over her chest, determined.

"Fine, but you're calling your mother and telling her exactly where you are."

"Agreed."

"*Exactly* where you are. Including the fact that you'll be alone in a house full of vampires."

"All right by me."

"Damn it. Fine. Stay," I muttered as I caught the look in her eyes. She knew she was going to win.

"Thanks, Aunt Sere," she called as I stalked out the door. "Be nice to him."

She was going to get herself in some serious trouble one day. Then again, she would just as easily get herself out of any trouble; she was like that. I was vaguely aware that Ray was following me to the car. He stood awkwardly shifting from foot to foot as I climbed in and started the engine.

"Get in," I called. "Where to?"

"Anywhere," he whispered, his gaze never leaving me.

"I don't want them overhearing."

I didn't have a clue where I was going. All I knew was those four vampires didn't need to hear what we had to discuss—even if I did end up explaining everything to them in the end.

"I'm sorry," Ray whispered after a moment.

"*Don't*," I snapped. "Don't you dare apologise for anything that happened."

The second the words were out of my mouth I felt guilty. It wasn't his fault he'd been turned into a vampire. It wasn't his fault he'd been caught in an unexpected air raid. Nor was it his fault that the result had been our separation for the better part of half a century.

For whatever reason, I'd survived the impossible, and now I had a second chance. Ray was here; he wanted to talk. Where things would go after that, I didn't know.

But after seeing him again, and staring into those eyes I loved so much, I knew one thing: if he felt the same way about me as I did about him, then I didn't care about anything else.

Chapter Twenty-Two

There was absolute silence as we drove. Eventually, I turned off and found a relatively secluded track into the middle of nowhere. By the time I pulled off the road, the last house we'd seen was several miles away. Open fields and a few scattered trees surrounded us, giving us the privacy we needed.

"We can follow the trail through the woods, if you like," Ray said hesitantly.

"Lead the way."

When we started walking, we lapsed into silence again. Resisting the urge to grab his hand, just to feel it in mine, I shoved my hands deep into my pockets.

I'd overreacted earlier. Of course there was a reason Issac had turned Ray. It wasn't as if he went around turning people for the fun of it.

"Did you ask him to do it?" I whispered, as we passed the first of the trees.

"No! Serenity, I would *never*." He grabbed my arm and pulled me to a stop. "I didn't know what was happening until it was too late."

I couldn't meet his eyes. "I'm sorry."

"What on earth do you have to be sorry for?" His hands were gripping my shoulders now, hard, but not too hard.

Pulling away, I cried, "Apart from the fact I just assaulted Issac Baruti? Everything! I wasn't there when you needed me. I couldn't find you anywhere when I came back. Lord knows I tried."

"Stop it. Please." He took hold of me once more, but his hands were gentler now, almost soothing. "You had to go away. William needed you. *Your brother needed you.*"

"I still should have been there!"

"Please, don't take this the wrong way, but I didn't want to *be* found," he whispered, stepping away from me.

"*What?*"

My world was already teetering on the edge. After so many years of not knowing, of being torn between the possibility of spending an eternity alone or him not wanting me, I'd finally found him only to hear the words that would send my world crashing to the ground, breaking my heart in the process. He didn't want me. It had all been too much, and he didn't want me to find him.

"I love you, Serenity. I will always love you . . ."

"Then why?"

"Look at what I am," he said, gesturing to himself. "I'm the very thing you have spent your entire life fighting against. I'm exactly the same as the rest of them."

"No," I whispered. "You're not the same."

"You can't know that. So many people died because of what I did to them. I may have had the restraint not to take that last bit of their life, but that doesn't mean I haven't come close." Such loathing on his face. "I came so close, and the worst part is I didn't want to stop. I *wanted* to drain every last drop of blood. And for some it was too close, so close they died anyway."

"And? It's in your nature to want to kill them. Do you really think that makes a difference to me?"

"It should. I remember the look in your eyes when you told me about Lona. I remember how you turned away from everyone to hide the burning anger you felt. I wasn't there, but I'm the same thing that killed her!" He was standing as far away as he could get, having backed himself up against a tall tree, putting as much distance between us as possible.

"I'll give you that one," I said, taking a step towards him to close the gap. "I'll admit I hate them for what they did to my family. I'll even admit it's strange seeing you as you are. But I could *never* hate you."

"You should."

"Why? Because you got caught in something you had no control over? Because I had to leave? Had to try to save my last bother? Or maybe I should hate you because you're trying not to be the same kind of monster the others are?" I continued, inching closer as I spoke. "But I look at you and I still see *you*. I don't see a vampire."

"How? How can you manage to see past what I am?"

"Because I love you. I've always loved you. The fact you're here, now, outside on a beautifully sunny day. Do you know how much that alone means to me?" He glanced up, as though he hadn't realised it was sunny. And that proved my point. "Do you know how many vampires are able to do that?"

"No."

"I know of maybe a couple of dozen who can do it on a regular basis. Most of those are living in Australia, living off animals daily because there are no humans for miles. But when they do see a human, they kill them." I needed to get my point across. "They slaughter them with no concern for any witnesses there might be, and absolutely no regard for the lives they destroy. Hell! If there *are* witnesses, then they're on the menu, too."

Ray was different.

"Can't you see why I didn't want you to find me?" he whispered, his gaze travelling anywhere but at me.

"I don't care!"

"You should!"

"You've already said that. You seem to forget, Ray, that I'm not exactly human. What matters is I love you, and I won't let you degrade yourself because of some idiotic notion that you're the same as the rest of them." There was absolute determination in me. I only hoped he saw it, too. "You're not the same as them, Ray. You're not."

Without giving him the chance to argue further, I closed the gap between us. He didn't look up until I was right in front of him, my arms winding their way around his neck. I pulled him down and crushed my lips to his.

So sweet.

He hadn't changed. He could try to argue the point of what he was until the end of time. I didn't care. I would never give a damn. Not as long as I was with him. The questions I had and the answers I wanted, none of it mattered.

He was unresponsive at first, rigid as he continued to fight. Then he caved, and it was more beautiful than I remembered. His hands found my waist, pulling me closer, half picking me up. There was the tiniest moan from his lips as he gave in completely, accepting everything I had to offer.

Each touch we'd shared was etched into my memory. Moments in time never to be forgotten. But this one had to be the best. That first kiss after so long without him.

"God, I've missed you," he whispered, head buried in my hair when we finally broke apart. "I'm so sorry."

"I love you, Ray. You have nothing to be sorry for. Just stop fighting this. Stop fighting me. Please." Leaning into his embrace, I was more than ready to beg if I had to.

"I don't think I could fight you anymore if I tried."

"Good."

I could have stayed like that forever, the rest of the world forgotten. Standing in the shade, cradled in Ray's arms was heaven. Eventually we changed positions and sat curled up together in the long grass.

"I'm curious," I said, after a moment.

"You always were."

"You never told them?"

"No. I couldn't. Of all the promises I made to you, it was the only one I could keep," he said.

"I saw Issac," I said, reliving that painful memory. "When I got back to the house, Helen was still there. Sam was missing, and no one knew where you were. I went to your house, then the university, and finally I ended up at the hospital. He told me you were dead, that he was with you when it happened."

"You didn't believe him?"

"Sometimes. I thought maybe my gift had let me live on, but why would any gift be so cruel? Sometimes I thought you were alive. How could you be dead? I hadn't felt anything, and I should've died with you. I thought . . . I . . . I thought you'd left . . ."

"You thought you'd scared me away?"

"Yes." I laughed, half-hysterical, as I remember my broken thoughts of that day. "Those were the good days. The days when I thought you were dead were worse."

"You could never scare me away, Serenity."

"Did you not know he'd spoken to me?" I asked, pushing those thoughts out of my mind.

"No. He never said anything. Not a word." He shook his head gently. "I thought for certain you were gone when I realised what had happened. Issac thought I was crazy for those first few years. I despised him for what he did."

"Why did you stay with him?"

"I didn't know what else to do. I didn't know how to stop myself from killing someone. As much as I hated him, I needed his help," he explained, lying back to look at the sky. "After the first decade, when the world continued as it had for years, I began to believe you were alive and I knew, with absolute certainty I knew, I couldn't end my own life. The only way to stop me from doing that was to find something to keep me busy."

"History."

"Yes, my only other true love," he sighed, finally smiling. "Issac helped me to get through my qualifications, and being around him and Poppy, then Al and Leo, it kept me busy. Stopped me from thinking too much. Leo always felt it when I was thinking of you, and she tried to help me, but I wasn't interested."

"Empath?"

"Yes, and a brilliant psychiatrist," he said. "Mostly."

"Mostly?"

"There's this habit she has of bringing her work home with her on occasion. In the form of missing people."

"She eats her patients?" I gasped.

"No, no. Not her patients. She can be vindictive when it comes to the worst of her cases. The people who cause them their troubles—child abusers and the like—they sometimes end up disappearing," he said, a small smirk on his face. "Even I have to admit some of them deserve it."

"I'm the first to admit the human race has its problems." All the races did. "Did you end up with a gift?"

"Not really. Well, not that we know of. I still have a passion for teaching history, and apparently my memory is better than average, but that's about it." He shrugged.

"You're fine just the way you are, anyway," I muttered, lying down with him.

"Lizzy said William didn't make it?" He wrapped an arm around me, holding me close.

"No. I didn't know she knew about that." I wondered how much she'd seen. "Elena was there when I arrived, and even then it was too late."

"I'm sorry. You don't have to tell me."

"I'd like to. I never spoke about it with anyone," I said, turning my head into his shoulder. "I knew what she'd done before I went into the house. Alison was too weak to survive the change. She died before Elena's blood had made it halfway through her system."

"Why didn't you kill Elena?" he asked, obviously aware she was alive and well.

"I should have, but I couldn't do it. She gave me the proof I needed to stop what was happening. A thousand years or so too late, but at least I stopped it." I still felt guilty sometimes for doing what I had, but the pain of losing Ray often overshadowed that.

"How?"

"She told me she would find my *Ray Willis*," I said, smirking.

"Willis?"

"When I was in Lyon, the first time I went away, Laura asked about you. I lied and told her you were Ray Willis. It was her family all along who'd been selling us out," I half growled; it was still a bitter memory.

"My memory is blurry. Laura was descended from one of your sister's children?"

"Yes. Lona had twin girls, Helen and Jayne were descended from one. Laura was from the other," I seethed. "They gave the vampires everything. Where we were, what they needed to do to end our race. Everything."

"What happened to her?"

"I didn't kill her, if that's what you're asking."

"The thought never crossed my mind."

"I don't think I could have gone that far. I wiped their memories." Which left me feeling guilty occasionally. "They're alive, but they know nothing of what they are."

"You erased her mind?"

It was one of those things we never talked about. The ability to take someone's memories wasn't recorded in our histories, and it wasn't something we told our children. It was part of who we were, as much as influencing minds was, but it was something that only became apparent when we matured.

"If all else fails, we erase the mind and start again. The only problem with it is that you end up with the same result every time. A power hungry, thirsty vampire with little or no control will still be a power hungry, thirsty vampire." It was something we didn't do often. If things got that far, we were more likely to end up killing the vampire than erasing their mind.

"Do you think you could do that to Poppy?" he joked.

"I thought she'd changed when she met Issac?"

"She has, a lot, but that hasn't stopped her from telling me to get over you for the past thirty years." He laughed, probably thinking of how he could rub that fact in her face now.

"She never mentioned she knew who I was?" I wanted to know why, but I doubted Ray could answer that.

"I was never sure if Poppy would have me killed for it, and she never mentioned knowing you," he said, sighing. "How much easier things could have been had I known."

"Or it could've been problematic," I offered. "It still could be a problem."

"To be perfectly honest, I have no problem disappearing if we need to." Good to know. "We shall have to see."

"Tell me some more about them?" I asked, wanting to know what I was facing when we got back.

"Leo and Al make a wonderful couple, and I'd say I'm closest to them. Issac and Poppy are perfect for each other, but Poppy irritates me at every opportunity. Issac is . . . well, he's like me in a lot of ways. Always wanting to learn, and he has such a passion for teaching. If it wasn't for what he did, I could see myself looking up to him."

"You seemed like a fairly protective group, especially the way Al and Leola were ready to defend Issac. But I didn't think you were all that close."

"We can be, mostly, but there are a lot of issues with us." He chuckled softly. "Me being one of them."

"How so?"

"I'm the odd one out. They never understood why I held on to you so desperately. Who would believe I was hoping to find you, yet hoping you never found me?" He shrugged awkwardly, his arms still wrapped around me. "I couldn't exactly tell them I was looking for a three-thousand-year-old immortal."

"Had you done that, Poppy might have said something."

"I really was never sure if she would turn me over if she knew," he whispered. "As far as I know, she has little to do with The Seats anymore. Her allegiances lie with Issac, and him alone."

"She'll be in a whole world of trouble if she attempts anything regarding you."

We spent the rest of the afternoon talking about the places we'd been. I told him of my brief time in Africa when the Congo Lions were having some troubles with the humans hunting them, as well as the time I spent dealing with the vampires that were hunting the Wolves in Russia. He told me of his studies and the different places where he'd taught over the years.

Not once did he let go of me, nor I of him. It was as if we were both afraid the other would disappear.

"So where does this leave us?" I asked, my head happily resting on his shoulder.

"I'm not sure. I don't think I want to ever let you go again, and I'm certainly still planning on marrying you," he said, smiling brightly.

"I'd like that, but I'm going to need some time. There are so many questions I want answered," I said. "Only I don't know where to look."

"Answers?"

"You know what happened to Lona. By all rights, I should be dead. I need to know why I survived and she didn't."

"That is more than fair. Although, is it not your gift?"

"Maybe." My turn to shrug. "I don't know enough about it to be certain."

"Can I help?"

"I don't know where to begin, Ray. There's nothing in our records about this. Nothing at all. Come on, I suppose we should be heading back before Lizzy says something she shouldn't." I sighed.

"We can stay if you like." His suggestion was a welcome one.

I contemplated it for a moment, but I couldn't. "As much as I'd love to stay here all day, I did leave Lizzy in a house full of vampires. That wasn't the best idea in the world."

"She'll be safe with them. Perhaps not with Leo, but she's had one too many brushes with The Seats to be comfortable around someone who knows our secrets. Al should be able to keep her safe, though." Both of us were reluctant to leave.

"How is she still alive?" One incident I could understand possibly surviving, but more than one?

"Poppy."

Ah. That explained so much. The woman held a lot of power.

We lay there for a while longer before Ray reminded me why we were supposed to be leaving. "Lizzy?"

"She'll know if anything's going to go wrong," I said. "At least, I hope she will."

"How?"

"Do you remember me telling you about my aunt?"

"The seer?"

"Yes. It seems Lizzy inherited the family's psychic abilities." She was good at what she did, even though she would never mature. "She's far from perfect, but she's the best we've seen in one of our un-matured descendants."

"She told me she was named after my mother," he said as we started walking back to the car.

"Jayne asked me to name her. She had this huge argument with her husband over what she was to be called. So they asked me to settle it, and Lizzy was the first name that came to mind." They had both fallen in love with the name straight away, and they knew where it had come from. Helen had sat by the bedside, a knowing smile on her face. She'd nodded once when I realised the name I'd said. It was her way of saying I'd done the right thing.

By the time we reached the car, the sun was already starting to set. It would be dark before we got back. There was something else I wanted to do first. Another way to procrastinate, but one I was sure Ray wouldn't mind participating in.

"I have some things of yours," I told Ray when we were driving back.

"Oh?"

"I took some things from your house when you disappeared. We could go get them if you like."

"If it means avoiding the inevitable encounter at mine, then I'd like that."

Chapter Twenty-Three

We drove back in silence, our hands intertwined between the seats. It felt right. Though his hand was cooler than the last time I'd held it, there was no real difference in him, not to me at least.

"I like your hair."

"You do?"

"It suits you," I said, turning the engine off.

As we sat in front of my house, something I realised was no longer needed, it became apparent that I had an eternity. There may have been many questions running around my mind, begging to be answered, but above all else, I wasn't facing the end anymore.

"This is where you live?" Ray asked, gaping in wonder.

"It was designed to be a safe house for after I was . . . Well, for after. Come on, I'll give you the tour."

It was the first time I'd really looked at the building since it had been built. Jayne had been in charge of all the final details, decorating and such. She had done a wonderful job. The outside was simple enough, brick walls and bay windows, but it was beautiful all the same.

"Impressive," he whispered.

"Wait until you see what's inside."

I planned on giving him the full tour, but when I opened the door, I realised that wouldn't be possible. There was a note on the hall table. Lizzy wasn't the only one waiting at the house full of vampires. Jayne had joined her after dropping Helen off for her evening at the movies.

I sighed. "Looks like the tour will have to wait."

"What's wrong?"

"Everyone is at your house." It wasn't a good thing.

"Not mine," he corrected. "I live about two miles away from Issac. Leo and Al live in another house, but we spend most of our free time with Poppy. We tried living together a couple of times. It drove me mad."

"Good to know. Let's head to the basement."

I wanted to return Ray's things before we went back. It was strange how I didn't think of Ray as a vampire. He was still Ray. It was clear what he was; I saw the differences in him. The predatory grace with which he moved, the shine of his eyes, and the distinct aura around him. It all screamed *vampire.* But the colour of his irises, the slight limp, his hair, and the way he smiled that beautiful smile, that was all Ray. *My Ray.*

The basement ran the entire length of the building. Every wall was lined with bookcases and books. The box I'd dragged down when I'd run was in the middle of the floor, contents spilled.

Picking it up, I led Ray to one of the desks. The portrait was the first thing I gave back to him.

"I thought everything was gone," he whispered.

"Gone?"

"When I went back to the house, before selling it, someone had broken in. Taken everything of value," he explained. "The only things that hadn't been taken were those in the safe. Fortunately, Mother had a habit of putting all of her valuables in there before travelling anywhere. I never got round to putting your book in there."

"I'm sorry I wasn't there with the two of you." There hadn't been much of a funeral for Liz, but it comforted me to know Helen had been there for it.

Ray placed his hand on my arm. "It wasn't your fault."

With a sad smile, I said, "You may want this then."

I handed him the book, watching as his face lit up in recognition. "I was so worried about this."

"I saved the best until last," I told him, smiling brightly.

"Is this what I think it is?" He was hesitant.

"Open it."

I swore his hands were shaking slightly as he lifted the lid. For a fraction of a second, he closed his eyes and his breath hitched. When he opened them again, it looked as if he didn't quite believe what he was seeing.

"Thank you," he whispered. "Thank you so much. *My Herbie.*"

It was fully dark by the time we left the basement. Ray asked if he could leave Herbie, and I agreed. He didn't want anything to happen to him and was sure something might if the others discovered him.

"Ready?" he asked when we pulled up in front of Issac's house.

"Not at all."

"We don't have to explain anything to them if you don't want," he told me, pausing at the door.

"Like hell you don't!" someone shouted from inside. Leola, I thought.

"Quit complaining," Lizzy said. That girl was going to get herself killed if she wasn't careful.

"Let's get this over with, before Lizzy gets served up as dinner." When I pushed the door open, I came face to face with one very angry vampire.

"Would someone please tell Miss Obnoxious Bitch to sit down and shut up?" Lizzy asked, indignant as ever.

"Watch your language, young lady," Jayne said, sounding exceptionally calm. The look she gave Ray, however, showed how angry she was. Fortunately, she chose not to bring up her complaints at that moment.

"Not until someone explains what we're doing discussing *anything* with these humans!" Leola snapped, snarling.

Poppy sighed. "Azrael is hardly human."

"And you expect The Seats to allow us to discuss anything with witches? Or whatever she is," she said, stalking back towards her partner. "The Seats hate everyone as much as they hate humans!"

"As you were told earlier," Poppy continued, "The Seats don't have a death wish. They wouldn't dream of coming near Azrael. Not anymore."

"I'd really rather you didn't call me that."

It was true The Seats stayed as far away from me as possible. After Elena fled from William's house, they'd only ever confronted me once more. They hadn't taken too kindly to losing two members of their largest group, both to snapped necks and removed hearts. I'd only removed the hearts so I could throw them at the feet of the remaining members. It had been a bad day. They steered clear of me after that. A good thing, too.

I'd certainly managed to live up to my name.

"Before I explain anything, I owe you an apology," I said, turning to Professor Baruti. "I'm sorry for how I reacted earlier, Professor."

"Please, call me Issac. I cannot say that I understand, but no apology is needed." It was more than I deserved for my actions. "An explanation may clear things up?"

"Are you sure you want one?" I asked. "My story isn't short, not by far."

"I can imagine. You must be at least as old as Ray."

"Ha! She wishes she was that young again." Lizzy covered her mouth, but her loud laugh leaked out around her fingers.

"Lizzy, be quiet or I'm sending you home."

"Fine." She stuck her tongue out briefly.

"How about some introductions?"

The angry brunette was Leola, Leo for short. Al was the German, her partner. Issac and Poppy I already knew. Still, it was nice to be officially introduced, and it helped me to delay for a while longer.

"Where should I start?"

"How about at the beginning, or at least at the part where we can kill you already," Leo hissed.

"Is she always like this?" I asked Ray.

"One too many brushes with fate," he answered.

"You want me to . . . ?" I tapped the side of my head. "You know . . ."

"I think she may try to kill you for that."

"You do remember I can't die, right?"

He nodded then said, "You're stalling."

"I know." I sighed. This was hard for me. The only vampires I talked to were The Seats, and that was more teasing and tormenting. "How about I start with a question? Did you ever wonder why The Seats order you to stay hidden in the shadows and punish you for revealing your secrets to the humans?"

The three vampires who didn't know me looked confused for a moment. Most vampires never thought about the whys of their secrecy. It had been drilled into them for centuries, millennia even, that they had to keep the secret.

"That's a stupid question. The human race isn't ready to know about us," Leola said.

"No, the human race is ready, it has been for years. Providing the revelation is handled correctly, they could know at any point. Anyone else?" It felt like giving a lesson to a bunch of hundred-year-old children. Though at least two in the room were far older.

"I have no idea," Issac admitted.

"It never crosses anyone's mind. Vampires are the ultimate predator. You have senses and abilities far beyond anything the human race is capable of destroying. You're virtually indestructible, with only a handful of exceptions. Those of you who kill have power far beyond compare. So why is it you have all these strengths, the motivation, and ability to enslave the human race, yet you hide in the shadows?" I moved so I was perched on the edge of my seat, leaning forward as I waited for their answers.

"That doesn't exactly tell us what you think you are." *Would she be missed? Could I kill her and not feel guilty about it?*

Perhaps.

"To understand what I am, you must first understand what I'm here for. Now, unless you have something useful to say, shut up."

Poppy stepped in with, "Do you remember my telling you about the Angel of Death?"

"Everyone knows that story," Al said, "but what relevance does that have?"

"She had another name," Poppy said.

"Serenity," I clarified. "Or Azrael, as The Seats often called me. I still hate that name."

Leola laughed, long and loud. "Please! Are you trying to tell me this *thing* is the Angel of Death The Seats fear so much?"

"I thought the race she belonged to was wiped out years ago?" Issac said suspiciously.

"Not quite, although they did a pretty good job of it. I'm the only one left."

It was harder than I'd imagined, telling them what had happened. I was light on the details, but they knew enough by the time I was finished. Leola quietly seethed as I spoke, glaring at Ray and me. Everyone else seemed content to sit and listen.

Time seemed to pass slowly as I told my story, and it continued to do so as they told me theirs. Poppy and Issac's I already knew. The supposed difference in Poppy was great enough that their tale spread through our race before Issac was barely a year into his new life.

As old as I was, Poppy was almost as old. She'd been born a mere three hundred years after I had. She'd met Issac on a dark night on the coast of Egypt or Yemen, only they knew which, and turned him after an attack. He hadn't tried to change her—he hadn't tried to change anyone. Poppy just had. There was something about Issac Baruti that Poppy found irresistible, and she'd given up her Seat, given up everything in order to stay with him. I could understand it, but I couldn't see what it was about Issac that was so interesting.

Leola was reluctant to share her origins. From her name, I deduced that she was Italian, or perhaps Spanish. She certainly had the appearance of having been born on the Mediterranean. Tall and elegant, she had darker than average skin for a vampire, but only went so far as to confirm her area of birth and a vague idea of how old she was. Everything else was apparently her secret to keep.

Al, on the other hand, was more than forthcoming with his origins. Born at the turn of the century, he'd survived World War I only to find himself at the mercy of a vampire after a night out. Walking back home, he'd come to the attention of the woman, and she'd almost drained him to death. At the last second, she changed him. Al had thanked her by taking her head.

They'd all come together as a matter of convenience. Leo was in trouble, which was apparently no concern of mine, and Poppy had bailed her out. Leola enjoyed Poppy's company, and Al was fascinated by Issac and Ray's devotion to not draining a human dry, so they'd decided to stick together. For Leo I suspected it had something to do with the sway Poppy held over The Seats. What better way to avoid death than to bring along the one they feared above all?

It was almost midnight by the time we'd finished exchanging stories. There was plenty I didn't know about each of them, but Lizzy and Jayne were getting tired.

It wasn't until they left, and I made sure to watch them as far as I could, that I returned to the house and was faced once more with Leola.

"Shouldn't you be going to sleep, as well?" she snarled.

"The last time I slept was in 1940. I don't *need* to sleep," I informed her. Turning to Ray, I asked, "Would you miss her?"

"Not really. Poppy might and Al would," Ray answered, reluctantly. "Was that truly the last time you slept?"

"I couldn't sleep without you."

"How sickeningly sweet," Leo interrupted.

"You are trying my patience, *child*. I suggest you keep your mouth shut, before I shut it for you."

As a vampire they were never anything more than a child unless they'd survived for at least half a millennium. Even then they were still a child. The most powerful vampires in the world had all been alive when the human race was beginning to realise its potential. A couple of hundred years old was insignificant.

There were muffled laughs as Leola stormed from the room, snarling. It was tempting to give her a little attitude adjustment, but I wouldn't. She'd done nothing wrong, not really, and until getting on my last nerve counted, I'd leave her alone. As much as was possible.

"No one has called her a child since she was one," Al said, not bothering to hide the smile on his face.

"I'm sorry. Some people just rub me the wrong way, and when I get angry, I have a habit of showing my age."

"No need to apologise, Serenity. I have not seen someone stand up to her like that since Ray did the first time. She is, however, my wife. I should perhaps check on her," he said, his voice still holding a thick German accent. He held his hand out. "You are welcome in my home. Despite what my wife will tell you."

I smiled, taking his hand. I'd become so comfortable with them in such a short amount of time. It was rather unnerving.

"I'm curious." It was time to ask some of my own questions, starting with Poppy. "You never told anyone."

"My reasons are my own," Poppy answered. "Nothing concerning you."

"I hope you'll understand if I'm wary. I'm not sure if you know exactly how much Ray means to me." I made sure to keep my voice low and my words even. Leola didn't need to understand exactly what he meant to me, either. She could cause a problem.

"Yes. I'm also aware of exactly what turning the two of you over to The Seats would get me. Having said that, it would reflect badly on me after all this time." One thing hadn't changed. Poppy always thought of the best outcome for her.

"I don't suppose you'd be willing to tell me where the nearest one is at the moment?"

"Finland recently relocated to Sweden, and London is still dealing with those events in Spain."

"Thank you," I told her. "I didn't expect you to be honest about it."

"You already knew."

"It's my job to know where they are."

That small piece of information put us on better terms. She'd been honest with me, a show of where her allegiances lay. Though I doubted I could ever truly trust her. There was still something she was hiding. I would have invaded her mind, but without her permission. I didn't want to chance a bad reaction if she found out. She could've turned Ray over to The Seats the second he came out of his change, but she hadn't. Even when she first saw me at the charity auction, she had the opportunity to say something. There must to be reasons behind her choices.

Unless I was just paranoid, which was a possibility.

"I was wondering . . . why here?" Ray said, breaking the silence of the room.

"I was looking for the Great Cats," I told him. "I needed somewhere for the safe house to be built, somewhere it would be protected."

"I thought the Great Cats were a myth," Issac interrupted.

"They're as much a myth as I am." And almost harder to track down. "I believe they're living inside the National Park. Hopefully I'll be able to find them on Saturday."

"Saturday?"

"Lizzy is going hiking with some other students, and ever so thoughtfully invited me along." She didn't realise she was about the only teenager I could stand. "Unfortunately, it will mean I'm going to be away for the entire day."

"I could come with you," Ray offered.

"As much as I'd love that, I'd rather not risk it."

"May I ask why?"

That made me laugh. "You can ask me anything, Ray. I'd rather not take you because Weres in general can be hostile. The Great Cats are the most reclusive, and there's every chance I'll run into trouble."

"Keep away from glass windows." There was a hint of laughter in his voice, but mostly there was concern.

"You remember that?"

"I don't think I'll ever be able to forget the sight of you covered in glass and blood," he whispered. "It was a bit of a shock."

"Come home with me tonight?" I asked at the same time he invited me to his own. "I haven't seen your home yet."

"Then come with me."

His house was everything I imagined it to be, and nothing like how I imagined the home of any vampire. Where Issac and Poppy's home was pristine, in order and perfectly clean, Ray's was the opposite. Homey. Various books dotted about the tables, chairs, and even a few on the floor in a corner, as though he'd run out of shelves or had forgotten about them being there.

The furniture wasn't the modern chic style we'd just been sitting on. It was mismatched, cottage style. Not all that different from my own. The room appeared as though he'd been collecting pieces over the years, adding them one by one so nothing was exactly the same. But at the same time it all fit perfectly.

"Alone again, at last," he whispered, locking the door.

"Does the rest of your house look like this?"

"I never was one for tidying."

"That hasn't changed."

"I'd like to show you some of the places I've seen," he said, pulling me close to him. "Unless you would rather get some sleep."

"Ray, we have all the time in the world. Sleep can wait. I want to know what I missed." I wasn't entirely sure if Ray slept at night. Most vampires didn't, only during the day.

We spent the entire night looking over some of the books he'd collected from various places. He'd travelled the world while we were apart. It had helped him to survive as the years passed. I knew the feeling well. It was how I'd spent my time, watching each second as it dawdled by.

Both of us had suffered while apart. More so than I'd care to admit.

Chapter Twenty-Four

The weekend came far too quickly. Every night with Ray wasn't enough, whether it was at his home or, as we were now, at mine. Being able to see him, away from the others, was wonderful. I'd only seen Leola on a couple of occasions, but on each one she glared at me and stormed off. Fine by me. The less time I spent with her, the better.

Al and I, however, were getting along wonderfully. For a military man from World War I, he was very laid back. When Leola stormed off, he shook his head and left her to it. She'd become more agreeable once she'd had a few weeks to adjust, or so I was told. That remained to be seen.

I got to know Poppy better. The more I saw her, the greater my understanding of why she'd changed. Her whole life revolved around Issac, as if he was the centre of her world and nothing could ever replace him.

"I don't want to go." Saturday morning had come all too quickly.

"Do you need to?"

"Yes. I can't ask them to move with me anymore, Ray, and I can't stay here, never aging, never changing."

"Why didn't you age?" he asked gently.

"I couldn't. I couldn't live a dream when the most important part of it was missing," I whispered, hiding my face as I spoke.

We were lying in my bed, not that I'd slept. Neither of us had slept. There were too many things we wanted to know about each other. It was as if I was meeting him all over again. The more time I spent with him, the stronger the connection I felt.

Whatever misguided thoughts I'd had about him not being meant for me had disappeared completely. It was as if the last thirty years had been a dream.

"I still need to go."

With great reluctance, I dragged myself from my bed. We'd spent most nights at his house, in his bed, but when Friday night came, we'd decided to stay at mine rather than be separated.

"You want some breakfast before we head out?" Lizzy called.

She and Jayne stood in the doorway. It had become a regular occurrence. They waited for me every morning and would offer me breakfast. I scared them half to death on the first occasion that I accepted, more when I actually engaged in the conversation they were having.

"Don't we have to leave in ten minutes?"

"We have a little longer."

"And if you don't have time for breakfast, then you at least have time to say good morning."

Ray froze at my side, gripping me tightly. The voice belonged to Helen, and until that moment Ray and I had either been at his house or he'd been working. I'd also been avoiding the confrontation Jayne was spoiling for.

Slowly, he turned. Helen brought her hand to her throat and gasped. Then she smiled, bright and wide, making her look much younger than she was.

"Ray," I whispered, taking his hand and leading him forward, "I believe you know Helen."

His mouth was slightly agape, eyes wide with recognition. He nodded once, working his jaw as though he wanted to say something but couldn't quite find the words.

"Why don't the three of us spend the morning together?" Jayne was the one to make the suggestion. I was too busy watching Ray.

Ray eventually found his voice. "We do have a lot to catch up on."

I squeezed his hand gently. "I have to go."

He leaned down, kissing me briefly. "I'll see you tonight."

Before I left, I took Jayne to one side for a second. "Be nice. It wasn't his fault."

She nodded once, but I wasn't convinced. Still, the quicker I found the Cats, the faster I could get back to Ray. That couldn't have come soon enough.

I left him leading Helen through to the living room, Jayne following quietly.

With a small amount of persuasion, Lizzy agreed to leave early. It was only by a few minutes, but those few minutes would be worth it at the end of the day.

"Aunt Sere, this is James, Andy, and Sophie," she introduced us when we picked them up.

James was the one she thought was a witch. She had a good eye. He wasn't much older than he appeared, but he certainly was a witch. The more years they had, the more power they radiated. We could see it in the same way we could tell who the vampires were. At best, James was in his thirties. Certainly no more than forty.

It was rare to see young witches. After being hunted to near extinction, most of them didn't dare tell any human their secret, much less reproduce with one. An immortal's genes were almost always dominant, especially witches' and Weres'. There was a ninety percent chance of changing with a Were as a parent.

"Did I hear Lizzy say you were related to someone we're seeing today?" I asked, shaking his outstretched hand.

"Yeah, Martin's my cousin," he answered. "Almost. We're related through my grandmother."

That sounded odd. Unless Lizzy was wrong and it wasn't the Cats he was related to. The races didn't mix. Weres didn't breed with witches, only humans. Witches were the same.

I hadn't heard of a new colony of witches popping up. That much energy in one place drew attention. Young witches could be reckless with their abilities. Many of them died because they tried something far beyond their powers.

Witches were also the only race who had a chance of recognising us when they saw us. They found each other the same way we found vampires. And though James didn't show any signs he knew what I was, he could have hidden it.

"I guess you're navigating," I said, smiling.

It was frustrating, having to drive at normal speeds, but there was no rush —other than my need to see Ray. I could have made it in half that time, but Lizzy was in the car, and so were her friends. They were good kids, more interested in their studies than dancing and discos. Lizzy was a great judge of character.

"We're meeting up with Martin outside the village, then we can hike from there," James said as I took the final turn, "if the weather holds."

That was a big *if.* The morning had been sunny and bright, but the further north we went, the darker the clouds had become. By the time we cleared the last few miles, it threatened to wash out the whole day.

Standing just off the road, sheltered by the trees, were three of the most obvious Weres I'd ever seen. While Ray towered a foot above me, they were nearly a foot taller. The physical appearance of each of the Weres differed depending on their animal. The Bears tended to be shorter, stout almost. The Wolves were almost as tall as the Cats, and similar in build, but with longer faces and more defined muscular structures in their human forms.

The long, sleek bodies standing beneath the tree clearly screaming animalistic power were the clearest indicator of what they were. The keen eyes that followed my every move gave them away even more.

As soon as I stepped out, they backed off, glaring.

"James, may I suggest you and Lizzy take the car into the village? I don't think the weather's going to hold for us." I kept a careful eye on the three Cats.

"I'm staying, Aunt Sere," Lizzy whispered, standing next to me.

"No."

"I'm not sure you can make me leave."

"I'll damn well try." Given the situation, I'd drag her away if needed.

"You hurt them, and you answer to me." The menace in her voice confused me.

"Go, Lizzy."

She didn't take much more persuading. I couldn't guarantee her safety. Though no Were could change when I was close enough, I didn't know if that would work with Lizzy by my side. I wasn't willing to test the theory using her life, and I didn't have time to wonder what her warning had meant.

"What do you want?" the one in the middle inquired, almost hissing.

"Martin, I presume?"

"That would be me, not that it's any of your concern, *vampire*," the one on the left answered, the shortest of the three.

"Okay. *One*, I am not a vampire. *Two*, I am curious to know how a Great Cat is related to a witch. *Three*, that isn't going to work." The last of the three looked as if he was desperately trying to shift forms. He was stuck as a human until he moved far enough away from me.

"How did you know if you're not a vampire?" the tallest one asked.

"I'm not a Were, I'm not a witch, and I am not a vampire. Clearly I am not human, so I would've thought you could put it together." They had their own stories, records of a kind passed from generation to generation. My race was part of their records. In passing at least.

"Why should we believe you?"

"I didn't come here to argue with you. I came for your help," I told them. "Who are your colony's elders?"

"I'm one," the tallest informed me. "The name's Alex."

"Nice to meet you, Alex. Mine is Serenity."

A light clicked on inside Alex's mind when I told him my name. He instantly relaxed, as though he knew exactly who I was. Only seconds later he agreed to take me to the other elders. The third Cat didn't seem happy about it, but Alex soon silenced him.

"If you don't mind me asking, Martin, how are you related to a witch?" I inquired as we walked the two miles to the village.

"My grandmother is a witch, my grandfather a Cat. My father got the Cat genes and James's mum got the witch genes." He rushed through his explanation, almost eagerly. "Who was the girl you were with?"

"Sophie?" He couldn't mean Lizzy.

"The one that looked like you."

"Don't get your hopes up, kid. She'll find her partner exactly how I found mine."

"She's pretty," he muttered.

We were the only race that found our mates as we did. Our lives were so busy with our work that we never stopped to check every face to see if they were the one for us. By having that pull towards them, that unbreakable connection, it made us stop and take the time to really see. Lizzy would find hers the same way, not quite as profound, but fairly close.

Unless . . . No, that is impossible.

It was one thing we knew for certain happened regardless of whether we reached maturity or not. All of our partners had been human. We'd never had a partner outside of the human race. Ray had been human when I met him. For those of us who found their partner before they reached maturity, reaching maturity didn't happen. Who wanted to live forever when your only partner was already dead and gone?

"If you don't mind me asking," Martin said as the first houses came into our line of sight, "why do you smell like a vampire?"

"Long story."

"Care to share?" Alex pressed. "The other elders may wish to know."

"I met my partner in 1940. I lost him the same year. Up until this week, I thought he was either human, living out his days away from me, or dead. As it happens, he was turned." It was the short version of my story, and the only one they were getting.

"I didn't think that was possible," Alex mused.

"How old are you?"

"Older than I look. Celebrated my two-hundredth birthday last year."

He didn't appear to be a day over forty. As with all of the immortal races, the Weres were ageless. Once they began their first shift, with the first full moon after reaching adulthood, they were frozen in time. As they grew older they mastered their abilities. When they were young they could only shift on the full moon.

Their ability to age came with their capability to control their shifting. They literally had to will themselves to age, and it was rare for any of their elders to look much above forty or fifty.

"I better give them some warning," Alex said, pausing in front of a small stone cottage. "I wouldn't want them to end up attacking you."

"Are they likely to?"

"After what happened with the Wolves, we normally kill vampires on sight," he explained.

I smiled. "Best let them know then."

I was left outside with Martin and the other very nervous-looking Cat. Neither of them was much older than Lizzy, though Martin was a lot more relaxed than his friend. They couldn't have been shifting for more than five years, at the most. Practically newborns.

"You two head on up to see James," Alex said, when he opened the door a few minutes later. "Elders only."

"No chance of me staying?" Martin asked.

"Not unless you want me to tell your mother what happened earlier," he countered.

"Fine." Martin sighed. "Still wasn't my fault."

"Go on, Son."

Son? So Alex was Martin's dad. "Come on in."

I was led into the brightly lit cottage. It was nothing like I'd expected a Were's home to be. Not that I'd actually been in a Were's home before. It was all rather normal. Coats slung over the banister, a vacuum cleaner peeking out from under the stairs.

Sitting around the table were two men and two women, one of whom I recognised immediately.

"Serenity Cardea. I never thought I'd see your face so soon," she said.

"Never thought I'd see you mating with Weres," I retorted, pulling her into a hug.

Georgianna Rose. At least that had been her name when I first met her. She was the oldest witch in the world, and the most powerful one at that. Standing at an average five foot seven, she was far from average. Her white blond hair contrasted almost starkly with her tanned features and bright eyes. I'd met her when the witches were being hunted in the 1600s. She was one of the few we'd managed to save.

"You assume too much, Serenity," she chastised me.

"Tell me I'm wrong."

"You, my dear, are never wrong."

It was good to see such a friendly and familiar face. She'd offered me anything I wanted in return for saving her. I'd refused. Though it had been tempting to call in that favour when I couldn't find Ray, I didn't.

"I take it you know my mother, then," Alex interrupted.

"Serenity doesn't merely know me; she's the reason I'm still alive." Her proclamation sounded more like something to be announced in front of royalty, not family. "Now, what can we do for you?"

I sat and explained everything to them. I told them what I wanted. It took almost the entire day to explain what had happened with Ray, and why I still needed their help, even after finding him again. It was the first time I'd admitted to anyone that I was fighting a losing battle. The world didn't need to know that sort of information.

As it was, I had to travel for at least a week once a year, every year, and that was just to keep my influence over The Seats. There were so many other incidents requiring my attention that I barely spent a full month at home without interruption. I wasn't sure if I could continue with Ray by my side.

"I think we need to discuss your request," Alex told me once I was finished.

Georgianna and I were led into the living room so the Cats could talk amongst themselves. It was a lot to ask, for them to protect my family as well as their own. I wouldn't have blamed them if they chose to deny me. I'd never done anything for them, but I had offered them anything they ever needed in exchange.

"And?" I asked when Alex returned almost an hour later.

"Provisionally, yes," he said, smiling.

"However?"

"We are somewhat concerned about what you told us regarding your mate." I hadn't lied to them about who Ray was or with whom he was travelling.

"I understand," I sighed. "I'm not exactly comfortable with them myself."

"If something were to happen," Georgianna added, "regarding a certain grandson of mine, would that change things?"

"What do you know, Mother?"

"I'm a woman of many talents, and I know a psychic when I get close to one," she said, glaring pointedly at Alex.

"What am I missing?" I asked, looking between the two of them.

"You know how I can sense power? It was how I knew Alex would be a Cat where his sister wasn't." I did know that. "A friend of mine told me my grandson would find his mate in a psychic. I believe that psychic is your niece."

"It doesn't work like that," I said. "We don't mate outside of the human race."

"Neither do we."

"How did that come about?"

"I don't know why I fell for him, I just did." She smiled, glancing back towards the kitchen. "The world is changing, Serenity. I found my mate, and he was a Cat. You found yours, and he was turned."

"Coincidence."

"I don't believe in coincidences."

Neither did I.

I thanked the elders for their time and asked Alex to show me where Lizzy was. The rain was starting to fall, so there was no chance of any hiking, and I missed Ray. Knowing exactly where he was didn't help. I wanted him by my side.

"They weren't as volatile as you thought, were they?" Georgianna asked me as we walked.

"I expected something different."

"It's because they recognised you," she whispered. "At least once they stopped believing you to be a vampire."

"You told them of me?"

"They know of the red-haired Keeper who saved my life."

"I'd do it again in a heartbeat."

"I know, and that is why my offer still stands. Four hundred years has taught me a lot, Serenity." She was hinting at something.

"That's not the kind of decision I can make without Ray," I answered.

"Talk to him. Anything is possible for someone my age."

She was implying the impossible. Changing Ray back. It would kill her, if she were able to do it. Not only could I not ask her for her life in exchange for saving it, I couldn't risk Ray's either. It was the sort of spell that came with no guarantees, for anyone involved.

"Nothing to think about," I said, closing the subject.

My hair was soaked by the time we walked the single street to Martin's house. It looked like the others, a small cottage made of stone. There was quiet music and distinctly hushed voices coming from inside. Excited voices.

Alex let me in then disappeared, leaving me with Georgianna. All of a sudden I felt like I was the grown-up crashing the teenagers' party. When I pushed the door open, I froze.

Martin was sitting on one of the chairs . . . with Lizzy firmly planted in his lap. There was an expression on her face that I knew all too well. I'd seen it on William's when he met Alison.

Lizzy had found her partner.

I growled, turning to Georgianna. "Damn you for being right."

"I only knew it was a possibility."

"Lizzy," I called, startling her. "Time to leave."

She'd been staring so intently at Martin that she literally jumped when I called her name. When she realised I'd said it was time to leave, her face fell.

"If he's allowed," I added, smiling tightly, "he can come, too."

"Thank you," she squealed.

Cats were sturdy, and it was a good thing. The way Lizzy dragged Martin from the room it appeared as if she was about to remove his arm. He didn't seem to mind at all. Everyone else stared after them, dumbfounded.

"How are we all going to fit in the car?" the other girl, Sophie I think, piped up.

"I have to drive to Newcastle anyway, I could drop you two off," Georgianna offered.

It was settled. Georgianna left with Sophie and Andy, leaving James to travel with me. I would be glad of the distraction. Lizzy was exactly like her mother, and that meant she wouldn't shut up for days. Weeks, more than likely.

"You know my grandma?" James asked.

"I met Georgianna a long time ago."

James turned out to be an all right kid. I wasn't too far off with his age; he was just older than I'd originally thought. Now that I was truly looking, I saw the resemblance between him and Georgianna. James had her eyes; ocean blue ones that were brighter than anything any human had. It was a witch trait, one we shared. Bright eyes.

Lizzy was beaming when she returned. "He has to run home, but I can bring him with us."

"Let's go home then."

Chapter Twenty-Five

The drive home was interesting. Lizzy climbed in the back with Martin and talked the entire time. James and I discussed various things, mainly revolving around Georgianna and what she'd been up to over the years. James didn't know why she'd fallen for his grandfather, only that they were happy together.

It reminded me of something, but I couldn't quite recall what it was. Couldn't have been that important.

James paused before opening the door when I dropped him off. "If you ever need anything—"

"I'll ask your grandmother."

He chuckled. "Thought you might."

James didn't bother to say goodbye to Martin; he was busy with Lizzy. He told her all about his first shift, the pain he went through, and the confusion. Lizzy just sat there, a look of total absorption on her face.

I almost had to drag the pair of them out of the car when we arrived home.

"Martin, I don't want you to panic," I said, noticing the extra car in the drive. "There may be a vampire in the house."

That brought both their heads up. Martin snapped to attention as if he'd been electrocuted. He was trying to shift. Fortunately, he wasn't able to. He was standing far too close to Lizzy and she would have been hurt.

"It's fine," I said. "It's probably Ray."

"*Probably?*" he growled. Realising he couldn't shift, he pulled Lizzy behind him instead.

I sighed. "Let me check."

Quietly, I stalked towards the house, careful of my every move. I didn't get further than the brown mini. It was Ray's, there was no doubt. Only

Ray's car would have an abandoned history book on the passenger seat, and another one on the back. How he found time to read while driving was something I'd have to talk to him about. He may have been much harder to kill since he'd been turned, but he wasn't completely indestructible.

"It's Ray," I called over my shoulder.

"How do you know?" Martin asked.

"There is only one man in the world that would think *The History of Ancient Egypt* was in-car entertainment," I told him, laughing. "Really, it's fine. We'll be staying upstairs anyway."

Lizzy calmed him instantly. She took hold of his arm, stood on her toes, and whispered something in his ear. I tried not to listen, but whatever she said made him back off. He was still reluctant.

The three of us walked into the house, and the smell of dinner wafted from the kitchen. Jayne was cooking, but there was no sign of Ray.

"He's upstairs, and Mum was invited out with her new bingo friends," she said when I poked my head around the door. "And yes, I was nice."

"We have company."

"Lizzy's friends?"

"Not quite. Maybe you should take a look for yourself." I winced when I told her that. I wasn't sure how she'd take sending her daughter to university and her finding her partner in the same week.

"What happened?" She dried her hands and followed me out of the kitchen.

"There may or may not be a Cat in our living room." I hung back a little as she walked in. Lizzy was sitting as close as possible to Martin without actually being on his knee. Her arms were wrapped around his waist, her head resting on his shoulder. It was a strange sight, seeing them so comfortable with each other.

"Lizzy Anna Johnson!" The volume of Jayne's voice made *me* jump. "What is going on?"

The pair leapt apart, and Martin sat there, head down, hands in his lap, as though he'd been scolded. Lizzy, however, showed no signs that she'd been caught in such a compromising position with a boy who hadn't met her mother yet.

"Mum, this is Martin. He's a Cat." She beamed as she introduced him. "Martin, this is my mum, Jayne."

"How is this possible?" she demanded, turning on me.

"Don't look at me! I don't know what's happening anymore."

"I assume you're staying for dinner, Martin?" Only her words suggested she was trying to be polite. Her tone was anything but.

"If that's all right with you, Mrs. Johnson," he answered, looking slightly afraid.

"Providing you don't eat me out of house and home, yes."

She was grumbling as she wandered back into the kitchen. Something about it being a good thing she always cooked too much.

"Is she mad?" Lizzy whispered, moving away from Martin.

"Come here." I opened my arms to her, knowing exactly why Jayne had reacted as she had. "She misses your dad. She doesn't want you to get hurt like she did, and being a Cat comes with its risks. Give her time, and she'll be telling you two to get a room before you know it."

Jayne had lost her husband not long after Lizzy was born. She was barely six months old, too young to remember what her mother was like before the accident. It had been a hit and run. Another driver ran a stop light, crashed into the driver's side of his car, and killed him on impact. The driver wasn't found until he crashed again three miles down the road. Jim had been a good man, and Jayne had been a wreck for months afterwards. I'd felt so helpless; all I could do was make sure they were taken care of. I couldn't offer any emotional support, not when my own feelings were still too raw.

It had taken Lizzy's first word to snap Jayne out of her grief, to give her a purpose again. It was hard for her knowing that Lizzy had found her partner. That Lizzy could suffer the same loss she had.

Jayne was back in the kitchen, adding to the already giant piles of food she'd prepared.

"You all right?"

"I will be. Ray is in your room."

"He can wait a second." Jayne needed me right now. "What can I do?"

"Tell me I'm not losing her," she whispered. "Again."

"You're not losing her, Jayne," I promised. "She won't be going anywhere, and he's part of the most reclusive of all the races. His father is two hundred years old, and his grandmother is the oldest witch alive."

"You work fast."

"Not really. I know his grandmother."

"From the witch trials?"

"Yes. She was old then." It felt good to be able to make her smile some.

"You saved a lot of them, didn't you?"

"Not enough, though I tried."

"You should go and see Ray." Her whole expression changed, and she looked concerned once more. "He didn't seem quite right and said he needed to talk to you."

I didn't spare a second to give Jayne a quick hug. I took off up the stairs faster than I'd moved in a long while. There was no conflict about barging through my door this time. If there was a chance anything was wrong with Ray, then a piece of wood wasn't going to stop me from getting to him.

He stood in the far corner of the room, as far away from the door as was possible.

"Ray?" I whispered, taking a step closer to him.

"Stop, please," he begged. "Please."

"What . . . ?"

Everything clicked into place, and I realised what was wrong. I'd found him on Tuesday. We'd spent every spare second together, day and night.

That meant that if he'd fed on Sunday or Monday night, he hadn't fed since.

A vampire couldn't die from starvation. It made them weak and sent them into a kind of delirium, but it wouldn't kill them. I had some idea of the feelings Ray would have been going through after just one week of not feeding. His senses would've been the first to fade—hearing and sight. His strength and speed would've been next.

All that came before the descent into madness. The need to feed would tear away at his sanity until there was nothing left but a killing machine.

"Ray," I whispered. "You need to feed."

"I don't want to hurt you." He moaned, trying to back away as I approached.

"You can't hurt me, remember? Why didn't you tell me sooner?"

"I didn't want you to hate me." His eyes were squeezed shut, his hands clenching repeatedly.

"Never. I could *never* hate you."

There was no choice to be made. No discussions to be had before I did what I did. Before he had a chance to react, or to object, I went to him.

The hiss that escaped him was like nothing I'd ever heard. Loud, animalistic, and meant to be a warning.

"Listen to me, Ray," I said, planting my hands on either side of him so that he had nowhere to go. "You can't hurt me, and I'm more than willing to let you feed from me. Please."

As soon as I said the word *feed,* his eyes locked onto my throat, and I got my first glimpse of his fangs. His canines were no longer short and human; they were utterly beautiful. Long, curved, *sharp.* On Ray they were nothing short of stunning.

"Please."

He didn't need me to ask again. With precision accuracy, he struck, sinking his fangs deep into my neck. A quick burst of pain flared through me as he broke the skin but faded quickly. My hands moved, gripping his shoulders. His moved to support me, cradling my neck and back.

I was aware of every tiny detail as he drank: The sharpness of his fangs in my skin. The quiet swallowing as he drank from me. My own deep, even breathing as I relaxed into his embrace and let him take what he needed.

It was actually quite pleasant. Not having him draw my blood; that wasn't so much painful as bearable. What I took great delight in was being able to give him what he needed.

Everything had been going well until I realised he wasn't stopping. Part of me didn't care. He couldn't exactly kill me. The more he took, the more I started to enjoy the whole experience, even when he sank to his knees, taking me with him, clutching my body to his.

"Ray," my eyes drifted shut, "you need to stop."

He'd waited too long to feed. If he didn't stop, he was going to drain every last drop of blood from me. I couldn't let him do that, but I didn't have it in me to stop him. I didn't want to. Somehow it felt right.

"Ray," I whispered. "Please, you have to stop."

I could've used my strength to force him, but I'd have hurt him.

Fortunately, Jayne had great timing.

"Serenity, do you want to come down for . . . ? What the blazes?"

She was at my side in a second, practically pushing Ray out of the way to get to me. Her face was frantic as she searched every inch of me before her eyes landed on my neck.

He was startled enough that he stopped, looking up, dazed and confused for a moment. A moment long enough.

"What did you—"

"Jayne, *don't*. It was my choice."

"You *let* him *bite* you?" she cried. "Are you mad?"

"Jayne, I won't justify my choices to you. Ray needed to feed, and it's not as if he can do any lasting damage to me." It had been my choice, and I'd do it again whenever he needed. The fact I was a quick healer helped.

"We are *not* finished discussing this!"

"For now we are. I'll be down for dinner in a few minutes." I hadn't discussed what happened with Ray; there was no chance I'd talk to Jayne about it yet.

Jayne had always worried about me, and I couldn't blame her for her reaction, though she'd seen me when I'd been suffering from far worse injuries than mere blood loss. I was already rapidly recovering, despite Ray drinking too much.

"Are you all right?" he asked once the door was safely closed.

"I'm fine. Just a little light-headed."

"I'm sorry," he whispered, eyeing the wound on my neck. "May I?"

"Mmhm." There was no point in telling him it would do no good.

A vampire would lick the puncture wounds on their victims' necks so they would close, leaving no trace of their presence. It didn't work on us. Every other type of wound healed in seconds, minutes for the larger ones, and a day or so for bones, but not vampire bites. There was something in a vampire's saliva that decreased our ability to heal. My body had already repaired itself from most of the blood loss I'd suffered. So when Ray's lips brushed against my neck there was nothing but pleasure on my part. His actions reminded me of a cat lapping up milk. Gentle, precise movements, nuzzling almost.

"Why aren't they healing?" Ray asked, brushing his fingers over my neck.

"They'll be gone by morning."

"Thank you."

"You never need to thank me, but I think we should talk . . ." He averted his eyes. "It's nothing bad, Ray. I wanted to ask you how you plan on feeding in the future."

"I . . . I hadn't thought about it."

"Would you consider using me?"

"Every week?" he asked. "Twice a week I need to feed, Serenity, sometimes more. I can't ask that of you."

"You're not asking. I'm offering."

He was understandably reluctant in accepting my offer. It all came back to the same thing: he didn't want to hurt me. Such a stupid notion. Even if he'd been thirsty enough to drain the life from me, he couldn't harm me. I'd simply be unconscious for a short time until I could repair myself.

"Let's go eat."

Dinner was a quiet affair. Jayne kept glaring in my direction, then at Ray and Martin. She'd calmed down considerably, but she was skilled at hiding what she felt. There would be a discussion after dinner, once Lizzy was safely elsewhere and Martin was out of earshot.

After dinner, sensing the tension that was looming between Jayne and me, Martin made his excuses for leaving. He promised to return as soon as he was able, and Lizzy didn't hesitate in promising she'd visit him as often as she could.

Before that could happen, Martin had to shift so he could run home. I offered to take him—anything to avoid the inevitable conflict with Jayne— but he insisted the run would do him good. Lizzy was also anxious to see what he looked like once he'd changed forms.

He jogged off into the trees that surrounded our house so he could shift. I wasn't sure of the exact distance he'd need to go, but it was far enough we wouldn't be able to see him. When he returned, he was completely different.

She was disappointed she couldn't see the shift as it happened, but it wasn't worth her safety. Even if Martin had been able to change forms with her near, there was no way I'd let her close to a Were that was about to shift.

His tall, six-feet-odd-inch frame had been completely transformed. In place of his arms and legs were the powerful limbs of a giant black cat. To the human eye, or at a glance, he was jet black with no variation. To my eyes, he was a myriad of colour: dark reds, deep black, and warm and vibrant browns. His thick fur rippled over strong muscles and limbs. I'd seen the Wolves up close. I'd witnessed the changing of a Bear or two, and a Lion from a distance. Never before had I seen a Cat.

He was beautiful.

Sleek, powerful, and so like a leopard that I could barely tell the difference. His pupils were human, and there was something off about him. The back legs were slightly longer than they should've been. His mouth, as well, was wrong somehow.

"Mum, he won't hurt me," Lizzy said when Jayne prevented her from moving forward.

I was tempted to pet him, as well, so I couldn't blame Lizzy for wanting a closer peek at her partner. That was going to take some getting used to. It always did. She was growing up.

Lizzy looked over almost every inch of Martin before he raced off into the trees once more. It would take him less than an hour to reach his home; all the Weres were fast.

Lizzy had a dreamy smile on her face when she skipped back inside.

There wasn't a smile on Jayne's face.

Chapter Twenty-Six

"Is she very mad?" Ray whispered.

Jayne had pegged us both with a level stare before heading into the house. She wanted to talk and there was no getting out of it.

She could have been angry with either of us, though my guess was her anger would be directed solely at me.

At least I hoped it would. There was no telling how I'd react if she started throwing accusations at Ray. I wouldn't lose him. Not again. And certainly not over something as trivial as him feeding from me.

I followed Jayne into the kitchen, where she started putting the last of the dinner plates away. Lizzy had retired to her room to work on her homework. There was nothing standing between me and the verbal lashing of a lifetime. Except perhaps Ray, who was behind me.

"Before you say *anything*," I said, deciding to confront her first, "I stand by my decisions."

"What if he'd drained you dry? Did you think of that?" she demanded, almost smashing the last plate she put away.

"He wouldn't have," I said, defending what had happened.

"You don't know that."

"You're right. I don't know that. I do, however, know it wouldn't have made a blind bit of difference. Regardless, it was *my* decision." When Jayne got hold of something, it was hard to make her let go. Chances were we could argue for days about what she'd seen, and she still wouldn't be happy about it.

"Your decision or not, we need you, Serenity. Do you know for sure whether you can come back from being drained?" I was pretty sure, but she had a point. Unfortunately. I couldn't recall any vampire getting so close as to try.

"What would you have me do? Let him starve? Leave your *daughter* vulnerable to a thirsty vampire? Leave *you* vulnerable? Helen? I couldn't do that. The same as I couldn't bear to let him feed from humans, not when I can give Ray everything he needs." She could argue her points all she liked. It would get her nowhere.

"Serenity," she sighed, "what am I going to do with you?"

"Nothing, Jayne. It was my choice, and I'll do it again."

"Is there anything I can say to change your mind?" She looked so concerned I almost caved.

Almost, because I knew Jayne far too well, and certainly well enough to know when she was faking.

"Ray, would you give us a minute, please?"

My eyes never left Jayne as I listened to his fading footsteps. What I was going to say to Jayne wasn't for his ears.

She knew not to say anything until I did. I could hear when Ray got to my room, where he was out of hearing range for us. If he listened hard enough, he would've been able to make out faint words, but he wouldn't.

"Don't make me pull rank with you, Jayne," I snapped, my voice low and hard. "*I* decided to let him feed from me, and *I* will be responsible for any of the consequences."

"Just because it was your decision, doesn't mean I have to like it!" she whisper-yelled.

"I'm not asking you to like it. I'm asking you to respect my decisions."

"I'm not going to sway you on this, am I?"

"No." My mind was already made up. "Feeding is an intimate thing, Jayne. I couldn't let him feed from some poor human." I couldn't blame him for keeping himself alive, but I couldn't stand by and let him continue to feed that way.

Besides, I'd rather liked it.

"I understand, Aunt Sere, I really do, but . . ." She sighed deeply.

"Please, let me deal with this myself?" I wasn't above begging her if I had to. It was better than pulling the age card.

"If he hurts you . . . " she warned, complete with wagging finger.

"*He won't.*"

She was only trying to protect me, even though I didn't need it. It was a habit of hers, as it was with Helen. It was their mothering instincts. Despite the fact I'd lived for much longer than either of them, there always came a time when they treated me as they had their own children. Once they hit that stage in their lives, it never ended.

Fortunately, there were a few years left before Lizzy took up that role.

Jayne and I were on better terms when I retreated from the kitchen. She wasn't going to be happy for a while, but she'd get used to the idea.

"Is it safe?" Ray asked, smiling a touch.

"She's upset, but she'll come around."

"Are you all right?"

"I'm fine. I recover quickly."

"Exceptionally so, save for that." He touched the bite mark gently.

"They'll be gone by morning."

We spent the rest of our evening discussing the merits of him feeding only from me. It took some gentle persuasion on my part, but eventually he started to listen to reason. Ray admitted he thought I'd see him for what he was and wouldn't want him anymore.

Of all the things for him to think.

"I wanted to ask you something," I whispered.

"You can ask me anything."

"How much do you remember of our last night together?" I needed to know.

"It's my fondest memory of us," he said, matching my quiet tone. "I remember everything. The tiny noises that escaped you. How your body felt under mine. How you blushed when you got nervous. How it felt to hold you in my arms afterwards. What it was like waking up to you, feeling every inch of you against me."

And now for the question I really wanted to ask. "Do you still want me like that?"

"More than ever, but not until you're ready," he vowed. "Things have changed since then, and I can't begin to understand what things must be like for you now. I'll always want you, in every way, but I'll wait."

"What you are isn't a factor. You are still you; I see that every day. I want you, Ray, all of you."

Neither of us hesitated once I'd finished speaking. He snaked his arms around my waist, pulling me closer as his lips descended. As we deepened the kiss, his hands left me for a moment and began undoing the buttons on my blouse.

Everything was so similar to the first time we'd been together—a blur of passion and need. It wasn't long before he gathered me in his arms and laid me out on the bed, naked in front of him. After he shed the rest of his clothes, I couldn't help but stare at him. He was as beautiful as I'd remembered, and more. So many things were the same, yet so much had changed. The scars, which had once been so stark, were now little more than a silvery design on his pale skin. He moved easily now, not struggling in the slightest. He lay next to me, running his hands over my body.

With each caress I let out a small moan. It had been far too long. The gentle feel of his fingers caressing my skin was so much better than I remembered. I struggled to open my eyes as he gently explored me, and found him watching me intently. His eyes were alive as they took me in, swimming as only a vampire's could. As he entered me, I marvelled at how good he felt. How different the cool of his skin was, but how amazing it was to be with him like this again. When he began to move within me, with so much more power, my breathing quickened, and my eyelids fell shut again.

I gripped his shoulders as his thrusts became harder, more urgent, feeling delight in the way his chest pressed against me, his arms holding me tight. I wrapped my legs around his hips, pulling him closer. I felt the familiar tingle of my approaching pleasure as he trailed kisses up my jaw, his breathing matching mine. Our cries mingled, growing louder as he thrust harder into me, nearing his own release. With a final push, my orgasm ripped through me, shattering the world around me and hurling me deep into a sensation I'd never hoped to feel again. Hearing my name fall from Ray's lips in the most reverent of tones was enough to keep me smiling for weeks.

"I missed you so much," I whispered when we were both able to breathe.

"You'll never have to miss me again," he promised.

His voice was the last thing I heard before I drifted off to sleep in his arms.

For a fraction of a second after I opened my eyes, I thought I was awake. But the room was too dark, and everything was wrong somehow, almost blurry but not quite.

I felt my body moving, but had no control over it as I walked along horribly familiar stone tunnels. Devoid of light, lifeless, and eerily quiet.

I was in one of the catacombs, though I couldn't say for certain which city I was in. It felt as if I was in Europe. The earth beneath my feet was damp, and the catacombs elsewhere in the world rarely were.

They'd been built when the first Seat was established. The rulers wanted somewhere safe to travel to when they needed it. Each one was well concealed, deep within the earth of various cities. I knew where each of them was; I'd been there when some of them were built.

I couldn't exactly place it, but it was one I'd been inside of. Possibly Russia, but London was more likely. Finland was the other possibility. There were some things I never forgot. Being frog marched into the catacombs to face The Seats was one of them.

As with all of The Seats, they had a permanent base of operations. Though they moved as often as needed, they always returned to their home when they were finished.

But this dream wasn't the past; of that much I was certain.

I heard the light, squelching footsteps of at least half a dozen vampires, but it was too dark to see to whom they belonged. Soon the stone walls opened into an underground chamber. The high ceiling was littered with skulls, casting long shadows that looked like demented pumpkins on Halloween. Each belonged to a vampire, someone who'd been on the wrong side of The Seats in such a way that their death was a warning to others. The fear I felt didn't come from the skulls, nor did it come from the half dozen faces staring in my direction. My fear came from hearing a whimper on the other side of the room.

I tried to call Lizzy's name, but my voice wouldn't work.

What was she doing here?

Frantically I glanced around, trying to get someone's attention. Everything came into sharp focus as I saw who was standing next to me.

Ray was by my side, a look of death etched into his features. Beyond him I could see Al and Leola, concern on his face and a sneer on hers.

I couldn't get their attention. My body wouldn't move. I was helpless.

It's just a dream.

Knowing it was a dream didn't prevent me from lurching forward, trying to reach for Lizzy.

There was a buzz of voices as I tried and tried again to understand what they were saying. They were so loud, yet I couldn't make out a single word. The only noise I could identify was Lizzy crying in the corner, tears streaming down her cheeks. Fear shone on her face as I continued to fight. There was nothing binding me, but I couldn't move.

My eyes were on Lizzy as she and I struggled uselessly, her against her binds, me against the dream. Kiros appeared behind her and dragged her from the floor. The chains bit into her wrists. I cried out when he bared his fangs, tearing into her throat.

As I was praying to wake up, I felt my own throat being sliced into. Lizzy's pain mirrored my own.

It felt so *real*. The slash of agony as the fangs pierced my skin. The deep, powerful pulls as whoever it was drank as fast as possible. It was painful, forceful.

Somehow I knew whoever it was meant to kill me.

I sat bolt upright in my bed, panting for breath, clutching my neck. Ray was frantically trying to get my attention, but all I heard were Lizzy's screams of pain ringing in my ears, loud and shrill.

It was a moment more before I realised they weren't in my head.

It was Lizzy.

Chapter Twenty-Seven

I was at Lizzy's door in seconds, clad only in my bathrobe. She was sitting up in her bed, tears streaming down her face, clutching her neck.

The catacombs were a far cry from Lizzy's teenage bedroom. It didn't stop my heart from lurching into my throat at the sight of her.

Without a second thought, I climbed onto her bed and took her into my arms.

"Lizzy, it's me. You're okay." My words were meant to comfort her . . . as well as myself.

It was a long few minutes before her sobs subsided to quiet whimpers, and she was able to speak. I was aware of Ray talking quietly with Jayne. None of it mattered, only Lizzy.

"It was a dream?" Her voice was so small as she looked up with wide, reddened eyes.

"It was just a dream, sweetie. Do you want to tell me about it?" She shook a little with fear as she nodded. "Are you sure?"

She nodded again, still rubbing her neck. "It felt so real," she whispered, curling onto her side.

I'd never seen her so distraught.

"Serenity? I'm going to check around the house, just in case," Ray offered.

I was surprised when Lizzy flinched at the sound of his voice.

"Thank you," I told him.

Lizzy didn't relax again until Jayne climbed onto the bed with us after Ray had left. Helen joined us a few moments later, sitting gingerly on the edge of the mattress, her hand resting on Lizzy's leg.

"Lizzy?"

"It never felt so real before," she whimpered. "The floor, the chains, the teeth, all of it."

"Lizzy, sweetie, I need you to tell me everything you can. From the start."

"I don't know how I got there, but I know it was one of the catacombs. I didn't recognise any of the faces, but I knew what they were. I was *so* scared. They kept taunting me, telling me they were going to kill me." She paused for a moment to take a breath, shuddering as she did. "Then Issac came in with Poppy. I think you were standing with Ray, and Al and Leola were next to you. I couldn't see you, but when the arguing started, you came forward. One of them was called Elena, and she was going to kill you, but you stopped her."

"Lizzy, it's all right," I told her. "Go on."

"You told her if she wanted you dead, then you wanted Ray to do it." That explained hear reaction to Ray's voice. "When he bit you, I felt it. I screamed for him to stop, but he wouldn't. He kept drinking until you collapsed. That's when I woke up."

"I had the same dream."

I didn't know what it meant, but I'd do anything to stop it from happening.

No human had ever seen the inside of the catacombs and lived. Lizzy was calmer when Ray returned, nodding once to indicate everything was clear. For that I was grateful. Too many of Lizzy's dreams had come true to disregard it. Too many of mine, as well, for that matter.

But if The Seats wanted Lizzy . . . there was *nothing* I could do to stop them. They had the power to do anything.

I needed more of us, more of my race. I couldn't do this on my own.

"You're more worried than you let on," Ray stated once we'd left Lizzy, Jayne, and Helen to get some more sleep, what little they'd be able to manage.

"You can't read my mind, Ray, you don't know that I'm worried," I said, trying to lighten the mood.

"I can't read anyone's mind, but that is hardly the point," he answered, stopping me in my tracks.

"You can't read *anyone's* mind?"

"No, but don't change the subject."

I sighed. I'd question him on his powers later.

"Yes, I am worried. We could watch her for every second of every day, and all it would take is one mistake."

"We can help."

"No. The more people I have looking after her, the more mistakes are going to be made. I think between Martin, you, and me we're covered." I ran through possibilities of how to best protect her. "Martin will want to help, anyway. I doubt I could stop him. You, I trust implicitly."

"But not the others?"

"It's not that I don't trust them . . ."

"You just don't trust them."

"I'm sorry. I really think having more vampires around at the moment would be counterproductive."

"In what way?"

"Have you noticed how The Seats have been more strict of late?" The more I visited, the stricter they became. "All it would take is for someone to see one of you with Lizzy and get the wrong idea. One word and they'd come for her. Not even I can stop them."

"Poppy could help."

"Just because she has kept her mouth shut for the better part of half a century, doesn't mean she'll continue to do so," I said without thinking.

"True."

"Can we talk about something else?"

"Anything you like."

It was the perfect opportunity to bring up his lack of mind reading skills. As young as he was, he should've mastered that skill decades ago. Apparently he never had, and neither had Issac. Poppy had given him a theory on why that was. As with all vampires, the more lives they took, the more powerful they were. It must affect their basic skill set, too.

"You're pretty *tame* as far as vampires go," I teased.

"Tame? I'll show you tame." I was flat on my back, Ray pinning me to the bed, fangs bared, by the time he finished the sentence. He knew I was stronger than him and could easily have stopped him, but I didn't.

"So all you do is drink blood?" I tilted my head back, exposing my neck. "So unbelievably tame."

"Don't forget, Serenity, it is my choice not to kill," he whispered, the tips of his fangs brushing against my throat. "I could, if I wanted to."

"No, you couldn't," I said, smiling. "You wouldn't be who you are if you were capable of the kinds of monstrosities the rest of your race is."

"Do you always have to be right?"

"Perks of living for three thousand years."

I surprised him with a kiss, pressing my lips against his, exploring his elongated fangs with the tip of my tongue. It startled him, causing him to pull away.

"They don't bother you?" he asked, confused.

"Why would they?"

"I thought they would."

"Ray, if I let you bite me with them, why would they bother me when I'm kissing you?" I pressed another kiss to his lips.

"Have I told you that I love you today?"

"I thought you loved me every day." I was in a teasing mood.

"I love you, Serenity Cardea, so very much."

"As you breathe, so will I," I whispered. It was an amended version of the words I'd used when I first met him. "I'm working on the rest. So for now, I shall tell you I love you, too."

We were standing in the back garden, scanning the trees, when dawn arrived. Both of us were wary, and though we pretended we were admiring the nonexistent sunrise, we were watching for anything unusual.

"How do you feel about helping me cook breakfast?" I asked, hearing the first movements in the house.

He raised an eyebrow at my request. "You do remember my last attempt at cooking, don't you?"

"Hmm, that would be the exceptionally poor job you did with the mashed vegetables."

"Would you like me to poison everyone?"

"All you have to do is keep me company."

"I may be able to manage that, though it's technically not helping."

We were in the kitchen before anyone else. I began pulling the things I needed out of the cupboards. Cooking was something I hadn't done a lot of in recent years. Ray perched on one of the chairs as I began making pancakes. The days when I made a full buffet breakfast were long gone. It wasn't long before the smell was wafting through the house and two high-pitched, excited squeals came from upstairs as both the girls realised what was happening.

There was a look of confusion on Ray's face as Jayne and Lizzy came racing in, only to stop dead in their tracks when they saw me. They were checking that I was indeed cooking. When they were satisfied, they flung their arms around me, each smiling. I could swear they were the same age, and not mother and daughter.

For once it was clear I planned on joining them.

It was a shame Helen was feeling tired and had opted to stay in bed. She would've loved to see me cooking again.

During those unmentionable years without Ray, food hadn't held the same appeal. It was fantastic to have that feeling of happiness again. The taste of fresh pancakes was something to be savoured.

"This is a nice change," Jayne commented.

The way she shovelled in mouthful after mouthful made me think she hadn't eaten in weeks.

"It is, but in the future can we have some warning? Martin would love this," Lizzy said.

"So long as it's only him I'm cooking for. I don't wish to know how much the Cats eat." With the amount of running they did, it was unlikely they'd have light diets.

"Well, for them to enjoy breakfast, they would have to stay overnight, and only Martin will be doing that."

Both Jayne and I cried out at the same time, "Oh no! Not in my house!"

"Not for that reason!" Lizzy defended herself as Jayne and I descended into fits of laughter at our matching comments.

"I should hope not. Besides, Ray and I would be staying up all night if you have him over." I looked to Ray for confirmation.

"I could read his mind . . . stop him from doing anything inappropriate," he bluffed.

"Can we *please* not discuss this?" She sat in her chair, arms crossed, pouting.

It was too good of an opportunity to pass up. "We have had the *Birds and the Bees* talk with her already, haven't we?"

"We did. She's never had a boyfriend before, though. Maybe it needs reiterating. Do you think Martin has had the talk yet?" Jayne was intent on being as serious as possible, but there was humour in her eyes.

"Mum! Aunt Sere! Please!"

"Perhaps we should take it up with his parents," I said. "I have met his father."

"Ray, please make them stop!"

"No can do, kid, you're on your own with this one," he said, enjoying the banter.

"All right, all right. You can have him stay over. *If* your mother agrees." Considering the look she gave Lizzy and me, it was a big if. "But he's staying in the spare room next to your mother's. If I find him in yours, or you in his, then I'll have the talk with both of you."

"Isn't that a little hypocritical of you?" Ray whispered.

"Different circumstances."

"I have a compromise," Jayne said. "He can stay, in the room next to mine, but instead of you giving them the talk . . . Ray has to."

I almost spat my mouthful of pancakes across the table. Jayne had a cruel streak. It was bad enough to force a teenager's boyfriend to endure a sex talk. It was even worse to subject them to it together, and by their aunt who appeared no older than them. But Ray was a vampire whose sexual experience was limited. Martin was a Were, and I didn't want to know how experienced he was, or wasn't. Forcing him to endure a sex talk from a vampire would be hilarious.

"Deal," Ray agreed.

"I am so dead," Lizzy mumbled.

Chapter Twenty-Eight

Three days later, Helen was admitted to the hospital. I'd gone in to wake her, only to find that I was unable. She'd been growing tired since the move, and at first we thought it was the daytrips and her evenings out that were the cause.

The doctors found nothing wrong, nor would they, but they were keeping her in for observation.

I knew what it was. I'd seen the symptoms a number of times. Tiredness was the start, and after that it wasn't long before the end came.

"Hey," I whispered when she opened her eyes. "How are you feeling?"

She smiled, but it was a sad smile. "Tired. I've been tired for a while now, Serenity."

I nodded. "I know."

"But?"

"But maybe I'm not ready to let you go just yet." I shrugged.

Helen reached out and patted my knee gently. She was so small lying there in her hospital bed. "You have him back, Aunt Sere."

And that was the reason Helen had held on for all the years following the death of her husband. She'd had a daughter to care for at first, and then Ray had disappeared. Not a word had been said about her reason for trudging through life, but we both had known it was for me.

"I'm still alone," I told her. "I still need you."

She made an unladylike noise and swatted at me. "Don't be so silly, Serenity. You have your partner back. That's all the reason you ever needed to keep going. Now, send that daughter of mine in, I would like a word with her."

We visited the hospital every day, but the doctors refused to let Helen come home. She was sleeping for longer and longer each day, and they were worried.

For the rest of that week following the dream, *absolutely nothing else happened.* Ray kept an eye on Lizzy while she was at the university, and Martin and I watched over her while she was at home or at the hospital.

I was bored. I'd found the Cats and secured their help. I wasn't due to visit another Seat for six months, and things were unusually quiet in the world. There was nothing left to do. Even translating the records was almost complete.

Ray had invited me to accompany him on a staff night out, but I was reluctant because Issac and Poppy would be there. Lizzy was part of a select group of students who helped the teachers. All of them had been invited, too.

"I'm not sure." I was hoping to offer a more agreeable alternative. "I'd love to spend the evening with you, but . . ."

"We could always put in an appearance and then leave," he offered. Apparently, it was something he couldn't get out of.

I still moaned. "I suppose if you must go."

"I must."

"Then we'll put in an appearance. We'll look devastatingly elegant, and we'll dance for a while and leave."

"*You* will look devastatingly elegant. Then again, you always do."

"You, my dear, are biased."

"Any man would agree with me."

When the mail arrived just over a week after the dream, I wasn't surprised. It had been too long since I'd received word of any troubles. It wasn't necessarily a bad thing, but vampires tended to head underground if something was coming.

As such, it meant I had to return from Ray's house every day to ensure there were no incidents to deal with. As much as I'd tried to persuade him to move in with me, he claimed that all of his books wouldn't fit. He still thought I'd see him as a bloodsucking fiend. Three times he'd fed from me, much to Jayne and Lizzy's displeasure. Then Helen had told them to drop the issue.

He'd spent every night in my bed and almost every second by my side. There was nothing fiendish about him.

Calling him tame had been an understatement. With the exception of his need for blood and his fangs, he was almost human.

"Work?" Ray asked.

"Germany." Which would mean a flight and at least a day away from Ray.

"You could always get a job with me," he joked. "We're in need of some more teachers."

"Yes, Ray, I shall come and work at a university whilst the vampires wreak havoc across the world." I rolled my eyes at him, barely resisting the urge to tut at him as well.

"How long will you be?"

"Too long. The Seats should have taken care of this."

It was a small enough problem to sort out, but big enough that I shouldn't have had to deal with it.

"I'd best make a couple of calls, then." He reached for the phone.

"No one needs to know I'm leaving, Ray." I sighed, briefly wondering who he'd be calling anyway.

"No, but they need to know I am"

"*I* am leaving, Ray. *Not you.*" I gave him a stern look when he tried to argue. "No arguments, I'm *not* taking you with me."

"Serenity . . ."

I cut him off with a wave of my hand, not wanting to listen to any excuses, and certainly not willing to change my mind. "No. I won't risk your life like that."

"It wouldn't be a risk. I can take care of myself."

"You mean more to me than anything else in the world, and I won't lose you. *Please.*" My voice was barely a whisper as I added, "I can't live without you again."

He sighed. "You never have to."

"Then stay here. I'll be back in twenty-four hours. Spend some time with your . . . what do I call them?"

"Well, we're as far from a family as you can get. We're too small for a coven or a clan, so I'm not sure."

"Go have some fun with the others." It was as accurate a description as any. "Take Lizzy with you. I'm sure Leola would love that."

"What planet are you living on?" He laughed, pulling me close.

"This one, as far as I know."

"Call me if anything goes wrong. *Anything,*" he stressed.

"I promise."

"Then I'll see you tomorrow."

He gave me a quick kiss, and then I raced to my room to dress. Light trousers would be no good, not when I was taking my bike. I changed into a pair of heavy jeans, boots, a woolly jumper, and my leather jacket.

Riding my bike was always enjoyable. She was fast and sleek and beat most of my cars. And she had the added advantage of being able to slide through the smallest of gaps in traffic. She was also more transportable.

"Zach! Just the man I need."

"Serenity, need to fly somewhere?"

Zach was my pilot. Since the invention of the commercial airplane, my life had been much easier. Zach's father had been my first pilot, and his son would be my third.

"I need to go to Hamburg. Can you get me to Hanover as soon as possible?" Fortunately, both were in West Germany. Had they not been, twenty-four hours would've been a lot longer.

"Hanover? Isn't that in the wrong direction?"

"Precautions."

"Problems?"

"In a manner of speaking."

"I can have the plane ready inside the hour." Zach always knew when not to question me further.

"Thank you. I'm bringing the bike."

"Ready?" Ray asked. He would've startled me if I hadn't heard his footsteps.

"I'll be back as soon as possible."

"Stay safe."

"Take care of yourself for me."

"May I kiss you goodbye?" The words put a smile on my face.

"No, not goodbye, but I'd like it if you kissed me." I was grinning over the fact he'd remembered.

I could never get enough of his kisses. So gentle and sweet, yet so demanding and fierce. All too soon he pulled away, letting me go and smiling sadly.

"I'll miss you."

"You'll see me soon enough."

With one last look at Ray, I started the motorcycle and sped off down the drive, pushing the bike to the limit before I'd hit the main road.

Zach would already be at the airport, clearing various things. I had neither the patience nor the inclination to learn to fly, so I paid Zach to be on standby when I needed him.

It was the first time I'd left since finding Ray again. That knowledge weighed heavy in my heart as I raced through the morning traffic. I was afraid he wouldn't be there when I got back. But as much as I wanted him to join me, I couldn't do that either.

Twenty-four hours, I told myself. That was all it was, twenty-four hours.

Chapter Twenty-Nine

The sun had just set when Zach touched the plane down at Newcastle airport after what had proven to be a very smooth journey. I asked him to pass on my regards to his wife and children but didn't hang around to chat. Ray would be sitting in my study grading papers or talking with Jayne and Lizzy. Either way, I wanted to see him.

The evening traffic was thin, and I made it back to the house in record time, a smile on my face. One that disappeared the second I pulled into the long driveway.

There wasn't a single reason for any of the Cats to be hanging around here, and certainly not in fully shifted states. Martin was the exception, but the snarling leopard that was hiding in the trees at the bottom of the drive was not Martin. Neither was the one further up.

I was off my bike before the engine had fully come to a stop. "What happened?"

"Nothing bad," Ray reassured me, waiting on the doorstep.

"Nothing bad? I can sense half the Cats are patrolling around my home! *What happened?*"

"Aunt Sere?"

"Would someone please explain to me why there is a need for the Cats to be prowling round the house?"

"Perhaps you should come inside," Lizzy suggested.

Something was very wrong. The Cats didn't leave their colony en masse for anything short of war.

Poppy, Issac, Al, and Leola sat around in my living room.

"What are they doing here?" I growled.

"We wouldn't be here if it wasn't for that little twerp," Leola snarled.

"If I find out you had anything to do with whatever is going on, *I will have your head,*" I warned her.

"Leo, back off." Poppy surprised me. "My apologies, we had a slight complication this morning, though I'm sure it's nothing to worry about."

"I think I had best be the judge of that," I said. "Explain *complication.*"

Ray had taken my advice; he'd taken Lizzy with him. Instead of driving herself to university, she'd hitched a ride with Ray, stopping at Poppy's house first. Leola was there visiting. She'd been enjoying some banter with Leola, irritating her more and more, when the phone call for Poppy came.

Leola had retaliated against Lizzy, not realising who was on the phone. "Listen, you pathetic excuse for a human being, I have no qualms in draining every last drop of blood in your body, your mother included."

By the time the words were spoken, it was too late. The person on the end of the line had heard Lizzy's laugh, Leola's retaliation, and Lizzy's comeback. They knew Leola was interacting with some very knowledgeable humans. That meant a death sentence for the humans and an audience for the vampires. The vampire would *have* to turn Leola and Lizzy over to The Seat or risk being called as an accomplice.

"Who was on the phone?" I asked, already planning what to do with them.

"That's the complication and why we're all here." Poppy was careful with her words, too careful.

"I swear, if you tell me it was Elena or Kiros, I will be tempted to kill you."

"It wasn't."

"Then who was it?"

"It was Paris," she answered, making my blood run cold.

Paris was a name that sent shivers down my spine. He wasn't part of The Seats but was one of the many hangers-on who they had following them around like rats. But he was different. He'd survived for centuries, and that alone gave him too much power for my tastes.

If Kiros was the vampires' self-proclaimed king, then Paris was their prince. Should a position within The Seats become available, then he'd be the one to fill it.

"Did he mention anything whilst talking to you?" I searched Poppy's face for any kind of treachery.

"There was a pause in his speaking. Other than that, nothing was said."

"Lizzy, you ride to classes with Ray, Martin, or me. No exceptions. Jayne, call work and tell them whatever you need. I want you here. No one is to tell Helen; we don't need her worrying about this."

Pulling everyone out of the area wouldn't be a good idea. I didn't want to have to move with Poppy or Leola anyway.

"Ray, go about things as normally as possible until this is sorted. The same goes for you four."

"Go to hell!" Leola said.

"You want to get called in for an audience? Be my guest," I snapped. "But I won't have you endangering my family, so I suggest you shut up and listen to me."

"She is right, *Liebste*," Al soothed her. "We do not want to tangle with The Seats again."

"I'd rather take my chances with them than take orders from this *freak*."

Ray snarled at her, baring his fangs and hissing in a way that made me want to retract everything I'd ever said about him being tame.

"I like you, Leo," he told her, becoming every inch the vampire, "but don't think I will side with you if you continue down this path. Serenity is everything to me, and I won't hesitate killing you if it meant protecting her."

The two of them stood eye to eye in the living room, neither budging. There was a look of pure determination on Ray's face. He was standing up to the people he'd spent his new life with in an effort to protect me. I didn't need protecting, but the gesture was nice.

"You know what? Forget it. Leola, you want to get yourself killed, be my guest. I won't miss you, but Al would. So, be a complete bitch, and lose your head in the process. I won't stop you," I said. "But I warn you, you put my family in danger, and I'll kill you myself. And I can do so much worse than The Seats could dream of."

"I'd listen to her on that one." Poppy chuckled. "They didn't call her the Angel of Death for nothing."

"Not many have lived to call her that," Issac added. Clearly Poppy had told him the stories.

"And that, my dear, is the point."

Leola never settled down. She grumbled at every plan we put into place, moaned at every precaution I insisted upon, but was wise enough not to openly object.

Lizzy and Jayne had agreed to stay home the following day. With Helen being in the hospital, they had all the time they needed.

"I need to know exactly what happened," I told Ray.

We were in the kitchen at almost midnight cooking for the Cats. They'd been prowling the house since morning without a break. I hadn't thought they would react as they had, but they protected their own.

"Poppy already told you everything."

"I want to hear it from you, Ray. I need to know when the Cats got here, who called them, what was said. I need to know everything."

He detailed the interaction between Leola and Lizzy, every word of it, and what he'd heard on the phone. I was surprised to hear it was Poppy who'd ordered everyone to my house and suggested calling the Cats. I was even more surprised when he told me she insisted on them coming to us.

She hadn't wanted to know where they were.

My opinion of Poppy Baruti was slowly shifting, from a menace to be avoided at all costs to a possible ally. I doubted I'd ever call her friend.

My opinion of Leola, on the other hand, was holding firm. I didn't like her, and I certainly didn't trust her.

"How did things go in Germany?" Ray asked, changing the subject.

"In and out. Nothing to report really." I shrugged.

"I'm glad you're home," he whispered.

"As am I. Though I do wish I knew more about what Martin will eat. I'm not sure this will be enough."

Ray laughed loudly, making me smile.

The kitchen was full of steam from bubbling pots of vegetables, potatoes, and the simmering meat in the oven. "If it isn't, then the Cats can cook."

Chapter Thirty

"Are you looking forward to this evening?"

"I'm looking forward to spending the evening with you."

"That's a no."

He could read me so well.

"It's not a no, per se," I said. "I'm just a little concerned about Lizzy and Jayne joining us."

Issac had arranged the extra invitation at Poppy's request. I had to agree it was better if they were where I could see them, but being in such a public setting was a worry.

For an entire week I'd been on edge. The others went about their business as normally as was possible. Work. Classes. Meeting up with friends. None of it went unsupervised.

Martin had practically moved in. I hadn't slept. Ray never left my side, except for work. Lizzy was never out of my sight. Jayne would be off as long as I needed her to be.

"They'll be fine. Jayne is going to get ready with Poppy, and Martin will be with Lizzy," Ray reminded me.

"That is the problem."

"If they're even a second late, I will have *the talk* with them."

"I have to be there to see that."

We were taking turns. Martin would take the first watch, prowling the dark, almost invisible in the trees. Ray and I took the second part. Once dawn came around, we all retreated back inside. Ray had had a couple of problems with the sun since he started feeding from me. He didn't need to kill me to gain power.

Our blood was more potent than that of a human. A layer of sunblock and staying indoors for most of the day did the trick, but there was a slight tan to Ray's skin. He looked good for it. So long as a tan was all he'd get from it, we eventually came to an agreement that he would use me, and me alone.

The sun had barely been over the horizon an hour when the mail van pulled up, depositing a stack of letters through the door. As soon as the van was out of sight, we jogged out of the trees and back into the house.

"Again!" I growled, perusing the envelopes.

"What is it?"

"Work again," I said.

"How can you tell?"

"You see the insignia by the return address?" It was part of the dead language we used. There was a set of five characters used to signify various things. Birth, death, partnership, maturation, and problems. It enabled us to send the letter to the right person, back in the days when the records were split. Now it helped me to see what I had to do.

Of course, the maturation symbol was one I longed to see again.

"When will you leave?" Ray asked.

"If I leave now, I can be back in time to meet you."

With everyone busy with other things, I could get to London and back in a day without any problems. Trouble in London was rare. Being so close to a Seat meant the vampires were reasonably behaved. "Strange," I murmured.

"What is it?"

"The London Seat must still be in Spain." The thought made me both smile and worry.

If they were, it could be that things were worse there than anyone wanted to admit. If that was the case, why hadn't I been called out there at least once in the last couple of years?

"Martin can't let Lizzy out of his sight," Ray said, obviously worried.

"Can Poppy be trusted?"

"I may not be overly fond of any of them at times, but if she knew all these years and *didn't* say anything, then I believe she can."

"Do you think she'd object if I read her mind?"

Normally I wouldn't have done it, or considered it.

"I don't see why not, but you can ask her yourself when she gets here." Ray smiled, chuckling when I scowled at him.

What was I supposed to say to her? *Hi, Poppy. I'd like to go snooping around your mind to see if I can trust you while I run off, deal with, and possibly kill, a few vampires?*

I didn't think that would go down too well.

"Or I can ask her for you," he offered.

"Thank you."

It turned out Poppy had no problem letting me into her mind; she only asked that I be brief. Once I'd requested that she think about nothing in particular, I was as quick as possible. What I found was . . . so very average. It wasn't what I'd expected from Poppy, the legend that she was.

Her thoughts were focused on Issac, what she needed to do to protect him. Her thoughts towards Ray were . . . well, they were almost *maternal.* There was no hint she wanted him anywhere near The Seats, and her thoughts about him were protective.

As far as vampires went, she was trustworthy.

"Thank you," I told her, offering a small smile.

"I can't say that Leola will ever warm to you, Serenity, but I know I have." Her words surprised me. "You make him happy."

It was the closest I'd ever come to calling a vampire a friend. Ray would never count.

It was fortunate that Poppy's idea of "getting ready" for a night out was a full day in a salon. She'd arrived just as Jayne was crawling out of bed. I'm not sure even I'd dare to try to wake Jayne up before dawn. When that woman slept, she slept.

"Will you be back in time?" Ray asked.

I was ready to leave, mentally calculating where I'd need to stop for fuel, and what the quickest route was.

"If I don't see you here, then I'll meet you at the pub," I promised.

"Do you have everything?"

"Yes, I even have my outfit so I can change in the car if needed."

For days he'd been trying to get me to reveal what I would wear. He hadn't stooped to snooping in my wardrobe, but I would've bet that he'd thought about it. He was desperate to know what I considered "smart attire."

Can't it wait? The answer to that was simple. It *could,* but things would only get worse the longer I left them. The worse they got, the more likely someone from The Seats would be there when I arrived. That was something I wanted to avoid.

I was back on the homeward journey an hour later than I'd planned. It meant I was going to be late, but finding the vampires had been harder than I'd expected. The three were relatively new, and were trying to stake a claim on a territory that wasn't theirs. The Seats weren't something that were available to just anyone.

Vampires fighting was never a good thing. They paid little attention to those around them, human or otherwise. When they started, they were loud, violent, careless, and noticeable.

So I was running half an hour late by the time I reached the pub. It was simple enough to change in the car. My hair was another matter entirely. I'd planned on doing something with it, anything. Instead I had to settle for leaving it down.

The back room of the pub had been reserved for the university faculty and guests. Jayne was chatting happily with Poppy. I spotted Ray as soon as I entered. His eyes lit up as though he was seeing me step into his home for his birthday all over again, and a brilliant smile spread across his face.

"Is that . . . ?"

"I thought you might remember it." Seeing Ray's face as he recognised the dress was worth the week of secrets.

There were few of my dresses that had survived more than a couple of years. The one I was wearing was special. It was the dress Ray's mother had given me for his birthday party. After the events of 1940, I'd kept it and taken care of it.

"You are as spectacular now as you were when I first saw you in it," he whispered, eyes wide with appreciation as I twirled for him.

"Where's Lizzy? She begged me to show her the dress"

Ray didn't answer. He looked around and then said, "I haven't seen her."

A feeling of dread built in the pit of my stomach.

"She was supposed to be here half an hour ago."

"Let me ask Jayne."

While he hurried through the crowd, I made my way to the bar and asked to use their phone.

The first number I tried rang and rang, but no one picked up. It was the same with all the phones I had at the house.

The second person I tried was the same. Nothing but a ringing phone whose only purpose was to make me more nervous than I already was.

The third number I tried, the most recently memorised, yielded some success.

"Alex, it's Serenity. Have you seen Martin or Lizzy?"

"No. He was with Lizzy this afternoon before taking her to that dance you were going to." I could tell he was frowning.

"They aren't here."

"I can be at your house in the next half hour."

"Thank you. It's going to take us an hour to get back. If they're distracted by each other, you mind if Ray gives them a sex talk?" I said, trying to ignore the rising dread I felt.

"Go for it."

With a slam, I put the phone back on its cradle, and quickly found Ray and Jayne in the crowd. "No answer," I said. "Tell me they're here."

"No one has seen either of them," Ray told me.

"Something isn't right," Jayne said, confirming my own feelings of dread.

"Can you ride with Poppy?" I asked, not waiting for an answer.

If anything was wrong, I wanted to get there first. Jayne didn't need to worry over nothing. And it was nothing. It had to be. I was kidding myself.

Even as I raced towards the car, Ray two steps behind me, I knew something was gravely wrong. It wasn't like Lizzy to get distracted, and especially not when things had been so unstable.

Something was very wrong.

"Serenity, talk to me." He took my hand in his for a moment. "Please."

"They have her," I whispered, my eyes never leaving the road. "I don't know how I know, but they have her."

I wove in and out of the tiniest of gaps in the traffic, desperate to get home.

Before I got out of the car, I picked up a frighteningly familiar scent. Elena had been here.

I raced into the house, desperate to know. There were no discernible signs of life, no heartbeats, no breathing, nothing. I swept every room in the house, hoping against hope that I'd missed something.

I hadn't.

As I passed the basement, something caught my attention. There was no need for Martin to have been there, but his scent was as bright as a beacon leading down the stairs. I was at the bottom of the steps before I'd taken another breath.

Martin's scent went as far as the desk, and presumably back again. There was a book on the floor, out of place in the neatness of the basement. I was sure it hadn't been there before.

It was William's family tree, a book I hadn't opened even to update his death. I couldn't.

The corner of an envelope was sticking out of the end of the book. Something that certainly shouldn't have been in there. Everything we sent each other was destroyed. It had to be. Whatever it was, it must have been important.

Hammering on the front door caught my attention. I stuffed the letter in my purse and returned upstairs. Alex was doing the pounding, looking like he'd just run a marathon.

"I got here too late; they were already gone," he panted. "Lost their trail three miles into the woods."

"Thank you."

A car—Poppy's—came screeching to a stop in front of the house. Jayne stumbled as she tried to move faster than she was able, fear etched on her face.

"Serenity, what is going on?" she demanded.

"I am so sorry," I whispered. "They have her."

"What!"

"I didn't have time to come home first," I explained. "I got changed in the car and went straight to meet Ray."

"We're going to go get her," she said calmly.

"No."

"I'm coming with you, Serenity. This is my daughter we are talking about."

"I know that, Jayne. I promise you, *I will bring her back,* but you are not coming."

"She's all I have left."

"They won't get away with this."

She was going to argue, to try to tell me anything to get me to let her come along, but the ominous ring of the phone cut through the air, silencing all of us.

Ray was closest to it, and he hit the speaker button as he answered.

I fought back the hiss that threatened to escape me as Elena's voice filled the room. "Put Poppy on."

"I'm here."

"My dearest Poppy, you remember the London catacombs? Bring the other human."

"Are you demanding an audience with me?"

"No, I am suggesting you show up and explain why you've been sharing our secrets with humans." It almost sounded as though she was bored. "Personally, I wanted to execute all of you, but I was overruled."

"After I slaughtered the best you threw at me, how fortunate for you. Should I be contemplating adding your head to my collection?" That was the Poppy of legends.

"Not quite. The humans will die for this; you can only affect what your fate will be. You have one day. Oh, and bring that freak show you hang around with. All of them."

Fortunately, she hung up just as Jayne lost it. She collapsed to the floor, tears streaming down her face. Alex moved to her side, comforting her and guiding her to a chair. I was on the phone.

"Zach, it's Serenity."

"Going somewhere again?"

"I need the plane, and I need it now. Be warned, we're going to London, to the catacombs, and we have guests."

"I'm coming with you."

"No, Jayne. I'm only taking them because Elena will come for them if they don't show." It was bad enough that Lizzy was in their hands; I wouldn't let them have Jayne, as well.

"I'll be ready within the hour," Zach promised.

"Thank you." I hung up the phone.

"I'll stay with Jayne," Alex offered.

"I will bring Martin back to you." I was already heading for the door.

What I had to say to Poppy and the others wasn't for Jayne's ears, so I waited until they joined me outside. It would be the first time I'd ventured into one of the catacombs in centuries, normally I didn't have to go inside to influence the vampires there.

"I know we've had our differences," I told them, "but I need you all to promise you will get Lizzy and Martin back. Alive."

There were solemn nods from everyone. Even Leola didn't look as harsh as normal.

"What are you planning?" Ray asked once we were in the car.

"I don't know."

I would keep both of my promises to Jayne. I would get her daughter back to her, and I would make The Seats pay. It was time they realised they were only alive because I allowed them to be.

Chapter Thirty-One

It was a ninety minute flight, and then a thirty-minute drive to the catacombs. The London ones weren't the easiest to find, not that I would've had any trouble.

It was far too long.

"You need to change," Ray reminded me. I was still wearing my dress.

God only knew what they were doing to Lizzy. They could've been torturing her, or putting her through all kinds of hell.

"Serenity," he pulled me against him briefly, "we'll get her back."

"I know. I'm just tired of this. Everyone I've ever loved has been taken from me, and now I am being forced to take you straight to them. I can't do this anymore, Ray. I can't lose you again."

"You don't have to," he promised.

"But I do. If we manage to get out of there alive, they'll come after you. There's nothing that can stop them. I can wipe every memory they have and the end result will be the same as always. All it would take is one person with any knowledge of The Seats and it would be over."

I rose and began pacing. I needed a plan, but nothing I came up with would work. The only thing that had any chance was me staying hidden for as long as possible and letting Poppy try to talk her way out of the situation. She was highly respected among The Seats.

Worrying about the situation would do me no good, and I needed to change, which would at least occupy me for a few minutes.

It was as I was changing, making sure I had everything I needed, that I remembered the letter. I grabbed the letter and returned to the main cabin, turning it over as I went.

The wax seal on the back froze me in my tracks. It was the one seal we never used, the one that struck fear into the hearts of everyone who saw it. Of course, it had long since been abandoned and would mean nothing to anyone looking at it today. I recognised it, and it shocked me that William had ever felt the need to use it.

Sitting in the nearest seat, I tore open the letter.

Dearest Serenity,

By now you are the last of us, and I know this pains you every day. Please forgive me for not coming forward with this information for so long.

Before your sister passed, she came to me, concerned about her daughters. She knew then that one of them was talking to the vampires, telling them our secrets, but she could not bear to tell you herself.

I am not so innocent either. I have always known who it was that betrayed us, and I have always known the way to stop it, the way to bring our kind back. But I could not tell you, not until it was time.

It is time, Serenity. You are the only one left. Yet you cannot fight much more, but love will do such a thing to you.

Please understand the separation you faced was needed. Had you found him again so soon after losing him, you would never have accepted what he had become. Given those years apart you have been able to do exactly that.

Your sister sat with me, telling me what was going to happen. She said that when we were all connected, as never before, it would be time. All of our partners have been human up until you. Ray was destined to be turned, and I am so sorry for the pain it has caused you both.

I know it will have taken a great loss to find this letter, and that is how it must be. When you read this, you will want to hate me, and I understand, but please, when the time comes make sure it is Ray who takes your life. Him alone, or your gift will not work.

Ray is unique in his creation. He is the only vampire ever to be created by one who had never taken a human life. He is the only one this way, as you are the only one left of us. Both unique, both drawn to each other like no other.

Please understand, also, the vampires are aware of this, but believe a different version of events will come to pass. They believe draining you will kill you because Ray is now a vampire. They have waited years to seek you out, and in the end you will go to them. Please heed my words.

You were never meant to be the last of us, Serenity. You were meant to be the one to change us.

There will be a difference this time around. We will have no weakness; it will be our choice alone to pass on. Thanks to you. You were always the strongest of us, and I am truly sorry you have to be the one to do this.

I will love you always, and I wish you did not have to suffer the pain

that is still to come.
Please find it in your heart to forgive me.
Your Brother,
William

"We're about to land." Ray's voice pulled me from my thoughts.

How long had I sat staring at William's words? With every part of me, I longed to hate him for hiding this. How could he? How could he have sat there across from me and not said anything?

"Serenity?" I folded the letter and handed it to him.

"Don't read it until I tell you to."

"What . . . ?"

"I have a plan, but please, do *not* read it until I tell you to."

We touched down in London, about twenty miles away from the catacombs. Dawn was fast approaching.

The drive was relatively quick, yet long. Each second dragged on, longer than the last. Yet the miles flew by as though they were moving and we weren't. As hard as I pushed the car, it wasn't hard enough. I couldn't take the bends quick enough or accelerate along the straights fast enough.

"Does everyone know the plan?" We were parked on a secluded stretch of road, half a mile from the catacombs' entrance. "Above all else, get Lizzy and Martin home."

Ray pulled me to a stop as the others set off on foot. "Serenity, what's in the letter?"

"Please, when the time comes, I need you to do *exactly* what I ask."

I almost told him how that single letter unlocked so many secrets I hadn't known. How it was the key to everything. But if he knew, he wouldn't do it.

"Promise me, Ray, that you'll do exactly as I ask."

"I promise."

"Thank you."

We were met at the entrance by a lone pair of guards. Neither of them recognised me as I stuck to Ray's side.

"What do you want?"

"I'm Poppy Baruti."

They must have been new not to recognise her.

"Are you expected?"

"I am *always* expected," she snapped.

The second guard whispered something to the first one, glancing at Poppy every few seconds. He was probably informing the sap who she was. He paled for a moment before pulling out a small radio. Speaking rapidly into it, he nodded, looked at me and then back at her.

"Is that the one you were asked to bring?"

"She is."

He spoke into the radio once more before shoving it in a pocket and nodding to us. "Come with me."

We followed them into the dark entrance, and I was thankful that I was something more than human. The tunnels weren't designed to accommodate mortals. Those who managed to survive an audience with The Seats then had to get out. One of The Seats' favourite sports was pardoning a vampire and then hunting them in the tunnels. There was a trick to it. Know the trick, and getting out was easy. Every second left followed by every first right. It was the same with all of the catacombs.

Everything was as it had been when I saw it in the dream. The high ceiling was covered in skulls, dark and unsettling. I couldn't see Lizzy, but she was here. Somewhere. The ground underfoot squelched, our footsteps echoing off damp rock and sodden floors.

I almost balked when we entered the main chamber. Half the members of the world's Seats were there. Black clothes, shadowed faces, and hungry, eager eyes. Kiros and Elena were in the middle, with the entire Russian Seat and half of Finland's. I was sure I spotted a couple of the Americans in the room. There was a representative from every Seat in the world.

Something was wrong.

They didn't assemble like this for a simple audience.

Unless it was because it was Poppy Baruti they'd summoned.

"Poppy, my dear, how good it is to see you," Kiros called.

"Cut the bullshit, Kiros. You *dare* to call *me* in for an audience?" Poppy stalked across the room, putting herself right in front of him. "I *invented* the damned things, and you have the audacity to use them against me?"

"Bring them in," Elena called, glaring at Poppy.

Wishing I could move a fraction and see what was happening, but not wanting to give myself away, I listened harder. I heard Lizzy, sounding strong as ever as she was herded into the chamber. It was so similar, yet so different from the dream. Martin was the difference. She was stronger for having him at her side.

"Get your stinking hands off me," Lizzy snarled.

"Silence, child," Elena bellowed.

"Go to hell! I'm not scared of you."

"You'll fear me when I'm killing you."

"Yeah, yeah. If I've told you once, I've told you a thousand times, you're dead when my aunt comes for me."

"What is this about?" Poppy demanded, barely glancing at Lizzy.

"You broke the rules," Kiros hissed at her, circling.

"We never broke your rules."

"How so? Both of these children know of us. They have shown not an ounce of fear since we captured them. If they did not come by the knowledge through you, then how did they acquire it?" Kiros asked, the picture of calm once more.

"They already knew of us when we met."

"That may be the case, but as a vampire, and a *former* member of The

Seats, it is your duty to eliminate them." Elena was pushing her luck with Poppy, even I could tell that.

"Back off, *Ellie*. Did you think to read their minds to see why they know?"

I was glad I wasn't the only one who called her that.

Kiros stepped in. "If it were possible, then we would have."

The self-proclaimed king did little talking, but the rest of the members of The Seats knew not to interrupt him.

"And what, pray tell, is the race we cannot read the minds of?" Poppy asked, a look of determination on her face.

"That is hardly relevant."

"And you are missing the obvious," Poppy muttered.

"Regardless of why we cannot read their thoughts, did you bring the other human?" Elena questioned, growing impatient. Not that she had a lot of patience to begin with.

"You hear a heart beating, do you not?"

"Read it," I whispered to Ray.

My lips were close to his ear, his hair tickling my face. I didn't dare look into his eyes as he silently unfolded the piece of paper.

"Well, come forward, child," Kiros called.

Why was it vampires thought they could use that term on everyone just because they'd been alive for a couple of thousand years?

"You did not call her that!" Lizzy said, laughing. "You really shouldn't have said that."

"Silence!"

"Your funeral," she murmured.

"Come out," he called again.

Looking into Ray's eyes, I knew he'd read the letter. He was willing, but reluctant.

"You are trying my patience, child. Come out now, before I take out my frustrations on this one," he said, moving towards Martin and Lizzy.

In a flash of movement, I was leaning casually against the back wall as if I owned the place.

"You know better than to call me *child*, Kiros," I said from behind him.

"Azrael! This is a surprise." He smiled as if he was my oldest friend.

"Is it? *Really?* Then you'll know if you have harmed a hair on my niece's head I will destroy you," I promised, smiling coldly at him. "I'll forget you broke into my home and kidnapped them. I'll forget you forced me into this godforsaken place to retrieve her. I will also let it slide that you threatened her life, but we will be leaving now."

"What makes you think you *can* leave?" Elena asked.

I caught a movement from the corner of my eye; all the exits had been blocked. It didn't matter.

"Because I can do anything I want. I can get inside your minds, and you are powerless against me." I tapped the side of my head, smiling brightly at them.

"That may be so, but you will not walk out of here," Kiros was almost excited as he spoke. Any other time I would've been amazed the man actually knew what emotions were. He spent so much of his life devoid of them.

"Why would you think that?"

"Do not play coy with us, Serenity." Elena had enough emotion for the both of them. "We are well aware you brought your partner with you."

"And? Do you have a point?"

"You are vulnerable," an impish voice purred from across the room.

"You brought yourself to the slaughter," Elena finished.

"Oh please! Pull the other one, Ellie. We both know I should already be dead, yet here I am. Do you really think you stand a chance at killing me?" I asked, pretending to yawn. "I honestly gave you more credit."

"I'll drain you myself," she hissed. "That will prove my point."

"Wait!" I held up my hand, and she stopped in her tracks. So well . . . *trained.* "If we are going to go through with this pathetic charade, can I at least get a last request?"

"Why should we give you anything?"

"Because you would be nowhere without me."

"I am interested to know what she would want," one of them stated.

"Have your say," Kiros said.

"If you want my body drained of blood, then I agree. On one condition. I get to choose who drinks from me," I offered. "May I advise that you take me up on this? You are well aware that I could kill you all."

"Who would you choose?" Kiros asked, a curious light in his eyes.

"Ray."

There was a shocked gasp that ran through the room, and it occurred to me that they knew who he was.

"Well then, that is something I would like to see. I never took you for the dramatic type, Azrael," Elena said, laughing.

Trust her to be excited that I'd requested that my partner drain me. She didn't pause to consider *why* I'd asked for him.

"Serenity," there was pain in Ray's voice as he spoke, "Serenity, I . . ."

He was playing his part well—the reluctant participant. "Please, Ray."

"Why me?" he asked, moving slowly to stand in front of me.

"It was always you, Ray," I whispered. "It was always meant to be you."

"I love you."

"Whilst you live, so shall I. When you sleep, so shall I," I replied. "I finally worked it out."

"Are you sure?"

"Yes." I *was* sure. I was absolutely sure William was right.

Every member of The Seats present looked on with expressions full of eagerness. Turning to face them, Ray at my back, I smiled. I tilted my head to the side, giving Ray the access he needed. The others didn't know this was all part of the plan.

They showed no signs of worry as Ray hesitated. They thought there was only one way to kill me, and they were right. For the most part, at least. If Ray were gone, I doubt I would want to come back.

That day was a very long way off.

I closed my eyes and let my head rest on Ray's shoulder as his fangs pierced my skin. It was a sensation I was used to, and one I was growing to enjoy. Giving him the sustenance he needed was its own reward.

This would be an unforgettable experience for him. The rush of power that came with the loss of life was a memorable event. No vampire ever forgot the first life they took.

As my legs collapsed underneath me, we sank to the floor. Ray's teeth never left my neck; his tongue greedily lapping up every drop of blood my body had to offer.

My vision started to blur, dimming at the edges. My hearing was weak.

I knew, with absolute certainty, my life was almost over. Everything seemed to have slowed to the point of stopping. The feeling was a strange one.

With my last few breaths, I recited the last words of William's letter. I wanted them to know they'd been mistaken.

"I was never meant to be the last of us." I gasped, struggling to breathe. "I was the one meant to change us."

My vision was almost black. *"Thank you."*

My last words, with my last breath, were thanks to The Seats of Power. If William was right, then it wasn't over.

Chapter Thirty-Two

I was dreaming, I must have been. Floating in the blackness, I felt at ease. There were bright lights surrounding me, illuminating nothing. Peace. Calm. Weightless. But . . .

Who was I?

Why was I here?

Where was here?

Why did it feel as if everything was as it should have been, but something was missing? Something I *needed* to know.

In the darkness I heard the faint echo of people speaking. There were worried cries and a frantic pleading. I felt the soft touch of someone holding me close, then the brush of fingertips against my hand. The sounds grew stronger.

Faint recognition stirred within me as I struggled to understand what was going on. I *knew* the voices that were crying and begging. With each new exclamation, my focus sharpened.

The arms around me tightened as a stir of air brushed against me.

"Don't touch her!" the voice belonging to the arms growled. What a beautiful voice it was.

"Ray, she's dead," a gentle voice whispered, causing the first to growl again. "You have to let her go."

"No!"

I wasn't dead! I could hear them! Every inch of me was aware of that fact. Nothing else made sense, but I knew I was alive. All that existed were the arms around me and the floating blackness. I couldn't move; I had no recollection of a body to move with. I couldn't make a sound; there were no words I could form and no mouth to make them.

If I couldn't speak, how was I supposed to tell them I was alive?

The arguing continued as I contemplated what to do.

Why was there a burning desire in me that said these people *had* to know I was alive?

Who were they anyway, and why did they seem to care so much about whoever I was?

There was so much *pain* in the voices, and I wanted to know why. I wondered why they were crying over me, I wanted to tell them not to and wipe away their tears.

My wishes were soon granted, but not in the way I expected. I wanted to talk, but I ended up screaming. I wanted to move, and I found myself thrown forward, a bubble of agony crashing through me.

It was as if I was being electrocuted, or struck by lightning. Perhaps both. I hurt everywhere, and nowhere, and for one brief moment everything was clear. I felt the arms cradling me to a hard chest. Their grip broke as my body flung itself forward. The floating blackness had disappeared and everything was in perfect clarity. The echoes of my tortured cries were fading, sounding like a million screams.

All I remembered was the sensation of the sharp heat, even though it had faded.

My chest heaved. Then the pain came back, crashing through me again, just as piercing and all-consuming as before. Another scream tore its way up my throat, and echoed off the walls.

I could pinpoint the origin now. It wasn't flowing through me at all. It was centred in my chest. The feeling was so intense in that single moment that it felt as if my whole body was consumed by it.

I watched with fascination as my fingers curled in reaction to the pain, slicing through the stone beneath them as if it was water.

There was silence again as I crumpled to the floor, curling in on myself, closing my eyes. I had no idea how long had passed before the final bout hit me, worse than ever. The white-hot strike pierced every piece of consciousness I was clinging to. I screamed again, unable to hold it in.

Then, as I felt my heart pounding in my chest, I knew what I was missing . . .

And I remembered *everything*.

"Damn, that *hurt*," I muttered, getting my bearings.

There was no way to tell how much time had passed in the catacombs. It could have been hours, days, or mere seconds. Almost every figure in the room was still, shocked, and staring. Lizzy appeared unharmed, but it had been her I'd heard crying. The tears stained her face.

Ray's hand was extended towards me. I needed the help; I still felt off after . . . what exactly had happened?

Slowly the pieces started clicking into place. William's letter. Ray drinking from me. My gift. It had all been about my gift, the inability to have my life taken from me. Or that was what I'd gathered from the words

William had written. Life, what a gift. A true immortal being only able to be killed by their own decision.

"You scared me," he whispered, cradling me in his arms.

"Don't worry, Ray. I think I know what happened," I told him, turning in his arms, smiling at him.

The rest of the vampires in the cavern were silent, shocked at what had occurred, waiting for some kind of order. No one wanted to be the first to make a move.

For all intents and purposes, I'd been dead. I understood what William meant about the pain that was still to come. My heart trying to restart itself was something I would never forget. Elena's face was the one that made me laugh. She was torn between utter disbelief and absolute rage.

"You really thought we were that stupid, didn't you?" I asked, taking in the room. "You really thought, with the gifts we had, we didn't see this coming."

I was taunting Elena, all of them, flaunting their blatant failure. Being the only female in a male-dominated world was hard enough. When they all wanted you out, it was even harder. Things may have seemed settled within The Seats, but it was far from it. They all wanted to be the self-proclaimed king, and they would all do anything to get there.

They'd thought that they'd won. They truly believed they had me beaten. The all-knowing Seats never failed. *In anything.* "We knew who betrayed us, and we took steps to make sure we would *always* survive. The time will never come when you are free to take over the world," I told them with utter confidence.

"I want to leave you with a message and a warning, all of you! I will stand between you and the rest of the world for as long as I live. I will never let you take over. As much as I want to destroy you now for what you've done to my family, I won't. You do a good job of sticking to *our* rules, and I would like to keep it that way. But if you *ever* cross my family or me again, I won't hesitate. I will destroy your world and everything in it."

They never moved, never flinched or blinked, not even when I stood in front of Kiros. He was their king, and he was the one who needed to know more than anyone. There was fear in his eyes as I spoke, fear that I would do exactly as I said. That I would take *everything* he valued, and *everything* he loved, just as he'd done to me.

I would've gone into their minds and taken their knowledge of my kind, but that was almost impossible. It was best to let The Seats remember, to know what I could do, and to be afraid of it.

I promised Jayne I would make them pay, and this was my way of doing so: by instilling a fear in them so deep it would never leave. I didn't have to enter their minds to do that.

"Release them," I called to the vampires holding Lizzy and Martin.

They hesitated for a moment, not moving, not daring to obey my command.

"Sometime today would be nice."

The vampires simply stood there looking back and forth between Kiros and me, unsure of what to do.

"Let's make this easy, shall we?" I offered, turning my attention back to Kiros. "Tell your little minions to let my family go and we will leave. You already screwed up the whole trying to kill me thing, and I, for one, would like to go home now."

Before I had a chance to react, Kiros lurched forward, clutching my throat and lifting me. "This is not over, Azrael. Your warning is meaningless. You never had it in you to destroy us, and you never will."

He was only partly right.

I didn't have it in me to kill them all; I only ever killed when I was attacked first. I did, however, have it in me to show him how much I meant it, the only way I knew how.

"Take a look into my mind, Kiros, and see just how far I am willing to go." There was no way he could resist a glimpse into any of our minds. Not when we'd been silent to them for so long.

It took little effort to flip that internal switch, to let go of whatever it was that stopped us from having our minds read. It was something I'd never done before.

As I felt the invasion, I remembered every ounce of pain I'd suffered at the hands of the vampires.

The exchange was silent, but it was profound. I'd seen so much in my time, more than anyone could see in a hundred lifetimes. The guilt I felt when I first had to defend myself and had killed the vampire I was up against. The grief I'd experienced with the passing of each of my mortal family members. The tears I'd shed at their gravesides. The pain of betrayal, of losing the last of my brothers, of watching my sister die so cruelly. And above all, the pain of losing the one person in the world I loved more than anything. That pain had lasted too long, every day, every breath, and every heartbeat for decades.

"You will *never* understand what that feels like," I snarled.

Kiros dropped me to the floor, staggering under the weight of my memories. "I have lived through far too much to give up now. I will do whatever it takes to keep my promise to you. Never think I won't follow through, and always remember *we were the ones who made you what you are.*"

"Let them go," he whispered.

There was a new look in his eyes, not one of fear, though fear was still there, but what appeared to be regret. That would be a first, but I'd have to check with Leola and see what she was picking up. For now, I wanted to get Lizzy and Martin home safely and go back to normal. Well, as normal as was possible for me.

Lizzy and Martin were released, and she practically flew into my arms.

She held me so tightly I thought for a moment she was trying to crush me. She wasn't, she was simply relieved. I had Ray on one side of me and Lizzy on the other. There was one more thing I wanted to say before we left.

"Oh, and when I say my family, I mean all of them," I told Kiros, "and that includes Ray, Poppy, Issac, Al, and Leola. You cross any of them, and I will keep my promise."

"They come under our rule!" Elena protested, finally coming out of her daze.

"Not anymore."

"You cannot do that!"

"I can do anything I damn well please, Elena. Get over it."

It was hard to believe they were actually going to let us walk out of there without a fight, but as we turned for the door it appeared as though they were. Each step we took was a step closer to freedom. As soon as they let us walk out of the chamber, it was over. They could try to hunt us through the passages all they liked; we knew how to get out.

"You're just going to *let* it leave?"

It? Elena had called me an *it?*

Elena hadn't always had the cruellest of minds. She'd forgotten how her life started out with the vampires—helpless at their hands. The years of working to be the best and trying to earn their respect had twisted her view of the world.

"Let her go," Kiros whispered, obviously not yet recovered from the influx of memories I'd revealed to him.

"Not this time."

Ray was already trying to move me aside, trying to stop me from getting hurt. I was moving in the opposite direction, getting Lizzy out of the way.

Neither of us was quick enough.

Chapter Thirty-Three

Ray's arms, tight around my waist, pulled just as I slipped my own around Lizzy's. I thought I knew what was coming. I expected to feel fangs piercing my skin, but it never came.

Everything went wrong, and the scream of pain that filled the air wasn't my own. It was Lizzy.

She'd been in my place when Elena's teeth clamped down on their target. What she was attempting to achieve was beyond me; they'd already seen what happened when drinking my blood. Fortunately, Lizzy's blood was as sweet as mine, and the flavour distracted Elena long enough for me to react.

The Seats had never tasted our blood before; they never got close enough. If they'd known how good our blood was, then we'd have been hunted for a whole other reason.

Elena was consumed enough with the flavour for me to pull Lizzy from her grasp. Handing her straight off to Ray, I growled, "Take her and leave."

"Not without you."

"I'll meet you at the plane. Go!"

Turning away from my mismatched family, I stalked towards Elena.

"You have kept pushing me, testing the limits of what I am willing to do," I hissed, daring any of them to attack. "I've had enough. You never believed we were capable of the things we claimed to be. That is going to change. Which memories of yours should I take, Elena?"

I stood in front of her now, glaring. Her eyes held no panic; she truly didn't think I was capable of it. She *refused* to believe there was someone with the ability to control their thoughts, actions, memories, and desires. She thought everything The Seats had was of their own doing.

How wrong she was.

The reason they had such little opposition wasn't because they were feared, it was because we instilled the fear of The Seats into every vampire we met.

If half the world's vampires forgot that fear, then The Seats would be faced with destruction. There were covens with the number and the power to destroy them.

We were the ones stopping them.

"I would rather tear your head off," she replied, fangs out, teeth bared.

"*Try it!*"

I was ready for anything. The other Seat members wouldn't interfere unless they were given a direct request to help. The fight, what there would be of it, was between Elena and me.

Our encounters had never come to much more than one pinning the other against a wall. Blood was rarely drawn, and never mine.

She didn't know I was armed. It was one of those subtle changes that had been made after losing Ray.

Elena and I were evenly matched, but I was working with an advantage. For once it was my short stature. Elena towered over me, meaning I could get in a blow before she had a chance to strike.

One thing I'd learned was to never make the first move. When she lunged, looking as though she was going straight for my throat, I let her come, waiting for the slightest move that would give away her real intention.

She wasn't that stupid. A head-on attack was pointless and so easily blocked.

She forgot I was faster than she'd ever been.

At the last second she changed her stance, just a fraction. She shifted to the left, going for my arm, which was slightly outstretched, balancing myself for any kind of impact.

Coming from the side was a mistake.

I threw myself in the opposite direction, twisting my body as I did. I brought my foot up, jamming it into the side of her neck. The ground was the perfect propellant, giving me enough of a boost to throw Elena off balance and send her tumbling. She'd made what was going to be a short-lived fight much easier with her ineptitude.

I pinned her to the ground by the throat, cutting off her air. Not that she needed it.

"Should I take the memories of your brother?" I asked and saw a flicker of disbelief in her eyes. "Or perhaps you'd like to see what *really* happened to your mother?"

Her brother was the reason she was so bitter. She'd never been a particularly kind human, but she'd loved her only surviving family member. Her upbringing had been harsh, more so when the vampires found they could use him against her.

She often thought her memories of her brother were a dream and struggled to hold onto them. She wished she could've saved him.

"Should I take those dreams, Elena?"

"You can't do that! You can't know that!" Fear was clear in her expression.

"I know *everything* about all of you, and you have pushed me too far. You murdered my sister, slaughtered my entire race, kidnapped my family, and threaten my life. *No more.*"

Reaching out with my mind, I entered hers. The hate that was her most prominent feature was gone, replaced by a fear that almost made me change my mind.

Almost.

I wasn't cruel, and I didn't remove those memories of her brother completely. Once they were gone it was almost impossible to bring them back.

It was simple enough to make her *think* she'd forgotten him. She would know she had a brother, but beyond that, it would be gone. When the influence I wielded faded, she would be able to remember. *If* I let her. *If* she'd proven she'd changed.

Until then, she wouldn't be able to recall his face or the way he held her when she was scared during those dark nights in the Russian mountains.

"If I ever see any of you near my family again, I will take what each of you hold closest to your hearts. I will not hesitate, and I will not forgive. You've had too many chances. I will not give you any more."

There was no reason to stay any longer. The message had been delivered. Kiros was reeling from seeing into my mind, as were the others who had dared to look. Elena was broken, still coming to terms with the loss of her most heartfelt memories.

I raced through the tunnels, desperate to see Lizzy again, to make sure she was well. The vampire bite shouldn't have affected her, but there was no way to know. It wasn't known whether our descendants were immune to being turned or if the healing properties in a vampire's saliva would have any effect on them.

Both of the cars were gone when I emerged. It was dark, which surprised me. By my count it had only been a couple of hours. The sun should have been rising in the sky, but it had already set.

"You got out alive, *human?*"

Of course there was someone waiting for me. It would've been far too easy for them to just let me go.

"No *human* walks out of the catacombs," I reminded him, watching carefully in case he decided to strike.

"I know that better than anyone." He smirked, licking his lips slightly.

"If you value your life, you'll let me pass."

"Let her pass," another voice called from the shadows.

"Yes, mistress."

What the . . . ?

"Serenity. It is good to see you again."

"Do I want to know why you have vampires calling you mistress, Georgianna?"

"I thought you might like to know why I'm here. I'd rather you heard it from me than from anyone else." She stepped out from a hidden recess, head held high.

The vampire slipped into the entrance, ignoring the pair of us as though we weren't there.

"What is going on?"

"How do you think young Lizzy was captured? Do you know how they found her at your home? How they knew nothing of my grandson being a Were?"

"You! You handed over your own *grandson* to The Seats?" I said, outraged. "How could you do that? They could've killed them both!"

"They wouldn't have harmed them," she promised. "It is well within my power to ensure their safety." And no doubt she was the reason Kiros couldn't read their minds.

"Does he know? Does your *son* know?"

"You cannot tell them."

"You ask too much of me."

"I owe you my life a hundred times over. I'm not asking anything of you; I know you will do what is right." She knew me far too well.

"And if I don't?"

"Do you think, as old as I am, that I cannot see your future?"

"Pull a stunt like this again and you'll not be seeing any futures."

"My husband is dead, Serenity."

The news caught me off guard. "When?"

"Yesterday morning. It's why Martin was so distracted. Ultimately, the timing made everything easier, but you will not see me again," she said, sounding so old.

"It doesn't give you a right to do what you did . . . but I am sorry, Anna," I whispered.

"You are dying to ask, aren't you?" she said, smiling a fraction.

"You know me too well."

"First, yes, I am older than you are, though I will not tell you how old. Second, they call me mistress only because I will it," she explained, knowing exactly what I was curious about. "Some things even you don't understand yet."

"Then I hope I never will."

"You will, but not for a very long time. Now, go. See to your niece."

"If it's your last request, then I'll not say anything about your hand in this, but my warning stands."

"You were always one of your word."

"And you were always full of surprises."

Neither of us liked goodbyes, and we left our conversation there. Her actions may have been unforgivable, but at least with a witch on our side, we'd had some say in the outcome. And I had to believe she'd protected Lizzy and Martin. Knowing Lizzy was safe didn't stop me from racing through the bitter London streets in an effort to see for myself.

The plane was on a small, rarely used airfield and was sitting, door open, waiting for me.

"Where is she?" I asked, not bothering with hellos.

"Bathroom. She's complaining she may have a scar, but other than that she's fine," Leola told me.

I would've been shocked at the pleasant tone to her voice, but Lizzy was my priority.

The second she stepped out of the bathroom, I engulfed her in my arms. "You scared me for a minute."

"Yeah, like you didn't already manage to give us all a heart attack with the whole dying thing you did," she answered, laughing.

"Still, never scare me like that again."

"We clear to take off?" Zach called.

I glanced at the door, half expecting to see Georgianna running up the steps after me. When I saw no one, I said, "Yes. Let's go home."

Lizzy spent the flight in Martin's lap. She would indeed have a faint scar from Elena's teeth.

It was clear she was comforting Martin, and I longed to offer my condolences, but I wasn't supposed to know about his grandfather. So I kept quiet, watching and waiting.

A couple of minutes into the flight the tension became unbearable. "Will you please ask me already?"

"What did you do to her?" Leola had a fierce light in her eyes.

"I didn't kill her, if that's what you mean."

"Shame, I always hated that bitch."

"You *didn't* kill them?" Al looked like I'd told him the most unbelievable thing in the world. "Then what *did* you do?"

"Perhaps I should explain something." No doubt one of many things I'd need to clarify. "I need them. More than you may realise. There is no guarantee there will ever be more of us, and I can't police an entire race on my own. They enforce your rules, and your race fears them. I need them to continue doing so."

"I can see your point. Even when there were many of you, we had troubles," Poppy said, eyeing me with interest. "But I always wanted to break Elena. I wish I could have seen it."

"You still have your sadistic streak, I see."

She smiled brightly. "Some things never change."

I explained what I'd done to Elena, avoiding the actual details of it. They didn't need to know how she'd suffered in her life. If Poppy was aware of it, she didn't say anything.

"Okay, I have a question," Lizzy said. "I know you let Kiros look into your mind, but what did you show him to get him to submit like that?" There was a fierce, almost excited interest to her words.

"That was easy. I let him see . . . ." As I started to speak, I felt Ray stiffen next to me, leaning away.

But he couldn't read minds. He couldn't have seen what I was thinking . . . unless . . .

"Ray?" I asked quietly. "Did you look into my mind, too?"

"I'm sorry. It just happened, I couldn't control it . . . I'm sorry."

I should've realised that by taking my life it would unlock something within Ray. It hadn't occurred to me that all he needed to gain those basic vampire abilities was to have his first taste of power.

"No. You never knew. Listen to me," I ordered, taking his face in my hands. "What I showed him was all the bad things I've seen. Fifteen-hundred years' worth of death and destruction. The pain I felt when I lost you is nothing compared to the happiness I feel when I am with you. Please believe that."

"But it was *so much*," he whispered, pain etched across his face.

"Listen to me, Ray."

I closed my eyes as I concentrated. They were private memories, feelings, and intimate touches. They were all Ray's.

I showed him everything. The overwhelming desire to stare into his eyes forever, the way his skin felt against mine, how I felt when I watched him sleep, and when I woke in his arms. The joy I felt at the secrets we shared, the way his smile lifted my heart as he picked bits from my hair when I returned the first time. The way I ached for him and the pleasure that each touch brought.

"Do you see?" I asked. "All of that is because of you. You are the love of my life, my reason for carrying on, and the reason I can never stop smiling. Any pain I felt is irrelevant because I have you."

"I love you."

"Whilst you live, so shall I. When you sleep, so shall I."

He smiled, and I saw it in his eyes—the belief I was not only telling the truth but I meant every single word of it, with all of my heart.

Once everyone had asked their questions, the atmosphere on the plane was a lot more relaxed. We all talked among ourselves for the rest of our journey. I found out everything that had happened had lasted much longer than I thought.

After Ray had drunk from me, I'd lain on the cold catacomb floor for hours while The Seats rejoiced in their victory. The crying I'd heard was because they wanted to do something with my "body." Only my screams had ceased their celebrations. The pain I'd felt hadn't passed in seconds. I'd then lain there for an hour or so between each bout of pain, passing out. Everything had seemed so much quicker from my perspective.

Thankfully.

Jayne was waiting for us with Alex and another Cat in tow. It was an emotional welcome home, for everyone. Alex pulled me aside before we left the airport.

"Have you seen her?" he asked.

I knew exactly to whom he was referring, but I answered, "No. Should I have?"

His eyes narrowed. Perhaps I should have played dumb when he asked.

"I had to check Martin's mind, so I knew he hadn't been hurt," I bluffed. "I assume Georgianna has disappeared again."

"Again?"

"When she lost her husband to the stake, she disappeared. It's how she deals with her grief." It was how all witches dealt with the death of their loved ones.

"She'll be back. She always comes back."

Somehow I wasn't convinced. She'd disappeared for centuries after the death of her last husband. This time, no doubt, would be the same.

"Do you need anything?"

"The funeral will be in two weeks," Alex told me. "You know we have to wait."

"I know. Let's go home."

Chapter Thirty-Four

The preparations for Martin's grandfather went well, and the funeral passed without Georgianna. It amazed me how deeply she was missed by the Cats.

They'd lost two of their elders in the same week, and it was a sad fact for those who took their place.

As the service drew to a close—a burial followed by a traditional speech and prayers—I looked around. Ray was by my side, my partner, my vampire. Lizzy was with her partner, half witch, half Were. With the human blood that ran through all of our veins, we truly were connected as never before.

Five races all joined into a single family.

Each holding a piece of the heart of one.

The impossible had come to pass.

"You ready to leave?" Ray asked.

"Come on, we need to get home. Now," Lizzy said, interrupting my reply.

She'd been excited all day; unusual for attending a funeral. She refused to tell me anything, smiling all the time. If I could have suffered from seasickness, her constant bouncing would've made me ill.

"Can you drop me off at mine? I'll be over in a while. I need to pick something up," Ray said. He was getting used to being out in the daytime again after feeding from me. My life hadn't been enough to make him incinerate before my very eyes, but we'd been given quite the scare. It was nice to be able to see him in the sun again without him wincing in pain.

After saying a brief goodbye to Ray, Martin, Lizzy, and I went back home, Lizzy fidgeting the whole way.

I slammed on the brakes as we pulled into the drive and leapt from the car.

"Samantha Louise Bryan!" I shouted. "What the hell are you doing here?"

She started speaking, explaining exactly why she was sitting in my driveway on the hood of my car, halfway around the world from where she should have been.

I was stunned.

She couldn't have been telling me the truth. I'd given up the hope of ever hearing the words that were spilling from her smiling lips. "When?" I gasped.

"Started just over a week ago," she answered, her words sounding strange in her American accent. "We didn't want to tell you until we were sure."

"We?"

"Me and mom."

For a moment I thought she was talking about others who had matured, but that was asking too much.

I'm not alone anymore.

There were more of us. One more, but still, that was one more than there had been in so long.

"I have something for you, but perhaps we should go inside?" she said, her sapphire eyes sparkling with excitement.

There was a subtle difference in her that screamed *Keeper.*

"Are you all right, Aunt Sere?" Lizzy asked. She had to practically drag me into the house.

"I can't believe it," I whispered. Then I started to laugh.

Of all the things that could have happened, Sammy showing up on my doorstep was not one I'd considered. We'd lived near them in America before moving back to England, and she and Lizzy had become friends. I'd offered to bring her to England with us when we moved.

"Here." Sammy handed me an unfamiliar box. The carving on the lid was done in our ancient language.

"Do you know what it says?" I asked, tracing the carvings with my fingers.

"*When you see how the world works,*" she quoted.

I had to laugh again. Sammy's ancestor had one of those talents we couldn't categorise. He could see how anything worked. Show him a human and he could tell you how their mind processed things, what made their inner clocks keep on ticking. Sammy would have been blessed with that gift.

"There were two letters in there. One addressed to you, and one to me. Mine was simple enough, instructions to find you. I have no idea what's in yours."

When I opened the box, I felt the colour drain from my face. Sitting neatly in the bottom was a delicate looking letter, one with familiar handwriting on the front of it. The last time I'd seen it, my sister had been smiling as she detailed my latest vampire encounter.

"Serenity, what's wrong?" Ray asked, as a tear slipped down my cheek.

Before I could respond, or even realised what was happening, Sammy was on her feet. I'd forgotten Sammy knew nothing of Ray being a vampire.

"Sammy, no!" I cried, dropping the box to the floor.

"Aunt Sere?" she asked, as I stepped in front of Ray.

"This is Ray. He's my *partner.*"

"I see that, but he's a *vampire.*"

"I know."

"*That's impossible!*"

I sighed. "I know."

I should've forewarned her, but my mind was so distracted by the thought of having another Keeper that it hadn't occurred to me.

"I can't explain it, Sammy. I wish I could, but I can't." I scooped up the box.

"Serenity?"

"I'm sorry, Ray. This is Sammy. She's—"

"Like you."

"Yes. How did you know?"

"I can see it," he said, smiling.

"He's been drinking your blood," Sammy told me, eyeing Ray. "It gives him more insight into what to look for when it comes to us."

Well, that was something I hadn't known.

"Are you all right, Serenity?" Ray asked again.

"Yes. I just had a bit of an unexpected surprise."

With careful hands, I picked up the box, thankful the letter was in one piece.

My Dearest Serenity,

Words cannot express how truly sorry I am to have caused you this suffering. Please do not think I am not to blame. I know this may be difficult for you to comprehend, but I have done thus in order to save us. Though the massacre you faced could have been prevented, we would have been destroyed had I not acted.

The vampires were supposed to kill us all: our children, our partners, and our parents. And I have known this for a long time, so I am giving them the information that will both destroy and save us.

Our seer, our aunt, told me what would happen long before I found my Henry. Please understand my actions are designed to protect us and those we have fought for all of our lives.

Have you never wondered why I did nothing to protect my partner?

You knew how volatile I could be. It is not in my nature to let someone defeat me. It is not possible for me to do nothing and let them kill the only person in the world I love.

Yet I know as I write this, I will do nothing to protect the love of my life. I will let them take him from me, and I am so sorry for what you will do for him. I never meant to put you in such a position, but I have no choice. If I do not act, we will lose everything.

There are few things I can tell you, but I can finally explain your gift to you.

My gift will not work if I live out a happy life and die when my time is due, and neither will yours. If I do not do this, then they will hunt our children, before they reach maturity, killing them, and us in the process. My gift, when I die this way, will stop us from maturing.

Your gift is the true miracle, my beautiful sister. Life. The ability to survive anything, no matter how hard it may be. We were two halves of a whole, you and I; one to end us and one to bring us back.

It will take a very special person to set in motion the events that will save us. Your partner is such a person. He is unique in that he was created by a man born of blood who chose a different path.

I am so terribly sorry for the things I have done to ensure this path is taken. The promises you had to make were unfair, but I could not risk you discovering these secrets. Had you done so, you would have stopped at nothing to prevent this course of action. Do not blame those I asked for help; they were merely fulfilling my request.

I cannot begin to imagine the wondrous man who will catch your attention. Ensure he knows to take good care of my little sister for me.

I would have also liked to have thanked you for trying to save me, though I know you cannot, and for standing as our last hope and succeeding. You have endured so much without ever being asked.

I truly am sorry for not telling you any of this before I had to leave you. It had to be this way.

I will always love you, my dearest sister.
Lona

"How could she do this to me?" I whispered, staring at the words. My breath was coming in shaky gasps, tears overflowing, dripping down my chin and splashing on the ink, joining the years-old ones of my sister.

"Could you honestly say you'd have let her do it if you'd known?" Ray asked, having read the letter with me.

Yes, I wanted to say. Yet, every part of me knew different. I would have never let her sacrifice herself like she had. I would have offered to take her place, to do whatever it took to stop what had happened. She was right. I would have done everything in my power to prevent it.

"No," I sighed, "I can't."

I dropped my head into my hands. Everything had been planned out from the start. Every last detail had been thought through, every change accounted for. It was easy to see why I had to be the last to know.

Some things are not meant to be changed, I told myself. *Some things have to happen.*

Here I was, standing with the next generation of my race. It was almost certain there were others experiencing the same changes I'd gone through three thousand years before: The increase in their speed, sight, and strength. The discovery of their gifts.

They didn't have me to thank for that. Everything that had come to pass was because of my sister's sacrifice.

Georgianna obviously knew what the plan was. How far did Lona spread the word about what needed to happen?

Ray wrapped his arms around my waist, holding me close. "I'd have liked to have met her."

"One day, many years from now," Lizzy said. "Many, many years from now."

Lizzy tended to break the tension with a well-placed comment, but something about this one struck me as true.

"I am a firm believer everyone has their time," I said, quoting Ray's words.

"You remember that?"

"I remember a lot of things, love."

Looking up, I stared at Sammy for a moment. She spoke quietly with Lizzy, whispering words of changes and excitement. If it was a choice between what my sister had done and leaving the world to the vampires, then it was no choice at all.

Yet, as much as I'd have liked to have known, here, now, seeing the faces of a new generation light up, it was worth it. It made me proud of my sister, and the lengths she'd gone to in order to save us.

Glancing back at the letter, I thought, *Of course I forgive you, Lona. You never had to ask.*

Chapter Thirty-Five

"There's someone here to see you," I told Helen.

The doctors refused to let her out of the hospital, and given that she was growing worse every day, I didn't blame them. Especially since she'd almost collapsed after finding out we'd taken an impromptu trip to the heart of the London catacombs.

My visit today was one I was hoping would help her. I hadn't told her our descendants were starting to mature; I planned on showing her.

When I opened the door, Sammy entered, a huge grin on her face.

I sat on one side of the bed, while Sammy went around to the other. "Hi, Aunt Helen."

"What are you doing here?" Helen's voice was quiet as she spoke.

"I had to come," she said, still smiling. "Sure shocked Aunt Sere when I showed up."

"In my car."

"I called Lizzy to arrange everything." Her grin widened as she prepared to give Helen the news. "I started maturing."

Helen's eyes grew wide, and she reached for Sammy's hand, gripping it tightly in her own. She opened her mouth to speak then closed it again, a tear slipping down her cheek.

"Oh my," she whispered. "Is it just you?"

"No," Sammy answered, "Aunt Sere's been getting all kinds of notifications."

Helen gasped and turned to me. She took my hand, squeezing it. The smile on her face was so bright, so proud.

"You're not alone anymore."

"No, I'm not."

We talked all day about who'd already called with news and who we were still waiting for. Helen smiled brightly, listening eagerly to Sammy's experiences.

A nurse bustled into the room late in the evening, politely informing us that visiting hours were over.

Helen grabbed my hand as I turned to leave.

"I told you so," she whispered quietly.

"You did. Go to sleep, we'll see you tomorrow."

"Take care of yourself."

I looked at Helen for a moment. There was a soft smile on her face as she closed her eyes and drifted off.

The doctors called at six in the morning. Helen passed away peacefully. They thought it was natural causes. I knew it was just her time. She'd suffered through the death of her partner and the loss of mine. She'd lived long enough to see me happy again, and to see our race reborn.

Jayne, Lizzy, and I held each other for a long while after the call came, and many times in the days that followed. Because, regardless of the life Helen led or the happiness she gained from seeing us reborn, we all loved her deeply. The house wouldn't be the same without her in it.

As the weeks passed there were many more phone calls, letters, and more than a few surprise visits. Each one made me long for Helen a little more. She would've been beside herself with joy to see so many of us maturing. It felt as though every descendant of every family throughout our entire race was reaching maturity in a matter of weeks.

I couldn't have been happier.

Everything was returning to the way it once was. The records would remain in one place; Lizzy was responsible for them.

She'd surprised us all.

Nearly two weeks after Sammy's unexpected visit, Lizzy started showing signs of maturing. Which was impossible, or so I'd thought. In the past, those who found their partners before they matured never did. It was a simple case of there being no point in becoming immortal when we already had a partner who wasn't.

Still, Lizzy's maturing shouldn't have been that much of a surprise. Her partner was a Were, one who was damned hard to kill at that. It had been unexpected, but it was a pleasant surprise.

"Serenity!" someone called.

I was stuck in the basement again, as if I didn't spend enough time poring over various books. It wasn't unusual for someone to have to drag me out for dinner or other events.

"I'm in the basement," I answered.

"Could you come up here, please?"

It was Jayne calling me, but I heard the excitement in her voice. I thought there must have been another surprise visitor I had to see.

I was wrong.

Everyone stood in the hall. Jayne, Lizzy and Martin, Poppy and Issac. Even Al and Leola were standing there, excited. They all were off to the sides, smiling brightly. Only Jayne's smile wasn't as wide as the others. It held a sad edge, and I smiled softly in return.

Ray stood in the middle of them, dashing in a pristine suit. He was shifting nervously, with his hands clasped behind his back, but he was smiling as brightly as the others.

"What's going on?"

Ray walked over to me, took my hand, and got down on one knee. "I wanted to do this the first time I asked, but it was somewhat difficult," he told me. "I was also going to use the same words, but I don't think they fit anymore."

"Ray . . ."

"Helen was kind enough to tell me where you'd put this when I told her what I had planned." He pulled the ring out of his pocket and slipped it onto my finger. "I never told you the story behind this ring. It's my grandmother's, but it wasn't the first one she had. She and my grandfather were walking home one night when they were accosted. The muggers took everything, including her wedding ring. They couldn't afford another one, so all of their friends and neighbours gathered every penny they could spare and they bought her this. It's not the same, but she treasured it every day. I wanted to give it to you because you remind me so much of the wonderful thing that they did for her. You are one of a kind, Serenity Cardea, and I would be honoured if I could call you my wife."

I was too stunned to answer right away. It was all too much to take in. My smiling family, Ray's touching words. It took a conscious effort to force the words out of my mouth, but it was well worth it.

"Yes," I whispered. "It was always going to be yes."

And the story continues in

Last Chance

Preview

"Explain to me why I just walked away from my *husband*," I growled into my phone when it rang. "And *damn it,* if there isn't a *bloody* good explanation, I'm turning this car around."

"Some of the records are missing."

Slamming on the brakes, I came to a screaming stop at the side of the road.

"*What?*"

"Some of the records are missing."

It took me a second to process Lizzy's words. "How in the hell are some of the *records* missing?"

Our entire race was in there. Everything. Everyone. Every place we had ever been and every place we currently were. Everything we had ever done. The explicit details of everything we were capable of.

How we forged The Seats. The details of what we did to maintain their power.

Everything.

If someone had taken the records . . .

"Take a deep breath, Aunt Sere."

"Lizzy, now is *not* a good time to tell me what to do. Explain to me how someone managed to get past you *and* the entire colony of Cats to get to the records in the first place." They should have been secure there.

Our whole history was in those records.

"We weren't home," she whispered. "We were up at the colony celebrating the newest Cats. *We weren't home.*"

Though it was clear she was beating herself up for not being there when it happened, I couldn't focus on that. "What's missing?"

"All of them." She whimpered, her voice shaking. "Every family tree we have. Every single one."

Time stopped. "What?"

"They're all gone."

"They can't be. *Not all of them.*"

Missing histories wouldn't be a big problem. They could be replaced. They weren't essential. Even the details of all of the gifts we had been blessed with over the years could be replaced. They weren't needed. The family trees? *That was what would wipe us out.*

It was a simple enough decision, but one that I did not take lightly. Once the words were out of my mouth, there was no turning back. "Move everyone."

About the Author

Michelle is 28 and has been writing and reading her whole life. Her earliest memory of books was when she was five and decided to try and teach her fish how to read, by putting her Beatrix Potter books *in* the fish tank with them. Since then her love of books has grown, and now she is writing her own, and looking forward to seeing them on her shelves, though they won't be going anywhere near the fish tank. When she's not writing, she's out and about on her motorbike, or sat with her head in a book.